Final Draft

ALSO BY DAVID CARR

The Night of the Gun

Final Draft

THE COLLECTED WORK OF

David Carr

Edited by Jill Rooney Carr

HOUGHTON MIFFLIN HARCOURT

BOSTON   NEW YORK

2020

Copyright © 2020 by Jill Rooney Carr
Foreword copyright © 2020 by Ta-Nehisi Coates

For information about permission to reproduce selections from this book,
write to trade.permissions@hmhco.com or to Permissions, Houghton Mifflin Harcourt
Publishing Company, 3 Park Avenue, 19th Floor, New York, New York 10016.

hmhbooks.com

Library of Congress Cataloging-in-Publication Data
Names: Carr, David, 1956–2015, author. | Carr, Jill Rooney, editor.
Title: Final draft : the collected work of David Carr / edited by Jill Carr.
Description: Boston : Houghton Mifflin Harcourt, 2020.
Identifiers: LCCN 2019038033 (print) | LCCN 2019038034 (ebook) |
ISBN 9780358206682 (hardcover) | ISBN 9780358310303 | ISBN 9780358310389 |
ISBN 9780358171928 (ebook)
Subjects: LCSH: Journalism—United States. | Mass media—United States. |
United States—Civilization—1970–
Classification: LCC PN4725 .C355 2020 (print) | LCC PN4725 (ebook) |
DDC 070.4—dc23
LC record available at https://lccn.loc.gov/2019038033
LC ebook record available at https://lccn.loc.gov/2019038034

Book design by Chloe Foster

Printed in the United States of America
DOC 10 9 8 7 6 5 4 3 2 1

Permission credits appear on page 377.

Contents

Introduction

WHEN MY HUSBAND, David Carr, died shortly after collapsing in the *New York Times* newsroom in 2015, so many of us grieved an epic loss —of a father, a life partner, a brother, a colleague, a friend, an extraordinary reporter and writer. Simply put, David was a glorious carnival of a human being, a guy who really lived three or four lives in his fifty-eight years.

In the aftermath of his death, I found that his words were still with me. I reread his magazine pieces, his spot-on profiles, his reporting in Hollywood for the *Times* (as the Carpetbagger, a mission he completed, mingling with show business media and film aristocracy in a $169 tux). David could go high, he could go low, and everywhere in between because he was fearless and deeply curious about the human condition.

His writing was a great comfort to me. His voice was so distinct, so original, you often didn't need to see the byline to know it was him. As time passed, I stopped feeling like I was falling backwards down the stairs. Grief has a way of destroying us, but little by little we climb back to a place where we are hollow but eventually capable of finding joy and wonder.

Over the last year I found myself gravitating to David's earlier work, the stories he wrote in Minnesota before I met him and those published in the early years of our life together. There was a desire to connect again with the remarkable man I fell in love with on the first date, a single father of twin girls, a recovering alcoholic and drug addict.

I cherish this diverse collection of work because it features the David I knew long before he became an icon of American journalism. The articles reveal what many would later see as trademark David Carr: an utterly bold approach to reporting, a desire to find the hidden truths people aren't eager to share and then write their stories, richly detailed, perhaps from a vantage point you hadn't considered. At his core, David was both a card-carrying contrarian and an empath in equal measure.

This trove reveals so much of David: a man of intense passions, strong convictions, and an appreciation for those among us who don't opt for the straight path. I believe these pieces are proof that David approached writing as a vocation. He really didn't have a choice in it.

Enjoy these treasures, large and small. For me, it's always a thrill to visit with David Carr.

—Jill Rooney Carr

Foreword

IT'S STILL ODD, after all these years, for me to think of David Carr as a writer. The broader world knew him as a writer, of course, and an accomplished one. David had a sprawling career that found him writing for alternative papers, doing longform magazine work at *The Atlantic, New York Magazine,* and *Washington Monthly,* and then finally as a writer for the *New York Times,* where he did everything from essays to straight news to (perhaps most famously) a column covering media. In 2008 he published a book—*The Night of the Gun,* an ingenious memoir in which David interrogated his own memory by interviewing the characters interspersed throughout his own rousing biography. Along the way, David cultivated sources and readers, collected friends, and enraged enemies. It is an enviable record, one that speaks for itself.

But there was the David the world knew and the one I knew. I met that latter David when I was a twenty-year-old faltering college student who had some vague ambition of being a writer. David was then one year into his stint as editor of the *Washington City Paper* and was, most importantly for my purposes, hiring interns for the summer. My application was underwhelming—a chapbook of poetry and some middling columns and reporting I'd done for my college newspaper. But David was looking high and low for storytellers, and he did not much care how or where he found them. I was hired for the summer, then extended as a staff writer, and for the next three years David both invigorated and terrified me.

David's staff skewed under thirty, and among them I was distinguished neither by talent or hard work. But David invested in me, if not in dollars, then in something more precious—time. He line-edited much of my earliest work—shifting sections, urging me on with comments, threshing wheat from the chaff. He was a stickler for names and facts—and if you missed one, he would think nothing of yelling at you and threatening your meager livelihood. I wonder now if all of that yelling was necessary. Probably not. But you take the bad with the good, and there was so much good.

David could be a terror when you got it wrong, but when you got it right—when you wrote something that made him smile—he'd make you feel like you'd hung the moon. I can remember coming to his office after closing a piece on day laborers and him looking at me and saying, "I was just talking about how fucking great your piece was this week." I was a kid who had never felt like he'd done anything great for anyone. And it was only when working for David that I came to understand that I might actually be "good" (to say nothing of great) at anything. Part of that realization wasn't just in what David said about my own work, but where he set the bar. David would bring in writers from *Vanity Fair* to hold workshops with the staff. He'd introduce me to journalists who were doing incredible work. He'd clip articles from the *New Yorker* or *Esquire* and leave them on my desk with a note attached: "This is the level of work I expect of you."

That kind of care and regard for young writers rarely happened in the '90s, when I met David, and happens even less now. And what followed in the wake of that mentorship was just as rare—David became my friend. What I remember are dinners out in Montclair with the Carr girls, lunches where he'd dispense the latest media gossip, pancakes at his cabin upstate. David didn't just love me, he loved my wife and my son. He always asked about them and would amuse them both with his wild stories and unique vocabulary—"Carr-isms," we called them. If he'd been working especially long hours, David would say he'd been "in the weeds" all week. Or if he had some secret to bestow, he'd say "this is just girls" talking. Later this evolved into taking a trip "out to girl-island." Carr-isms aside, David had an inbuilt sense of the significance of family ritual that I lacked. You didn't go visit the Carrs and-sit around and watch TV. You played touch football. You hiked. You rode bikes.

David was a ferocious advocate of those he loved—his efforts on my behalf are matched only by those of my wife and parents. He was violently loyal. Once, he heard an editor I'd worked with disparaging me in front of a bunch of other editors, at a time when I was on unemployment. David, as was his wont, informed the editor with a flurry of colorful language that no such further talk would be tolerated. I don't think I'll be getting more friends like that in this life. I knew that at the time. I used to stop past the *New York Times* building to stand outside with him and shoot the breeze during a smoke break. I didn't even smoke. It didn't matter. *This was rare. This man was rare.* I knew it. And when people like this have time to bestow upon you, you take it. You take as much of it as they will give. My only regret is that I did not take more.

I guess it's for that reason that I am particularly thankful for *Final Draft*. These pieces represent one last conversation with David. Much of what is here I'd read at the time of publication, so the most striking material for me is the work David did while in Minnesota and in his emergence from rehab. It's in his own self-assessments, as a recovering addict and a father, that I see an earlier David that I did not have the privilege of knowing. But my interest in this earlier portion of the book is a subjective judgment.

More broadly, what you see in *Final Draft* is not just the thing that was hard for me to recognize as a former pupil—that David was a writer— but that David was a writer of uncanny gifts. He was already, as a relatively young journalist, in possession of the easy voice and understated humor that would later bloom in his later work for the *New York Times*. He didn't waste his readers' time, and he knew how to get to the heart of the story with velocity. In memorializing Brian Coyle, a politician fighting the good fight, a young David wrote:

> Brian Coyle made certain that his fight to live with AIDS became
> a very public one. Dying with the disease was necessarily a private
> matter.

And just like that, you're in the story. No throat clearing. No hemming or hawing. No philosophizing on the nature of death. You see the same efficiency years later when David profiles Robert Downey Jr.:

> Look at him standing there, a great big movie star in a great big movie, the Iron Man with nary a trace of human frailty. A scant five years ago the only time you saw Robert Downey Jr. getting big play in your newspaper came when he was on a perp walk.

There's the whole story in two sentences—a hero once laid low, now back in the saddle. And then there is David's sheer fearlessness, which bled over from the man onto the page. For thirteen years, he was a media reporter for the *Times*, writing a column for the business section for nine of those years. This latter venture was something of a promotion, but it was also a risk. Columns are where great journalists go to die. Unmoored from the rigors of actually making calls and expending shoe leather, the reporter-turned-columnist often begins churning out musings originated over morning coffee and best left there. But David rarely, if ever, published a column without calling someone—often people who were, themselves, the subject of that particular column's ire. For that reason, David's columns had heft without devolving into an unwieldy mess of "on the other hand."

That style of reported, researched, pointed opinion reached its apex in David's exposé of the billionaire Sam Zell's purchase and pillaging of the once great *Chicago Tribune*. This was a story made for David, who loved newspapers and hated bullies. Through detailed and damning reporting, David showed how Zell acquired the *Tribune* with little of his own money, transformed its offices into a frat house, decoupled the *Tribune* from its journalistic reputation, and then paid his execs millions in bonuses. It was a tour de force of journalism and in so many ways presaged this tragicomic era.

How many times have I wished David was alive right now? Media—from mainstream to tabloids to reality TV—was instrumental in the rise of Donald Trump. David would have loved this story as much as he hated its implications, and very few reporters would have been more equipped to detail those implications. But David is not here. And our coverage, and our country, is poorer for it.

Some of David's journalistic gifts were obvious to me at the time. Many were not, and even those that were, I poorly understood. He worked us all so hard, as an editor. And then, as a writer, he worked himself even harder. I could see this at the time, but now reading *Final Draft*, I wonder how much of that was rooted in his earlier brushes with death and his constant struggle with sobriety. When I was younger, I imagined substance abuse as a foe David had conquered—a slain dragon. Only later did I understand that the dragon was reborn each day, and every morning, David had to wake up and go off to battle.

David won much more than he lost. And I think those victories were tied to this fact: No one had a better sense of the brevity of life, and how essential it is to live as much of it as we can. I think now that that is why he worked so hard—that the work (and the play) was how he fought back. And I now think back to David as an editor, and think that's what he wanted most from us. To battle, every day. To wake up in the morning, ready to face the dragon.

—*Ta-Nehisi Coates*

Final Draft

1

Early Freelance in Minnesota

After he finished college at the University of Minnesota with a double major in psychology and journalism, it seemed quite natural for David to begin contributing pieces to local media. What was not so natural for him was to pursue these writing gigs while struggling with alcoholism and substance addiction. He sought treatment, and the rehabs both saved his life and provided exceptional material for some of his early articles.

In the late 1980s, David began reporting regularly for Minneapolis's alternative weekly paper, the *Twin Cities Reader*. At first he freelanced (his first article was based on a story he's heard from his own father), but within a year the *Reader* hired him full-time.

The paper had become well known for its coverage of Minneapolis's vibrant music scene, but David's writing honed in on municipal politics, local heroes and gangsters. While his burgeoning success was again interrupted by his ongoing addiction struggles, the *Reader*'s ownership was tremendously supportive of David during his difficulties and recovery efforts, and by 1991 he had fought his way back to solid work and respectability. Two years later, now a single father of young twin daughters, he was offered the post of editor, overseeing a staff of about thirty, bringing new prominence to the *Reader* with sharp-eyed features, attention-grabbing headlines, and most important of all, first-rate writing.

New Home Isn't Pretty,
but I Came from Hell Anyway

Saint Paul Pioneer Press, FEBRUARY 1989

I OFTEN HEAR the sounds of sirens at the rehab center where I live, but for the most part, my emergency is over.

No more scrambling to score cocaine, lying to cover up, or sitting down with the boss to explain why the work never gets done.

I'm sober.

The place where I live isn't pretty. But then, I came from hell anyway. Although the treatment center is jammed with recovering drug addicts and alcoholics, it seems relatively quiet compared with the insanity I left behind. This is the place where the merry-go-round stops and something resembling life resumes.

I spend my days on simple things. Preparing food. Picking up ashtrays. Talking about what life was like on the "outs." The "outs" meaning the outside, where most people go to work, raise families, and spend their leisure as they please. That wasn't what life was like for me. I have a primary relationship with cocaine. That makes me dysfunctional as a human being. Not that I didn't try to imitate a human being.

I'd be sober for a while, hanging on by my fingernails. Then I'd gradually lose my grip, and finally the wheels would come off. I'd hit the wall. My drug use wore down the most understanding of bosses, the most supportive of parents, and the most giving of lovers. They all found out what I had known all along: cocaine was the most important thing in my life. No matter how much they cared, I would always end up choosing to feed my monkey.

The words of the people who supported me echo in my head: "I think that *this* time David is really serious and he's going to do what it takes to remain sober."

The sad fact is, I *was* serious, each and every time. I left treatment with an earnestness and determination that even I found convincing. But three separate times I started using again, throwing away months of rebuilding and hard work. Even after ten years of cocaine addiction, I am at a loss to explain it myself.

Everyone has read the disheartening stories of young urban kids who turn to coke as a source of contrast to their dreary existence. That wasn't me. My life had no gaping holes. I came from a warm, loving family, received a better-than-average education, and was blessed with a talent for writing. I worked for a weekly newspaper covering cops, robbers, media darlings, and the powers that be. Every day was different. I was good at my job, and I was recognized as such on a daily basis.

It wasn't enough.

I can clearly remember my first exposure to the drug. On my twenty-first birthday a customer at the restaurant where I worked gave me a little coke as a birthday treat. I knew right away that I had found a friend. I stepped out into the evening with a feeling of power, a smile fueled by the knowledge that I had a little extra edge on anybody I was likely to encounter.

I *needed* to have that racer's edge in my pocket, the little paper bindle of powder that told me that I could go faster, have more fun, and go home later than anyone else.

It made for some tough mornings.

I would race the sunrise home, mumble a not-so-convincing excuse to my significant other, and then lie in bed for a few hours, maybe dozing, maybe not. I usually decided to head for work when the anxiety of being later and later became too much. If I had any, I'd do a toot of coke to get me started, and then I'd head into work, talking and laughing as if there were nothing wrong. If I was really in bad shape, I'd quickly hop onto the phone so I'd look like I was working. More often than not, I was calling the dope man, not the sources for the next story. When the boss came in looking for copy I had promised the day before, I'd explain that I had one more lead I wanted to check out before putting the finishing touches on the story.

In reality, I hadn't made the first phone call. But somehow, some way, I'd pull it off. By the afternoon, with my head clear enough for a flurry of calls, I'd get a story together. Then, about the time everybody else was going home, I'd make plans to write.

The plans usually began with cocaine.

I'd slip out, score some coke, and come back to the office with a new attitude. I came to feel that cocaine was an essential ingredient in my formula for success. There were a lot of stories that I was paid two hundred dollars to do that cost me three hundred dollars to write.

Cocaine's effects on my life were subtle at first but grew to be profound. Because cocaine intoxication has little effect on the user's motor skills or speech, for a time I was able to abuse cocaine and work without getting into trouble. If I tended to be a little glib and hyperactive in my role as media critic and news reporter, people wrote it off as youthful enthusiasm or hyperactivity. I was competent enough as both a reporter and an interviewer to overcome lapses in preparation and thinking, but the stress began to show.

I can clearly remember interviewing a sitting governor and having my nose begin to bleed as the result of the previous night's abuse. Deadlines began to get stretched to the breaking point. My editors' nerves got more than an occasional workout. A gradual increase in both dosage and frequency of use cut into work time more and more, to the point where both coworkers and bosses expressed their concern. I would shrug off their good intentions, mention something about "slowing down a bit," and plunge out into the night for another tour of the dark side.

Although my days were spent with cops, reporters, mayors, and legislators, my company changed when it got dark. I'd be out with night people—dealers, rockers, and women who gravitated to people who had cocaine. I often marveled at my schizophrenic existence and even reveled in the reputation I was developing. I took pride in my image as something of a "gonzo" journalist, a local echo of Hunter S. Thompson. But even if I managed to keep myself employed, my personal life was a mess.

An early marriage to a supportive woman fell apart under the weight of drug abuse. I was losing track of my old friends. I began to think of myself as some kind of half-assed gangster, buying and selling drugs and intimidating those who didn't have the money when I needed it.

After a time, it's difficult to avoid a sense of isolation and detachment from the people around you. The transition from abuser to addict is costly in terms of money, sanity, and relationships. A habit that grew out of a need to have just a little edge on the people around me was now leaving me alone in a crowd. My little secret became a big, ugly secret that wasn't so secret after all. Family and friends intervened, and I found myself admitted to inpatient treatment.

It didn't take much sober time to figure out how important drugs had become in my life. Virtually every aspect of my adult life had come to be focused on cocaine; while I was taking coke, the coke was taking me, in agonizing bits and pieces. In treatment, I resolved to reclaim myself and my future. I managed to remain sober for eight months.

My relapse was accompanied by a gnawing sense of fatalism. Even in my deluded state, I knew I could no longer be functional on a drug that had demonstrated tremendous control over me in the past. To make a long story short, my next treatment resulted in six months of sobriety. The next, a mere two days. In that time I chewed through automobiles and credit cards and, when there was no money left, the people around me.

My addiction reached the point where I was willing to sacrifice the relationships that had kept me alive in the past. I lost an important job and screwed up a number of lucrative outside assignments. My reputation as a journalist was trashed. I responded by being utterly consumed by the cocaine lifestyle, scraping to feed my habit and lying around watching cartoons when I couldn't do that.

There was plenty of time to figure out that I had no future if I continued to use, but I had lost the capacity to care. Then, about three years ago, I—along with the rest of the nation—was introduced to smoking cocaine.

Crack, as it has come to be known.

There was no honeymoon with crack. Crack is like smoking death. Each puff increases, rather than reduces, the craving for the drug. In its smoke form, cocaine reaches your brain in four seconds and winds the user's mind up so tight that he can't think past much more than where his next hit is going to come from. Crack users are universally paranoid consumptive eunuchs who show little interest in things unrelated to their addiction.

Because the drug must be smoked in fairly obvious fashion, the user becomes a prisoner of his own space, rarely leaving home. Going to a bar to hear a band was out of the question. Just going to the 7-Eleven for a pack of smokes was a genuine challenge. When the user is on a binge, the only outside trip that seems doable is the trip to the dope man's house.

And I was drinking. I used alcohol as a leveler and a type of medicine, a mood-altering depressant that was strong enough to hew some of the rougher edges.

Cocaine enables, and in fact nearly requires, the user to drink enormous amounts of alcohol. There are times when the body reaches the upper limits of its tolerance for a blood pressure twice the norm and a heartbeat that threatens to explode its source. That's where alcohol comes in. Alcohol was about the only way I was able to end a binge when the coke ran out. I would drink past the point of intoxication and into an oblivious state where the mind became less obsessed with getting high.

Cocaine people tend to operate at the upper limits: the upper limits of their credit cards, the law, and their health. Even as a well-paid professional writer with a steady gig and lots of freelance work, I was constantly scratching for enough money to buy cigarettes or food, on the off chance I had an appetite.

All of which testimony would seem to offer compelling motivation to stay away from the drug once the body heals and the spirit is revived.

There is no more grateful recovering person than someone who has come off years of cocaine abuse. The financial and emotional burden of maintaining the addiction is so corrosive that it is initially just a pleasure not to have to fight to live. Recovering cocaine addicts experience a particularly powerful "treatment high," a sense of well-being, and a wish to share it with everyone. Unfortunately for the user and society as a whole, this state of bliss and this commitment to wellness evaporates when the user is exposed to cocaine. Let me state flatly that in the periods of sobriety I have managed to put together I have never been exposed to cocaine.

Unlike an alcoholic, a cocaine addict is not confronted with his drug of choice every day. That's a damn good thing because I have never looked at cocaine and not done it. Just as surely as Pavlov's dogs came to salivate at the sound of a bell, the coke user will use if he is presented with the opportunity.

In support groups for alcoholics, it's not uncommon to encounter people with years of sobriety. In support groups for coke people, someone with a year of sobriety is a miracle. Cocaine addiction is highly resistant to treatment and rife with the potential for relapse. Former cokeheads are continually plagued with dreams of using, and deep-seated, palpable cravings for the drug.

A wise counselor once told me that "you just aren't going to go that fast ever again, and you might as well get used to it. You liked cocaine because it made you feel good, and there's nothing in the world that is going to make you feel like that again."

I am now approximately sixty days into recovery. Life is sweet and simple compared with where I came from. I get up when the sun does and start to yawn not long after it goes down. Just a few months ago, I would have been tuning up for a night in an ugly little subculture of crack pipes, twenty-dollar bills, and people who were being destroyed from the inside.

Near the end of my last run, I didn't even mix with other users. I would spend my nights with my nose pressed up against the window, searching for signs of approaching trouble. In retrospect, I know that the real menace was the reflection in the glass. I managed to destroy myself more efficiently than any cop or robber ever could.

But I'm surprised by how little that last relapse matters now.

The contrast between my old life and my current sobriety is immense. At times I feel good to the point of giddiness. Simple things please me enormously. As an addict, I was missing out on almost everything. Skiing, horseback riding, and going out on passes—all those little activities they have recovering people engage in—bring me great joy. Friends who noticed a while ago that I had fallen off the map are beginning to find out where I am and are checking in. They all say the same thing: "It's good to have you back."

It's good to be back. Having membership in the normal things of life is more than enough for the time being, and I'm at a point in recovery where the cravings of addiction are infinitely quieter. I watch people come and go from the place I will likely be for a few months, and some make it and some don't.

No one here is telling me that "this time" is the last time I'll be in treatment. But that's okay. I sit on the edge of my skinny little bed and hear the chatter of a therapeutic community in the background while I type. It isn't exactly the highlight of my professional career, but it feels right for now.

Fishing Trip to Boundary Waters

Saint Paul Pioneer Press, JUNE 11, 1989

SUPERIOR NATIONAL FOREST —There was talk around the campfire about drunken motorboaters from Canada: guys with Mercury outboards, twelve-packs of Bud, and what seemed like a prurient interest in the women of our group. Would they try to mess with us?

Marion Moses, a felon turned camp counselor, a rope-muscled black Hercules in ever-present mirror sunglasses, had to laugh. "There are twenty-three of us," he reminded the campers. "We are people who have been cut up, shot, beat with chains. Some of us shot dope into our eyeballs because that's where the best veins were.

"Nobody in their right mind is going to mess with us."

Looking around the campfire, I could easily see why. After a few days in the north woods, our group—twenty recovering drug addicts, three Eden House staffers—looked more like bloodthirsty pirates than your average band of weekend walleye hunters. With his massive chest and arms, Marion Moses would be nobody to mess with in a dark alley or on a remote wooded island. After years on the streets as a career criminal and a doper, and a long stint behind bars, Moses turned it around and became a counselor at Eden House, a last-stop Minneapolis treatment center for people who have defied every previous effort to separate them from their dope.

For Moses, as a camp counselor, his job on this island, forty miles north of Grand Marais and a couple of hundred feet from Canada, was mostly pulling in walleyes with the rest of us. But when squabbles did crop up, he'd suck in his breath and show teeth: "Knock that s— off."

At Eden House, it's Moses's job to convince residents that there is a life apart from crack and booze, robbing and stealing, pimping and whoring. That there is more to life . . . like going fishing, for instance.

Eden House, founded in 1971 from cultish beginnings, is a world unto itself, a regimen of confrontation and conflict far from the open air and beauty of the Boundary Waters. Privileges are strictly regulated, from phone use to going to the corner store. It's a kind of junkies' boot camp, where a screw-up might lead to scrubbing the stairs with a toothbrush. It is housed in a dowdy building in a crummy neighborhood. It's a noisy place, where a page system constantly orders people to report here or there.

Most of the referrals are from jails. Most new clients are surprised to find out they have fewer privileges than they had in jail. "This ain't no goddamn game we're playing, folks. We are battling for your lives," the staffers are fond of saying.

The doors aren't locked. If you leave before your program is finished, it's generally in handcuffs, or else you slink back in the middle of the night to your own personal prison on the street.

The springtime trip north is an Eden House tradition, but it's more than that. It's a chance to wake up on your own schedule, to relax when you choose, to take a vacation, to do the things normal people do.

About forty clients entered the lottery to take the weeklong canoe trip, and twenty got lucky. Among them: two convicted murderers, at least one rapist, and a few canoe loads of strong-arm robbers. Not the kind of guys you usually see on the Saturday TV fishing shows. There were also two women, one a client, one a counselor, who by now were used to macho posturing.

"What could go wrong?" said Tak, an Eden House client who helped organize the trip. Surveying all the fillet knives and axes being loaded into the vans by all these convicted felons, I kept my darker thoughts to myself.

As we loaded the van, though, I couldn't help but think of those boyhood trips when we assaulted the woods with our pocketknives and laughter. We would survive by gang-tackling the wilderness. And maybe this trip wasn't all that different: a group of outsize Boy Scouts gone bad. All of the adolescent energy and horseplay was there, along with the whining. The clients, mostly in their twenties and thirties, were people who probably hadn't found much time for fishing while they were out on the street feeding their habits. Their obsessions went beyond walleyes.

Fowl Lake's warm spot in the collective heart of Eden House is more about legend than accessibility or beauty. The spring rains had turned the island we camped on into a swampy, jungle-like place. And while there was an old logging road that came in from the Canadian side, it was of no use to our expedition. Our crew's extensive resumes as felons would have made a border check problematic. Instead, we paddled and portaged through three lakes and two rivers from the Minnesota side.

Jerry Peterson, senior counselor and nominal leader of the canoe outing, said such trips have no concrete objectives. "Its most important function is really in the building of memories. Sure, it's to see how people function up here, but it's mostly just spontaneous, mostly just fun," he said beneath the brim of a well-worn cowboy hat.

Some people took their fun more seriously than others. Takashi, a compact Asian man with a fondness for heroin, was a professional fisherman back when he was going good. He hadn't lost his touch. Early mornings, he'd paddle out with his boat mate, Dave J. They'd limp back just as darkness fell, legs stiff from being confined in the canoe all day.

Their smiles were usually accompanied by huge stringers of walleyes. "Yeah, we got a few," Tak would say quietly. Along with a few other serious fishermen, they served as the group's fish locaters. We'd all paddle out to the hot spots in their wake and beat the water to a frenzy with our crisscrossing casts.

You could almost hear the street when the group gathered to talk fish: "Where'd ya find 'em? What were you using? Do you think they're still there?" It was the kind of intense, searching discussion that probably characterized their pursuit of drugs a few short months before.

There were times, mostly at nightfall, when the hustles and addictions that had ruined our lives would seem a long way off. The moon would reflect off our rod tips as four or five canoes encircled the day's hot spot, and we razzed each other about our respective fishing talents.

As the week wore on, the shore of our island became lined with stringers from guys who were more used to hooking potential dope clients than fish. It made for a lot of knife work. David L., a huge, jowly man with a bushy moustache, had never fileted a fish in his life. He ambled down to the sandy point on Fowl Lake with a stringer of day-old walleyes.

This wasn't Dave's first trip to the island. Sixteen years before, he entered Eden House because he was addicted to shooting drugs. That was back in the days when a potential client had to stand on a chair for a day or two and scream for help before he was accepted into "the family." Dave stayed at Eden House for two years, remained sober for six, and then began drinking a little "socially."

Thirteen DWIs later, Dave L. found himself back in Eden House. As "chief elder," or client-in-charge, he was instrumental in organizing and funding this year's fishing trek. It took him days to get his first fish, and when he finally did, he didn't know how to filet it.

"Before I leave this point," he announced, "I want to know how to filet fish. What if I took my kid fishing, and I didn't know how to clean them? What would he have thought of me?"

Dave learned. "I feel like a butcher. I'm a real woodsman now." But teaching a kid how to filet fish is a ways off for Dave and just about everyone else on the trip. Most are cut off from their families, relationships that collapsed under the weight of years of drug abuse and prison time. For the time being, the trip with Eden House is the only family function we'll be invited to for a while.

Scott S. didn't really want to come. Seems there was a girl, "the only one I ever really loved," who grew tired of his fascination with drugs and returned to the North Country. "This is where she's from," Scott said, gesturing into the darkness beyond the campfire. "Being up here makes me miss her a lot."

Scott hadn't had much luck with women since. His hang-ups eventually turned into rage, and one day he jumped out of a tree and onto a woman who just happened to be walking by. He nearly killed her. Scott explained to the judge, and anyone else who would listen, that he was out of his mind on cocaine and alcohol—that's how he ended up in Eden House instead of Stillwater.

It was ironic, then, that Scott designated himself as the protector of the women on this trip. Not that they needed protecting. Client Kathy E., who did her makeup every day before leaving her tent, and Beth Knudsen, a counselor, endured all of the boy talk with ease. They also caught their share of fish, although they tended to make more noise when they did. The only allowance they required was a wide berth when they announced that they were heading up to the camp's open-air privy.

Thankfully, they didn't run into Vinny on one of his moonlight patrols. Vance W. lost his medications—tranquilizers and antidepressants —in a spill on the river on the way in, and he wasn't having much luck fishing, so he took to wandering around the swampy terrain at night, collecting things and muttering to himself.

One night, he came into the glow of the campfire and stuck out his tongue. A little turtle was perched there. Midweek, Vinny finally caught a northern, and there was a collective sigh of relief. Vinny wouldn't let go of his pet northern, walking him around the campsite with a Charles Manson–like leer that would have created discomfort in your average citizen.

"God answered my prayers on the spot. I cast out onto the water and said, 'Lord, gimme a northern,' and my pole started bending," Vinny explained without smiling.

John X. didn't show a lot of interest in fish stories or fishing. He spent most of his days straddling a canoe, sunning and staring down into the water. He must have been thinking bad thoughts. John, twenty-one, was back in Eden House just a few nights when he was caught slipping in a back door. He was seriously "geeked"—high on cocaine—something he probably already had decided to do out on the waters of Fowl Lake.

Like a lot of guys, John probably thought he was too young to give up partying forever. He was one of the guys on the trip who still might lay legitimate claim to adolescence. There was also Brett, a straw-haired eighteen-year-old who smiled a lot about nothing in particular.

Brett fished some, slept constantly, and stirred up a little trouble when he got bored. Brett apparently didn't find what he needed up in the woods. On the way back in the van, he got hyped up about something and took all of his medications that he had squirreled away. Brett's health wasn't in danger from the stunt, but his future at Eden House got a little darker. Two nights after we got back, Brett gathered up his meager belongings and slipped back onto the streets. He didn't take a good prognosis with him.

I remember sitting out on the sandy point near our camp with Brett, holding the flashlight while he gutted a fish. "You go in here," he said intently, "and then just cut along the backbone . . ." He was obviously proud of his skill; Brett P. could filet one hell of a fish. I hope he's as slick on the outside. He's just the kind of smiley-face that gets squashed in a hurry on the street.

When the first serious rain of the week began, Jerry Peterson announced, "We're moving out." Even though it was a day early, the tents were down in twenty minutes. "You don't have to tell us twice," somebody said.

On the way back, territorial squabbles began in earnest, old behaviors kicked in, and the camaraderie of the island faded with the highway stripes. The trip provided more of a respite and a detour than any kind of epiphany.

Jerry Peterson was happy, anyway. "We weren't expecting anything like that. We caught a lot of fish, we had a good time, and nobody got killed. That was enough."

Drinking and Flying

Former Northwest Captain Norman Lyle Prouse
Tells His Story in an Exclusive Interview

Corporate Report Minnesota, FEBRUARY 1991

LES STENERSON SOCIALIZED with three hard-drinking out-of-town-ers through much of an evening last March. The men, he learned in conversation at the Speak Easy bar in Moorhead, were Northwest Air-lines pilots. Stenerson, a lumberyard worker, suspected that the pilots would be flying out of Fargo the following morning, and at 1:30 a.m. he placed an anonymous phone call to the Federal Aviation Administra-tion to report the activities of his new acquaintances.

One of those pilots recalls that he felt pretty good on the morning of March 8. When his alarm went off at about 4:30 a.m., Captain Nor-man Lyle Prouse did thirty push-ups, a routine he suggests wouldn't have been followed if he were feeling the effects of the previous night's drinking.

Prouse and copilot Bob Kirchner met in the lobby of the Moorhead Days Inn motel and proceeded to the airport. Flight engineer Joe Balzer told them he wasn't feeling well and took the next van to Fargo's Hector International Airport.

At the airport, Kirchner went out to inspect the plane and Prouse went inside to fill out paperwork for the 6 a.m. flight. That's where Prouse met Verl Addison of the FAA.

"When he came up to me, and said that he had received a call at one-thirty in the morning about pilots drinking, I'm thinking 'Okay, he must be assessing me right now,'" Prouse says. "He's checked my ID, we're standing very close, and he's looking at me, observing me . . . and I'm wondering, What did he think? I'm not feeling clumsy at all, but I am extremely uncomfortable . . . and let's just say I'm scared, because I am.

"He knows about the Speak Easy."

A combination of denial, lack of information, and fear left Prouse wondering how to proceed. He decided to let Addison control the situation.

"He's talking about intoxicated pilots, and I'm thinking he's either gonna okay us or not okay us," Prouse says. "I thought for sure he was going to say something somewhere along the line that would indicate what we should do, but he never did."

Prouse walked with Addison out to the plane, where they met Kirchner in the cockpit. The three chatted for a while about the report that had been received. Addison has said that he told both of them that he could detect the odor of alcohol. Prouse is adamant in his contention that Addison never said he could smell alcohol on their breath. "If he would have told us that, we would have had no choice. We would not have started the engine," Prouse says.

The FAA requires an eight-hour gap between any drinking and flying, and Northwest has an even stricter twelve-hour bottle-to-throttle regulation. Prouse's recollection of the previous night is spotty, but he is fairly sure of two things: "I thought we were okay on the eight-hour rule, and I was sure we had broken the twelve-hour rule."

Without a clear directive from the FAA's on-site observer, Prouse says, he wasn't prepared to make a move that would threaten his career. "My feeling was that if [Addison] wasn't saying anything, he was giving us tacit approval [to fly]."

Addison has said that he made a point of telling both the pilots that there would be no violation if the plane didn't move. On his way out of the plane, Addison met Balzer and talked with him about the report. Balzer immediately asked to take a blood or urine test. Addison, who says he told Balzer he didn't have the authority to order such a test, then went to call his superiors at the FAA Great Lakes office in Chicago.

Addison also has said that while he was on the phone, he noticed the plane was pulling away from the gate. That statement more or less implies that the pilots spirited away a 727 despite unresolved questions concerning their compliance with the eight- and twelve-hour rules. Prouse counters, "That is the most asinine thing I have ever heard." He has since listened to the tapes of the ground conversation and contends that there were at least fourteen minutes from the time they called for clearance until the time they took off.

Prouse is asked whether he might have been playing a game of high-stakes chicken with Addison. "No," he says. "I just thought [pulling away] would be the final test."

And why didn't he directly ask Addison's opinion of their airworthiness?

"I just honestly didn't think to do that," Prouse says.

He admits, however, that the question might have been one he didn't want answered. He and the other two pilots were well aware that their careers were at stake, but Prouse says he never felt for even a moment that his fifty-eight passengers were at risk.

"I knew that if we didn't go, if we didn't push back, that we were going to be fired. That was a given," Prouse says. "Losing our jobs was the extreme max, capital punishment, but if the thought had occurred to me that maybe these people are at risk, I couldn't have and wouldn't have gone."

He adds: "We didn't have time for a group discussion. I just turned to the copilot and said, 'What do you think?' and he said, 'I don't know.' I know I'm dead if we don't move—so we pull back."

Alcoholics frequently talk about something called a "bottom"—an event or series of events that serves as a period, putting an end to one's drinking life. It is a time of reckoning, an end that marks the beginning of recovery.

Norman Lyle Prouse's bottom was trumpeted in big, headline type. On March 8, Prouse, a former marine flyer in Vietnam and a standout pilot at Northwest Airlines, fell about thirty thousand feet. The twenty-two-year veteran of Northwest Airlines and his crew were placed under citizen's arrest at Minneapolis–Saint Paul International Airport for flying passengers from Fargo to Minneapolis when their abilities might have been impaired by the residual effects of a night of heavy drinking.

Prouse and his crew were convicted on federal charges last summer in what was the first use of a common carrier statute that became law in 1986. Prouse's captain's bars and vocation are gone. He began his sixteen-month sentence in the Atlanta Federal Prison Camp just after Thanksgiving.

The man who sentenced Prouse, US district judge James Rosenbaum, deployed a tidy bit of understatement when he called it "a most unusual case." As Rosenbaum went on to say, "Who can comprehend an entire crew alcohol-impaired?"

Certainly not the Federal Aviation Administration. The FAA regularly deals with reports that a particular pilot may have a problem with alcohol, but the system was dysfunctional when three allegedly impaired pilots showed up together to pilot an aircraft. The FAA's on-site official in Fargo — Addison — was completely unaware that there was a relevant federal statute addressing intoxication. His primary concern seemed to be whether the FAA's eight-hour bottle-to-throttle rule had been broken.

Prouse and his crew ended up in federal court in part because Addison failed to stop the plane from leaving, even though Addison testified that he smelled alcohol. Addison told the court he didn't think he had the authority to prevent the plane's departure. The US Department of Transportation gave Addison its "Way to Go" award for his actions.

By all reports, Prouse and his crew executed a flawless flight and landing, despite difficult conditions caused by sleet and rain. The men were met in Minneapolis by Northwest security personnel and were given blood alcohol content tests. At 9:15 a.m., more than nine hours after he had left the Speak Easy bar in Moorhead, Captain Prouse registered a blood alcohol concentration of 0.128, above the legal limit for driving a car. His hangover will likely last into early 1992, when he is scheduled to leave prison.

In his first extensive interview since the incident, Prouse spent four hours recalling one of the most notorious aviation stories since jets began taking wing. His lawyer, Minneapolis criminal defense attorney Peter Wold, says Prouse turned aside interview requests from most of the nation's major news organizations, as well as the calls that came in from the producers of the *Oprah* and *Geraldo* shows as often as three and four times a day.

But on October 25, a day before his sentencing, Prouse, fifty-two, and his wife, forty-eight-year-old Barbara, met with a reporter at attorney Wold's house on Medicine Lake in Plymouth. Prouse had decided it was time he offered some personal perspective to an incident that positioned him as a punch line for Johnny Carson for several months.

Many others in the incident still aren't much interested in talking. Citing pending litigation, the FAA declined comment. Northwest Airlines spokesman Douglas Miller was less than expansive: "We have never experienced anything like this . . . one of the last ways we have of ensuring that some impaired pilot isn't flying is having the other pilots there to monitor the behavior of their peers. That system didn't work in Fargo."

Since his arrest, Prouse has been dealing with his alcoholism, spending sixty days as an inpatient and uncounted hours subsequently in various support groups. The former captain explains that, by giving an interview, he hopes to help get out the message that people can and do recover from the disease of alcoholism. He is noticeably eager to share the message of recovery but chuckles bitterly at the suggestion that he might be on the type of "treatment high" experienced by newly recovered people who seek to let the rest of the world in on their secret.

"I certainly don't have anything to be high about," Prouse says. "For fifty-two years I set very high standards for myself and the people around me, and I was lucky enough to hit most of them. Then this happened."

He adds: "I betrayed the public trust. I betrayed my employer. I betrayed my fellow employees terribly . . . they have suffered terribly because of this. But the person that I betrayed the most was myself. I had set all of these Great Santini standards. Everything was either black or white, and I didn't equivocate on anything. I don't do that anymore. I had all of these standards. I was an honorable man, with good character and good principles. I fell so far, so fast, that my mind has had difficulty catching up."

Prouse spent his adult life avoiding gray areas. He entered the marines in part because there would be no confusion about who the enemy is. He was, according to his family, a reliable provider who insisted the trains run on time around the Prouse household.

"The way I always looked at it, everybody's got a pair of bootstraps and they better damn well yank on them," he says.

Prouse gave his own bootstraps enough of a tug to catapult himself out of a chaotic childhood and adolescence and into a winged version of the American dream . . . great job, beautiful wife, good kids, and a comfortable place to land. The Prouse family survived the strikes that ripped at Northwest during the sixties and seventies and eventually bought a respectable house in Conyers, Georgia, a suburb of Atlanta. As a captain, Prouse made more than $100,000 a year. But his autocratic demeanor eventually left him isolated in his own castle. Ironically enough, both of his sons entered the marines, but all three of his children eventually left Prouse and his impossibly high expectations.

When Prouse's adopted daughter left in 1988, Prouse became obsessed with what he perceived as her disloyalty. He spent many angry nights in hotel rooms all over the country, drinking alone and a lot. Even so, Prouse was very protective of his career — he had made captain that same year — and carefully planned any drinking so it wouldn't take away his opportunity to fly.

Reggie Butler, a Northwest pilot who chairs an Airline Pilots Association committee on substance abuse, says it's a familiar pattern: "It's a curiosity of the airline pilot profession. They let their home and social life deteriorate, but they will do anything to hang on to that job."

Prouse brought the same kind of discipline and penchant for organization — this is a man who changes the oil on his car every two thousand miles — to his drinking.

"I would look at the layovers, and I would know when and where I was going to drink. I was very good at observing the clock, but I would do all of the things that alcoholics do," Prouse says. "I would look and say, 'It's one in the afternoon,' and I would need to be to bed by eight, so I would need to be done drinking by six, which means I could buy a pint. If the takeoff was later, depending on the time, I might buy a fifth.

"And then what I would do is sit there and drink by myself. I would sit there and reflect most of the time, thinking about what was happening with my family."

The evening of March 7, 1990, was unusual for a couple of reasons. Perhaps most important, Prouse's drinking that night was of an uncharacteristically social nature. The captain generally preferred to drink alone and was wary of having someone identify an entire crew together in a bar. For reasons he still can't explain, he walked to the Speak Easy bar that afternoon with Kirchner and Balzer.

Once there, the drunk in him found expression. "I had one drink, I had two drinks . . . I'm talking and having fun. I don't remember seeing a clock," Prouse says. "And I simply sat there and had more and more and more. I didn't go out that night and say, 'I'm going to have nineteen drinks and then fall out of a chair.' The clock just stopped for me as long as the waitress was coming by. I just continued to have drinks. That's the nature of alcoholism."

At least two years of binge drinking came in for a landing the day he got busted. But Prouse has come to grips with reality at a time in his life when the picture isn't too pretty. "I'll be fine for a little while, and then

I'll start thinking about going to prison, about leaving Barbara alone, and how I'm going to make a living after I get out. And my mind will start cartwheeling again."

On this day, there is a respite created by the need to remember. As the Prouses sit on the couch in Wold's den, their hands frequently intertwine as Lyle talks; Barbara's gaze rarely drifts from his face. Both traffic in the rhetoric of recovery with ease.

Prouse agreed to talk in part because he was given assurances that he would be able to address some of the mythology that has been built up around his case.

"I'm not interested in some story that says I'm a neat guy, so I'm entitled to drink nineteen rum and Cokes. What has hurt me a lot is that people have a very different perception of me than what I really am," he says. "Today, I'm willing to just be me, and people can make their own judgments. I'll take my chances with that.

"Part of the reason that I agreed to talk is that I would like to give back a little to Northwest, I would like to pay back a little bit for all of the terrible shit that rained down on them. I'm not talking with the idea of getting my job back. I just think it is the honorable thing to do."

The day before the interview, Wold had received a letter from Judge Rosenbaum, who wrote that he was contemplating an upward departure from the twelve- to eighteen-month sentence recommended by federal guidelines.

"This time of my life has been marked by a series of crises, and [the sentence] is just one more of them. Each one of them has been an escalation, and each one on its own has been a tremendously crushing, hammering blow," Prouse says, his right hand tracing his expansive jawline. "But I'm thankful that never during any of these events, some of which were literally driving me to my knees and taking my breath away, never did the idea of drinking appeal to me."

For reasons he declined to explain, Judge Rosenbaum eventually backed off from his threat and, on Friday, October 26, sentenced Prouse to sixteen months in prison. Prouse asked to be allowed to serve his time in the federal prison facility on Maxwell Air Force Base so that he could attend college full-time in order to find a new career, but federal prison authorities said they were concerned Prouse might hop a fence and steal an aircraft.

Instead, he has to make his way at an extension of the Atlanta Federal Prison. Unlike Maxwell, the facility has no Alcoholics Anonymous program and a limited number of educational offerings. "I have been through some fairly tough situations in my life, and this is just one more of them," Prouse says. "It wasn't pleasant going to Vietnam, but at least there was a sense of honor and purpose to what I was doing. This doesn't feel like that."

The case was the first Wold had tried in federal court. He took the conviction hard but has come to understand that, in this instance, the justice system had to demand retribution.

"I think that his treatment was within the realm of fairness," Wold says. "We don't have to agree with the result to agree that he was given a fair trial."

Wold is pursuing an appeal on constitutional issues, as are the lawyers for the other two pilots, who both received twelve-month sentences. Prouse, however, has elected to enter prison while his case takes its course.

"Can't get out till I get in," Prouse explains, then he says: "If you ask me whether I think it's productive for me to go to jail for a long time, the answer is no. I don't think that I'm being incarcerated to prevent me from getting drunk and going and stealing an airplane. But if the dictates of society say that I need to go and do some prison time, I'm not going to go kicking and screaming."

That kind of rationale is what Ken Watts has come to expect from his former colleague. Watts is the chairman of the local Airline Pilots Association and a Northwest pilot.

"As a pilot, Lyle was a very competent flyer across the board and adhered very closely to Northwest standards and procedures. I really don't have any insights about how this ended up coming about," Watts says. "But now that it's happened, he is just going about the business of dealing with the reality of the situation. I think that Lyle has a lot of inner strength, and he focuses on what happened instead of what would have been, what might have been, or what he might have wanted to happen."

Indeed, Prouse sees little sense in focusing on the past. "It is so easy to get into the victim role and the self-pity, but when it comes right down to it, I did something that needs to be accounted for. I am responsible for it, and I accept the responsibility. Period." He leans back and meets the gaze of his wife. There is a sigh that seems to come from somewhere in between them.

Prouse goes out of his way to defend the airline that fired him and the coworkers he left behind. In an age riddled with convicted felons who blame everyone but themselves, Prouse is an exception. He harbors no small amount of bitterness, however, about the public aspect of his abasement.

"In a way, I feel like the media took the opportunity away to accept responsibility for what I had done," he says. "I have seen the power of the press. I was seeing stories that were sent down to me in treatment, and by the time I was finished, I felt that nothing short of a public execution on Nicollet Mall was going to satisfy people.

"It got to the point where it was very difficult to convey what actually happened. People had this mental picture of some pilots stumbling out of the bar and flying an airplane.

"Now, I was in treatment with several anesthesiologists, and they said that there were entire days where they could not remember what happened. Now, that's a scary thought to me, but it doesn't play the same way as fifty-eight people thirty-one hundred feet in the air with three pilots who may or may not be all screwed up. There is certainly a much greater sense of terror and drama in that situation."

It began innocently enough. Three pilots on a layover in Fargo were staying in neighboring Moorhead and walked a block and a half from the Days Inn to the Speak Easy bar at about three-thirty in the afternoon. Kirchner and Balzer shared a pitcher of beer, while Prouse opted for a rum and Diet Coke.

"The first mistake was going to the bar to begin with. We were crowding the clock," says Prouse. Northwest's twelve-hour bottle-to-throttle rule would have required that the pilots be out of the bar by 6 p.m.

Initially, Prouse told investigators that he had left the bar by 8 p.m., 8:30 at the latest. Witnesses testified during the trial last June that Prouse didn't leave the Speak Easy until 11:30. To a comment that he must have been fairly intoxicated by then, Prouse responds: "Yeah, I might have been. Yeah. I'm sure I was . . . I'm sure I was screwed up. Plus, I had taken a hell of a crack on the head when I fell out of the chair. I really hit my head big-time."

Witnesses testified at the trial that near the end of the evening, Prouse fell off of his chair and hit his head, sustaining a cut above his eyebrow. Prouse suggested during the trial that the chairs in the bar were unsteady to begin with, but now he admits that the alcohol may have made him unsteady as well.

"I can remember starting to get up and then losing my balance . . . now I'm sure nineteen rum and Cokes sure as hell helped me lose my balance.

"I can remember getting up, but I don't remember walking out."

Just a little more than six hours before he was scheduled to captain a 727, Prouse was wandering around on the street in front of the bar.

"I didn't have my glasses on, and it was dark. I don't know where I ended up wandering around," he says. "I just don't know." Yet Prouse refuses to characterize what happened to him as an alcoholic blackout.

According to published reports, the other two pilots made moves to leave the bar midway through the evening, but Prouse encouraged them to stay. Prouse was asked whether his failure to leave the bar in a timely matter was in some sense a failure of leadership.

"There is a real misconception about that," he says with a chop of the hand. "I'm the captain of the airplane. I'm not the captain of layovers. I'm not the social director, and I'm not in charge of who goes where."

While Prouse and his crew were knocking them back at the Speak Easy, a local slid alongside them and began talking about Vietnam.

"That is not one of my favorite topics," Prouse says quickly. "Now that they have quit spitting on the people who served and have decided that we did a pretty good job, like our country asked us to do, there are people who want to get into the act, and I just didn't think that this guy had been there. He was pretty flip about people getting their heads blown off, and I guess this guy didn't seem real to me."

Witnesses testified that Prouse swore at the guy and told him to leave.

"He came and sat down at the table totally uninvited and started talking about this stuff," recalls Prouse, "and I eventually asked him to leave. I was very courteous the first three or four times, and then, yeah, I finally stood up and told him he ought to go. I thought he was the one that phoned in the tip." Not so.

Since the morning of March 8, Prouse has not had any significant interaction with either Kirchner or Balzer. Prouse says he felt initially that it was important the three keep their distance to avoid the appearance that they were cooking up some explanation; they have never reconnected. Prouse was asked whether that seemed odd to him.

"I have no problem with either of them, but I think we are each dealing with what happened in our own way," Prouse says. "It's true we all went off a cliff together, but I think we landed a lot differently."

During sentencing, Judge Rosenbaum said he received what he described as an unprecedented number of letters—about seventy—on behalf of Prouse. The letters detailed Prouse's leadership during combat in the early years in Vietnam and his solid reputation at Northwest.

Much of the correspondence displayed an almost tribal loyalty to Prouse, consistent with his background as a marine and his ancestral roots as a Comanche Indian. He had—and still has—the kind of friendships that are formed when men are under attack. Although Judge Rosenbaum felt it was his duty to ignore the pleas for lenience, the letters and some four hundred calls of support have given Prouse sustenance throughout his ordeal. His fellow pilots have supported him financially, emotionally, and unconditionally. At Prouse's sentencing, other pilots showed their support by taking up an entire row in the courtroom.

"I didn't expect . . . I couldn't have expected the good things that
have happened to me since this incident," Prouse says. "I don't know
why I have gotten this tremendous outpouring of phone calls and letters. So many good people have jumped in on my behalf."

There is a bittersweet pause. All of the letters in the world couldn't
change the fact that there was going to be hell to pay the day following
the interview and for a long time afterward.

Prouse sinks back into the couch, nestling closer to Barbara. Theirs
was a union shot whole out of every flyboy movie ever produced. She
was a small-town girl from Beeville, Texas, who finally said yes to the
attentive pilot in training. He was a stand-up marine who got a shot at
flight school after a life of unrelenting upheaval. They married and he
went off to Vietnam, flying A-4 Skyhawks low enough "for the rabbits to
jump over the cockpit.

"I enjoyed the single-seat jets. It was just me and my buddies, and we
each had an airplane."

Prouse, an enlisted man without a college degree, never thought he
would get the opportunity to fly. "I can remember winning some contest and getting to ride in a jet with some marine captain when I was an
enlisted man. I remember fantasizing about what it would be like to fly
that plane."

He certainly never envisioned being assigned to the first marine attack squadron and flying into a postage-stamp-size landing strip in the
middle of hostile territory. Prouse got started flying in 1961, got his
wings in 1963, and went off to the war in 1965. His tour lasted thirteen
months.

"It was close-in work. Mostly naping [laying down napalm] and straf-
ing," he says. "Initially, we hit a lot of what were called suspected targets,
and I thought that a lot of it was just sound and fury, but as the war
heated up, we became part of the first marine ground offensive. We
would get called in when they got pinned down."

The momentum hisses out of Prouse's voice, and his gaze drifts to the
rug. "We lost five of our twenty airplanes while we were there. We lost

two of our friends." He stops, starts, and then says simply, "I didn't feel so good about that.

"Later on, when everything got played out over there, I thought they were wasted."

He makes a strategic shift in topics to regain his emotional equilibrium. "The marine corps was my kind of thing. It was tough and it was organized, and I got enmeshed with it immediately. I kind of escaped into the marine corps when I was seventeen, and out of sixty-eight of us in boot camp, three got private first-class stripes. I was one of them."

For Prouse the marines offered the kind of structure and consistency that had never been a feature of his home life. Born poor in 1938, Lyle came of age struggling through the Depression. He and his sister followed their parents around Arkansas and Kansas as they attempted to scratch out a living.

"I remember as a child, a young child, we had a diaper service business in Fayetteville, Arkansas. It was rough. All of the work had to be done by the old wringer-type washers. We lived in a house in front of the diaper service building that was condemned by the city. There was no paint on it, and all of the boards were rotted. We moved out of there and into a converted chicken coop outside of town. We didn't expect things because we never had things."

When the family moved back to Wichita, Prouse remembers, both of his parents were drinking heavily. His father later took Prouse into the bathroom—the only place in the tiny house where there was any privacy—to tell him that they were divorcing and that the children could not stay with their mother. Lyle and his sister moved with their father into the slums of Wichita. Three years later, when Lyle's mother had a nervous breakdown, he was the one who picked her up and drove her to the state mental institution. "I just kind of deposited her there," Prouse says. He was seventeen. His father eventually died of alcoholism.

Among the things that sustained Prouse during his teens was a growing awareness of his Native American Indian heritage. He is part Comanche—from his mother's side of the family—and he found himself drawn to the dances and rituals of his people. One family nurtured his burgeoning interest, taking him along on trips to Oklahoma to, as he says, "do Indian things."

It is apparent that Prouse feels his heritage as a Native American Indian imparts a sense of responsibility as well as a sense of belonging. Fear of failure was brought into sharp relief by the value placed on his accomplishments.

"When I was accepted into flight school, the Indian people had a big go-away dance," he says. "All I could think about when I was in flight school was that I could not wash out and go back to the Indian people. It was something like the Asian loss of face."

He excelled at his classwork and as a pilot. He returned to the Indian community with a shiny set of wings that had been pinned on by his new wife. It was a little harder to go back after his arrest in March.

"I felt that in a way, they went down with me. It was very difficult to go back and talk with them.

"I got a phone call from a Comanche brother a while back—I tensed when I found out who it was. I told him how ashamed I was and that I couldn't bring myself to call anyone," he says. "This was a guy who spent six years over in Vietnam and had been terribly shot up."

Prouse's voice wavers as his wife rubs the back of his neck. "He told me that I was forgetting what our people respect the most . . . honesty and humility. He told me I still have that."

The man shared with Prouse a membership in two tribes: the marines and the Comanche. "He sent me a very sacred item that is called a Comanche prayer stick. He put some items on it that had a high, high value to him personally."

"It's been difficult to come to terms with what I did, but the fact that so many people have been willing to forgive and support me has made a big difference," Prouse says. "To begin with, I was so crippled with shame and humiliation that I couldn't do anything. I spent a week in the hospital looking at my shoe taps."

Prouse watched the televised reports from a bed in the chemical dependency section of Anchor Hospital in Atlanta. "The initial stories were just like a red-hot poker to my gut," he says.

Originally, Prouse felt that "none of the people that I was [in treatment] with had the kind of trouble I had . . . nothing could be as severe as what happened to me." But "I didn't have to sit in those groups very long to figure out that the trauma these other people were going through was every bit as severe as mine."

The turmoil created by the charges and concurrent media attention came at a time when Prouse was confronting his addiction to alcohol. At one time his doctors sat him down to tell him that federal marshals might be coming to take him away in handcuffs.

Offered the benefit of hindsight in treatment, Prouse realized his drinking career had escalated just about the time he received his captain's bars. While he was off taking his exam to become a captain, his teenage daughter gathered up her things and left. Prouse turned inward, and his drinking was often as hard and bitter as the feelings he had about his daughter's decision to leave home.

She married without her father's blessing, which was hardly forthcoming. "I didn't go to her wedding, and I didn't go see her baby. I didn't even want to know its name."

Barbara Prouse has noticed a change in her husband since the events of last year. "Lyle is," she stops, catching herself, "Lyle was a very controlling person. He was like a little sheep dog running around behind us, trying to keep us all in line so that we would be perfect. He was never abusive, but he had strong ideas about how we all should live our lives.

"Both of his parents were alcoholics, so he was very aware of it. There were a bunch of times when he said, 'Okay, I'm not going to drink,' and he would go a week or a month when he would not drink, but once he had that first drink, it was like, 'Well, why not kill the bottle?'"

Prouse says the segue from being a hard drinker to a drunk is difficult to pinpoint in time. "It's pretty tricky trying to figure out where you went beyond abuse and became an alcoholic. That is a journey and not an event. I was a binge drinker and I drank periodically . . . it wasn't like I drank all the time, but if I apply the criteria that I learned in treatment, I was probably an alcoholic some time ago."

In between his trial and his entrance into the Atlanta Federal Prison Camp, Prouse filled large parts of his days with the nuts and bolts of recovery: aftercare, meetings with "Birds of a Feather" (a pilot support group), and lots of interaction with folks who have quit drinking.

"I was in a pilot support group, and someone in the group had slipped for the second time, and he was being given the chance to keep his job if he was willing to go through treatment a second time—he was all haughty about it. The group asked me what I thought about it, and I told them if I were given a chance to get into the cockpit, I would consider it a miracle of the highest order."

Perhaps, it was posited, he had lost the right to fly. "Maybe I have, but if I have, it's because of the publicity," Prouse says. "There are over fourteen hundred fifty pilots who are in recovery and have been reinstated."

Says Wold: "This whole thing will come full circle when Lyle is back flying again and the people on the airplane know exactly who is flying the plane. His recovery will be validated at that point."

Butler, chairman of Northwest's abuse prevention committee, gives Prouse credit for initiating his own treatment the day after his arrest, before anyone suspected that he could end up in federal prison for his decision to fly on the morning of March 8. "I'm pleased with the kind of program Lyle is running," Butler says. "He's serious, and he knows what is at stake."

Douglas Miller, a Northwest spokesman, was noncommittal when he was asked whether Prouse might ever again be at the helm of a Northwest aircraft. "It's very difficult to say. There have been other cases where we have brought people back as employees. It's hard to say what is going to happen in this instance."

Miller admits that Prouse and his crew mates created "a significant public relations challenge. We realized early on that it was a black eye that was going to play out over a long period of time. It didn't surprise us that it was food for comics, but it was carried long beyond the point where it was humorous. That certainly didn't help at all . . . but I think that the traveling public understood that this was a very unique, unfortunate event and that Northwest is a very safe and reliable airline. We haven't experienced any drop-off in the number of passengers as the result of this incident."

Prouse has no trouble understanding why Northwest distanced itself from the three pilots.

"I have had people ask me, 'Has Northwest contacted you?' and I have told them that I never expected Northwest to. They have distanced themselves from me as quickly as possible, and there is nothing else they could have done. The company couldn't defend what I had done. That would have been ludicrous. I think I was treated fairly by Northwest."

Prouse has willingly surrendered his medical license to fly, and his love of flying will be confined for a time by prison fences and the magnitude of his mistake. But his punishment will not rub out his newfound ability to put his mistakes in a manageable perspective or his well-grounded belief that there are no real limits to what he can accomplish.

"I would take my kids out in the yard and say that if I got on the roof of the house and wanted to fly to that pine tree in the yard, I could," Prouse says. "If I don't make it, it's because I don't want to do it badly enough."

The former captain was asked whether he ever tried to prove his claim to his children. "I suppose maybe after nineteen rum and Cokes I could have done it." The visitor waits until a smile breaks Prouse's face before he laughs out loud.

Faegre's "Women Who Run
with the Wolves"

Corporate Report Minnesota, MAY 1993

HOP A SCHEDULED flight into Anchorage and find a ten-seater that
will trace the Cook Inlet before landing out on the Kenai Peninsula.
After renting a car in the shadow of the Redoubt Volcano, drive into
the town of Soldotna. Take the K-Beach road, bang a left at the Sizzler
and another louie at the National Bank of Alaska, and pull up to the
wood-paneled office next to the travel agency.

Carefully sidestep the moose droppings, and notice the homemade
shingle announcing the presence of the law firm of Faegre & Benson.
Depending on the time of year, you might find three Faegre & Benson
lawyers inside, poring over files.

Exposure, northern or otherwise, is part of what brings these three
lawyers—who happen to be women—to this office on Cook Inlet and
their eight hundred or so salmon-fishing clients.

The salmon, along with the entire ecosystem of southern Alaska, suffered a ferocious blow when the Exxon *Valdez* ran aground in Prince
William Sound on March 24, 1989, spilling some 11 million gallons
of oil.

One of the more predictable results of the spill has been the huge
in-migration of people with Juris Doctors. But whereas most big firms

flew in and out, Faegre has established a beachhead on the inlet, which is tucked around the Kenai Peninsula from Prince William Sound and received massive secondary damage from the spill. The firm has eschewed a class action, preferring instead to take on the giant oil company one client at a time.

Faegre's Lori Wagner explained her involvement in a phone interview from the road. "I like the idea of suing Exxon, and I wanted to go to Alaska," she says. Team members were initially asked if they wanted to go to Alaska for a week and a half. "That was four years ago, and we are still going up there," she adds. "There's still no end in sight."

During a recent break from their far-flung efforts at frontier justice, two of the other lawyers on the case agreed to meet at the Loon for a chat. Sarah Armstrong and Melanie Julian Muckle showed up bearing handfuls of pictures and no shortage of anecdotes.

Prominent among the photos is the company moose, who returns the favor of carrots and other goodies with redolent gifts on the office steps. According to Armstrong, a thirty-two-year-old cum laude graduate of the University of Minnesota Law School, protocol must be observed in all lawyer/moose interactions. It is best, she established empirically one morning, to maintain a certain distance.

"I was trying to give him a saltine by hand, and I guess he just got impatient and he charged me," she recalls.

Asked whether she offered the moose any tactical advice at that critical juncture, she says, "Nothing that could be printed. I just ran." The two lawyers roar with laughter.

Brian O'Neill, who heads Faegre's environmental law team, encourages interaction with the community as well. "If we were going to represent hundreds of fishermen, I thought it was important to learn what their lives were all about, so we all went out commercial fishing," he says. "I think it made us better lawyers in this case."

Wagner suggests that a full-time presence has been essential to advancing the relationship with the firm's clients.

"Alaska is not a culture where people deal with lawyers all the time. Around the rest of the country, people have come to view lawyers as a minor annoyance. But in Alaska, the only thing they know about lawyers is what they see on *L.A. Law*, if they see it, although they have probably seen far too many lawyers since the spill," she says.

Armstrong recalls that when the team first landed on the Kenai Peninsula, "we had about ten people and five of them were women. We were informed that we probably had more women per square foot than almost anywhere in Alaska."

The three have spent a lot of time hiking, fishing, and, yes, even mushing, when not preparing cases. Faegre lawyers working back in the gleaming, hermetic confines of Norwest Center have a hard time picturing life at the top of the continent.

"There's a lawyer in our group who calls us 'the women who run with the wolves,'" says Muckle. Others from the firm came to help with depositions a while ago, and, she recalls, "there was a tax lawyer who was standing in the office and somebody dropped off six fresh salmon. He couldn't believe it. He said, 'You just open the door and they bring fish in?'"

Even with fresh fish flopping next to deposition files, the lawyers from Faegre always remember that they are up against the legal equivalent of a force of nature.

"This is going to be a long war because Exxon has a lot of money at stake," Armstrong says. "They have been just shameless because they don't have a case on the merits, so they have tried to get rid of fishermen by setting up all sorts of procedural requirements."

Muckle has been handling the 1.5 million pages of documents that have been created so far, documents that are fast filling up a room at the Faegre office in Minneapolis.

"This is very sophisticated, big-time litigation that just happens to be going off in a very remote part of the world," says a proud O'Neill.

"The success of our team thus far has been the result of the work that these three women have put in," he says. "They have taken years of their lives and dedicated it to this battle."

Karen Hanson, a lawyer from Opperman, Heins & Paquin who represents native people in a class action related to the spill, says the thousands of miles logged by Faegre's lawyers have put them far out in front of the case.

"These three women know more about this case than anyone else. When they talk, the other lawyers involved in this case listen and listen good, because to ignore what they know is suicide," says Hanson.

Part of their edge is that they know the conflict goes beyond Alaska's resources.

"The oil is a temporary resource, and it will eventually be gone," says Armstrong. "When the oil companies take that with them, it's important they leave behind a place where people can still make a living."

Brian Coyle's Secret

The Very Public Minneapolis City Councilman
Has Kept His Exposure to AIDS
a Very Private Secret for Six Years

Minnesota Monthly, MAY 1991

AFTER COAXING HIS two little dogs, Shannon and Toto, from the room, Brian Coyle shuts the door to his bedroom sanctuary. There's the canopy-topped bed, the candles, the host of religious objects, and just a foot away from the bed, a bookshelf overflowing with seemingly endless literature about AIDS and chronic diseases.

With morning light barely appearing through the west-facing window, Coyle drops a black, pill-shaped pillow to the floor and quickly folds his long frame into a cross-legged position before a statue of Buddha on a makeshift altar. Coyle closes his eyes and begins to meditate. In a few short minutes, his increasingly rhythmic breathing fills the room.

The Minneapolis city councilman uses this morning ritual to help cope with the tensions of fighting the many public battles he has waged. For the last six years, he has used it to fight a battle that until now had been very private. But for the next twenty minutes there is silence, inner peace.

An internal clock signals, and Coyle rolls onto his back. His long hands arc over his head until they hover just above the ground with a slight, but noticeable, tremor. Coyle's purple jogging suit seems a size too big, the extra material bagging and twisting at odd junctures on his attenuated frame.

He moves steadily through a series of yoga positions until he turns soundlessly toward the northern wall, which is dominated by a picture of friends Dick Hanson and Bert Henningson. Both are now dead from AIDS. He raises his arms above his head for a full minute, staring at the picture. Later he'll say he remembers how they died, but mostly he remembers how they lived. After concluding his private ritual, he changes quickly into his blue pinstriped suit and heads down the block to catch a bus to Minneapolis City Hall.

Hours later he concludes his day with a ritual of another sort. He spikes his last pink phone message, says a quick goodbye to secretary Lori Komar, grabs an elevator to the first floor, and heads to Metropolitan–Mount Sinai Medical Center. Here he enters Clinic 42, where he greets folks behind the desk and heads back to the treatment room with its eight curtained cubicles, each with its own big, black, comfortable chair. Jorge Chorens, the respiratory therapist, sees Coyle arriving and begins hooking the air hose to a valve in the wall. None of the people in the chairs looks up. None makes conversation.

As Coyle eases into a chair, Chorens hands him a clear plastic mouthpiece that has a small bottle of fluid riding on its underside. A fine, bitter mist of antibiotic Pentamidine hits Coyle's tongue, and he settles in to watch the local news on the small TV in front of him. His breathing becomes rhythmic once again.

The two rituals, the first practiced each morning and the second each month, are part of Brian Coyle's battle against AIDS. He is HIV positive and has been for at least six years. All this time this very public man has kept a very private secret. In 1985, right after being elected to a second term with 85 percent of the vote, he decided to test what his body was already telling him and walked the few short blocks from city hall to the Red Door Clinic. He had intuited the results long before the guy with the clipboard told him the news was not good.

Coyle, who was forty years old at the time, says, "I wasn't at all surprised. Looking back, what was going on with my body and what was going on with the spread of the virus, I would say that I was exposed as early as 1981. I had inklings way back then."

Nineteen eighty-one was a turning point for other reasons. Coyle, who had spent most of his life raging against the status quo, was doing his best to take his progressive agenda in-house, into the chambers of the Minneapolis City Council. Deploying a ragtag army of gays, tenant activists, and neighborhood types, he challenged incumbent Jackie Slater and came within a hair of denying her endorsement. Ever the planner, Coyle spent the aftermath of the 1981 race laying the groundwork for a successful bid in 1983. He arrived as a force to be reckoned with in the community at large, and within the gay community he was viewed with a combination of affection, pride, and envy.

For Coyle, the early eighties was a time of liberation and exploration, just as it was for many of his gay peers.

"Like a lot of gay men in the rest of the country, it was a time when we were finding out what sex was really about. But Minneapolis never had the kind of rampant promiscuity that was part of gay life in other cities. We had no back rooms filled with group sex. I went to the bars, I met a lot of people, and every once in a while I went home with one of them."

Coyle was never one to patronize the hypersexual gay bathhouses —he later voted to close them down after it became obvious they were fertile transmission grounds for HIV—but he acknowledges he was sexually active with a number of partners.

There was more flirting than serious cruising at that time, but he took risks he had no idea he was taking, engaging in sexual liaisons that occurred before it became evident that unprotected gay sex had the potential to kill. As a newshound and a well-networked gay politician, he was among the first in town to recognize the menace HIV represented to the gay community. His sexual lifestyle changed in 1983—he found a lover and was monogamous for the next two years. Coyle doesn't talk to his former lover these days.

"I've tried calling, but he doesn't seem to want to talk."

The city's first openly gay council member decided a couple of things in the weeks following his test results: He liked his job, he was excited about the future, and he was certainly not ready to die. There was, of course, the rather knotty issue of disclosure.

First he went through the denial, as a survival mechanism, and then "there's been the very real fear of telling my story, because I can lose my contacts, and eventually lose my job." But trying to keep the secret while in public life has finally worn him out. There will be no more avoiding support groups and slipping into the AIDS treatment clinic after hours out of a fear of recognition. Brian Coyle has decided there is life—political and otherwise—after disclosure.

"You have to weigh and balance the gains of being in the closet— again—or coming out. First it was the issue of testing; now, six years later, it's a matter of telling my story. I think I'm ready.

"At the risk of sounding hokey, I believe in honesty, and I really have been compromising my own sense of integrity by having to keep this a secret. From the standpoint of my health, the people who have been out in the open and dealing with it seem to have benefited. And I need all the help I can get.

"Plus, whether I live for many, many years or for a brief time, I want to make a contribution to the larger AIDS community that I feel a part of. I think that the only way we are going to destigmatize the disease is by coming out, by saying that we have it, and by saying we are living with it."

Whether the public and specifically his coworkers are ready for the information is another matter. Coyle's decision to tell will no doubt set off a power scramble within city hall. Historically, it's a culture where a hint of vulnerability can spark the most venal kinds of self-interest. There will be support, but some of it will be offered in the context of other people's ambitions.

"The keepers of the lists and the watchers of the horse race are going to start crossing your name off . . . They'll say, 'He's a dead man, so

we'll chalk him off the list.'" This last observation is delivered without
rancor or indignation, but Coyle thinks the political vultures may be in
for some lasting disappointment.

"The untold story in America right now is that there are many long-
term survivors of AIDS. Increasingly, people who are working with HIV
and the specific manifestations of AIDS are beginning to see it as a
chronic disease. It has the potential to be fatal, but there are increasing
numbers of people around the country who are fairly long-term survivors. Eight to ten years."

So far Coyle has had the makings of a long-term survivor, but he
knows that could change in a matter of days.

Riding uptown on the way to his doctor's appointment, Coyle explains
that the mental approach to living with disease is critical.

"The meditation is important because you can return to the breathing throughout the day when you are in stressful situations. When you
begin to panic, it's important to remember your breathing. Panic is very
destructive."

Today, because a series of rashes on his face is not responding to
treatment, Coyle heads to the office of Dr. John Weiser, an old friend.

"I'm not the beauty I once was," Coyle says, tilting his face up into the
examination light. Weiser enters the examination room and chats about
vanity while he examines the pronounced bumps that ring Coyle's face.
He and Coyle decide to switch Coyle's medication.

There is a short discussion about the semantics of AIDS, and the doctor begins talking about his patient of the past five years.

"He's the worst patient you could ever have . . . totally noncompliant," jokes the doctor, who looks a lot more like a weight lifter than a
doctor, even in his white coat. "Brian is HIV positive, he has none of the
opportunistic infections associated with AIDS, but he has skin manifestations associated with AIDS-related complex."

Weiser admits that working with AIDS patients can be fairly grim
work, "but after ten years, we are beginning to get a lot better understanding of AIDS, and we are finding ways to help people live with it as

a chronic disease." The talk ends on that bright note, and Weiser heads down the hall in search of some new medicine for his patient. Coyle meets him at the supply closet just short of the lobby and is handed a pink bag stuffed with six boxes of pills. He opens his briefcase full of city paperwork and finds a place for the bag.

On the way out, Coyle spots a number of acquaintances in the waiting room who may or may not be there for the same reason he is. He nods hello, and the glances he receives in return are a weave of mutual recognition and discomfort.

Coyle steps out onto Hennepin Avenue and speaks with regret about the furtiveness HIV has engendered anew in the gay community.

"Everybody is so damn worried about who knows what," he says, his voice colored with aggravation. "The irony is that I am a public person, and I have a lot more to lose, but I'm tired of sneaking around. I don't skulk anymore . . . I'm almost brazen," he says, holding the door as we walk into Calhoun Square.

He buys the coffee and we take a seat across from Odegard's bookstore, a place where Coyle spends two hundred dollars a month feeding his appetite for books. A woman walks by in a striking purple beret, Coyle's favorite color.

"I've got to have that hat. Wouldn't that go over well in city hall?" he says, smiling at the prospect.

We return to the subject of his beloved books. "They're very important to me. I've decided that when I do die, all of my books on AIDS are going to the Quatrefoil Library," he says, referring to a local gay lending library. "It's just one more way of leaving something behind."

His father's death in January after a long illness sparked a number of responses in Coyle, including a leisurely tour of his own house in which he indexed all of his possessions on little pink cards. He spent an afternoon organizing the cards, deciding who would get what in the event of his death.

"You have to be prepared to divest things. I love all of my things very much, and I love life, but it's still important to face up to the inevitable reality of death."

Among the many good things that have happened to Coyle since he was elected to represent the Sixth Ward are buying a nice house in the Whittier neighborhood and filling it with nice things. He makes an effort to hide his annoyance when it's suggested that AIDS could put his lifestyle, as well as his life, at risk.

"I spent a lot of my life being partially employed. I know what it's like to have three dollars for the next two weeks . . . to go to the co-op to buy just carrots and a loaf of bread. Yes, I worry about income and especially my home, but as long as I have supportive friends I'm not going to get stressed out about those things," he says.

"I guess my worst nightmare is what all people who have a chronic disease must think about—blindness, dementia, and a prolonged decline. I can put up with anything as long as I can write, read, and think."

Coyle grows weary of the direction of the questions and begins to take the offensive.

"All of you goddam media people are so intent about talking about AIDS as some kind of death sentence," he says, his face friendly but resolute. "While I don't want to deny the possibility of death, I have been living with this disease for a while, and I'm interested in talking about how me and a lot of other people are surviving with AIDS."

Every day, Coyle executes a regimen—of diet, meditation, yoga, and the drug AZT—which is bearing fruit far sweeter than simple survival. His quality of life and his professional output are high by almost any objective standard. That's why Coyle still has a choice. In spite of an incredibly distressed T-cell count—one of the primary indicators of AIDS —he has no opportunistic infections, no gaping skin lesions, and no catastrophic weight loss. His symptoms—indeed, his disease—remain manageable.

Coyle reminds me often that 20 percent of the people diagnosed with AIDS are still alive after three years. "But," he admits, scratching his left shoulder, "there are a lot of folks who get very sick right away. I've been lucky.

"I am honest enough and realistic enough to realize that I'm living with a compromised immune system. I'm HIV positive, there is no question about that. While I haven't had any major opportunistic infections, I am experiencing some of the symptoms associated with AIDS. I guess you could say that on the continuum of this disease, I'm somewhere in between," Coyle says.

"Essentially, I'm living as a thinner person, a person who can wear down more quickly, and therefore I have to moderate and control my time. I have some skin eruptions and itches that are pretty common to HIV-positive people. There is some dry cough . . . that's been going on for a good three to five years. Some people notice it, some people don't notice it at all. But the cough is hard to pick up in the wonderful world of politics because people are constantly clearing their throats and harrumphing quite frequently as they prepare to speak. I always fit right in. I still do.

"I have to be realistic though," he says. "I mean, I could get a massive opportunistic infection and die. Wouldn't that ruin the story?" he says, before unleashing a witchy cackle, along with a pronounced arching of the eyebrows.

The possibilities of sex, once one of Coyle's many preoccupations, have been ground down under the weight of his HIV status.

"After a while, you just get tired of all the negotiation that has to go into it. After a while you just don't want to go through that," he explains.

"The AZT depresses the sexual drive, and apart from that, you aren't exactly feeling like Mr. Prowess because of the changes that are going on in your physical self."

Besides, he says, "there's no way in the world I would transmit this virus to somebody else. To me, that would be like taking out a gun and shooting somebody. I know that's a loaded statement, but I just couldn't morally live with that. I can assure you, there will be no drunken lapses or excuses or maybe-just-this-one-time with me."

His solitary lifestyle lends some irony to Coyle's compromise victory on the domestic partners ordinance, which granted sick and bereavement leave to registered gay and straight couples. The author of the ordinance has no practical use for it. For Coyle, it was a political issue that stemmed from the personal, but not in the strictest sense.

In his speech on behalf of the ordinance before the council, he reacted with some frustration to other council members' suggestion that gay orientation was "a lifestyle choice."

"I spent the better part of my adult life trying to choose to be a heterosexual, over and over and over again . . . I really worked hard at being a good heterosexual," he told the council.

"This notion that we choose our lifestyle . . . I don't think of myself as a lifestyle statement. This suit," he says, pulling up the lapels on his black pinstriped Armani jacket, "is a lifestyle statement, but it certainly does not represent the core of who I am. The only real choice is to be honest with yourself about who you are."

"I think this will be great for him," says Coyle's roommate and friend Roy Schmidt. "The fact that he hasn't spoken out before has really troubled Brian. He has never been in the closet about anything, and I think having to remain silent on this has been contrary to what he is all about." As a staffer at the Minnesota AIDS Project, Schmidt has seen his share of AIDS casualties, but he suggests the number of long-term survivors is growing. He is convinced that the folks in city hall and elsewhere who attempt to bury Coyle will be in for some disappointment.

"There will be those who reject Brian when they find out, and that's just the sort of write-off that's happened to Brian before. They wrote him off in 1981, they wrote him off in 1983, and they will try to write him off now that he is out as HIV positive. I think that's a big mistake."

Coyle is noncommittal about his specific political plans. "I don't feel I have to run again in 1993 to prove myself, but that's a decision I will make at some time in the future."

Publicly announcing he has AIDS is complicated business. One morning I show up for an interview, and Coyle's face is taut and speckled by a noticeable rash. There is an uncharacteristic hesitation to both his speech and his movement. Absent any prompting, he admits his participation in the story is wearing on his physical and mental health.

After one particularly productive interview session, I clap him on the back to punctuate my appreciation. He lurches forward a full foot as I recoil from the feeling of lots of bone and very little tissue. Our eyes share a moment of recognition, and then he begins talking.

"There are a lot of adjustments you make. You have to be careful what you sit on because you don't have a fat butt anymore . . . There are small adjustments and large ones. I think that the biggest trauma of this disease—or any other chronic disease—is that it dramatically alters your sense of your own future. You have to begin to say, 'I'm not going to just survive, I want to plan for the future,' even though you may not accomplish as much as you would like."

The only elected official in a position to know about the political impact of Coyle's health is council president Sharon Sayles-Belton. She is the one person on the council Coyle chose to tell about his HIV status. She says Coyle will still be in the driver's seat.

"Brian is a very determined man, and I think he is doing a good job of representing the Sixth Ward. As long as he can do the job, he is going to do it, and if he can't do it anymore, he will say so. He has a tremendous amount of integrity."

Coyle says, "I have told her that I was thinking about stepping down from the vice presidency of the council, less for health reasons than just wanting my old independence back, and she said, 'Don't you dare.'

"If there comes a time when I can't do the job, I'll deal with it. This has definitely altered my sense of the future, but that isn't all bad. I will make my decision when the appropriate time comes."

Because the city council now has four-year terms, Coyle's need to decide is less than imminent, which may have had something to do with the timing of his decision to go public. The council will not come up for election until 1993, leaving both the voters and the council members plenty of time to process the impact of Coyle's HIV status.

Of course, if he runs in the next election, he will be knocking on doors as a person with AIDS.

"It would be real rough," he says, "but then again, you have to remember that I have door-knocked as an openly gay person and had an

average of one out of three doors slammed in my face every day endlessly for two hundred days. I have been accepted and rejected more
times than even the worst barfly in the Saloon or the Gay Nineties. I'm
used to it."

His days of knocking on doors began in his hometown of Moorhead
in the 1950s, when he was a twelve-year-old campaigner for Ike and later
head of something called 125 Teenagers for Nixon.

"Brian got sent to this Republican function to do a report for school,
and he came back heading up this group of students for Nixon," says sister Kathy Coyle. "When Nixon came up to Minot, Brian got his picture
taken with him. We still have the picture. It's funny when you think he
ended up . . . as part of the effort to get Nixon impeached in seventy-
two."

Kathy Coyle is a forty-year-old news anchor for KXJB-TV in Fargo,
and after seventeen years in the news business, she has some concerns
about how the latest chapter in her older brother's career will play out
in public.

"I worry that when the story that he has AIDS gets out, that is all
people will focus on, that they will not focus on his total life," she says.
Her voice breaks with emotion before she continues. "I want people to
remember Brian as my big brother who taught me how to make snow
forts and run neighborhood puppet shows.

"I want them to think about his dedication to Minneapolis, helping
victims of poverty, working for better housing, working long and consistent hours to open people's hearts to accepting minorities.

"Over the past few years," she says, "Brian has been more at peace
with himself and a lot easier to be around. It took me a while to figure
out that the change corresponded with him being diagnosed."

Kathy says that serenity was not always a prominent feature of her
older brother.

"I remember after he moved to Minneapolis to go to the U, he came
back very opinionated about what was wrong and he would give these
big lectures at the holiday dinner table. *Bourgeois* was his favorite word
back then."

But Coyle's anger and radicalism eventually found a focus in his second campaign for the Minneapolis City Council. His sister remembers the victory party on election night in 1983 very clearly.

"Brian had been an underdog for a long time—he lived in poverty —and all of a sudden it became apparent that he was going to win election to the city council. We went downstairs to the party, and all of these people were there, all of the television stations were there . . . and it was like the rest of the city had finally discovered what we had known for years. He proved you can be honest about who you are and win," she recalls.

Coyle came to the council with an odd resume. He was a founding member of Students for a Democratic Society, a successful draft resister, and an advocate of an open system of higher education. In 1972 he was part of a national student effort to impeach Nixon, and in 1974 he went to Hanoi.

Once the war—and the focus it lent to dissent—evaporated, he moved to tenant advocacy, eventually shaking change out of the federal housing establishment.

He came to the council with six older neighborhood-based candidates with a progressive neighborhood platform that has dominated the council ever since. He has pushed his personal and political agenda with a style that is a marriage of equal parts flair and ambition. By the mid-eighties, people mentioned the possibility Coyle would be the city's first gay mayor, and he was elected vice president of the city council.

For the past six years Coyle also has been part of a national lobby that has seen the funding for AIDS go from $200 million to more than $3 billion. On March 11 and 12 of this year, Coyle and other gay elected officials again lobbied Congress, trying to ensure that AIDS isn't relegated to passé status in the media or allowed to tumble off the government's agenda.

He did so as a gay elected official without publicly revealing his HIV status, but he will go back next year as both a politician and a person with AIDS, a PWA. He is one of the leading voices for "A Call to Action in '92," which will feature a million or so gay people marching in Washington to remind government officials that every half hour someone in the United States dies from AIDS.

While Coyle understands the ultimate consequence of being HIV positive, he is not yet ready to die. A timeline he has drawn for his future includes a number of possibilities, but dying of AIDS is not one of them. By surviving, indeed thriving, he is negating the odds and making a fool of the experts. It's a role he's gotten used to.

Even in Facing AIDS,
Coyle Served Truth and His City

Star Tribune, AUGUST 1991

BRIAN COYLE MADE certain that his fight to live with AIDS became a very public one. Dying with the disease was necessarily a private matter.

Coyle's death took its course over two months in the Southside house he loved, in the Whittier neighborhood he fought for, in the city he helped lead. His dying lacked some of the cinematic elegance we all grew up on. Yes, there was nobility, and a degree of acceptance. But Coyle's march toward AIDS's inevitable upshot was on the whole a bum deal.

Both his prognosis and his personal outlook were guardedly optimistic just four months ago. The process of disclosure had been cathartic for Coyle, combining his love of a focus with an innate need to be honest. But the planning and execution of his decision to go public as a politician with AIDS likely cost him some days, weeks, or months. Coyle recognized all along the risk of disclosure.

We worked together on his AIDS story last winter, talking about what it was like to be a public person with a terminal disease. On one gray, snowy afternoon in February, we walked from city hall to the clinic where he took treatment. He wondered aloud whether it was wise for him to abandon a survival strategy that was built on nondisclosure, a strategy that had sustained him through six years with HIV.

He admitted then that the process of coming out—again—was already having telling effects on his health. "I do worry," he said, "whether I'm making the right decision."

But a magazine editor and a TV reporter had already been contacted; the genie was out of the bottle. The question drifted away for good. Coyle never said so, but he probably felt he made the right decision. It was AIDS that killed him, not the strain of being honest about it.

The big media splash that followed required an enormous amount of his limited energy. For two weeks solid he made the media rounds—hammering home the message that he was *living* with a chronic disease. Then the splash subsided and Coyle, ever the planner, was left without an obvious mission or challenge. A peptic ulcer—perhaps unrelated to his AIDS condition—was diagnosed in June, but by that time he was already very weak and skinny.

I stopped by the hospital in June to chitchat and practically fell over when I saw him.

"I look like an AIDS victim, don't I?" he said, his narrow face creasing with a grim smile of recognition.

He was in and out of the hospital after that, losing weight and losing ground. A system of round-the-clock home care was set up, and I took some nocturnal shifts.

The last visit should have prepared me for what was to come. The plans for recovery that had been discussed on previous shifts were replaced by talk of wills, fear, and spirituality. It was a bumpy night, with Brian stirring and sitting up frequently. It was not quite morning when he finally began resting easily, but even that was disquieting. I leaned over him in the dark—just to be sure.

"I'm still breathing, David," he said without opening his eyes. "Go away, please."

We shared a quiet laugh as I ambled back to the couch. Even at 5 a.m. in an incredibly stressed state, Brian was a terribly witty, funny man.

• • •

In the matter of Brian Coyle, I crossed the line of objectivity—from reporter to pal—almost exactly one year before he died. I had long admired his dedication to his inner-city ward and his willingness to tweak the mighty when he asked me out to lunch and said he wanted to spend some time talking.

I wondered what naughty bit the best source in city hall had been hoarding. In his three terms on the council, Coyle made an elegant transition from a combative left fielder to a mature city leader, capable of productive compromise without becoming an ethical eunuch. During the same period there were changes in his physical appearance, but it seemed impolite to ask someone as vain as Brian why his suits seemed to be hanging on him.

Lunch on that hot August day was outside, at a table with a view of the pond in the middle of the park. I was jabbering about my latest journalistic conquest and noticed Coyle, a chronic interrupter, was simply waiting for me to finish.

"Well, I've been taking the week off," he said, turning to gaze out into the park. "I'm feeling a little guilty because my dad is real sick and I haven't been home [to Moorhead]." It was suggested that maybe he *should* feel a little guilty.

"I've got my own stuff to deal with," he said quietly, his gaze fixing mine.

I swore aloud and girded myself.

"Do you have *it?*"

"Yep."

The acronyms HIV and AIDS weren't mentioned that afternoon. We talked a great deal about *it* instead. He concluded lunch by saying at some point he would be interested in telling his story.

Eight months later the story rolled out in print and on TV. It was a case study of media manipulation, and he took a politician's pride in pulling it all off.

Toward the end there were no phone calls being made and no horses being traded. Coyle chatted if he felt up to it, ate when he was able, and slept whenever his illness would allow. If he wasn't destined for recovery, last Friday afternoon was probably as good a time as any to punch out.

It was far too soon for me and a lot of other people in this town.

As a political person, he was a weave of calculation and compassion who worked both to comfort and empower the afflicted. Coyle never became unmoored from the grass roots that pushed him into office in 1983. Discrimination and poverty were hardly academic for the gay politician who had doors slammed in his face every time he went out door knocking.

For Coyle, the political was always personal; his battle on behalf of others was a primary tool of his own survival. Brian fought for his people as if his life depended on it—because in a fundamental way, it did.

2

Family Times

While toiling assiduously at his day job at the *Twin Cities Reader*, David also began contributing to a monthly local publication called *Family Times*. Once or twice a month he would write a first-person column—entitled "Because I Said So . . ."—about being a single father. It was candid, intimate, funny, and outrageous, and it put a real-world spin on the typical parenting advice. He continued this labor of love, this autobiography of a family, for decades.

Because I Said So . . .

Musings of a Single Father

MOST PEOPLE USE their annual vacation from work to revive and get focused, but to my mind, a good trip can be one of the most confusing things in the world. I left town for ten days and went to a place a long, long ways from home. It was everything a vacation is supposed to be: adventurous, too expensive, and a diametric shift from my workaday life here.

Before I left I was sincerely worried about leaving the twins for ten whole days. Once I hit the road, however, I barely remembered I had kids. That may be overstating it a bit, but running around being spontaneous and self-seeking was something I had thirty years of practice doing. This team concept thing is a relatively recent development in my life. Let's just say that I got into the vacation swing of me, myself, and I without much trouble.

It made for a tough landing. The girls were frantic to see me, and I was overwhelmed by love in abeyance. And the awesome responsibility that it represents. We had a tough week of readjustment, and I found myself feeling pretty punk about the tall challenges of making like Ozzie without Harriet in the picture.

A couple of corners of reality had me feeling all the more conflicted.

Part of the reason that I savored my vacation so much was that we had such a tough winter around my house. I spent quite a few months very ill and struggling. The three of us were out in the tall waves for a while, just hanging on for a seriously ugly ride. And even though my health has returned, the peek at my own vulnerability—and by extension my own mortality—frankly scared the hell out of all of us.

It isn't just the big stuff that grinds you down. So much of the business of running a family seems hopelessly mundane after a peekaboo at life absent commitments. For ten days I woke up and was presented with choices—like heading to a volcano for the day or opting to go to the ocean. Two days after I got home I found myself in a fugue state at Rainbow trying to remember which flavor of Berry Bears the girls prefer.

Paying for the Berry Bears is a whole other bag of snakes. The economic vagaries of life in the freelance lane indicate that we will be heading into the summer with significantly less moola to throw at the business of living. That doesn't mean that the monthly nut is no longer manageable, it's just a lot less fun in an era of family limits.

When I landed back in my life, it was the battles big and small that preoccupied me. I felt worn out before I even punched back in. While my vacation had indeed provided a much needed break, it seemed to have sucked a lot of the momentum out of my confidence. I guess I lost some of the hopefulness about our collective future.

That's where my friend Dave comes in. We were pals in the bad old days, fellow fun seekers who didn't plan much beyond the next twelve-pack. Oddly enough, after all these years, Dave and I still have some things in common. In fact, it turns out we're both custodial parents of twin girls, although Dave has a younger daughter.

We got together for a rare lunch, the first part of which I monopolized with a lot of pissing and moaning about how tough it was to be me. Dave listened politely and quietly mentioned that his family had some medical stuff going on. Seems Heather, one of his ten-year-old twins, had a tumor attached to her optic nerve. There were many months of doctoring, some of it from an occasionally indifferent medical team. One of the things that sustained me while I was in and out of the hospital this last winter was the realization that it would have been infinitely more difficult to bear if it had been one of my kids instead. And yet here was Dave talking in very reasoned tones about an illness that could have profound effects on his daughter's future.

After suspense beyond what any parent should endure and more indignities than should ever land on a kid's shoulders, Dave and his daughter came out the other end. He spoke with visible choice about his daughter's resiliency and toughness—and then managed to articulate a tremendous amount of gratitude about how his little family had been blessed.

My face warmed about the edges with discomfort. I asked David how they were getting by financially. "We're on welfare," he explained matter-of-factly. "This is a time in my life when I needed to be home with my children, and I just decided that we are going to try and make it on AFDC. We're not going to be doing it forever. I'm going to school, and in a few years we'll have something."

I have never been silly enough to buy into the redneck notion that welfare is some kind of cushy gig. The grinding, chronic dilemma of never enough would wear me flat inside of two weeks. How Dave could be sitting there being upbeat and positive about getting by on an impossibly low amount of money was beyond me.

The old cliché about the educational value of shuffling along in somebody else's moccasins—even for just a few minutes at lunch—was a real wake-up call. I had spent so much time staring at my own belly button that I lost track of my place in the world and in my family. It's a nice family, a nice world, a space where me and mine have every opportunity to make the kind of life we choose.

SEPTEMBER/OCTOBER 1992

Traffic is building up very heavy on all of the entrance ramps on this the opening day of the Mall of America.

I pushed the ten-year-old Volvo into fifth and headed north, setting out toward our cabin near Hayward and away from all of the foolishness down in Bloomington. The radio—for as long as the signal lasted—continued to issue breathless bulletins concerning the megamall's giant baby steps into the consciousness of Twin Cities shoppers.

For the time being, I will have to experience it through the magic of radio. It was probably just a coincidence that the family's week of mosquito hunting in the untamed resort country of Wisconsin happened to begin August 10—the very day the largest mall in the galaxy was opening for business just ten miles to the south of our home.

Yeah, coincidence—happy, happy coincidence. Now, all of you black belt shoppers needn't feel compelled to set down the paper. This isn't another of those screeds against the mall's Godzilla-esque embodiment of America's culture of consumerism. Me and mine will no doubt end up dropping some bucks in the neighborhood of Snoopy's outsize doghouse . . . eventually . . . someday . . . like whenever the entrance ramps finally begin to clear. But for now, the Mall of America is just as remote as Disneyland in the minds of my little family. I have maintained my advantage over the kids by shutting off the television every time the mall or Snoopy is even mentioned. Hopefully, the rest of the kids at child care will keep their mouths shut even if they go.

But any adult who sat through the media blitzkrieg concerning the Eighth Wonder of the World can understand why it felt so good to be heading north on the Shopping Opener, north to a cabin that will likely never have to bear the weight of a purchase from the Mall of America.

For this week at least, our version of family fun will not require spending fourteen dollars every time we take three steps. As I sit huddled over a little portable in the corner of my shack writing this column, Erin and Meagan are crisscrossing the space between cabins, offering long squeals as they trail layer upon layer of bubbles in their wake. Honest John, who happens to be my father, along with being the uncrowned king of the yard putzers, is fighting through the bubbles as he tries to find the right piece of lattice to fit beneath his cabin. It is a generational dance of the most delicate variety, an exquisite present-tense memory.

True enough, the economic prerogative that allows us to have a cabin in the first place is the same one that is sending people to Macy's in droves. There is an undeniable sense of privilege that girds either escape route—whether it leads through Bloomie's or to a dilapidated cabin. And for any family to have any money that can be defined as disposable in this day and age is remarkable in and of itself.

But the *eau de commerce* that probably whooshes out the minute you finally get rid of your car and get into the mall seems a million miles away right now. Situated as I am in a little cabin three hours north of any commercial node, I wouldn't know what to buy right now even if I had any money. Besides, the nearest store is fourteen miles away and is stocked with little more than Rolaids and Ding Dongs.

The simplicity of our week here has been almost overwhelming. Whenever I manage to spend more than a day or two up here, I am absolutely astonished at how little it takes for us to proceed through life. The huge infrastructure that our life in the city requires, which places like the megamall are designed to fulfill, loses all relevance out here on the shores of Blueberry Lake. Right now our available assets consist of four bratwurst and three hamburger buns . . . and that sounds just about right.

The process of simplification begins the second we head north and amplifies with each passing mile. By the time we reach our destination, we will probably get exactly what we want precisely because we have ceased wanting much.

That's really the heart of the problem I have with the Mall of America and other playgrounds that are allegedly monuments to family fun. If we all had such a good time, then why are the exits all filled with screaming kids? The wailing of fulfillment gives the lie to the notion that we can and should want it all. It's all part of the fallacious set of assumptions that we and Madison Avenue use to train America's future army of consumers. If the things we buy could truly change our lives, we would be the happiest culture on the planet. But we are not.

People who can't figure out why our kids are so disengaged from the business of living should keep in mind that a lot of them are spending their summer vacations watching greedy you-can-have-it-all-without-messing-up-your-hair rockers on MTV before heading out for a big day at the mall.

There's no doubt in my mind that there will be things worth seeing out at the mall, but will there be things worth remembering? Watching my girls surprise their grandma this afternoon with a bunch of wildflowers they found on our hike leaves me wishing that I could keep them at the cabin till they are about, oh, let's say nineteen years old.

But come Sunday afternoon, some unseen alarm is going to go off and we will be piling back into the car and back into our rut in town. By that time, some of the crackle will have hissed out of America's mall and the newspapers will resume publishing their daily diet of murder and mayhem. Maybe then the mother of all malls will take its rightful place in our family hierarchy—as just one more spot where we won't have enough money to satisfy consumerist dreams we never should have had in the first place.

NOVEMBER/DECEMBER 1992

If memory serves, my last column was all about what wonderful little grownups my four-year-olds had developed into and what fun we were going to have now that they were capable of the true give-and-take that characterizes the commerce of human relationships.

That lasted about seventy-two hours.

I couldn't help but notice that just about the time my kids became interesting as people, they lost interest in me. Does that seem fair? I mean, now that they are sentient, thoughtful presences—with very clear tastes in things and people—they all of the sudden figure out I'm nuthin' special.

I'm dealing with it maturely, responsibly, and directly. I'm pounding away on their sense of pity in a frantic search for affirmation.

"C'mon now. You still think your dad is the smartest guy around, don-cha?" I say, making big moon eyes at the both of them.

"Oh yeah," Erin will say, turning back to her sister to discuss their plans for the rest of the day.

"Sure we do," her sister chimes in absently.

To be sure, much of the change that is underway is a function of age. Somewhere past four, kids seem to sense that the challenges that lie ahead will be met principally as individuals. It may work to their advantage, but I'll be darned if they didn't begin untying the apron strings just about the time I was finally getting used to being connected to something besides my own wants, needs, and desires.

This most recent joint declaration of independence has been discon-certing for a number of other reasons. It's clear that both Erin and Mea-gan seem to be turning away from me—and toward each other. It is as if they still believe in the team concept, it's just that the team got smaller. I guess I'm wondering how I ended up on the bench.

My sudden irrelevance is different from times past. It is not the will-fulness of a two-year-old that is pushing me away, nor the burgeoning snottiness of a three-year-old that keeps me at bay. Naw, this is differ-ent, this has more serious and lasting implications. Time and again of late, I have searched the eyes of both of my daughters only to bump up against a quiet insistence that there is indeed a point where I end and they begin.

I guess this is how they make kindergarteners. I feel as if the bus showed up a half a year early and the door opened to scoop up my little babies and they were kids by the time they came home in the afternoon. They will still cuddle, but more often than not the quiet little interludes are interrupted with talk about what the agenda is or some statement of strong preference. In recent weeks I have heard the girls have long, windy discussions about whether so-and-so at child care really is "ishy" or whether a particular character in a video was truly scary or just silly. Less and less, they call out for me to settle differences of opinion.

I always knew that at some point in their lives, my children would

head off to deepest, darkest Girl Island, a place where boys, and especially daddies, are never invited. I have had enough experience with
grown-up women to know that some type of indoctrination takes place
—an extended seminar during which the ways and wiles of befuddling
grown-up males take center stage. There have been times of late when
I have felt awkward around my children, caught off-guard by the things
they are saying and doing. While much of my parental struggle in the
past was about maintaining my sanity, these days it is more of an en-
deavor for equilibrium, a search for a firm place to stand in order to
have a vantage point from which to watch my kids' oh-so-rapid individ-
uation.

One of the rankest, most visceral fears I have as a parent is the loss of
relevancy, an inexorable slide into obscurity that will render me invisible by the time my girls are thirteen years old. Around the fearful edges
of my mind's eye, I can just make it out. They'll come walking into the
house with their pals, tossing their bangs and rolling their eyes as they
pass the inarticulate lump on the couch—that would be me—before
heading into their room and closing the door behind them.

At this point their secrets, to be sure, will not be about me.

I used to know everything about my kids. For the first four years of
their development, they didn't believe something happened unless they
ran it by me. I would take in the experience they were sharing, turn it
over, validate it, and then hand it back to them—a newly minted memory that was real because I said so. If there was a flare-up between forces
at child care, I would hear about every detail and then be asked to make
a judgment about what was fair or just.

These days, Erin and Meagan display a thoughtfulness that can be
breathtaking. They have a separate take on the world that may or may
not be consonant with what I have tried to teach them. They have begun to trust their own instincts and intuitions, a growing tendency that
should give me satisfaction as a parent. But it also leaves me feeling
about as useful as earrings on a pig.

Last week both of the girls came trailing out of the house and got into the car with smiles that suggested they had something very sweet and delicious behind their teeth.

"What's up?" I asked, peering into the rearview.

"We've got some secrets," Meagan said evenly.

"Secrets. About me?"

"Not tellin'," Meagan said, crossing her arms.

"Just give me a sample."

"Nope." Eyes straight ahead.

"If you have *lots* of secrets, you may certainly share one of them with me."

Meagan could not hide her annoyance. She exhaled her exasperation as she spoke.

"Daddy," she began, finger wagging as she went. "We have some secrets, and if we told you those secrets, they wouldn't be secrets anymore. Understand?"

My head just about came flying off. Now, I have gotten a few lectures from these little girls before, but the condescension was coming in bunches. She was talking to me as if I were a complete knucklehead. I looked at Erin in the mirror.

"It's starting, isn't it, Erin?"

"Yep."

FEBRUARY/MARCH 2003

EVERY FAMILY HAS its rituals, and the Carrs have more than their share. Whether it's a Memorial Day marked by a profoundly unskilled game of touch football or a Christmas Eve appetizer contest, we are more than happy to embrace tried-and-true observations, the cornier, the better.

No one knows how this stuff gets started. Someone has an idea, the rest of us go along, and before you know it, we can't live without it.

This year, it was Jill who had a notion that it might be fun for us to spend New Year's Eve up at our cabin. While that sounds simple enough, the cabin is in the mountains of New York, it has no insulation, and there was twenty-eight inches of snow on the ground.

The morning we set out on our little caper, the weather was mild. But as we drove north, the snow deepened and we began to wonder what we had signed up for. There was a little space plowed out for our car when we got in, and we pulled our supplies on sleds over the snow for the last fifty yards. It took about a half an hour to shovel out enough of a space to open the door and bust our way in. A fire was lit, and the girls went off to explore the common areas of the lake association we are a part of.

Erin and Meagan came back an hour later with a report that some other people who lived nearby had built a tubing run, complete with a steep start and huge bank turns. Inside, it was warming up, but there was the small matter of not having any running water. We'd brought our own, but then there are other ways water comes in handy. Without getting into too many specifics for a family newspaper, we had some devices that fit over the toilet that Jill's mom, a nurse, provided. We were only staying for a night, so it was suggested to the assembled that it might be best to wait until we got home for certain bathroom activities. Maddie, however, made it clear right away she wasn't prepared to wait that long. Jill did the dirty work, but it was a moment of high comedy when she made a beeline for the door. As for the rest of it, let's just say that it's good to be a guy in times like these.

The tubing run was a revelation. Although it was hovering just above freezing and misting a bit as it got dark, the folks who built it left some tubes out and we whooshed our way down the course and spilled out onto the lake. We went back to the cabin for hot cocoa, and then, rather than mess with a bunch of dishes, went out to the Rustic Inn for a dinner filled with lots of fried food and some serious pinball.

Back at the cabin, some friends stopped by and we decided it was time to teach the girls poker. Jill broke out the champagne, and Erin and Meagan got their annual taste of the forbidden grape. They watched in amusement as their dad declined, as he always does, because alcohol transforms him into a lunatic. The card game that followed was a little like our touch football games—very enthusiastic but a little short on finesse. At midnight we broke for a countdown, kisses and hugs were passed around. Our friends left soon after, and I banked the fire to the gills as we settled in for the night.

I woke up in the middle of the night, but it wasn't because I was cold, it was out of a need to, ah, visit, ah, well, you know what I mean. It was still warm as I padded my way to the door and gave it a push. Nothing happened.

As it turned out, the warmth of the fire floated right up through the roof and melted the pile of snow there, which fell in a three-foot heap in front of the door. Nature called, but I was unable to go out and answer. I waddled back to bed.

In the morning Jill volunteered to climb out a window and re-shovel a path. We punched through and enjoyed a morning on the tubing run. After a quick lunch, we packed up for home because we had business back in the city. The ride home was brutal, with lots of traffic and steady rain, but we rode along happily, secure in the knowledge that we had christened a ritual that would be part of our lives for years to come.

SUMMER 1999

Sometime early this fall, Erin and Meagan will wake up and crawl out from under the same quilts in the same bunk beds in the same room. And they will likely have the same eggs—if their dad is feeling in a cooking way—or English muffin if he isn't. They will each take a vitamin, and drink exactly the same amount of orange juice.

They're twins, after all.

But after they shuffle up to the room to get dressed, Meagan will come down the stairs in the latest little number she has put together. Erin will come down in plaid, as in parochial plaid.

Erin and Meagan, twins by birth and by nature, are going different ways this school year.

Meagan will be attending the same public school she has attended for years, finishing out the sixth year in a place she has come to love and that loves her back. Erin is switching to the school at our church, beginning a new epic in her young life. She will head off to school by herself, waving goodbye not only to us but to her twin sister as well. And Meagan will do the same.

The story of how they got here is one more reminder that twins, at least fraternal ones, are not clones.

In the past year Meagan has thrived. Academically and socially, she is the queen of all the surveys. Her standardized test scores, her steady smile, her complete eagerness to get back to school, all tell the story of a kid who has found a place to stand.

Erin, bless her gracious self, was pounded to a pulp last year. She experienced the kind of casual meanness that fifth-graders specialize in. While her sister has a black belt in fitting in, Erin has not a calculating bone in her body. Erin meets the world with complete openness, a lack of pretension and artifice that adults find charming—and that her peers cannot abide.

She is not without blame. She can be a geek, tends to seek attention in sometimes inappropriate ways, and doesn't really give other kids a chance to come to her in their own time. But what should be a misdemeanor in the game of life becomes a felony in the wild kingdom of classroom hierarchies. I told myself that it would work itself out, but it hasn't. A couple of little monsters in particular have made it their hobby to make sure that every one of Erin's days has at least a little misery in it.

The effect has been predictable. Erin is a creative, skilled scholar, with a history of solid and occasionally exceptional academic achievement. But as the rest of her life slipped out of round, her grades tanked and so did her sense of self-worth. Her standardized test scores at the end of the year were frightening compared with the fall.

Throughout the year, we met with the teacher, we grilled Erin about how her day went, and we poured on the homework and oversight. But she finally told me late in the school year, "I keep expecting it to get better, and it never does." All of the platitudes I had been spouting at her about keeping her chin up, nose to the grindstone, and eye on the ball sounded a little hollow after a while. I wanted to step up to her and tell her something real, something practical.

That's when I decided that it was time for her to switch schools, even if it meant leaving behind her sister. I don't do that lightly. Their status as twins is one of life's singular gifts to them. Even on Erin's worst day, her sister was always nearby, loyal and steadfast. But Meagan can't single-handedly keep the world at bay.

It took a lot of lifting to switch schools at such a late date. Deadlines had passed, waiting lists had been formed, but Jill and I pulled, lifted, circulated, and finally weaseled her into a new school. (We'll get to the business of figuring out how to pay for it in due time.)

We decided to try a different school because that is what parents do. There is no overarching logic to it, and certainly no sure expectation that it will change the fundamentals. But you can't march into a school where your kid is getting boxed around and alter your child's social status. You can't get that one mean kid to get off her case. You can't live your kid's life for her. The only thing tangible I could come up with was the geographic cure, a switch in space that will give a basically wonderful child such as Erin a place to start anew.

Erin's ready. She isn't fond of new situations and I'm sure will have her share of butterflies walking into her new school—especially without her sister—but that isn't stopping her from seeing that she is leaving some old problems behind and jumping into something that is genuinely new.

It snaps my heart in half to be the one breaking up the team. For years they have had one name—ErinandMeagan. They have always been part of a single breath and a common thought. But I have a growing awareness that this is just the beginning of a time in their lives when they will declare themselves as individuals, over and over. Life as a pea in a pod can get pretty oppressive at times, and I have to think that each will find adventure in getting the chance to bloom in her own light. They will find their way into adolescence as individuals whether I like it or not. But I'm still hoping that they will be holding hands as they make their way.

MAY/JUNE 1999

It is an exquisite family gathering, full of crosstalk, shouts, and teasing
—the best kind of chaos. Erin, Meagan, and I flew in earlier in the day
to celebrate the fact that eleven years ago I called my mother and told
them we had a gorgeous new pair to shuffle into the deck of our family.
The celebration of their birthday was impromptu—my father went and
picked up the fried chicken, my mother-in-law procured an ice cream
cake, and other family members trickled in as schedules and other commitments allowed.

Erin and Meagan were at the center of it all, maturity and grace
etched into their every move. They were so impossibly tiny and challenged when they were born, little more than two pounds apiece. Yet,
here they were, small women that filled everyone around them with
pride. Me most of all.

The presents poured forth, clothes mostly, and a fashion show en-
sued in the living room, which was now overflowing with wrapping. I
can't remember the last time I was so filled with joy. I looked around the
room. Everything was perfect. Well, almost.

There was the mother-in-law's hair, very little of it, and a different
color than it was a few months ago. My aunt, after having crawled
through all sorts of medical complications, was fresh off the news that
there were "spots" on her lung and liver. And my mother, even though
she was running the show, had an oxygen tube on, the bulk of it trailing
upstairs where a machine gathers and compresses sustenance for her.
And there was the son—me—marks all over my neck from the biopsies
that marked my own battles.

Our family has just a little touch of cancer. A survivor here, a radiation
candidate over there, and a two-time veteran in the middle. The odd
thing about the festive cancer ward at our house is that it is not at all odd.
Families everywhere have their own stories and their own battles about
the implacable foe of cancer. I've always wondered why people even
bother to watch monster movies. I mean, what could be more scary than

an insidious organism that spontaneously appears deep inside you and then grows at uncontrolled rates until it threatens to take over your life?

Stephen King never, ever came up with anything this evil. And yet it is everywhere.

We are dealing with it by dealing with it. My mom's case is not good. But she is. Right now in the happy part, where we can all give and receive tremendous comfort. And we are not missing a minute. Breakfast in my mom's bed is an event. Flowers on the tray. The bacon extra crisp just like she likes it. Erin and Meagan slicing and arranging the fruit until it becomes a bouquet. We gather in close, chat about going to radiation later in the day and then maybe sticking a movie in the video for the afternoon.

And we talk about what a wonderful party we had the day before.

And it was. Not in spite of the cancer but precisely because of it. The gifts of illness are meager compared with its consequences, but you grab what is good and make it your own. Erin looked around near the end of the party and sensed that this celebration—with these people in this place—may not happen again. She suddenly asked everyone in the circle what they thought heaven was like. Each person, in turn, speculated about what that next place might consist of. Erin had her own ideas. She has a blanket that her grandma made for her many years ago. It has been mended and patched over and over, each incarnation becoming more worn, and yet more loved. Erin thinks heaven will be "like one big blanky."

And that sounds about right. Heaven, right now, is a place where the tears and the laughs weave together into a fabric large and sustaining enough to provide comfort for each of us.

SPRING 1999

As the proud parents of a profoundly precocious two-year-old with a mental age of—by our expert estimates—a six-year-old, we took a lot of comfort in knowing that Maddie mowed through the behaviors commonly associated with her development in a few short weeks when she was eighteen months old.

Ha. Nice try. Good thought there, but wrong, oh so painfully, terribly wrong.

To avoid cliché, let's call them the horrible twos. Nah, how about the freakishly maniacal twos? Or perhaps the wretched, excruciating twos?

You get the picture. It's Maddie's world, and we just happen to be in the way of it. Who gets her up, who takes her potty, what she eats, when she sleeps, and what she is willing to wear—those decisions suddenly belong to her. "You are not the boss, Maddie."

"Oh yes, Daddy, I am the boss."

It depends on the day, actually. Jill and I are both parental fascists and believe that the big people should be in charge of the little people. But our "Lords of Discipline" routine does not include corporal punishment, which, if I am reading the right magazines, seems to be making a comeback. After a few days locked in a death match with Maddie, I can understand why. But I'd just as soon our house not be a place where people hit one another.

That leaves the dreaded "Time-out!" Oh boy, is she ever terrified of the old time-out. Up to the roomful of toys you go, Maddie—and stay there. She caught on fairly quickly, not even bothering to apologize on her way to the anointed sentence.

Last week she robbed candy from her sister's backpack right after breakfast and snuck under a table in the living room and began jamming it down her piehole as quickly as her hands could get it there. She was deeply hidden beneath the table, and I demanded she come out. She demurred. I demanded, Maddie ignored. I reached under the table—not in anger, of course—and pulled Maddie out into the light of consequence. She smiled through a mouthful of Jolly Ranchers. I squeezed her cheeks until the candy popped out, and then we went up to the dungeon.

I was yelling and gesturing wildly. Maddie, on the other hand, remained calm. I took her into the room and told her she was staying there until she was willing to apologize. "Are you ready to say you're sorry, Maddie?"

"No."

That settles it. I closed the door with as much emphasis as I could without actually slamming it and was walking away when I heard a sound inside. "Baa, baa, black sheep, have you any wool?" How nice. Maddie was singing to herself. Probably her way of processing naughtiness. Either that, or she could care less that she got busted for candy theft. Truth is, Maddie could have easily remained there all day. For all I know, she probably had a nice stash of Jolly Ranchers somewhere in the room to sustain her throughout the ordeal. I came up ten minutes later, and she took enough pity on me to mumble that she was sorry so she could get back downstairs and begin perpetrating anew.

Maddie has officially become a piece of work. Yes, her verdant curls and angelic face are impressive, but it's a little hard to enjoy when the horns and tails keep rearing into view. She is capable of enormous sweetness and gigantic insight for a person of her size, but she can turn into a dynamo of nastiness in a hot second. And thank God she inherited both of her parents' legendary stubbornness so each conflict can mushroom into an international event.

I know, I know, it will pass. Like El Niño will pass someday. But in the meantime, each day produces the kind of tribal warfare that makes Bosnia sound pretty pleasant this time of year.

She is still a peach. On a pure cost/benefit level, I could accept the sour with the sweet for the rest of my life and count myself lucky. But I'd just as soon book in an exorcist and consign this particular piece of development history to the past. I've thought about getting out the video camera to document this amazing transformation from angel to the Dark One's evil little wonder, but something makes me think that I will never, ever want to see it again.

FEBRUARY/MARCH 1999

In a world where people go about their business without a thought for others, can the concern of strangers be anything but a blessing?

Well, yes, in a word, when it goes past common courtesy and into something else. Or maybe that's just me.

Walk with me a second, and you can be the judge. A few weeks ago, Erin, Meagan, and I decided—actually, it was just me, but that's an old story—that we were going to go on a long bike ride down to one of the sights in our city. The goal lay at the end of one of those gorgeous bike trails most cities have, but like all things wonderful in a busy place, many people try to occupy the same space. It was a particularly stunning break in the winter weather pattern, so the trail was a little like 35W on a late Friday afternoon, but we had a talk about staying in a line and made sure our helmets were extra snug.

On the descent, we stayed to the far right of the path and out of most of the traffic, but it was still disconcerting to have so many people whizzing by. I kept the girls in front of me to make sure that they were staying out of harm's way, but then a particularly fast jerk came whizzing by without warning just off my elbow. I watched with concern as he whipped by Meagan and got queasy as he overtook Erin. She seemed surprised by the quick commotion off to her left and veered slightly off the path. Then it was slow-motion torment as I began to watch her seesawing in broader arcs, gradually losing control and getting tossed onto the tar of the bike path. Her head bounced hard once, and then she skidded off into the leaves and dirt.

I was off my bike and had every inch of her ten-year-old self gathered onto my lap in seconds. Many people saw her fall and were reasonably concerned. It looked and no doubt felt nasty, and they gathered in close to watch and listen. Erin quietly sobbed responses as I gently moved parts of her and asked whether it hurt. She was shaken to her core, but there was nothing broken. Meagan said nothing, just silently picked bits of leaves and dirt out of Erin's hair and mouth.

My fears gave way to anger at the moron who flew past her, and I began to notice two women had come in close. They talked only to Erin and ignored me, asking what happened and then repeating the litany of questions we had already gone through. With Erin wrapped up on my lap, they nonetheless began reaching in and stroking her hair and squeezing her hand. That might sound lovely, but you know what? I don't like strangers touching my child ever, under any circumstances. And it became clear from the clucking noises that they were making that they thought Erin needed her mommy.

They didn't choose to see it, Erin was already on her mommy's lap. It's my conceit that the mommy role is fluid, that it belongs to the parent the child is with and needs. When Erin and Meagan are with their mother, Anna, they are in their mother's care. And the times when their stepmother, Jill, is there, the mom's role belongs to her. And during those many times when it is just me and them, I am their father, protector, guardian, and yes, mother.

As somebody who spent a fair amount of time as a single parent with the twins, I grew to hate the intrusiveness and patronization of strangers. We were a family complete and whole, no matter how many people at the grocery counter stupidly commented about how cute it was to see Daddy "babysitting" his little girls. Women have primacy in parental matters as a matter of cultural and history practice, and I'm fine with that. But please don't suggest that my lack of ovaries makes me somehow less able to care for my distressed child. I appreciated the concern from the bystanders, but when it became clear that they thought they were filling a role that I could not, I thanked them for their interest and politely asked them to leave us alone. They seemed taken aback and kept throwing looks of concern over their shoulder as they got back onto their bikes, but I can tell you that Erin began to perk up when she had a few moments just between her and me, and we began piecing ourselves back together to go slowly back home.

3

Twin Cities Reader

Prodigal Clown

Tom Arnold, Whose Romances with Roseanne, Goldfish, and Cocaine Are the Stuff of Tabloids, Explains Himself to His Hometown

AUGUST 14–20, 1991

OF ALL THE institutions Tom Arnold has visited—as often as not in handcuffs—marriage seems to be the one that has done the most good. Arnold, who got his comedy start in Minneapolis, married the former Roseanne Barr two days out of drug rehab. He entered their nuptials as a recidivist dope fiend who had sold information about their intimacies to the *National Enquirer* to finance his cocaine habit.

Two years later, Tom Arnold has, or shares, control of nine separate film and broadcast projects. Following his counsel, the former Ms. Barr has changed lawyers, managers, producers, and her name. Upon becoming executive producer of *Roseanne*—one of the top-rated television shows in the country—before last season, Arnold fired most of the people associated with it yet managed to maintain not only the show's ratings but its creative momentum.

Arnold is clearly in charge of their joint production company, Wapello County Productions (named after the Iowa county where they are building a prairie getaway). He recently produced and starred in his own highly rated HBO special, and a fall TV movie starring Roseanne and him, called *Backfield in Motion,* is in postproduction. Arnold will be shooting two sitcoms this fall, *Roseanne* and *Jackie Thomas.* The latter is an ABC midseason replacement that Arnold will produce and star in. He'll play a meatpacker from Iowa who gets struck by show-biz lightning and becomes an entertainment maven extraordinaire—in short, himself.

Roseanne explains Arnold's frenetic business activity simply: "Tom's a monster."

But many people see Arnold as an ogre for other reasons. Against a backdrop of skepticism and outright contempt, Arnold has insinuated himself into every aspect of Roseanne's business life. While his powerful influence on Roseanne is reminiscent of Colonel Tom Parker's on Elvis or Nancy's on Ronald Reagan, he seems less inclined to keep his mate in a bell jar, away from public scrutiny. He would argue that, yes, he is protective of his wife's interests, but he certainly is no more parasitic or controlling than the phalanx of lawyers, managers, and agents that preceded him. At least this way it stays in the family.

Arnold and Roseanne have a reputation for being joined at the hip, and a *Reader* interview the day before their show at the Orpheum Theatre last month was no exception.

Although the interview is exclusively with Arnold, Roseanne remains near, feigning disinterest but breaking in at strategic junctures. By the end of the two hours, it is a dual interview, the two of them kibitzing and cooing between questions. They dote on each other to the brink of credibility, but it's undeniable that there is some powerful human chemistry at work.

On this July day they are spread out over a couple of rooms at the top of the Whitney Hotel. Arnold is wearing his uniform: a sport shirt and a pair of stonewashed jeans. Arnold the success is as physically imposing as he was in his Minneapolis bottom-feeding days, but for different reasons. Then, he weighed three hundred pounds. His head is just as massive as it ever was, but now it sits atop a muscular and articulated frame. Arnold steps over an electronic treadmill to greet me.

When he lived in Minneapolis, Arnold was a comic whose life imitated—and often destroyed—his art. The farm boy from Iowa with a goldfish act was also a cokehead and a fifth-a-day drunk who spawned chaos wherever he went. People in the Twin Cities comedy community would say, "Sure he's funny, but . . ."

Arnold eases back in one of the chairs in the Whitney penthouse to recall the bad old days. He is less frenetic than he was then, but his ever-present leg twitch is still in evidence.

"I mostly just think of how many times I fucked up in this town—how many times my life was screwed up," Arnold says. "I can't help but feel a little sense of dread when I come here."

Despite the money, the notoriety, and the willingness to butt heads with LA's powerful, Arnold admits that he wants to explain himself to Minneapolis. "It's my hometown in a way," he says.

Roseanne, in a sweatsuit, plops down sideways in a chair an arm's length from her husband and begins absently leafing through a magazine.

"I could not let myself get ahead. I sabotaged myself at every possible point," Arnold says. "My addiction and other things in my life made me think that it just wasn't possible to be successful. I didn't think I deserved it. But you know, there was two of me. There was the fuckup, and then there was this guy that busted his ass to make sure it would happen, and he had to work twice as hard because of what the fuckup was doing."

The Minneapolis Tom Arnold seemed to have an insatiable need for negative attention. In the process, he managed to get thrown out of just about every bar in town.

"I got eighty-sixed from Moby Dick's," Arnold says. "You know what kind of shit you got to do to get eighty-sixed from Moby Dick's? They just said, 'We're not serving you anymore.' And I didn't even remember what I did. They said, 'You know what you did!'

"And Moe [the proprietor of the CC Club] banned me from the CC forever," Arnold says, mentioning the bar that was just a beer-bottle toss away from his old house on Lyndale Avenue.

I was there one of the times Moe tossed Arnold out of the bar at Twenty-Sixth and Lyndale for the umpteenth time. My friendship with Arnold dates back to his arrival from Ottumwa, Iowa, in 1983. We were pals and fellow coke fiends for the next six years. We now talk on the phone occasionally. A few months ago I went out to Los Angeles to watch him marry Roseanne for the second time. This time the groom was a newly minted Jew.

Arnold is a likable guy, and I am not allergic to his rather outsize charms, but that doesn't necessarily translate to trust. One of the first stories I did after I took the cure was a feature for the *Reader* about the rumors of a romance between Arnold and Barr (who was still married at the time). Arnold swore that there was nothing to the rumors. And I bought the lie.

"Roseanne made me," Arnold says, glancing sheepishly toward her.

"Well, I was in New York and I didn't want my kids to find out from the newspapers," Roseanne says. "We had a big fight about it, but yes, I asked Tom to lie about it."

A week later, stories were splashed all over the country about Roseanne and her drug-addict boyfriend. Suddenly Tom Arnold, comedian, was a household word—at least in households that keep the *Star* on the coffee table. What was missing from the stories, though, was that Arnold was a pretty talented guy before he met Barr.

That's not to say that he would be taking meetings with the president of ABC if he hadn't become involved with the number one female comic talent in the country. He wouldn't. But quite a few Twin Cities comic talents have made their mark nationally—names such as Louie Anderson and Joel Hodgson spring to mind—and had Arnold gotten his cocaine habit under control, he might have been one of them.

"I was working at Hormel killing pigs, and I got fired," Arnold says, beginning his career resume. "I went to school in Ottumwa for a couple of years, and then I went to the University of Iowa. I decided while I was there that even though I didn't want to kill pigs, I didn't want to be a stockbroker, either. I saw Joel Hodgson, along with Stephanie Hodge and Scott Novotne. Joel really stood out, and I thought I should come up with some kind of gimmick. That's how I ended up with the goldfish."

Thus began "Tom Arnold and His Fabulous Goldfish Revue." At least Arnold was billed ahead of the fish. Unfortunately, once the gimmick caught on, he was stuck splitting his fee with a Ziploc bag of fish for a few years. His props-with-a-heartbeat shtick involved high-concept comedy such as putting a pope's hat on one of the fish and taping another to a tiny motorcycle.

"It was a huge pain in the ass keeping those fish alive," Arnold says. "I would forget to put that dechlorination stuff in the water, and I would open up the bag and sing 'Here are the goldfish!' and they'd all be dead, so I'd have to keep them moving," he says, making a swirling motion with his hand, "to pretend like they were alive."

Although Arnold placed high in a number of comedy competitions at the time, things didn't move quite as quickly as he planned. "I had done about three open-mike nights in Iowa, and I moved here and thought I would be on *Letterman* in about six months."

In 1983 he met Roseanne Barr when she was in Minneapolis on a gig.

"We slowly became writing partners, and I watched her career take off," Arnold says. "I was living vicariously. I was in a rut and her career was taking off. It was fun to watch from a distance."

With that Roseanne breaks in.

"Can I say something about what I thought about him? I don't think he gets this about himself, but the thing that is so funny is that there is a charm and innocence to him. He is just a huge kid. He's standing there and saying things like, 'Pooh-pooh,' and other bad words, and I think that's why the audience loves him so much. He is so rude, and you *have* to laugh because it is like a little kid doing it. The things that he would say to people from the stage just blew me away."

But even as Arnold's reputation with the local comedy community expanded, his career faltered. "I had a lot of opportunities to work on the road, and it would have been very good for me, but I just kept screwing up. I would cancel or not show up. I had to get booked with guys who had cars because I had three DWIs, and I ended up touring with the biggest nerds in town."

Even Roseanne has her favorite Tom-the-loser story. She had managed to get him a performing slot in front of a gathering of big-shot promoters in Saint Louis.

"He was going to open for me, and I told him that he was the greatest opening act in the world. And he was. And he still is," she says. "He came down there and he started drinking about three in the afternoon. I guess I was drinking too, because there's this picture of us both from that time and I was just shitfaced and I had put on my own makeup and I had eye shadow going way up here," she says, indicating a spot most of the way up her forehead as she cracks out a laugh that fills the suite.

"He drank a whole fifth in about an hour," she says.

"I always did that," he says.

"He went out and he killed," Roseanne says with pride. "He was really hard for me to follow because he was so great. Then he drank all the way through my show too.

"But anyway, these promoters really loved his act and couldn't believe how great he was. We went out afterwards to talk with them, and he got kicked out of the club and got the cops called on him. He went up against the plate-glass window where these two old ladies were eating and did this," she says, standing up and miming a spread-eagle against glass.

"He wouldn't move, and they called the cops on him. The promoters said, 'He's so funny, but he is too crazy. We can't work with him.'"

Later the same night Arnold succeeded in getting tossed out of the Improv Club in Saint Louis.

"Yeah," Roseanne says. "They were doing improv, and they asked for suggestions, and he screamed out, 'Jism on a stick.'" They look at each other with a shared moment of pride at this comic moment.

"They called the cops on him there, too," Roseanne concludes with weariness. "He'd always blow it when he had done real good."

● ● ●

People close to Tom Arnold know that the kind of success he has been experiencing has historically been a toxin to him. Three days before he was to be filmed for a role in Roseanne's HBO special in 1986, Arnold got thrown in jail in Rochester for pissing in a McDonald's parking lot. When a cop asked him what he was doing, Arnold said, "I'm making you a cocktail." Minneapolis attorney Ron Meshbesher sprang him just in time to appear in the show.

Later, a week before he was supposed to begin writing for Roseanne's show, he began hemorrhaging from his nose—one of the less attractive symptoms of cocaine abuse—splattering blood all over the apartment he shared with former Minneapolis comic Sid Youngers and his girl-friend, Michelle Larson. Larson called Roseanne, who was about to be reunited by the *National Enquirer* with her teenage daughter, Brandi, whom she had put up for adoption when she herself was a teenager.

"She called me and said, 'I think Tom is going to die if you don't come over here,'" Roseanne recalls. Roseanne took him to a hospital, got him patched back together and put back on the wagon. Two weeks later Arnold found a bag of dope when he was cleaning his apartment and he fell off again.

Although the Arnolds speak of the bad days with relief, as if the war is won, it's hard to put a lot of stock into what Arnold, or any cocaine addict, says about sobriety. But it's doubtful that he would have been able to sustain his production and competence over the past eighteen months if he was using.

Arnold admits that his track record makes it hard for people to trust him. "I don't have any control over that shit," he says. "People are going to believe what they believe."

Part of the negativity floating around Tinseltown is connected to his past failings, but more of it, Arnold suspects, is generated by his recent success. Arnold shares Roseanne's disrespect for the entertainment power brokers, and the two have continued to succeed while blowing off the supposedly important people.

Roseanne's popularity is a durable, highly bankable commodity, and

Arnold has parlayed her half-hour weekly show into a web of projects. Youngers has been a friend of Arnold's since they did pizza sculpture on the walls of the house they shared on Lyndale and is now a writer on *Roseanne,* one of a number of Twin Cities comic talents Arnold hired when he took over the show. Youngers says he isn't surprised by Arnold's success at dealmaking.

"Regardless of how he got there, you would have to say that he is operating at the level he is at," Youngers says in a phone interview from Los Angeles. "He is very good at what he does—all of it.

"Tom always was good on the phone," he says. "He was getting work back when he had no business working, and that was because he knew how to negotiate."

Arnold is a physically imposing person who gets his back up when he feels strongly about something. Like when he was convinced that Roseanne's creative authority was being undercut on the set of the *Roseanne* show by the producers and writers who were supposed to be working for her. He sprang to her defense, almost literally, sparking on-the-set wrestling matches that became the meat of the tabloids.

But the guy who stood up unflinchingly to entertainment moguls and their lawyers was still cowering before his own demon.

"I would find the stuff on the floor," Roseanne recalls. "I would taste it and it would taste like cocaine, and he would say, 'Well, we had that party and there were people back in that part of the house.'"

Roseanne eventually saw through the lies and left. Arnold limped into treatment in Century City and has managed to stay on the wagon since.

While Arnold is infatuated with the visibility and power he has gathered through Roseanne, he is less a virtuoso at handling money. The very definition of nouveau riche in all its tackiness, Arnold still hasn't lost his meatpacker's concept of the value of the dollar.

Earlier this summer, Arnold stood outside his leased Rolls in front of a Santa Monica hotel an hour before his wedding. The guy who never bought a round at Moby Dick's was fishing through a wad of hundreds as thick as a paperback, digging out tips for the scurrying hotel staff. Arnold riffled past the hundreds to dole out one-dollar bills.

"The biggest problem with being rich is who to tip and how much to tip them," he says defensively. "If they go get my car, I give them two bucks. If they drive us around for a night, I give them a hundred dollars."

Arnold allows himself a bit more than he does parking attendants. "When you are first rich, you go out and buy everything."

Including something called a Bentley Turbo, his current rolling office. A Harley, looking a little forlorn, was parked outside their house this summer. I asked Arnold if he paid someone to drive it for him. "No, I only have to pay someone to start it. I actually ride it once it's running."

The blue-collar concept of money appears to apply to the family finances in general. "We run it even. Rosie makes ten [million]. I make two or three, and it all goes to the same place. And when we die, it goes to our kids, slowly."

Any way you look at it, be you cynic or romantic, at the heart of Tom Arnold's success is Roseanne. He struggles when he tries to explain the relationship.

"We're great friends, we talk about everything, and we're, um, I don't know, we're each other's biggest supporters," Arnold says.

"Lemmesee," he says, his head turning into his wife's ample bosom, "having sex is very important, though. You have to have sex every day, or tempers start to get short.

"Every once in a while, she gives me a message," he continues, "and that message is, 'I want to be with you *now*.'

"And she might be all dressed up in a sexy outfit, and I'm watching *Arsenio,* and I'm saying, 'Hold on, honey, I think they're going to talk about us,'" he says, taking a swipe through his thinning hair with his left hand as he looks at Roseanne.

"Once she put on this special outfit," he continues. "It's a maid's outfit, and she went to all this trouble, and I was watching sports and ignored her. She took off in the car and her feelings were hurt.

"When she came back home in the car, I had that fucking outfit on and met her at the door. It was humiliating, but I had to do it."

Tom Arnold is addicted again, this time to the Spotlight. Things like his weight loss and gain, the public declarations of sobriety, and the graphic public demonstrations of affection spring to mind. And, of course, the trademark exhibitions of bad taste.

"Hey, it's hard to do anything when you can't pick your butt in public," Arnold says in defense.

"And Tom won't let me pick my butt in public," Roseanne offers cheerily. "I do everything that Tom tells me to do, and he doesn't allow me to burp or fart in public anymore."

"Goddammit," he says, lecturing her. "Just not farting or burping in public still leaves you a lot of room for shit. It isn't like I'm running your whole life or anything."

Maybe not, but finally Arnold seems in charge of his own.

Paranoid or Positive?

Behind the Red Door

A VISITOR WALKS into the clinic dragging a backpack and silently hands the receptionist a yellow slip of paper. The paper looks as if it has been folded and unfolded many times since he was tested for HIV two weeks prior. She motions him toward a chair in the mostly full waiting room and says his name will be called.

The young man takes a seat and stares straight ahead, seeming not to notice the kids playing on the floor or the song about love playing in the background. His left leg begins bouncing almost immediately, tapping out a fearful rhythm that has nothing to do with pop music.

In a room brimming with intensity, the man—who appears to be somewhere in his mid-twenties—looks as if he is grinding his way to the center of the earth as he chews insistently on his lower lip. The anxiety comes off him in silent waves as twelve long minutes pass. A middle-aged woman in a white lab coat comes out and summons him by his first name. He leaves his chair as if a large spring has been released and trails her closely down the hall.

Forty seconds later he comes around the corner with a small but noticeable smile on his face. He exits the Red Door without looking back to the place where negative is positive and the kindnesses are unspeakable.

In a waiting room in which your very presence implicates you, the courtesies come quickly. The unloaded smile of the receptionist settles you down, and the chatter of the staff puts a welcome patina of normalcy on an uncommon experience.

The Red Door is a place where our community stores secrets. All of the festering externalities of our collective sex life can be diagnosed and sometimes treated in a clinic that has been built on discretion. Everyone from the street prostitute who tests routinely to the terrified forty-five-year-old suburban housewife who's convinced her lone indiscretion was a big one can find badly needed information and even a degree of solace behind the Red Door.

The door isn't red these days, save for the square of red tissue paper that covers the glass window in the middle of it. Until a few years ago, people walked up to a big red door in the McGill Building. The portal gave its name to Hennepin County's outreach to people with diseases arising from sexual activity. Since 1972 the Red Door Clinic in downtown Minneapolis has served as a point of entry for people who either have, or fear they have, a sexually transmitted disease.

Currently located in the basement of a twelve-story building at Sixth and Portland in downtown Minneapolis, the Red Door has seen its mission (like that of its Saint Paul counterpart, Room 111) change as its client population began to show up with sexually transmitted diseases for which there is no cure. In the summer of 1985, when the acronyms HIV and AIDS became part of society's lexicon, testing for the virus became a major function of the facility, which currently has an annual budget of a little more than $1 million, funded entirely by the county. The clinic is available to whoever walks in, at no cost.

Anybody who has been there will tell you that the Red Door is a safe place to bring unsafe behavior. The staff is an exemplar of nonjudgment. They take a cliché like "respect for all people" and infuse it with compassion and professionalism on a daily basis. "We don't make people earn our trust," says one staffer. "We give it away freely."

It is a contract that is implied from the moment you arrive. A client who comes in for HIV testing sits down in a private examination room and discusses his or her sexual history, with an emphasis on risk behavior. The clinician reminds the client that test results will remain confidential unless he or she signs a consent form allowing the clinic to forward the information to the State Department of Health. More than 99 percent decline to share their results with the government. Blood is drawn and the client receives a yellow slip of paper with an ID number and the date when his or her results will be ready. Results are not given over the phone for obvious reasons.

Red Door staffers guard the confidentiality of their testing procedures most gingerly. Margaret Heinz, the clinic's director, would allow neither a client's nor a reporter's visit to be journaled for publication because she considers the testing process itself to be proprietary.

Last year the Red Door saw 6,500 clients for HIV testing. Although only a little more than 2 percent tested positive for the virus, one quarter of the clients who were tested did not care, or could not bear, to come back for the results. Of the 5,536 people tested in 1991, 121 tested positive. More often than not, it's "fraids"—the fear they contracted the virus somehow—and not actual exposure to AIDS that brings people knocking at the Red Door. Heinz, a registered nurse, says that 80 to 90 percent of the clinic's clients are at very low risk.

People who have been tested for HIV will testify that dread is not easily compartmentalized during the wait for the results. Seemingly unconnected parts of life suddenly hew to that moment in abeyance. Turn on the radio for a bit of distraction and Tom Petty will suggest, "You take it on faith, you take it from the heart . . . the waiting is the hardest part." In those two weeks, the sweetness in day-to-day life is often pigmented by foreboding.

And even if you manage to keep "the test" off your screen, the return visit for results is a lonely moment, a time when everyone, regardless of sexual history, gnaws on the bone of regret—sitting in a cloistered examination room with a relative stranger whose manila folder contains a verdict on the future. Both guilty and innocent, the client waits for that moment when he or she will be handed permission to leave this place and never screw up again. On the one hand, if the test is negative, the folks at the Red Door hand you some rubbers and tell you to do what you can to remain negative. The other hand strikes more ferociously.

"Most people don't hear a thing after you have said, 'I'm sorry, your test came back positive,'" says Heinz.

Two weeks seems an interminable time to endure even the possibility of a positive HIV test, but due to the limited testing capacity of the Memorial Blood Bank, where the Red Door sends its samples, results can't be obtained any quicker. It also means that it's difficult to get a test in the first place. HIV testing is by appointment only, and a reporter had to call three days in a row to get past a recording that told potential clients to call back later. Once the appointment is made, it can be three weeks to a month away. The Red Door has added phone lines and a full-time receptionist, but demand continues to surpass capacity.

"When I went to get tested, it seemed like someone implanted a clock while I was there. It ticked very loudly for the two weeks while I waited," remembers Sandi, a recovered IV drug user from a very high risk area of the country with a large percentage of infected addicts.

"The first time I went, it was the old place and it was pretty much of a bus terminal for marginal people. I was sober at the time, and there I was sitting with what looked like street-boy prostitutes and sick-looking people. The staff was pretty grim, the building was pretty grim, and so was I. I was prepared to be HIV positive," she recalls.

"And then a guy in a lab coat sits me down while he stands up and says, 'We received your results,' and he pauses for a second before he says, 'and they were negative.' Then, without pausing, he says, 'What are you going to do about changing your behavior?'"

Both the clinic and the testing process lost a measure of spookiness when the Red Door moved from its dilapidated offices in the McGill

Building to the shiny glass-and-brick county building at the corner of Sixth and Portland. But it's still not a walk in the park. The clinic is downstairs, tucked into the basement at the end of a tendentious one-floor elevator ride.

"I don't think our clients miss the message. If you push the button to go down in this building, there's only one place you are going," says Hank Jones, a community health specialist at the Red Door. "We did not choose to be in the basement. This is a statement of how we are regarded."

The Red Door is a dissonant place. The walls offer muted fields of maroon and gray that frame soft, atmospheric art. All of the ambient crackle comes off the people occupying the chairs, making the Red Door's reception area a place where the waits are delineated by uncommon anxiety. Kids who come with their parents take advantage of the toy box, oblivious to the emotion and experience churning just over their heads. But the staff has been immunized by years of exposure to the dread that brings their customers to them.

People from all walks come to these examination rooms to drop their pants and some of the inhibitions they have about talking about their sexuality. A permission of sorts hangs in the air, allowing the staff to cut through the bullshit with directness, the anxiety with humor. To a person, staffers will tell you that it's the best place they have ever worked. Margaret Heinz has run the clinic for five years. During her tenure, only five of the clinic's positions have turned over.

"This is a very dedicated group of people," says Heinz. "They are the most talented small group of people that I have ever worked with. I can't think of a single person who works here who doesn't have something unique that they bring to their job."

Heinz oversees a bunker of sorts, a corner of the medical system where the symptoms are impolite. If you hang around her staff long enough, you might get the feeling you've wandered onto the set of *M*A*S*H*.

An alloy of streetwise social worker and latex evangelist, Kirk Harrington could easily have been assigned to the 4077th. As a regular part of his Red Door duties, he hits the streets with a large black box that he slaps for emphasis as he talks. He opens it and watches a visitor's reaction as a very menacing penis rises into view.

"You bet I hit the streets with it—a portion of my job is outreach, and all the condoms in the world aren't going to do any good if kids don't know how to use them."

Harrington jumps up without a word and shuts off the light. Through the darkness he asks how easy it might be to put a condom on correctly in complete darkness.

"See what I mean?" he says as he switches on the light. "This," he says, gesturing toward the bobbing, spring-loaded penis, "is my biggest tool." There's no indication on his smiling face whether the irony is intended or not.

Within the clinic, Harrington is the first person kids under eighteen see when they believe they may have a sexually transmitted disease. The amount of misinformation he encounters on a daily basis makes him shake his head of short-cropped hair.

"Girls come in here saying that they've been told they can't get AIDS if the guy withdraws. We have young female clients who come in and have condoms still inside them. These kids need answers."

Harrington prides himself on his ability to make adolescents feel comfortable in his tiny, windowless office, but he says it takes a little more salesmanship out on the street.

"You have to approach in a nonconfrontational way. Once I'm chatting with them, I just say, 'Bet you can't tell me what's in this box.' And then I tell them if I can do a demonstration, I will give them free condoms. But that's the catch, they have to stick around and make sure they know how to use them properly."

Talking with young people about the most intimate part of their lives is something most parents dread. Harrington considers it a privilege.

"I have to go within myself and think about the unique opportunity I have to talk with kids on a personal level. It seems tough, but it becomes a thing where you get into a zone and mentally condition yourself to feel good about what you are doing. I have an opportunity to give them exclusive information about their sex lives."

Jenny, a thirty-year-old who has been to the Red Door three times, was diagnosed with herpes on her first visit and has returned twice for HIV tests. She was negative both times.

Although she has her own doctor, she says, "I have my reasons for going to the Red Door. There is the issue of confidentiality and privacy, for one thing. Medical doctors look down on you when you ask them for an AIDS test. You get this look like you are promiscuous, and you don't find that at the Red Door. I guess most of them [doctors] like to think that their clients wouldn't come down with something like that."

David Swarthout, a psychologist who serves as the Red Door's community health specialist, is in the business of meeting his clients where they are, instead of lecturing about where they are supposed to be. A big bowl of rubbers sits on his desk, partially covering a little furry animal that has a sign reading, THIS BEAR LOVES YOU. Just to the right of his desk, a sign opines that KINKY IS USING A FEATHER, PERVERTED IS USING THE WHOLE CHICKEN. And tucked inside the desk is a large, white latex penis for demonstrating proper condom use. The action created by the protruding metal crank is probably just a bonus.

"It *does* set off alarms at airports, in case you were wondering," he says, his eyebrow arching for emphasis. Although he is mostly bald and wears glasses, Swarthout's quick mouth and wit make him well positioned to occupy the Hawkeye niche at the Red Door. Like everyone else at the clinic, Swarthout has a seamless ability to shift from the comic to the tragic in a nanosecond. It's a highly adaptive behavior, he explains.

"This is fast-paced, high-stress work. Some people thought the *M*A*S*H* humor and all of the liver jokes were morbid, but we talk about sexual topics in exactly the same way around here. We need to keep perspective."

For the past five years, Swarthout has been the person clients see immediately after they have received a positive HIV test. At other times, he delivers the word in the first place.

"I don't preface it by saying, 'I've got bad news,' because I don't think it is. I don't believe that being HIV positive is a death sentence. It's true that some of my clients are devastated when they find out, but it's my job to put things in perspective. AIDS is a chronic disease that many people are living with."

Swarthout is calm and direct when he talks about his work, unless the topic turns to media coverage of HIV and AIDS.

"One poorly written article can bring hundreds of people in for the next few months. Our clinic has not slowed down since the 'doctors with AIDS' stories were blown up all over television and the newspaper. What they did was disgusting," he says, his nose wrinkling toward his glasses with the memory.

A controversial investigation launched by the *Star Tribune*, which contended that AIDS was a noncrisis, particularly riled Swarthout.

"I don't think fifteen thousand cases of HIV is *acceptable*. And I don't think that seven hundred cases of AIDS is *just fine*," Swarthout says, his voice dripping disdain. "Most of the media doesn't know or care what they are talking about."

Life on the front lines is more sobering. Better than half of the clients who test positive are gay men who are repeat testers. Knowing they are at risk doesn't necessarily translate to good decisions when desire peaks.

"What people know and what people do are often very different. Many gay men continue to engage in high-risk behavior," says Swarthout.

"When I first came here, I was frustrated. My expectation is that every person is eventually going to make changes to reduce their risk, and the reality is that some people just want to be treated and aren't interested in making any behavioral change. And that's their business."

Sandi, the former IV drug user, says people who go to the Red Door for testing make umpteen pacts with God about how they will never do anything that will make them feel the need to get tested again. But risk is relentless.

"I don't think that people understand that things like drug addiction and relationships can take people to places they would never elect to go in a single moment," Sandi suggests in a phone interview.

"It's hard . . . to have to explain it to some guy wearing a lab coat."

Sandi remembers her most recent HIV test as less fraught with contrition and uplifting in an almost spiritual way. "You can tell that the people there care about what they are doing. When you go there, it just seems like life is going to go on and that you might have a shot at being part of it."

There are times when a few well-placed words from a clinician can create a bridge sturdy enough for people to step away from their old ways.

"Sometimes, I do come off like their mother," admits Sandra Graham, a registered nurse who heads the clinic's youth intervention project. She's a woman who shows her big smile often.

"You have to have the right tone of voice and the right amount of concern so that what you are saying gets through to them. You have to be direct if they are making poor decisions, but you cannot condescend to them.

"I have been here long enough [twelve years] to know that if they keep making bad choices, they are going to end up with a positive [test] result. When a fourteen-year-old girl is sitting in front of me telling me that she has had unprotected sex with three people and her current boyfriend is twenty-one years old, I just have to say, 'If I were your mother, I wouldn't want you to be making those kinds of decisions.'"

Josh is a thirty-three-year-old gay man who's been to the clinic five times, in part because he believes his privacy will be respected.

"My friends and I call it the Rouge Porte," he says, laughing into the phone. "I think it's a tremendous asset to the community.

"Even though it's one floor down from the entrance, when you are going to pick up your results, it's the longest elevator ride of your life. It's a relief when you get a negative result, but I think you have to keep in mind what brought you there. It's not like, 'Thank God I'm negative. Now let's go fuck our brains out.'"

Hank Jones's job is to get the Red Door to clients before HIV gets to them. After eight years of living with HIV, Jones does not see it as an

academic issue. He spends much of his day mentioning the unmention-
able, his efforts aimed at breaking through walls of shame and isolation.
He works on the HIM (HIV intervention models) program, a safe-sex
education outreach program for gay and bisexual men.

When he lived in Chicago, Jones found succor and support in a community that had broad-based sensitivity to living with the virus. That has
not been the case in Minnesota. "It's fortunate in Minnesota that the
rates of infection are very low, but it's bittersweet in that there is not a
good understanding of the reality of HIV."

Jones's agenda includes creating outreach that connects with the
Red Door's target audience—an agenda he claims creates tension with
county administrators who are leery of offending their superiors, the
Hennepin County Board. Jones believes administrators should listen
to the clinicians and community health workers, the people who daily
make their way through a sea of sexual discharges from people who
are underinformed or misinformed. And under those circumstances,
fashioning a message that is palatable to a straight, fifty-eight-year-old
Hennepin County commissioner should be a lower priority than it inevitably is.

"I was a little bit disillusioned when I came here," Jones says. "From
a distance, you hear that this state is a very progressive place, but the
progressive part ends with social programs. It's a very sex-phobic place.
Some of the ways we need to communicate with people in order to do
the job are bound to run up against puritan standards. And vague, fear-
laden messages aren't going to do it."

The clinic and county administrators are currently working out a review process for outreach materials. In the meantime, a brochure produced by the Minnesota AIDS Project titled *Fucking and Sucking* is not
going to be among the resource material distributed by the clinic.

Nor will the clinic be targeting identifiably gay men only. "The higher-
risk groups are people whose behavior does not match their identity. If
someone identifies themselves as a heterosexual but has sex with men,
they are at very high risk," Jones says. An ad he placed looking for mar-

ried men who have a sexual life with other men sparked more than six hundred responses last year.

"These are very closeted people, so I think the response is an indication that there is a lot more out there. I think people would be astounded how prevalent the problem is and how serious the consequences can be."

Bruce, a thirty-one-year-old with a complicated heterosexual history, suggests that the testing process at the Red Door goes beyond information, offering a therapeutic element to those who are willing to listen.

"When you go there, everything seems very normal, like any doctor's office. But the feelings that go with being there are tough to manage.

"I don't especially like going to any medical place, but to go to some office and talk in detail about your sexual behavior is worse still," he explains. "On my last visit, I talked about what I had been up to and the woman gave me a pretty hard look and suggested I might want to consider making changes.

"It was a gentle kick in the ass," he recalls softly. "And sometimes, that's the friendliest thing in the world."

IR Queer

Gay and Republican in the Age of Quist

JUNE 22–28, 1994

DELEGATE MIKE GALLAGHER bends over a sheet of paper, furiously tracking Allen Quist's June 17 ascension to a first-ballot endorsement for governor at the Minnesota Independent-Republican convention. The lionization of Quist is minutes away, but it can't arrive soon enough for Gallagher.

"If we as a society do not begin to conform our behavior to biblical principles, we will perish as a society. Homosexual behavior is a mortal sin and a deadly, disease-ridden lifestyle. The homosexual agenda means the destruction of the American family," Gallagher says, lifting his pen from his pad and waving it in front of his big eyes during his elegy. "If we do not restore the family, we will be punished, as God did to Sodom and Gomorrah."

Steve Swonder stands off to the side, confronted by a sea of delegates sporting royal-blue Quist visors. They are tickled to death, abuzz at the prospect of their intrepid Christian warrior winning the endorsement. A twenty-year veteran of politics, Swonder is one Republican delegate who knows how to count and who realizes he is outnumbered many times over. As someone who is moderate *and* gay, he will have trouble finding a comfortable place to land at this convention. The fraternity of conservative IRs frothing about "the sodomite agenda" continues to grow, and being gay in the age of Quist shapes up as tough duty. Swonder smiles quietly at the organized mayhem around him, showing no indication that he will turn into a pillar of salt anytime soon.

"I am no threat to these people. I am certainly not anti-family—I love my family. I mean, I have my grandmother's china in my cabinet," he says, keeping his hands on his hips and his eyes on the other delegates. The sweat on his brow and his weary mien reflect the close, hermetic confines that define the battle at the Saint Paul Civic Center.

Any way you look at it, Swonder belongs to a profound minority. His candidate for governor, incumbent Arne Carlson, is about to be thoroughly spanked by the Quist insurgency. Swonder's status as one of the few homosexuals in plain sight doesn't offer much succor as the Christian soldiers march past him to support Quist.

In a just world, there would be room in the Grand Old Party for an economic conservative who both votes and giggles with metronomic regularity. But Quist's thumping of Carlson is not a minor course correction in the body politic—it is a hard jerk to the right that left many fearing that individual rights will be trampled in the pursuit of moral rectitude. The moderates in attendance are horrified, suggesting that Minnesota's Republicans are fast becoming a party at the end of the world.

Kathy Worre, a longtime Republican activist, stands next to her delegation, beaming and bouncing to the political music of the next millennium. She is blissed out by the trouncing of Carlson, a governor who has made a career out of snubbing her party. Worse still, from her perspective, in 1993 Carlson's signature turned into law a bill that granted equal rights to *avowed homosexuals*.

"The people that are here today," Worre says, indicating the blur of blue and yellow Quist shirts, "know and understand the homosexual agenda, which is to remove the traditional definition of the family. Hey, I'd like special protection because I own a maroon VW. But that's not the way it works. Quite honestly, the lifestyle is abhorrent, it is deviant, and it is a disease spreader. We," she says, gesturing toward her fellow delegates, "certainly don't believe that kind of behavior deserves special protection."

As Worre fades back into her reverie, a tall, blond man sidles into view and begins speaking in a hush as his eyes ricochet off of the crowd.

"There are many, many people in this room who don't believe a word that she just told you," he whispers. Asked for his name, he rolls his eyes. "In this madhouse, with these people running around? Are you kidding? Just say, 'an unidentified Republican,'" he says. He walks away without looking back.

Swonder isn't shy about offering his name. He's not shy about his sexuality, either—although it's not something he features. Swonder is gay because he was born that way, but he made a conscious lifestyle choice when he became a Republican. The forty-one-year-old former president of the religious youth organization Luther League in Crosby, North Dakota, grew up in a family composed mostly of staunch Republicans. While he doesn't mind being identified as gay, he eschews the term "queer," suggesting it connotes a level of activism and passion about gay issues that he has never displayed.

Swonder's passion is clearly the Grand Old Party. He thinks Barry Goldwater was politically correct, Ronald Reagan was cool, and Gerald Ford's son Steven was a dreamboat. For two decades Swonder has been carrying water for the elephant. He's a true-hearted Republican who believes government is most effective at throwing money down a rat hole. As an office services specialist for the Chemical Health Division of Hennepin County, Swonder sees clients who tap into federal largess by obtaining disability benefits for their addictions.

Swonder's ardor derives from a fairly common—at least in political circles—combination of naivete and cynicism. As former presidential candidate Gene McCarthy once said of politics, "It's a lot like being a high school football coach: you have to be smart enough to know how to win, but dumb enough to think it matters." Swonder fits the description nicely.

"Reagan was not as bad as anybody predicted. My civil rights were not hampered by him one little bit. I mean how bad could the man be? His children weren't exactly repressed," he says, arching his eyebrows for appropriate emphasis.

Any doubt among his fellow delegates about which master Swonder serves should be wiped out by his support of Ronald Reagan. In his own affable way, Reagan initiated a cultural war that has targeted gays' and lesbians' very right to be who they are. Swonder's fealty blinds him to the fact that Reagan responded to the greatest public health crisis of our time by taking a nap. Reagan didn't even use the acronym AIDS until late 1985, after thousands had been infected.

While his support of much of the Republican agenda seems counter to his self-interest, it's not hard to fathom Swonder's passion for things political. He is an inveterate gossip, loves keeping score, and doesn't mind working hundreds of hours for nothing.

"Steve has distinguished himself as one of the workhorses of the Republican Party," says Sarah Janacek, a Republican lobbyist and Swonder's friend. "Steve is known for what he does, not the fact that he is gay." Party insiders say Swonder's abundant technical political skills qualify him to be a consultant, but Swonder says he isn't much interested in operating out of that particular closet.

"I suppose I could get a hair transplant, lose fifty pounds, and become one of those people in blue suits with a red tie," he says, indicating some of the slicker functionaries working the mezzanine. "But what would be the point of working for something if I had to pretend to be somebody else while I do it?"

"People should be able to be supportive of the American family without being called a bigot," says Julie Quist, watching from a distance as her husband is interviewed by *Nightline*'s Cokie Roberts. "The big problem that we have right now is that we are raising children that have no idea what a family is supposed to be. The family is under attack."

Genetic predisposition aside, Julie Quist possesses the gestural elegance of a candidate and a firm understanding of what she believes is wrong with contemporary American culture.

"The homosexual agenda is wrong," she says with quiet certitude. "The gay agenda would like to legally define the family as something it is not. To say that it is appropriate for a man and a man to be a family, well, that means it could be anybody. A family could be a man and woman, a man and a man, or three women and a man. There has to be some parameters to be a family."

After weeks of fanning homophobic and pro-life flames through the mail, Allen Quist seems to be softening his rhetoric now that victory is nigh. There is room in the IR tent, according to Quist.

"I have friends and workers who are gay, but I'm not convinced that they need any greater level of protection than anybody else," he says as his media handler ushers him off to his next exposure.

All the chatter at the convention about "special protection" is just coded invective, of course. There is nothing "special" about extending the rights of the Constitution—a document the Republicans hold so dear—to people regardless of their affectional preference. And even though Quist is fond of making passing reference to his gay pals and workers, that wasn't who he was hugging in the feel-good videos that preceded his speech. Nope, father and man's man that he is, Quist spent most of his time on camera squeezing the ten children he has sired.

Swonder thinks it's disingenuous to say you are okay with gay people but not gay rights: "You know, it's not that I want any more protection than the rest of these people, I just don't want any less," he says.

Swonder is justifiably proud of the fact that it was a Republican governor who signed the bill extending civil protections to gays and lesbians. But that's just one more reason why the assembled flock is intent on driving Arne the False Prophet from their number.

Although a lot of the people around him at the convention are talking about the homosexual menace, no one confronts Swonder personally. At the convention and elsewhere, he may notice more conservative members of his party whispering and pointing, but he says, "They're probably saying that I'm a secular humanist or something *really* horrible like that."

He is active in the Republican Organizing Committee, which employs the Constitution's sixth article as the basis for its efforts. The article states that "no religious test should ever be used as a qualification for any office or public trust under the United States."

"We chose it because it's real simple," says Swonder. "There are no big words in it. It clearly indicates that there should be a separation between church and state." But the Chesapeake, Virginia–based Christian Coalition, one of the galvanizing forces behind Quist's candidacy, sees no reason to wall off government from religion.

"We vehemently disagree that there should be a separation between church and state," says Bob Beale, founder of the Minnesota chapter of the Christian Coalition. The coalition is rooted in bedrock televangelist conservatism — pro-family, anti-homosexual dogma with abundant conspiracy theories.

"Allen Quist drew people out of the woodwork who would be interested in the Christian Coalition. All we did was incorporate," Beale says. "Quist and the coalition care about the same issues." Interviewed on the floor of the convention, Quist claims he has no sense of how much support he has gotten from members of the burgeoning coalition of fundamentalists.

Nationally, the Christian Coalition helped Oliver North advance in Virginia and has made waves in seven other states. The surge of fundamentalist imperatives makes sense to Dave Jennings, a former Republican leader in the Minnesota House.

"There are a huge number of people, not just in Minnesota but everywhere, who believe that their way of life has been under attack — under attack by the press, by the politicians, and by the entertainment industry," Jennings says. "Quist is having success because he is telling people that he knows how to fight back."

Gays, Jennings suggests, have drawn the target on themselves.

"The gay community has been flaunting it in the face of Middle Americans with gay pride parades and things like that. Gay people are politically aggressive, and it's left people feeling threatened."

Steve Swonder isn't one for flaunting. His lapel pin at the convention features the Jerry Falwell quote "God created Adam and Eve. Not Adam and Steve."

"It's a nice color," he explains with a broad, friendly smile as he speaks over the roll call vote. "See how it picks up the purple in my shirt?"

Swonder continues to show up, and continues to work hard for a party composed of "self-appointed, self-anointed holy rock throwers," as one moderate described them. For a number of years the party has had a plank in its platform specifically condemning Swonder's lifestyle. It mentions that "homosexuals should not be able to obtain the right to enforce their status as a special interest group." And judging by a plank in the health care section, the IRs would rather eliminate homosexuality than the disease that occasionally afflicts them: "We support state and federal funds being allocated to AIDS research in equitable proportion to cancer, diabetes, Alzheimer's and heart disease."

"Oh well, my state party has planks against just about everything," Swonder says, dismissing the passage. "I mean, I haven't checked yet this year, but we usually have a plank against fluoridated water. Does that mean I'm going to quit drinking water? No."

Watching Swonder move through the convention, waving to some delegates and leaning in to chat with others, one wonders what some of his more conservative brethren would do if they knew that *one of them* was actually among them. Would they come with the nets and try to deprogram him from his godless ways?

"Look, I've never denied it, but I have never made an issue of it either," he says. "In all my years in Republican politics, I think only one person has asked me, and he said something like, 'Are you a sodomite?' Well, I just clutched the imaginary pearls around my neck and said, 'Moi?'"

• • •

Just prior to accepting the nomination, the Quists stand stage left, smiling at each other. Swonder comes up behind them and says, "Hey, Allen, give us a smile." Both Quists turn and flash world-class grins, which promptly melt when Swonder drops the camera from his face and they see who he is.

Quist is a portrait of shopworn humility as he ascends the podium amidst a custom-designed presentation that is equal parts charm and spectacle. Speaking from behind the words "Empower People," Quist keeps his acceptance speech short, both in terms of length and specifics, instead allowing the energy of the crowd to roll over him in wave after wave.

The animation and charm of the Quistians gives the lie to all of the press about Quist supporters being zombies, although some of the speeches from the floor sound as though they've been piped in from another dimension. The candidate himself shows much greater capacity for modulation than the public has been led to believe he is capable of. He pounds on economic issues with ardor and does a fine job using his aw-shucks offhandedness to get his friendlies in the audience excited. In the wake of his nomination, the Civic Center is the scene of good old-fashioned political theater, not a religious revival.

But there is a rural dimension to the proceeding that shows up in countless ways. When Barbara Carlson aired interviews from a hot tub wearing an evening gown and gargantuan fake pearls, the delegates studied her as if she had just disembarked from a flying saucer. In the mezzanine, a cappuccino cart that inspired block-long lines during the Democratic convention two weeks ago sits empty for most of the convention. And the rabbi, just after giving the invocation, has a single urgent question on his lips: "Which way is out?"

When the avowed enemy of the Quistians, Governor Arne Carlson, spoke, there was none of the divinely inspired booing and hissing that had been predicted. As their leader had requested, the Quistians sat politely on their hands. Some took the time to do some knitting, while the handful of Carlson delegates kicked up as much noise as they could muster.

Mike Triggs, a former executive director of the IR Party and the man who earlier this year ran Carlson's reelection campaign, couldn't get elected as a delegate to the convention. Triggs's experience on the Carlson campaign convinced him that the governor's support for the state human rights bill cost him dearly within the party.

"I really don't understand it, though. If the truth be known, many of these delegates have a nephew or a niece or a son or a daughter who is gay," Triggs says, his eyes traveling up to the ceiling, where hundreds of balloons await a Quist victory. "In a political party that's based on individual liberty, I guess I don't understand the fixation. We're supposed to be the party that keeps government out of people's lives."

Quist does a wonderful job of being the modest farmer-servant who just happened to step off his tractor in time to lead the prairie fire of discontent. But who is providing all the organizing muscle? Julie Quist may be an outstanding organizer, but she did not fill the Civic Center by herself. And where is all the money coming from? Quist may say that he doesn't know how much support he's been receiving from the Christian Coalition, but its director and many members of his family have already maxed out on their contributions to Quist.

"They have a national agenda, they make no secret of it. It's printed for all to see," Steve Swonder says. "These people are not kooks. Pat Robertson is not a kook, Pat Buchanan is not a kook, and Allen Quist is not a kook. They have money, they have experience, and they have a plan," he says, gesturing down the row of tables to where the Christian Coalition has set up a booth.

Even though Quist was busy telling Cokie Roberts and every other national newsie that there is no Christian conspiracy to take over the political apparatus of the country, the Christian Coalition's materials at the convention seemed to suggest that something resembling a call to arms is reaching the pews in the churches of America.

And even though the local chapter of the Christian Coalition is just five months old, they plan to grow the franchise fairly quickly, with a "Leadership Training Conference" on August 26 and 27. Topics will include "God's System of Delegated Authority" and "Organizing and Winning Your Precinct." Expect the homosexual agenda to be mentioned more than a few times.

"Most of the people who come from a religious background into politics are lacking in perspicuity," Swonder suggests. "In fact, many of them have the critical capacity of ferns. [Conservatives] may be running the party, but they are not putting forth electable candidates." He points out that while Republican moderates have not had an easy time getting endorsed by their own party, they have a history of good relationships with the voters.

The hothouse confines of a political convention usually end up reflecting and amplifying ideological extremes. But endure enough of the Quistians' chant about how they represent the mainstream of American values, and you begin to wonder. Maybe creationism will end up being lesson number one in schools and queers will be forced back into their closets.

Steve Swonder says when the smoke clears, he will still be here.

"What happened here is nothing more than great theater," he says, sweeping his hand over the crowd, which is beginning to thin as the excitement over Quist's endorsement dissipates.

"They storm the caucuses and write the platform, but nobody in the general public supports this stuff. Beginning tomorrow, this convention will be over and the primary will be under way and I will again be part of Republican politics in Minnesota. They can have this weekend, but that's it."

Still Life with Alien

How the Monster from Inner Space Took Over My Life

FROM THE TIME I was little, I loved watching movies about aliens. Years after I saw *The Day the Earth Stood Still,* my dreams were filled with steel-noggined guys who spoke in detached, tinny voices as they ordered the world to submit. Their invasion was relentless but seductively ordered and controlled. Those aliens of my childhood seemed very far away—just so many dots on my parents' crappy black-and-white TV. They didn't scare me, and if they did come, well, I'd know what to do.

The aliens became more menacing with the passage of nights. They arrived in the longest part of sleep, when consciousness steps back and reveals a darkness within. In that nightmarish reverie the invaders seemed more explicitly interested in me than in world domination. They didn't wear helmets or live on TV. In these dreams they appeared as a part of me I couldn't quite recognize, with an intimacy that made them infinitely more confounding.

When the alien of my dreams made its presence known in my waking life on December 10, 1992, I stepped aside immediately, regarding myself and the alien with inexplicable detachment. I couldn't bear sharing space—even for a second—with something that was after me . . . in me.

During the time of occupation, I answered my phone with excessive cheerfulness, wrote reassuring notes to old girlfriends, and smiled knowingly whenever someone in a white coat revealed something sharp in their hands. I put my fingers in my ears and hummed tunelessly until someone told me it was gone. I acted as if I had been merely interrupted.

I can remember the day cancer came to me in the mirror. I am not one to study myself, at least not in mirrors, but a distortion in my reflection caught my eye one cold December morning. It looked as if, overnight, someone had inserted a large sausage underneath the skin on the left side of my neck—part of me was clearly under invasion. The next morning, I was absolutely certain the incubus was bigger. I called a clinic.

From the instant the doctor entered the room and stared at my neck, the firm line between nightmare and reality dissolved. I remained inert, waiting for a cue to panic, but each technician, nurse, and doctor I encountered riveted me with their devotion to routine. From the outset, I mimicked the detachment surrounding me, even when someone mentioned a lymphatic cancer called Hodgkin's disease.

I remained awake while they surgically removed a piece of the mass in my neck for biopsy, and in spite of myself I asked for a look at it. The small but ominous specimen bobbed in a vial filled with iridescent, greenish fluid. I swore under my breath when its ugliness came into view.

Four days later I got a call from the surgeon, Dr. John Delaney, telling me my neck sausage was cancerous. I thanked him for the call, if not the information, and went to my bathroom mirror. The tumor was there, no different, just as alien as when it first arrived. My eyes were another matter, offering a sober flicker of recognition that I was sharing space with my nightmares. As I watched, I saw myself going away.

In the first five months of 1992 I underwent radiation therapy for the treatment of Hodgkin's disease, a "good" cancer with a high cure rate. The regimen was unpleasant but manageable. I hung on to my job, my kids, and my equilibrium by concocting enough denial to get from one day to the next. But my pretense that nothing horrible was underway left me with a persistent feeling that all of it was happening to someone else.

This summer, more than two years after being treated at the University of Minnesota Hospital and Clinic, I felt compelled to review my medical records — to revisit a part of my life during which I'd made a point of not paying attention.

There was nothing significant or noble about my treatment for cancer: the four inches of files depict a routine case with a successful outcome. The records are mostly indecipherable, full of hard and fast data that betrayed no hint of the unreality gripping me during those months when I felt as though I was being forced out of my body.

I continued to pretend it never existed even after it was gone. The treatment, the rhetoric, and the pity engendered by diagnosis left me feeling abashed, as if I had woken up and found someone I did not know touching me. It set off a deep, inexplicable sense of embarrassment that took years to dissipate.

Even now, the word *cancer* sounds dreadful to me. It's still the big C, with an eponymous power that makes it difficult to insinuate into polite conversation. Cancer sounds horrible and it is, an inexorable mutation of the flesh that leaves the host beleaguered and friends speechless. Once you're diagnosed, people loop around the word so often you begin to think you have a disease called *it*. "So how is *it?*" they say. Every once in a while I wanted to interrupt the séance of avoidance and say, "Oh, you mean this large cancerous mass on my neck?" But that would have scared people and me even more. Instead, I'd tell them that *it* was fine and so was I, even though the cancer was still there, strengthened by its ineffability.

I was unable to wrap my lips around the word until my second day at the hospital, when I was sent over to the Masonic Cancer Center. The people who work there call it the Masonic Day Hospital, which sounds infinitely more comforting and less chronic. I stopped and read the writing on the sign, trying on the sound and reality of cancer. It made me feel sick.

• • •

In my experience, even medical people don't like talking about cancer unless they have to. It's too dreadful, too unfathomable — even to them. Its persistence is an affront to their belief system, a whisper of unadmitted mortalness and mortality. Doctors respond to cancer by becoming monster-movie heroes — those plucky guys who make it to the end of the story. When something goes wrong and the alien takes out another hapless victim, they shake their heads, then get back to fighting that damn alien.

In order to maintain their equilibrium and your sanity, there are doctors who act as if they can kick the shit out of cancer, but even they know it's a crapshoot. While medicine has made enormous strides — many of which personally benefited me — doctors are clearly at a loss to explain why certain parts of people's bodies metastasize into killing fields.

When someone is completely overtaken by cancer, the patient's caregivers offer spoken homage to the good fight. I know from sitting in a lot of waiting rooms that many people with uncontrollable cancer don't fight the good fight. They fight a miserable fight, full of unspeakable pain and physical abasement — and then they die.

There aren't a lot of ways to avoid this blind spot in American medical brilliance if it's your turn. Alternative medicine seems a little speculative and freeform in the context of something as beguilingly poisonous as cancer. In allying with mainstream medical doctors, I found a gauzy assurance that somebody was doing something about the monster from inner space.

For most of my life, my operating principle was blind aggression. If I thought someone was coming after me, I contemplated poking their eyes out as a defensive strategy. If I didn't like the way the game was going, I'd tip over the board and walk away. But cancer shrugs off belligerence with its implacability. Once I became a patient, I became a model of compliance — my records duly note my persistent acquiescence. I made friends with my doctors because I found their uniforms and presumption of expertise comforting. I was impressed and nourished by their hubris. I let them shower me with radiation, excise my spleen, and dissect my neck whenever they asked. Given a medical directive, I became Forrest Gump in hospital pajamas. Patient is as patient does.

I remember my initial consultation with Dr. Greg Vercellotti, a hematologist eminent in his field who possesses social skills not normally associated with medical professionals. After I was diagnosed, Greg and I acted as though we were auditioning for roles in a made-for-TV movie. He'd say things like, "We're going to beat this thing, buddy," and I would respond with a determined nod. I often felt a very shameful urge to giggle.

During that first visit, Greg was upbeat, saying that the scans and blood tests seemed to indicate that I had Hodgkin's 1A, which is the disease's earliest and most treatable form. The cancer likely was located only in the lymph nodes of my neck and probably had not spread, even though the tumor was expanding in size into cantaloupe range. He went on to say that "just to be sure," they were going to perform a staging laparotomy, which involved making a ten-inch cut in my abdomen, biopsying all of my major organs, and even taking my spleen out. I noted the organ I'd be losing was elemental to my disposition, but Greg said they wanted to take it and squeeze it to make sure that the Hodgkin's disease was not on the march through my lymphatic system. I was stunned that major abdominal surgery could qualify as diagnostic work, but Greg told me it was the most conservative approach.

Even in medical parlance, which is the most euphemistically infected language in the world, "conservative" seemed like a reach. *Conservative* is a doctor code word for patent aggression in the name of survival. Cancer produces the same reaction as the monster who pops up in the midst of a well-armed landing party: everybody starts blasting away with everything they've got. I found solace in the trips from clinic to clinic at the U, submitting my problem to the serial expertise of a big hospital, but there were moments when I felt that they were taking my life in order to save it.

Half an hour before the staging laparotomy, a doctor—whom I had not met—came into the room and introduced himself as an oral surgeon. He and his "team" had determined that my mouth was in for a lot of radiation because the cancerous node in my neck was high. His team had decided to take out twelve of my grinding teeth as a preventive measure against radiation cavities and ensuing necrosis of the jaw. Sitting in just my surgical gown, I was loath to make a major life decision without my pants on. I gathered my thoughts enough to tell the doctor, whose name I never knew, that his timing was poor and that I was only willing to donate my spleen on that particular day. He used cryptic jargon to indicate I was going to dearly regret my decision. I don't. I think of him every time I order steak.

Other procedures were just to be gone through, part of an endurance contest that left me progressively desensitized over the course of the five months. At the beginning of my treatment I submitted to a bone marrow biopsy to determine the extent of the Hodgkin's. Bone doesn't anesthetize well but has a surprising amount of nerves, which is an unfortunate combination. The doctor who was after the marrow in my pelvic bone was furtive and clumsy. "You might experience a little sharpness here," he said, just before the needle penetrated some white-hot place. Sharpness.

Doctors are wrenches, biological mechanics who head into the shop looking to solve problems. On the whole, I liked my doctors. My surgeon found out I had cancer, my hematologist decided what to do about it, and my radiation doctor used one of her machines to make it go away. They cured my cancer, and while I hated what they did *to* me, I appreciated what they did *for* me.

Treatment regimens for cancer are full of painful realities and powerful ironies: Radiation can cause cancer or wipe it out. Toxins in the body can create an opening for cancer or be used to shut the door. In order to fight cancer, I had to sit very still. Being a cancer patient required spending much time alone in rooms of white that hosted shiny medical appliances. In those hours, I often wished I could leave while my neck was being treated, that I could dissemble into a form in which the tumor —and what it represented—wasn't part of me.

Many of the machines I encountered had a peculiar ability to see what I could not. The CAT scanner would rotate around me, a huge whirling doughnut of metal that seemed as if it was preparing to take off. I was conveyed into the device's tube and listened to the mechanical voice repeating instructions from the small speaker. *Hold your breath. Relax.* I came out of the tube smiling beneficently, lulled by the Zen rhythm of diagnostic hardware.

I never came close to dying from cancer, but the first month of my treatment made it look as though I might. In those thirty days I had a neck biopsy, a bone marrow biopsy, major abdominal surgery including a splenectomy, and thousands of rads of radiation. I went from a fat, self-involved creep to a skinny, almost beatific soul who could only handle a bite or two of white rice. My gaze averted every time I caught a reflection.

Bystanders react in different ways to having cancer in their midst. Some of it was predictable. My parents and siblings were perfectly pitched throughout, relentlessly optimistic when things were tough and indignant when things went wrong. Many good friends were unconditionally available for the length of my illness. Other reactions were understandable but less foreseeable. There were good friends who went away because they truly didn't know what to say. And there were men and women whom I had viewed as near-mortal enemies who showed up with hot dishes and wan smiles while I was ill. I was gratified by their interest but mortified by my own vulnerability.

The compassion of others can be a tremendous burden. When people would call or show up, they'd inevitably ask, "How are you?" Which meant they wanted to talk about it until I told them I was fine, even though some days that was not the case. I stopped telling the truth about how I really was for purely practical reasons. When some of my strength returned, I began pushing people out of my life. I ended a long relationship with a woman, in part because I couldn't bear to have someone looking at me from an intimate distance while I was in a state of contamination.

When I was alone, I spent time speculating about why the alien chose me. I was certainly a juicy, deserving target—the big-chested blonde in the monster movie who is a little too slow to outrun the beast. There was a long and glorious history with cigarettes and a romance with alcohol and class A narcotics that had cooled not long before the beast came after me. But Hodgkin's isn't like lung cancer, a swift and sure punishment for ignoring both your mother and your doctor. It's a kind of malignant opportunistic invasion—an uncontrolled proliferation—that lays siege to otherwise healthy middle-aged people. My doctors were loath to speak of causality, preferring to focus the discussion on making the cancer go away.

My speculation came to rest on an old microwave, a fixture in my home for many years. It was ancient, an appliance of doubtful structural integrity that throbbed and buzzed with radiant energy when I used it to warm a bowl of frozen corn. Maybe, I thought, my microwave leaked cancer into my life.

Once I had cancer, my prescribed cure involved being led into a room by chirpy technicians who positioned a couple of tons of radiation-issuing machinery over me, then ran away behind lead doors. Other than the hum and throb of the machine—which reminded me of the microwave—it was pretty quiet in there. I passed the time by staring at a tropical tableau above the machine, put there for that very purpose. (Which might explain why I left for a vacation in the jungles of Central America eight days after my final radiation treatment.)

Dr. Chung K. Lee, a physician eminent in the therapeutic effects of highly targeted X-rays, decided that about ten million volts would be sufficient to send my cancer back where it came from. She warned me that I might lose "a little" hair on the back of my head. It was the only lie she ever told me. During the initial stages of treatment, I'd wake up with a face full of fur, as if I had been sleeping with a Saint Bernard that had a shedding problem. I was left with a small skullcap of hair that fit right in at First Avenue but looked pretty weird everywhere else. I took to wearing a Public Enemy cap one of my daughters gave me. I thought it enhanced my profile at a time when I was consummately concerned about appearances.

While I was undergoing radiation, I went to see an old boss of mine who had bone cancer. His bones were disintegrating, and from what I had heard, his head was gradually dissolving into his shoulders. The pain was said to be beyond expression, yet there he was, sitting at his desk. We talked for a half hour, mostly about hair. Neither of us mentioned the word *cancer*. He died four months later.

As my treatment progressed, I began to ignore the culture at large and see myself in the context of other patients, like the wino who rolls over in the gutter hoping to see someone just a little farther down the hill. On a day when I was feeling low about the radiation-induced burns all over my ears and neck, I was seated in the waiting room next to a dairy farmer from Luverne, Minnesota, who had a metal hoop screwed into his skull. The hoop helped hold his head very still so the radiation killed the tumor in his brain and not him. "How's it going?" he said cordially, peering up from beneath his steel halo. "Great," I said, not mentioning that part of the reason I felt okay was that I wasn't scheduled to have any metal components screwed into my head.

On my last day of treatment, I brought flowers to the radiation technicians and told them I would miss our daily visits.

Cancer returns often enough after its supposed demise to leave a palpable vapor trail of fear. Cancer patients are said to be in remission, not cured. Four months after finishing treatment, I returned to see Dr. Vercellotti: my neck had enlarged again. As I walked in, I noticed him eyeballing my neck as so many doctors before him had. I watched his eyes with the same intensity and noted the shine of concern. He probed my neck, then moved down to the lymph nodes in my armpits. With his hand in my armpit, he spoke quietly. "I feel a mass in here."

The message was clear, the space between us electric. Not only was my cancer back, but it was on the move. I never made a peep during the alien's initial visit, but a return engagement meant more than a temporary interruption. Greg's note in the chart indicates I had a "vaso-vagal episode" when we talked about a recurrence. He means I fainted straightaway.

An ensuing battery of tests—neck biopsy, CAT scans, and bloodwork —revealed that my swoon was premature. My denial had been built on a belief that the alien was only visiting, and when I was confronted with the possibility that it was back to stay, along with a much more acute diagnosis, my brain shut down. Greg and I had a laugh about it after the biopsy came back negative.

Illness has ennobling effects that are difficult to adequately describe. The waiting room for therapeutic radiology was often suffused with an undue cheeriness. I saw people with holes burned in their heads smiling and chatting like it was just another day.

I know what they were up to. To acknowledge, even for a moment, the seriousness at hand would have corroded my infrastructure of de-nial. I needed to pretend everything was under control so I could re-main in check. In order to avoid a sudden tumble into despair, I spent an enormous amount of time pretending to be happy while I was sick. The first expression of my cancer-free life was the return of my historical prickliness. Beneath the practiced diffidence, I was really pissed that the alien had landed on me.

But now I'm fine. Really. Friends who haven't seen me for a while ask after my health with more than passing interest, but I pretend I don't know what is behind their concerned perusal of my face. Because the cigarettes are back for occasional, guilty visitations, their faces darken every time I light up. Having cancer certainly spoiled my ability to truly enjoy a cigarette, but I still like them just as much as I ever did. I'll smoke for a month every now and then before the fear and guilt overtake me.

I lived to inherit "the gifts of illness" term I swore I would never use. My innate fatalism has not been supplanted by an enhanced lust for life, but cancer did make me a handsomer person. I arrived for treatment as a prototypically obese American male with a gut and an early onset of jowling about the cheeks and neck. The radiation made me too sick to eat, so I lost a lot of weight. Some of the pounds have returned, but the jowls are banished. The radiation that killed all of the cancerous cells in my neck took the fatty ones, too. I now have an elegant pencil neck and clearly defined jaw. It's a pleasant reminder that cancer changed me.

• • •

Cancer narratives hew to words such as *bout, battle,* and *fight,* as if the patient is in the midst of an exceptionally long boxing match. Combative rhetoric offers the comforting illusion that a disease will somehow respond to the will of the host. But I never threw a punch. The period of occupation was a time of endless surrender—to my doctors, to the corruptive immigrant within my body, and to my fate, which turned out to be a happy one.

At thirty-seven, I have developed the mind-set of a grandfather, swallowing pills every day while squeezing and probing every lump and bump, searching for a reason to worry. In a way, I should be honored. Maybe now that I've had a little touch of cancer, it will be someone else's turn.

My doctors tell me that I am free of cancer, but that's not really true. When I catch an image of myself in a mirror, it is apprehension, not vanity, that is reflected. The frightful alien in my dreams is now in remission, and if he returns, he will be in a form I now recognize. He will look like me, except he will have cancer.

Indictment City

Durenberger's Arrogance Remains at Large

APRIL 7–13, 1993

> I believe that fairness will prevail. So will the ideal of justice.
> And so, in the end, will I.
>
> —*Senator Dave Durenberger*

> Now don't be sad.
> 'Cause two out of three ain't bad.
>
> —*Meat Loaf*

SOMEWHERE DURING HIS slide from Mr. Clean to the uncrowned king of Senate money launderers, you'd think Senator Dave Durenberger, IR-Minnesota, would have caught the drift. In between all of his keening about crazed federal prosecutors and bad legal work, a little voice should have popped up and whispered: *Hey, Dave, maybe your time is up.*

Instead, this guy has been a model of reckless consistency. As of last Friday, Dave Durenberger had enough operational denial to rail indignantly against "senseless felony charges" leveled against him by the US Department of Justice.

The charges *were* senseless. If Durenberger had done the chaste thing and fallen on his sword while Bush was still president, the Justice Department would have lost interest in him a long time ago. But his ferocious arrogance and apparent lack of a vocational future induced him to hang on to a point where most of his constituents feel compelled to reach for a clothespin every time his name comes up.

Minnesotans have given up on the idea that the fifty-eight-year-old senator will take responsibility for his behavior. We mostly just wish he would go away.

The feds offered him just such an opportunity, suggesting he go down on a misdemeanor charge last Friday. He told them he wasn't dealing. Snubbing the misdemeanor offer was a big mistake. The government's willingness to deal on a lesser count was consistent with an underlying theme Durenberger and his buddies have advanced since the investigation began — that while they may have fraudulently obtained taxpayer money, it wasn't a *lot* of money. Durenberger merely used a combination of greasy lawyering and phony documents to advance his personal financial interests. In his statement following his indictment, Durenberger went to great pains to point out that he was *only* being charged with defrauding the taxpayers of $3,825.

It may be news to the senator, but out here in the real world, money starts at a hundred. We haven't forgotten that he was forced to pay back $40,000 in condo reimbursements. Or $93,000 more in speaking fees. We're mindful that Durenberger was smoked out by the *Star Tribune* and federal law enforcement officials. Durenberger never disclosed anything — unless you're talking about closely held US intelligence secrets.

At the time of Durenberger's denouncement, Democratic senator Howell Heflin of Alabama, chairman of the Senate Ethics Committee, described the senator's behavior as "a knowing, deliberate, and calculated evasion." Not a lot of gray area there. Heflin, the Senate, and now the US Department of Justice reached the same conclusion: Durenberger has consistently pushed the ethical envelope, going beyond wiggle room and into a variety of schemes that were plainly lawless at their conception.

What else do you call a deal, first entered into in 1983, in which he switched condos with a pal and then billed the Senate for staying in his own place? When that pal dropped out, Durenberger and his staff frantically searched for another "partner." It took six months to wire up another arrangement, but Durenberger was not content to merely resume the scam. Instead, he and his lawyers backdated documents and created sham billings to cover the six months.

Through it all, Durenberger has tried to build a ledge out of the fact that he's continued to do a good job on behalf of the state's citizens. He misses the point. It's not his politics that are out of step with Minnesotans; it's his ethics. His willfulness in advantaging himself at every turn has nothing in common with the fabric of this state and its history of political leadership.

Durenberger still postures about his past leadership and current work on health care, but those efforts lost a little of their sheen recently when it was revealed that nobody in the entire Senate has taken more money from insurance companies and other medical special interests than Durenberger.

A day after his indictment, Durenberger was being coy about his plans for reelection. The man is humility-impaired and remorse-deficient. And his political antennae are in a wee bit of a tangle. The text of his statement delivered to "the people of Minnesota" following his indictment offers a picture of a man whose tether to reality is tenuous at best.

"You will always have the very best that's in me, as a person and as your senator, every day of my life. I will continue to prove that to you as I have every day for the last fourteen years."

Assuming, of course, he remains at large.

A League of His Own

THE NUMERICAL DAVE DURENBERGER

- Number of sitting senators in US history to be indicted: 9
- Number of senators ever denounced by his or her colleagues: 9

- Number of years in prison Durenberger faces: 10
- Vote count in favor of Durenberger's denouncement: 96–0
- Amount of money Durenberger owes his lawyers so far: $400,000
- Number of times the senator has actually accepted responsibility for his behavior: 0

Jackpot City

THE CASE OF Reva Wilkinson, gambling addict, is fearfully average. An otherwise law-abiding person, she had a fondness for gambling, lost big at the tables, and allegedly ended up ripping off her employer. It's a doleful litany that unfolds every single day in the state of ten thousand jackpots. Wilkinson's case made news only because she is the wife of the Anoka County sheriff and she stole from a highly visible institution, the Guthrie Theater.

The month before Wilkinson was busted by the feds, the public discovered that Hennepin County commissioner Sandra Hilary had jammed her whole life and reputation into a slot machine along with $100,000. The year before that, it was the promising law student who took to robbing banks after she began losing big at the casino. And so on.

People who dig themselves into a hole through gambling rarely just push back from the table. They stay put, putting ever more precious resources on the line in the hopes that they will crawl back out. Gambling odds being what they are, most continue to lose. One recent study suggested that a third of compulsive gamblers have been arrested for gambling-related crimes.

A decade ago, Minnesota was an island of Vegas-free sanity in a national sea of gaming. Since then, we have sunk into a double-or-nothing morass, a lotto hell. You can't buy a can of pop without being confronted by four separate instant opportunities to enrich yourself. Turn on the TV to catch the news, and you are confronted by the state-run scam. The commercials that follow remind you that the place for fun in your life is in front of a slot machine.

But all this bullshit about treasures and jackpots being a short car ride away never includes mention of the unexpected potholes on the road to the big payoff. Common, ordinary people are being transformed into liars, perpetrators, and thieves by the persistent allure of gaming.

Where else does the $4 billion spent in Minnesota on gaming last year come from? Do people really believe that you can suck billions out of residents and not tear significant holes in the social fabric? Billions don't come from painless, goofy fun money. Billions come from people ripping their lives apart to feed their jones. The gambling industry may welcome and market to the marginal player, but it is the hardcores who pay the bills, very often with money they have stolen from employers or loved ones.

Gambling's pervasiveness in Minnesota means that we are always going to be reading some story about the knucklehead of the week who didn't know when to quit.

Consider the depth of the pathology that would drive the wife of a sheriff to steal $300,000 after dropping every available nickel her family had at the blackjack table. Doesn't the dealer have some culpability? If this woman had thrown away that much dough on crack, the people who sold it to her would be sweating bullets. But the entrepreneurs at Mystic Lake Casino in Prior Lake are comfortably busy making half-million-dollar payouts to lucky shareholders.

A certain percentage of people are going to be hardcore players regardless of where they live. But logic suggests the rampant availability of gambling action has actually infected otherwise marginal gamblers.

Calls for help to the Minnesota Gambling Hotline have nearly doubled in the past two years, while the number of Gamblers Anonymous meetings has increased at the same rate. As access to gaming has been democratized, so apparently have the consequences. The people calling the hotline and showing up at the meetings are not marginal creeps who owe money to the mob. They are mothers who can't buy groceries for their kids because their account was closed after they kited checks at the casino. They are grandmas who can't go to Florida this winter because they went to Hinckley too many times last winter. They are the midlevel managers who can't do their jobs anymore because they are obsessing about their next piece of action.

For every public abasement like Reva Wilkinson's, you can bet there are a thousand other stories of quiet heartbreak. Stories that miss the front page but exact a tremendous human cost.

Public Dis'course

AUGUST 17–23, 1994

"WILL YA LOOK at this, Ronnie?" she says, rattling the newspaper at her husband in disgust. "Look what these monsters did to this apartment building—covered the damn place in graffiti. Oh Christ, there's a picture of 'em in here, too, doing all that gang stuff. Paper here says they're taking over, that they got a plan to kill more cops."

The *Star Tribune* took its readers along on an inner-city parade of homes last week, dutifully photographing the graffiti-covered lobby of an apartment building and following up with a photo of the alleged Bloods who showed up to be part of the media event the paper staged at Thirty-Sixth Street and Clinton Avenue South in Minneapolis. Reporter Kevin Duchschere transcribed while Minneapolis police gang investigator Mike Martin translated what he suggested were threats against police officers.

"This is the kind of stuff that affects what we do on the street and who we stop," Martin told Duchschere. Not much translation required there. If you are young, black, and live on the South Side, you can expect to be shaken down at will because some knucklehead scribbled "Copkilla" on a wall in the 'hood.

I am not compelled by the atavistic splendor of graffiti, regardless of the motivation or message behind all the symbols. But the *Star Tribune*'s fear-driven coverage serves the same purpose as the alleged gang graffiti — marking turf.

The black-pen rantings are no more of a cartoon than what appears in the paper every day. Consider the level of discourse President Clinton rolled out for our fair city and network cameras when he came to pimp for his faltering crime bill: 100,000 cops; three strikes, you're out; death to the really bad guys.

There isn't an abundance of nuance there, either. On the off chance that folks on the street didn't understand that the war on crime is really turning into a war, Clinton surrounded himself with a sea of blue, row after row representing an organized, well-armed gang that will really get down to business if the president passes his $33.2 billion bullet allegedly aimed at crooks.

The gangs on the street, in the newsroom, and in the White House are all using similar iconography to convey the same message: the streets are up for grabs, and it ain't going to be pretty. Everybody, it appears, is playing for keeps.

US Senate candidates Ann Wynia and Tom Foley trade sharp elbows to stand by their gang leader; Bloods act the fool for a *Strib* photographer. Is one inherently more meaningful than the other? Hell, no — white people have a bigger gang, printing presses, and a presumption of the higher moral ground, that's all.

Graffiti and daily journalism have become barely modulated expressions of rage and fear. Gang members really think cops are out to kill them. The white majority really believes that gangs are formed to rape their daughters and murder their mothers. When people come to believe that they are at risk, they inflate themselves and start talking shit. The debate is endlessly embroidered as opposed to advanced, so we end up with apartment-building hallways filled with inarticulate threats and a crime bill that's all guns and no butter.

The daily paper has no more salience to a black American than inner-city graffiti has to people from Fridley. That paper is full of jobs he can't get, parties he ain't invited to, and a government that is currently divided on just how hard his ass should be kicked.

Not long ago, Representative Jim Ramstad got stapled in this space for carrying water for the National Rifle Association by opposing a ban on semiautomatic weapons. In last week's test of the president's crime bill —which includes just such a ban—Ramstad was one of just eleven Republicans in the House who shook off the NRA, voting for a bill that he believed to be in the interest of his district. It was, as they say inside the Beltway, a tough vote. Regardless of how I feel about the crime bill as currently configured, I have been proven wrong about whose interests the congressman from the Third District is ultimately serving.

4

Washington City Paper

In 1995, Carr received a call from the management of another weekly newspaper, albeit one in a larger market—and on a larger stage—than Minneapolis. *Washington City Paper* offered him the chance to move east and take over as its editor. This was a grand opportunity, with the promise of a higher budget, a bigger staff, and the chance to hire new talent to cover a much underreported city where news from the White House and Capitol Hill overshadowed municipal happenings in a woefully impoverished city. Though some members of the longtime editorial staff were initially distrustful of an outsider such as David (especially an outsider with a bad midwestern accent), he eventually earned their loyalty and respect with a fresh approach to local news coverage and his inspired recruiting of young writers (such as Ta-Nehisi Coates, Erik Wemple, Brett Anderson, Jake Tapper, and Amanda Ripley). Though focused primarily on overseeing the paper's news content, David came to frequently write articles and commentary himself, displaying his shrewd, mordant wit, irreverent yet informed media coverage (especially of the *Washington Post*), and an unerring sense of stories that other journalists had missed. By the turn of the twenty-first century, *Washington City Paper* had significantly increased its circulation and garnered a new level of critical respect.

Andrew Sullivan Out at *New Republic*

1996

LET'S SAY YOU are the brilliant young editor of a weekly opinion magazine and you are being assisted out the door by your publisher. Do you: Smile and wear beige? Backchannel like crazy about what a meddlesome brute your publisher is? Or disclose your HIV status? Let's just say it was a busy week for *New Republic* editor Andrew Sullivan, who told the *Post*'s Kurtz last week that he was relieved to be both out of the HIV closet and out of a job.

Sullivan's decision to go public with his personal health status on the day he left is odd. For years, people who are positive have struggled to make the case that HIV is a chronic condition that has nothing to do with a person's ability to perform at work. By revealing he is HIV positive on the day he announced he was leaving his job, Sullivan created a subtext that suggests that the one had something to do with the other.

Sullivan's unparalleled promotional moxie was never matched by a congruent editorial vision for the *New Republic*, but he successfully introduced slices of the broader culture into *NR*'s weekly wonkfest. He left behind a larger magazine, with a bigger editorial palette and increased ad sales, but his tenure will be defined by his intermittent last year. Sullivan was out of the shop a great deal while it was becoming apparent that rising star Ruth Shalit was really a misguided bottle rocket. Sullivan hung in with Shalit, racking up a year of bad headlines and a potentially expensive libel suit. He finally put Shalit on perma-leave the month before he left by the same exit.

Good News Traveling Too Fast

NOVEMBER 1996

TWO OF THE nation's premier news organizations recently published stories about AIDS that lit a powerful candle, bringing light and hope into what has been a very dark place. Within three days of each other—on November 8 and 10, respectively—the *Wall Street Journal* and the *New York Times Magazine* each published first-person essays by HIV-infected gay men that brimmed with optimism.

The *Journal*'s Page One story by one of its Page One editors, David Sanford, chronicled his odyssey from the brink of immune-system collapse to his current state of paunchy wellness, courtesy of a new regimen of protease inhibitors. Former *New Republic* editor Andrew Sullivan's cover piece in the *Times Magazine* was a political and spiritual treatise on what happens "when AIDS ends." Although they wrote very different pieces, Sanford and Sullivan merged on one critical point: AIDS is finally on the run. The stories were lovely to behold. Would that they were true.

Early in his story, Sullivan does the responsible thing, pointing out that the vast majority of people who have AIDS or HIV cannot afford protease inhibitors, and acknowledging the paucity of evidence that science is finally trumping the virus. But he breaks out of his cautionary gait, writing, "The power of the newest drugs, called protease inhibitors, and the even greater power of those now in the pipeline, is such that a diagnosis of HIV infection is not just different in degree today than, say, five years ago. It is different in kind. It no longer signifies death. It merely signifies illness."

Sanford's *Journal* piece is even less restrained. "I've outlived friends and peers, and now I find myself in the unusual position of telling people how I've survived this scourge, something I never thought would happen. My condition could change for the worse tomorrow. But today I feel well again."

Two major pieces on vanquishing AIDS coming so closely together mark a change in the way the disease is being discussed. And just as the public developed a new and deeper understanding of the pandemic when important people started dying or coming out as positive, Sullivan's and Sanford's stories will no doubt bring a measure of assurance to the rest of us. But it may be fleeting.

The cover for Sullivan's beautifully rendered piece featured a lift from the text of the story in type that goes from sickly to elegant as your eyes drop down the page. "A difference between the end of AIDS and the end of the many other plagues: for the first time in history, a large proportion of the survivors will not simply be those who escaped infection, or were immune to the virus, but those who contracted the illness, contemplated their own deaths and still survived." The headline comes quietly at the end: "When AIDS Ends."

Sullivan must have drawn tremendous satisfaction from penning an obit for a disease that has wiped out so many people he loves, but AIDS has shown a mutational resilience that suggests that it is premature to finally dance, however tastefully, among the graves. Like all plagues, AIDS will eventually slither back where it came from, but people who spend their days treating and tracking the disease say it has a ways to go.

"If you talked to the researchers who are doing the work on these drugs, most of them believe that these patients will not be cured. I don't think there is any evidence that we have gone beyond that," says Spencer Cox, director of the Antivirals Project for the Treatment Action Group, a major AIDS advocacy organization based in New York.

Still, Sanford and Sullivan clearly believe that they have dodged a bullet and that science has spawned something that allows them to shoot back. While Sullivan doesn't spill his vital signs in newsprint, Sanford's story includes a quarter-page graphic depicting his T-cell count, which has bounced back over the critical 200 mark since he started taking protease inhibitors along with other powerful antiviral medications. His viral load—a crucial indicator of disease progression—has dropped sharply in the past few months.

"Thanks to the arrival of the new drugs called protease inhibitors, I am probably more likely to be hit by a truck than to die of AIDS," Sanford wrote.

"There must be some pretty bad truck traffic in his neighborhood," says Carlton Hogan, a training director at the Coordinating Center for Biometric Research at the University of Minnesota. Hogan has been tracking AIDS treatment regimens for six years, but his interest in protease inhibitors is more than professional. Hogan has had a T-cell count in the neighborhood of 50 for some time and recently began a regimen of protease inhibitors.

"I would love to believe that what they are saying is true, but in the one pivotal trial that people cite [among people with highly compromised immune systems], about half as many people died as might be expected. Now, that's very encouraging, but no matter how you slice it, that's an alarming death rate," Hogan says. "The trial certainly shows that the drug does something, but it doesn't sound like the end of AIDS to me. I'm glad that they are having these epiphanies, but I don't think it's based on enough science," Hogan says.

The stories bring to mind the fanfare of trumpets that accompanied AZT back in 1987, the last "miracle" in AIDS treatment. Desperate AIDS victims and pharmaceutical companies relentlessly fanned the hype and spoke of putting the acronym AIDS in the past tense. But widespread use flushed out AZT for what it was: an effective, if punishing, tool in slowing the progress of a chronic and usually fatal disease.

"I don't fault them for telling their stories; that is certainly legitimate," says Cox. "But this all sounds a lot like back when they did the first study of AZT. They studied the drug for six months, and people taking the placebo were nineteen times more likely to die than people taking AZT. There was dancing in the streets as I remember it, but as time wore on, it became clear that people on AZT were still dying, and at the doses we were using at the time, the drug was incredibly toxic.

"There was a huge letdown and an even bigger backlash. I am afraid we are doing the same thing all over again . . . that we are overselling what these drugs can do and setting ourselves up for the same kind of backlash," Cox suggests.

Cox and Hogan agree that it isn't just patients who fall victim to the happy talk. "There are enormous marketing pressures to downplay the risks of these drugs from the drug companies. And the researchers are all desperate for some good news, and this is a genuine breakthrough," says Hogan.

Because the protease cocktails are being pressed into service hastily, there is a dearth of data about when patients should begin taking them, what combinations are most effective, and most important, what the long-term consequences of the regimen are. And though they have proved effective in reducing viral loads, nothing in the data suggests that they are any more a cure than their pharmaceutical precursors.

In the margins of both pieces lies an issue even more delicate than the authors' illnesses. As Sanford points out, the Centers for Disease Control and Prevention estimates that some 900,000 people in the United States are infected, and only 100,000 are taking protease inhibitors. Part of the problem with the pieces by Sullivan and Sanford is that they are not a good measure of the reality that most seropositive people are living. Sullivan and Sanford are rich, powerful men with big-league connections. In a weird arc across the stories, Sanford mentioned that Martin Peretz of the *New Republic,* Sullivan's old boss, introduced him to Dr. Jerry Groopman, Harvard professor and chief of experimental medicine at Beth Israel Deaconess Medical Center. Although Sullivan doesn't go into details, he reportedly shares the same doctor, which puts them both in the vanguard of AIDS treatment.

Dr. Peter Hawley, medical director of the Whitman-Walker Clinic, says the talk of a miracle drug has some of his patients feeling mighty left out.

"Their stories are very misleading to all of the people who can't afford the drugs. Right now, there is a freeze on HIV assistance money in the District, and they are not taking any new people for these drugs. The people who are getting them are people who have very good insurance or have money of their own. We have patients who are asking us all of the time whether they can get on these drugs, and until the HIV assistance program begins taking all comers, we can't help them. It's very frustrating for them and for us," says Hawley.

Hawley worries that Sanford's and Sullivan's optimistic pieces will hurt AIDS awareness in the long run.

"I get the feeling when I read these stories that people are pausing in their battle, but I'm hopeful that they will get reenergized to make sure that these advantages are more universally enjoyed. At least in the beginning of his article, Andrew points out that not everybody is participating, but [that message] sort of gets diluted out after you read the whole article," Hawley says.

In the District, gay white males with the wherewithal to follow complicated treatment regimens are no longer the big local AIDS story. Today, the city's biggest at-risk population is poor, black, and often homeless.

"There is some question whether it's ethical to prescribe these drugs for homeless people because they require a level of compliance that's very difficult to achieve even if you aren't on the street," Cox points out. If a person is noncompliant, he runs the risk of allowing the virus to mutate—which raises the specter of a virus loose in the street population that is resistant to protease inhibitors. Transmission of AZT-resistant strains of the virus is a scientific fact.

"All it takes is some people who don't follow through, who are sexually promiscuous, and suddenly there is a virus out there that is already protease-resistant," adds Hogan.

"I think that what Sullivan is doing is very parallel to what a number of researchers have been doing. They won't come out and say that they have a cure, but they are certainly suggesting it between the lines. And they are all doing it for the same reason . . . We are all very desperate for some good news," says Hogan.

Sanford's *Journal* diary was a jarring departure for the nation's daily business paper. Even a few years ago, who would have predicted that the *Journal* would use its front page to showcase a first-person piece in which a *Journal* editor admits he may have been infected during anonymous sex at a bathhouse in the East Village? The publication of his story clearly demonstrates AIDS's transformational power in contemporary culture. It's too bad that in deciding to publish the story, the *Journal* didn't hold it to the same standards of fact and precision that most every other story in the paper meets.

Sullivan's story is much more difficult to fault, in part because he does a good job of anticipating his critics. And from a literary standpoint, Sullivan's story is a sprawling, majestic thing to behold. He manages to weave a thread through the Holocaust, circuit parties, AIDS conferences, and personal anecdotage to elegantly demonstrate how AIDS engendered mainstream acceptance of homosexuality and forced gay men to go beyond self-seeking. It would have been a tremendous read with less dramatic packaging—the pages were stamped with a little tombstone at the top that read "After AIDS"—but the *Times Magazine* was clearly interested in putting its readers on notice that this was not just another AIDS story.

Even those who find fault with the message are thrilled by what is happening to the health of the messengers. Hope is such a precious commodity in the AIDS community that most people will take it any way it comes.

"I'll be very frank. I know a lot of upper-middle-class gay males that I very much want to live, and if I can see them cured and no one else right now, I will take that and then keep working on everybody else," says Cox. "I don't think anybody is of the mind that we shouldn't take the cure until there is a cure for everybody."

Gored

SEPTEMBER 12, 1997

VICE PRESIDENT AL Gore was on the ropes all last week, his rise to presidential inevitability imperiled by revelations in the *Washington Post* about his alleged campaign finance transgressions. On Tuesday, Martin Peretz, editor in chief and owner of the *New Republic,* wrote an item for the Notebook section of the magazine arguing that Gore was being unfairly worked over. Michael Kelly—hired as editor of the magazine with much fanfare less than a year ago—spiked the item, saying Peretz's take flew in the face of widely reported realities. Three days later, Peretz fired Kelly in a quick phone call.

Any editor who takes a job at *TNR* should know that Peretz goes batshit on occasion and that certain issues are off-limits. Writing about Arabs as human beings, for instance, has been an institutional taboo since Peretz bought the magazine in 1974. But working around Peretz's Gore fetish when the vice president has moved to the center of the most important political story of the year proved too much for Kelly.

"He always knew he was going to get fired," said one staffer. "He just thought it might take a couple of years." It took all of nine months.

Peretz apparently couldn't sit still and watch Gore, his friend for three decades, get roasted in campaign finance stories. In a signed column last March he defended Gore against a "scandal hungry press," calling the veep "bolder and more nuanced than any other person in public life." Peretz's ability to anthropomorphize, and even deify, the lifeless Gore has always been a source of wonder around the magazine. His decision to fire Kelly because he chose to Mau-Mau the Clinton-Gore administration in the TRB column week after week ensures that *TNR* will go back to being a pointy-headed brochure, narrowcasting to a thin bandwidth of Zion-worshiping, Gore-hugging former liberals looking for affirmation of their superior intellect.

Reached this week, Kelly still seemed stunned that he was out so quickly.

"I guess it isn't that big of a deal in the broader scheme of things," Kelly said in a phone interview. "People who own magazines hire and fire editors all of the time, [although] Marty hires and fires a little more than most. He didn't give me a reason initially, but I pressed him and there were two strains. One was that I was not sufficiently bending to his will in operational matters, and the second was that I would not get off the subject of campaign finance scandals at the White House. Those two strains met in a confluence after Marty sent in a Notebook item about Gore that I didn't think we should run.

"It's his magazine, so I guess he can do what he wants, but to fire somebody over the editorial content of a signed column is not the same as firing somebody for incompetence. I don't think it reflects well on the integrity of the magazine," Kelly said.

Some *TNR* staffers don't think so, either. "Marty's line was that Michael 'violated the spirit of the magazine' by what he wrote in TRB. I don't think that people necessarily agree with that. Michael did this unhinged, obsessive thing in the front of the magazine and made sure that many of the other people here did great work in the rest of the magazine," suggested one staffer.

Kelly's "unhinged, obsessive thing" was something to behold. While many of his campaign finance columns were just clip jobs that did little to advance the story, Kelly did manage to frame the Clinton presidency in newly devastating ways. In panning Clinton's search for a place in history, he described a "hummingbird in chief" who flitted from issue to issue in search of something that might stick around after he left. And Kelly's take on the Paula Jones affair was a work of seething brilliance, in which he managed to pose Clinton as a draft dodger and a butt pincher in a single sentence.

Peretz says Kelly isn't the editor he thought he hired.

"If I were Michael Kelly, I would be devastated by the people who have leapt to his defense: Cal Thomas, Robert Novak, Hilton Kramer. The people who are up in arms about his firing are the ideologues from the far right who understood that Michael was their ally," Peretz said in a phone interview.

Kelly clearly loved taking a baseball bat to the current administration —he left the magazine's White House Watch column vacant so he could have the field to himself—but he also devoted himself to building a magazine, something he didn't have the chance to do as a writer at the *New York Times* and the *New Yorker.* Kelly invigorated *TNR* not by bringing in a bunch of ringers—*Post* staffer William Powers was his only major hire—but by squeezing great work out of the people who were already there. He got excellent, counterintuitive stories out of *TNR* staffers, including Peter Beinart, Hanna Rosin, and Stephen Glass. Even Ruth Shalit cranked out a couple of covers for Kelly, and the magazine was neither sued nor accused of plagiarism following publication. Kelly's *TNR* was less thinky and more narrative-driven, with stories that had real live people—of all things—in the middle of them. With the talk value of an over-the-top TRB and cover stories that were actually being read, *TNR* was in danger of again becoming part of the conversation of common folk in Washington. Now it's back to the Ivy tower.

"Michael was not one of the [Ivy League] boys here. Never was," said a staffer. "Where did he go to school? The University of New Hampshire? He was a total breath of fresh air. He sparked the best in people. You wanted him to like your story."

But Peretz, who reportedly had to hold back the tears when he introduced Kelly as "the best hire" he had made since he bought the magazine, fixed all that with a phone call.

"When we first talked, we talked about a magazine that was open to dissenting opinions, but he was intent on limiting the focus. Politically, he is on the fringe, and I was stupid not to recognize that," Peretz said.

Charles Lane, who has had his eye on the job and his lips on Peretz's ass since he had his first *TNR* byline, was named as Kelly's successor. (Earlier this year, senior editor Lane wrote an article suggesting that Peru's hellish prisons were "a drastic but defensible response" to the antigovernment guerrillas, a point of view that any dissenting *TNR* staffers had best keep in mind.)

William Powers, the senior editor hired by Kelly, quit immediately. "It seems like a huge, foolish mistake to me, but it's not like it's going to sink tomorrow. This magazine has been through many mistakes and it has a wonderful brand name, but for a media critic or a political writer of integrity I don't think this is a magazine to be at anymore. It has been compromised, possibly irreparably," Powers said.

"It's sad, because Marty built the kind of magazine that could attract the likes of Michael Kelly, but there is another side to him that keeps undermining what he has built," Powers said.

Some things won't change now that Kelly is out. *TNR* survived Michael Kinsley's coming and going (twice), Hendrik Hertzberg's leaving, and Andrew Sullivan's anguished goodbye. And Clinton's most vitriolic critic should have little problem finding a prominent outlet for his columns. When I tried to call Kelly at home, his phone was busy for two days solid, more than likely clogged with job offers. He will be heading off to the Jersey shore for a bit, but when he goes back to work, it will likely be as a writer, not an editor. "There aren't that many magazines out there to edit, and there aren't that many that I would want to, anyway. I never wanted to become an editor just to be an editor. I was interested in the *New Republic*."

Sidney Blumenthal

First Amendment Warrior

FEBRUARY 27, 1998

OF ALL THE feats of prosecutorial muscle displayed by Kenneth Starr, his single-handed transformation of Sidney Blumenthal into a poster boy for a free and unfettered press is the most amazing. The special prosecutor is currently hammering the White House aide to find out who is spreading dirt about his investigation.

Until last Tuesday, Blumenthal had busied himself puncturing the fourth estate's First Amendment prerogatives. Blumenthal, you may recall, took time out from his duties as Washington correspondent for the *New Yorker* two years ago to assist Hillary Rodham Clinton in conjuring an enemies list of media ne'er-do-wells. And once Blumenthal had turned in his notepad for a White House pass, he built a grassy knoll out of his belief there is a vast journalistic jihad trying to deprive President Clinton of his birthright. In between drawing conspiracy trees on a whiteboard and channeling for Hillary's darker side, he paused to sue the hell out of digitainer Matt Drudge for publishing a false report alleging that Blumenthal was a domestic abuser.

Blumenthal, like any bona fide Washington player, invokes the Constitution when it suits him. Now that his new career as White House media monitor has yielded a grand jury appearance in Starr's chamber,

Blumenthal has his own personal mouthpiece sputtering about free speech.

"We view it as an assault on the First Amendment, and I think this is obviously intended to . . . intimidate the press," Blumenthal attorney Jo Marsh told the Associated Press. The proceedings are secret, so who knows—maybe Starr is just pulling Blumenthal in for a little advice on how to bring the media jackals to heel.

Blumenthal, by the way, will be back in the very same courthouse on March 11, but then it will be as a plaintiff asking for damages inflicted by the deleterious effects of Drudge's inaccurate free speech. (Among Blumenthal's initial demands: "the name of the 'White House source' whom you purported to quote.")

The irony would be too delicious to bear were it not for growing fears that one of the casualties of the pissing match between Clinton and Starr may be the Constitution. The specter of a White House aide being compelled to divulge any and all contacts with reporters is hateful, and per se contrary to the notion of a free society. But it's hard to forget that the guy with his nuts in Starr's vise is Blumenthal, a campaign consultant who has masqueraded as a reporter. Journalists have been dutifully horrified, although a dash of schadenfreude always seems to go with it.

"It would take an awful lot to get the honest press to rally around Sid Blumenthal, but if anybody can pull it off, Ken Starr can. Not everybody is blessed with that kind of adversary," says *National Journal* and *Washington Post* columnist Michael Kelly.

Kelly succeeded Blumenthal at the *New Yorker* and immediately tore down the façade of respectability Blumenthal had erected around the Clinton White House. Kelly isn't surprised that when Blumenthal switched estates he turned around and opened fire, saying it's consistent with Blumenthal's MO when he worked at the *New Republic,* the *Post,* and the *New Yorker.*

"I think he believes that everyone operated the way he did. He got a lot of information from people who trusted him as a politically reliable propagandist. It's understandable that he would think that is the way that the rest of the world works. The con man always assumes that everybody else is in on the game," Kelly says. Even if it is Blumenthal in the middle of it all, Starr's subpoena-happy offensive is a menace to the free flow of information and may derail his role as special prosecutor; Stuart Taylor called for Starr's resignation in the *National Journal* even before his latest witch hunt. As frequently happens in politics, both sides have come to deserve each other: a president who allegedly has his way with those around him and a special prosecutor who doesn't care whom he screws in his effort to bring that same president down.

Sally Quinn on Vernon Jordan

FEBRUARY 27, 1998

ANYBODY WHO THINKS Washington lacks the kind of loyalties that quilt together other cities might want to take a look at the tidy circle of wagons around Vernon Jordan. Al Hunt of the *Wall Street Journal*, R. W. Apple of the *New York Times*, and Sally Quinn of the *Post* have all paid tribute to Jordan at a time when he is being investigated for suborning perjury. The defense has been stalwart and fatuous: Jordan, the ultimate fixer, was simply bamboozled by those crafty little buggers from Arkansas. Quinn, in particular, offered inspired palliative measures. In a *Post Magazine* piece that presented a clear view into the skull of Washington's permanent class, Quinn put the rest of the world on notice that the tribe would look after its own:

"When Vernon Jordan stood in front of the cameras in late January to declare that at no time did he encourage Monica Lewinsky to lie, most of the country observed a solemn and resolute man defending his reputation before a horde of unruly and scandal-hungry journalists . . . When Jordan looked out from the lectern that day, what he saw was in fact not a mob of rabid reporters, but a collection of friends and colleagues, people with whom he had dined and socialized and transacted business for many years."

The doyenne of Washington's cocktail nation was not content with providing additional Teflon for Jordan. She made it clear that in a choice between Jordan and the president he served, it wasn't even close.

"Scandals can also be cohesive, in part because the elite rallies to preserve its institutions against interlopers who might corrode or undermine them, and in part because everyone understands exactly how to behave, what role to play, what position to take," Quinn wrote. Her role, in case you missed it, is to distinguish the silky Jordan from those crass elected arrivistes at 1600 Pennsylvania Avenue. In addition to her bon mot in the magazine, she offered the *Times* the following cat scratch:

"Vernon has a place in the community," she said. "He knows where he's going to be for the rest of his life. If you consider the life of Bill Clinton—whenever he leaves the White House, he's going to get on a plane and where is he going to go? I mean, when you think about it, he's homeless." There, the clothespin is finally off. The smart set hates that trailer-trasher from Little Rock almost as much as old what's-his-name the peanut farmer. To Quinn's gimlet eye, Clinton's current travails are the ultimate expression of bad breeding.

A lifelong observer of the Washington social and political scene thinks all the Jordan hugging provides an equally disgusting spectacle. "It's as if it's OK if a presidency is toppled by indiscretion, but God forbid that Vernon should be sullied by this," the observer says. "I mean, who are all of these people who decide this stuff? The thirty people she has over on New Year's? People don't care who gets invited anymore."

If Quinn does speak for an upper crust, it's one that seems to be crumbling.

"Her quandary is starkly confronting the specter of her own irrelevance," says James Warren, bureau chief of the *Chicago Tribune*. "Every time one sees her, you see someone grasping to be taken seriously. I don't know the woman personally, but she is one of the last people that should be opining on office relationships." Quinn and the rest of her

tea party obviously can't wait to get their hands on Al Gore, a nice St. Albans boy who still knows the value of the A-list. She concludes her magazine piece with the following embossed invitation: "The line most often
heard inside establishment Washington after the scandal broke was this:
'I think Al Gore is a truly decent man. And I just adore Tipper.'"

Kids Say the Darnedest Things

JUNE 26, 1998

LET'S CALL IT *Post* lightning. A person, critter, or group will do something heroic, heart-wrenching, or tragic that is then captured in the random spotlight of the *Washington Post*. The singled-out entity is promptly inundated with flea collars, diapers, cars, guest appearances, and sometimes cold hard cash—all from readers moved by the pathos/nobility of a single news story.

That's what happened to seven-year-old Latia Robinson. On May 21, *Post* reporter Maria Elena Fernandez wrote a Metro piece lauding the four-foot-four-inch child for seizing the wheel and driving her unconscious dad to Howard University Hospital. Like any tale of precocious indomitability, Latia's feat captivated the country: she got a call from President Clinton, feature slots on the local news, a *People* mag splash, and the promise of a guest appearance on *Oprah*. Michael Jordan phoned, and Mayor Marion Barry even came through with a savings bond. Those windfalls were joined by an agent, a lawyer, a budding stage mother, and a trust account, all common byproducts of *Post* lightning. The *Post* tossed in a few more bolts for good measure in a June 11 page 1 feature on the child's sudden renown.

Fernandez's first two stories on Latia were over the top, but the Metro beat doesn't turn up stories on seven-year-old chauffeur/heroes every day. The odyssey began a month ago, when Fernandez was assigned to check out a rumor that a child had driven her father down a busy four-lane street four blocks to the Howard emergency room after he passed out at the wheel of his Honda. The incident was more than a few days old when she began reporting it, but Fernandez interviewed the father's doctor, who termed her act "astonishing." With that it was off to the races. No one in the story actually saw her driving, but a few touted her composure.

Great story. Not true. That's something that the *Post* eventually got around to telling its readers on June 18. A four-foot-four-inch child might be able to see over the wheel and touch the pedals, but the notion that any seven-year-old could drive a car under any circumstances is nonsense or wish fulfillment, depending on your level of cynicism.

Common sense, never in abundance in the *Post* newsroom, would have suggested that her chronicle needed some looking into. Fernandez is on vacation and did not return a call left on her voice mail at the *Post*. Assistant city editor Paul Duggan, who edited the story, says, "Anybody in this business who doesn't think this could happen to them is fooling themselves."

Veteran Metro reporter Vernon Loeb agrees.

"If I am a reporter and I get to an emergency room and I come upon a doctor who says to me, 'This little girl drove her father to the hospital and is a hero,' I'm not sure I have any cause to probe that much deeper. I have no reason to think that this guy is making up a story. I mean, what's in it for him to make up a story?" Loeb says.

Like all of us, the guy in the lab coat wants it to be true. But even rudimentary reporting on the feasibility of Latia's amazing driving skills would have busted her out. I mean, wouldn't you have liked to hear from someone who actually saw her do it?

Staring back at the paper's decisions in the rearview mirror, Duggan took some comfort in the fact that all the important facts in the initial story were at least attributed — to a seven-year-old girl.

"A small girl told us a story. We looked at it, turned it over a few times, and decided she was credible. In retrospect, sure we could have done more investigating, but once we had an indication that something was amiss, we went back and vigorously reported the story," Duggan says.

Duggan and managing editor Robert Kaiser credited themselves with doing the footwork to finally print the truth about Latia. All they really did, though, was pick up the phone: the person who actually drove the car—an emergency room technician—came back to town and told them they were printing fairy tales.

The make-good story that resulted may have been "vigorously reported," but it was mendaciously rendered. Latia was front-page news when she was riding the crest of a *Post*-inspired wave of coverage back on June 11, but the minor fact that she made it all up was tucked at the bottom of Metro with a headline asking, "A Story Too Good to Be True?" Well, yes, it clearly was, and by the way, what's up with the question mark? How about "*Post* Story of 7-Year-Old Driver Was a Total Fabrication" instead? Doesn't quite scan so nicely, does it? Many people I called about the story had no idea that it was eventually smashed flat, a tribute to the disingenuous packaging and placement.

The piece revealing the hoodwinkery was not a correction by any stretch, just so much featurized butt-covering, replete with cute little interruptives such as "a story to make you smile" and "a story to amaze you." Clearly written by committee to dig out of a deep hole, the piece laid the blame on a fanciful kid with an overactive imagination. Since the woman who actually drove the man to the hospital had left town, the story implied, Latia was able to tell tales to her heart's content. Nowhere in the postmortem was any indication of how a seven-year-old got over on a big metropolitan newspaper.

Kaiser pointed out that the initial story was very carefully worded. "We didn't claim to have seen or known that she was driving. And we didn't play it on the front page. We played it on the Metro."

Which is where, I guess, the *Post* plays stories that may be a little less true. And if the paper had enough doubts about this holy-cow story to minimize its play, why not spend the shoe leather and time to make it right?

"In terms of how we treated [the story] once we found out that her claims were untrue, we saw no value in slamming a seven-year-old girl," says Kaiser, who is now in his last week as managing editor.

Not everybody in the newsroom was impressed by the paper's fixer-upper.

"I could see how it happened in the first place, but I wish our correction story had been a lot more about our own reporting," says one staffer. "I think you should report on yourself when you screw up, and you should do it rigorously and not be so goddamn protective of your own people. If we knew someone else had done something like this, we would rake them over the coals."

The need for unalloyed remediation seems all the more important given the amount of bounce the *Post* got out of the story. Duggan says it wasn't the *Post*'s problem if a bunch of other media outlets picked up a seemingly astonishing story on the strength of the paper's substantial brand name.

"We didn't seize on the story. We wrote a [small] story in Metro, and it took on a life of its own. I have no control over what other [media outlets] decided to seize on," Duggan says.

Nah, all the *Post* did was light the fuse and then cover the hell out of the results.

The page 1 follow-up included the following shiny diamond: "Before her infectious personality and sassy ways earned her national celebrity, Latia was debating whether to become a doctor or a firefighter. Now, she has added movie star to the list. And she wants Sinbad—who reminded Latia during [her appearance on his] show that it is illegal for a 7-year-old to drive—and Eddie Murphy to have roles in her movies." Latia was also lauded as "poised beyond her years," "pretty and spontaneous," and "on the fast track to stardom."

Yeow. Brushing off the execrableness of the writing—no small effort there—the story offers a picture of a newspaper hyping the hell out of its proprietary find. How much different is "Twenty days after the *Washington Post* reported how Latia took control of a Honda Accord . . ." from some witless hairdo hopping around on TV frothing about his "exclusive"? But if the first story was underreported, and the second story was overhyped, it was the third in the suite of Latia stories that was the most incredible.

As the *Post* suggested in the same piece, it's "a story to make you wonder."

Road Trip

SHE'S IN THE middle of a glorious bunch of players on the stage of the Birchmere, a portrait in reverie as she plays the hell out of her new record. But however content Lucinda Williams looks, trust that the bus is idling just outside, ready to pull out on a moment's notice. Williams is good at a lot of things, but staying put ain't one of them.

The tour behind her took-forever *Car Wheels on a Gravel Road* is just one more stretch of Williams's endless road trip through life. By the time she kicks into her fourth song, it's clear that she never met a town —or a man, for that matter—that didn't look a whole lot better in the rearview mirror.

With its Greenville, Lake Charles, Jackson, and countless unnamed juke joints, the record sounds like an invocation of place, but it's really more about placelessness. The title cut, "Car Wheels," is about a little girl with a fixation on passing telephone poles, one who apparently comes to rest only when she is in motion. Four decades later, Williams is still in gear, looking for a safe place to pull over. Last Sunday night, the Birchmere served as a rest stop—she called it "the most comfortable place we play."

It must feel swell to finally be on the road, touring behind a real, actual album. In the six years since she made *Sweet Old World*, the industry, the press, and frantic fans have been banging on her for the follow-up. *Car Wheels* is an old record by now, having been through three separate recordings and mixing sessions over a number of years. As Williams bounced from label to label and went through producers like so many packs of cigarettes, the industry whispered about her being hung up on the capital letter in the word *Artist*. In interviews, she pleads guilty only to searching for a perfectly imperfect reflection of the way she hears her songs. Chalk it up to fickleness, but clearly some of the delay may be the growing tyranny of the "No Depression" country ethic — it takes a lot of trying to make it sound like you're not trying, after all.

The record came out June 30, and even though it is a rough-cut gem, it will probably come up short of her expectations, just like the other four she has made. If the forty-five-year-old resident of Nashville — for now, anyway — were a dark, brooding male, she would no doubt be lauded for her stubborn genius and unwillingness to settle for less. As it is, she's just a girl who "Can't Let Go," as she admitted in one of the songs she dropped on the adoring upturned faces at the Birchmere.

As if to put an exclamation point on her impetuosity, the trademark bleach-blonde strode out to the mike as a shockingly brunet, country-singing archetype. It nicely accessorized her current fascination with unadorned music-making. She is a songwriter of proven economy, having not wasted a single word in all of the records she has made. (The precise gift for language is a legacy — her father, Miller Williams, read his poetry at President Clinton's second inaugural.)

She opened with *Sweet Old World's* "Pineola," in which slide king Bo Ramsey did spooky fills to nicely etch the graveside tribute. Even the casual listener would end up noticing that the men Williams takes a liking to have a tendency to expire — I counted at least four dead guys in her two-hour set. It's a testament to her wry durability that the audience laughed heartily the second time she introduced a song by saying the intended was no longer among us. "Why do people always laugh when I do one of my songs about death?" she complained through a smile.

Williams has a singular facility with Kaddish. Both "Drunken Angel" and "Lake Charles" are edgy, funny tributes that include a little swift foot on the backside for the departed. Like her signature song, "Sweet Old World," they suggest that the boys are idiots for checking out of the party so soon. In "Angel," she asks,

> Why'd you let go of your guitar?
> Why'd you ever let it go that far?
> Could've held on to that long smooth neck
> Let your hand remember every fret.

That hanging on to a guitar, even with bloodied fingers, would strike Williams as a route to salvation fits perfectly. It's worked for her.

There were four guitarists onstage at the Birchmere, counting warm-up act Jim Lauderdale, who sang perfectly measured harmony throughout the twenty-song set (and on the record). While she and Lauderdale stuck mostly to rhythm on their acoustic guitars, the electric bookends of Ramsey and Johnny Lee Schell offered separate arguments for the primacy of the guitar in every genre Williams touches. Schell, a punk-geek boy complete with odd-shaped Coke-bottle specs, came through several times with tasty forty-second revelations before stepping just as quickly back into the pocket.

The best instrument onstage was inarguably the one that lives between Williams's heart and soul: she leaned into her new songs with nicely pitched abandon. On "2 Kool 2 Be 4-gotten," a tribute to Birney Imes's photographic book *Juke Joint,* she chanted her way through the verses like a southern Rickie Lee Jones, before breaking her voice to high and beautiful effect to punctuate each chorus. She reached up for the chorus of "Car Wheels" and stayed there, bolstered by Lauderdale as she belted out the lone anthem on the new record. And her straight-up country hymn "Jackson" was sung in a voice that seemed to rise up out of a valley of its own accord.

The séance broke only when she reached back to cover songs that are as close as she has ever gotten to hits. When she introduced "Passionate Kisses," she said that Mary Chapin Carpenter sent her roses when she played the Birchmere last year—a floral acknowledgment that a song that sold 4 million for Carpenter was bought by fewer than 100,000 when Williams sang it. (The dreaded first-person interlude: I was in the Zona Rosa bar in Austin five years ago, home court for Williams at the time. She kicked into the domestic paean that asks, "Shouldn't I have all of this and passionate kisses?" I was stuck to the wall, ruminating about being a single parent with armloads of laundry and not much else. A real live Texas girl in one of those gingham swing dresses pulled me onto the dance floor, hard. Case closed. You can have it all.)

Her other high-profile outing, an ode to a stalker called "Changed the Locks," was gender-bent a few years ago by Tom Petty to good effect. But what would be jewels in any other songwriter's discography were rendered as so many tin cans by Williams. She seemed content to phone in her best-known songs for greedy fans before heading back into the beautifully grinding gears of *Car Wheels*. She may have lots of misgivings about what gets committed to record, but her commitment to the songs on the current record was implicit in every note she sang.

Like almost all of her writing, *Car Wheels* is about men, a species that sounds like a very tall child when Williams is doing the explaining. Yes, they're cute and adorable, but they are usually shitloads of trouble, she seemed to be telling the crowd. By her lights, it's less about standing by your man than picking the knucklehead up and dusting him off when he falls down, which is all the goddamn time. And when that doesn't work, well, there's always a proper burial. Williams has a blind spot for assholes, which probably explains the number of men in her audience. The portraits of men as not-so-beautiful losers were delivered without rancor, just gorgeous regret.

In lesser hands, all of the romantic autopsies would wear an audience down. But just when you thought Williams believes guys really are good for nothing, she delivered "Still I Long for Your Kiss" and the album's single "Right in Time," both coming across in all their girly, naive-again splendor. The only time she sounded at all forced was when she talked about a love imprisoned behind "Concrete and Barbed Wire." The corn-pone weeping — she spent part of her six-year hiatus in the sway of country god/devil Steve Earle — about a feeling bigger than a building didn't sound like anything Williams had ever lived.

Her first encore, a three-song suite of dead-on blues, was the only abject failure of the evening. Williams may have the blues big-time, but when she sings them, she's toweringly average. Bonnie Raitt, whose current work wouldn't entitle her to carry Williams's guitar pick, could pack more white-girl blues into a single phrase.

This clubfooted blues turn was quickly erased as she headed for the bus with manifest goodbyes. "Sweet Old World," "Jackson," and "Big Red Sun" showed again that when it comes to sendoffs, a real southern girl will always leave you wishing you could stay a little longer.

Crash Course

FOR THREE DAYS, the carful of Montgomery County teenagers tumbled across the front page of the *Washington Post,* rolling over and over until they began to look as if they were trapped inside some horrific spin dryer.

It was a common story that received uncommon play: the hotdogging teen drove his pals from summer school, lost control, and creamed another car and a pickup before his car came to rest on its side. Three people died: two kids inside the Subaru Outback and the pickup's driver. In a series of front-page stories beginning on July 15, readers learned that the sixteen-year-old driver had been behind the wheel for only two weeks, that the now-dead man in the pickup had attended morning Bible classes, and that one of the surviving teenage passengers had since decided to turn his life around.

The carnage alone does not explain why the *Post* could not look away. Multiple-death motor vehicle accidents are news in any medium and any city, but it's usually the definition of a one-day story. The MoCo tragedy, however, was rendered as a suite, writ so large and in such detail that something larger, less fickle than an "accident" was at work. It was a story about "the recklessness of youth and the vulnerability of life," according to *Post* writers Marcus E. Walton and Fern Shen.

It was oddly touching, a rare display of heart and emotion from a big daily paper that seemed to feel the pain of the community for a few days. "He's with His Maker" quoted one headline, of the pickup driver, who left three kids behind.

The teens were treated with less deference, especially the driver. The paper's tone was overwhelmingly parental, all tough love and concern. Kids drive too young. Kids drive too fast. Everybody drives too fast on East-West Highway, dammit. And just in case the message didn't come through between the lines, a follow-up story, in which the *Post* decided to use a radar gun, demonstrated that the average speed on the highway was 38 miles per hour, a whopping 8 miles per hour over the posted limit. The *Post* obviously believed it had a morality tale in its possession, a story of youth and death with implications far beyond, say, the dozens of kids getting mortally perforated every year in the District. The *Post* covers the hell out of teenage driving gone awry because we can do something about it. We, as good and true citizens, can band together and teach our kids that showy driving can have unforeseen ends. It's not intractable, not insoluble, like, say, kids killing kids with guns. The teen driver story merited the kind of coverage that begets change. A dialogue has been joined about when kids should start driving. Enforcement and traffic patterns are being reexamined. The cops are on the case.

But imagine if the *Post* brought the same rigorous, impassioned reporting to gun violence. Imagine if, instead of a cube of type buried in Crime and Justice on page 7 of Metro, in which nameless youths are killed by other nameless youths, we found out that the killed kids had mourning families, had attended Bible classes, had been turning their lives around. You know, stories about "the recklessness of youth and the vulnerability of life."

The reason that a pileup in Bethesda owns the papers for three days while gun victims in the District die on the margins is a matter of class expressed through geography: many of the decision makers live within an easy walk or drive from the crash site, which means their kids could have been in that car.

"We all sort of wondered why the paper was going on and on about this, but it's a neighborhood issue to the editors here," says one staffer.

The *Post* apparently thought that the number of bodies merited going over the top in coverage, but back in 1995, when three coworkers at a Southeast McDonald's were shot like dogs in a basement cooler, there was no third-day story, no investigation into the underpinnings of the tragedy, no sense that the loss was one held in common. If you want big treatment of a triple homicide, you'll need a different brand name (think Starbucks) and a different neighborhood (think Georgetown).

Newspapers always express the interests and biases of their minders. The *Washington City Paper* seems constantly stuck on a cow path between Dupont Circle, Adams Morgan, and Mount Pleasant because most of the writers and editors live there. We don't have a lot of employees or affiliates in the tougher parts of Shaw, or some of the scarier corners of Southeast.

The *Post* is run by people who often don't choose to live in any part of the city. Out where they live, gun crimes are something horrible that happens to someone else. When viewed from a great distance, there's an easy, helpful suspicion that the victim is somehow complicit. At the beginning of this month, there was a story about Kimberly Moore, a seventeen-year-old who was found dead in the 200 block of Atlantic Street Southeast. Didn't see it? It appeared on page 7 of Metro. Not enough room on the front of Metro that day, what with the go-cart accident out in Prince William County.

The Prince William story was a tragedy; a ten-year-old named Nathan Trammel was killed when the go-cart he was driving hit a car driven by his brother. The ten-year-old Trammel was brought to life through a thorough story about his death.

Moore, however, remained imprisoned in the tiny space where murder victims in the District generally go. Police arrested the alleged shooter in the Moore case last week (page 3 in Metro), and it turns out she wasn't the intended target. No more than Nathan Trammel. But her story lives in a place where we don't live, where we don't go, where we don't want to know about.

Somewhere on the way to DC's tenure as the nation's murder capital, the daily paper of record lost its ability to report the chronic, ongoing accident in its midst. The one in which a bullet always seems to find someone who doesn't deserve it and doesn't see it coming. The *Post* no longer covers murder with any enterprise or interest. Real reporting, real empathy, is reserved for the people down the block.

Death March

1998

THE PRESIDENT'S PRINT and broadcast pursuers continue to grind it out amidst the current lull in the Lewinsky story, but to be honest, it's just sitting there. Nobody I know is reading or watching with any gusto. I have friends in town from a place where the Beltway is found only on a pair of pants, and they had one question after a few days of reading the *Washington Post:* "What is it with you people?"

Even though "the presidency is at stake" and "an issue of national moment is at hand," my Clinton-hating wife—who was treated for carpal-remote syndrome back in August—flips past the *Post*'s scandalfest to catch the celebrity fluff in Style.

It should just be getting good for the armchair presidential scholar: High crimes have been alleged, perjury seems manifest, and the creaky but reliable articles of impeachment have been renewed.

But a city that first responded to the notion of a Clinton barbecue by all but offering to buy the charcoal seems to have lost its appetite. In that respect, Washington is just catching up with the rest of the country. Even the best pornography lacks staying power after the money shot has come and gone. The coming impeachment story is a hell of a comedown from the giddy heights of the president's nonconfession and nonapology, Starr's Scud-like report, and Lewinsky's oral admissions.

Those who have enough distance to detect patterns don't even experience the middle part of a Clinton scandal, the part that involves doubt and suspense about his viability.

Pity the poor schmucks who are still cranking it out as if we cared—they can't let the lack of an audience get in the way of a good story. The *Post*'s Peter Baker has carried his share of the slime buckets the scandal has produced, and his arms are getting pretty damn tired.

"It's like covering a disaster, but it's as if the hurricane keeps hitting the town over and over and over again. It is unrelenting and never-ending," says Baker, who has many more twists and turns to follow before he gets to type 30 on this story.

His competitor over at the *New York Times,* James Bennet, says that the story punishes him the most during those odd times when the eye of the hurricane hovers over Washington. "There have been many exciting and intense episodes, but the problem is that it always settles back into this chronic, incremental, leaden saga. And that's a problem, because it is a very competitive story and you can't afford to let your guard down."

And when will he let his guard down?

"I've given up trying to predict what will happen . . . I try not to think about covering it for another year, but I can't imagine being the president. We have to write about it; he has to live it."

So do regular folks, but that doesn't mean they will religiously turn in for the moral jihad of *Hardball.* People will show up O.J.-like when the verdict is in, but don't look for a lot of attentiveness in the meantime. While the public may not know when it will all end, it knows how it will all end: with a crippled president, a maimed Republican majority, and the people's business sitting in a huge neglected heap.

Alexis Simendinger of the weekly *National Journal* doesn't have to worry about getting an 11 p.m. phone call from a crazed editor because Baker or Bennet has something she doesn't, but she says this story won't end because it keeps starting over. "We've had a lot of beginnings. We had a beginning back in January, a new beginning back in August, and another beginning when the Starr report came out. There is no calendar that says when this is going to end, but because it is historical and serious, it makes you try to be up, up, up, all the time."

Simendinger says not all the fatigue stems from the tactical battle of covering a massive scandal: "I think part of their exhaustion with Clinton just comes from covering him for six years. It happens to beat reporters all the time, even at the White House."

The public feels their pain every day, and Simendinger acknowledges as much: "I hear a lot from family and friends who say that they feel like they have gotten to the end of the novel and wonder why there are six more chapters tacked on."

Getting a D on the First Draft of History, the *Post* came out of the gate quickly and cleanly on the Lewinsky story, but as the tempo drops and the stakes rise, history and import hang much more near in the *Times*. Francis X. Clines is writing beautifully about why, and how much, it matters. Meanwhile, the *Post*'s David Maraniss and Bob Woodward —Clinton's biographer and a man with a presidential pelt on his wall, respectively—are sending their thoughts out into the ether of Talkland in between attenuated appearances in print. "I think the great paper of Watergate has not done a great job of putting this story in context," says one *Post* writer. He believes the only serious attempt at framing the story outside the daily ticktock came on the op-ed page. In that piece, former Virginia Republican representative M. Caldwell Butler suggested that the whiners who long for the bipartisan days of Watergate are forgetting that Democratic House Judiciary chairman Pete Rodino showed a tolerance for the opposition that brought to mind Chairman Mao. It was a rare burst of context from a paper that should be rife with it.

"It's a shame," says the source. "We have missed out on many chances to tell our readers how this story compares and contrasts with Watergate, and we are sitting on top of a vast repository of talent and information. There are all sorts of comparisons to be made. We should show a time line of the polling data on Nixon. I think it would demonstrate that he wasn't in trouble until the very end. But our readers still think [his resignation] was a foregone conclusion from the start, which it wasn't."

People (Not) Like Us

NOVEMBER 6, 1998

AT A PARTY in Georgetown last Saturday night, Vice President Al Gore and wife Tipper offered hosts Sally Quinn and Ben Bradlee a toast of gratitude in front of 250 other denizens of the innermost loop of the Beltway.

It was a gesture of fealty that will serve Gore splendidly should he succeed William Jefferson Clinton, a rustic from one of those middle places who never got the hang of local ring-kissing rituals. Unlike Clinton, Gore—son of a senator, nice St. Albans boy, and all that—has always had a place in the heart of Quinn and the rest of Washington's permanent class. It was no surprise they were in the midst of it all as Quinn and Bradlee celebrated their twentieth anniversary.

But enmity between the doyenne of DC's cocktail nation and Bill Clinton is as old as the president's tenure, and now that he has shown himself to be every inch the Philistine she judged him for, Quinn and her familiars can't contain their contempt. (For the record, Quinn says she has a fine relationship with the first lady.)

That bile boiled over last Monday in "Not in Their Back Yard," Quinn's first *Washington Post* Style byline since she came back on staff. The piece amounts to a focus group among the Georgetown set on the post-Lewinsky Clinton, and the results are conclusive: the president is not one of us. Quinn sells the story as the product of reporting enterprise: The "disconnect between the Washington Establishment and the rest of the country is evident on TV and radio talk shows and in interviews and conversations with more than 100 Washingtonians for this article."

What follows, though, is a vapid spin through her Rolodex and a long snake of predictable cluck-clucks and how-could-he's from DC cognoscenti. Her point, apparently seconded by every one of the one hundred like-minds she talked to, is well-taken: The president's behavior has deepened the country's cynicism about the city we live in. But since Quinn has played majorette in the parade of civic disdain for Clinton, making the decision to hand her a journalistic megaphone is silly.

Since the beginning of the year, Quinn has been pointing the crooked finger at Clinton in other publications and on televised blabfests. She provides dynamic, attention-getting commentary, but it's not the kind of cant you usually shop for when making a writing assignment. Quinn doesn't buy that for a second.

"Whatever people's perception of me, the fact remains that I am very much a journalist—and this was not an editorial; it was a reporting job that I felt did a good job of analyzing a situation people don't understand very well," she says.

Style editor David Von Drehle referred calls about the piece to *Post* editor Len Downie. According to staffers at the *Post*, Downie reportedly championed and edited the piece along with front-page-feature editor Mary Hadar. Downie saw nothing inappropriate in having Quinn reporting on a phenomenon she has served up like so many canapés.

"She did a reported piece that is not straight news, which is very much in the Style tradition. I think it is very consistent with the kind of coverage that we do in that section of the paper," Downie says.

And Quinn's tenure as the social secretary of the upper crust doesn't trouble Downie, either.

"Howie Kurtz is a reporter, and he covers the media. This doesn't seem all that much different," Downie says.

Many others in the newsroom do not share their leader's enlightened perspective. Says one of Quinn's colleagues, "I think it would have been a much more honest story if we had put it in that Saturday real estate section called 'Where We Live.'"

Not a bad idea. After all, Quinn opened her Monday piece with a scene from the village square, detailing a high-bucks fundraiser attended by the likes of Rahm, Madeleine, Donna, Alan, and Maureen. The jeweled scene-setting was meant to establish that there really is a there here—that she and her pals care about each other and the city they own. And even though the rest of the country has clearly stated that they have no appetite for lynching Clinton, Quinn goes on to consult the Muffies, Tishes, and Cokies on her way to this epiphany: "Bill Clinton has essentially lost the Washington Establishment for good." It would have been a nice conceptual scoop back in January, a decent observation midsummer, but as an anchor Style piece in post-confessional November, it's a dusty cultural artifact, a paean to the Lost Tribe of Washington.

"They call the capital city their 'town,'" says Quinn of the cluster of her friends and neighbors. "And their town has been turned upside down."

In an interview, Quinn says Washington's story isn't really being told.

"There were plenty of surprises in the piece. Everybody is writing about what people in Oregon and Montana think, but nobody has written the piece about what people here really think. I have a certain expertise, because of the kinds of friends I have, and where I live, and what I do. Those things give me access and allow me to get quotes other reporters can't," she says.

Jill Abramson essentially did the same piece last July in the *New York Times*, but instead of proprietary tang, her piece was synthetic and full of social nuance. Style needs to work this story, but Quinn's spanking machine was not the way to go. She recently returned to the section part-time after ramping down her career for many years in order to look after her son. Since coming back, Quinn reportedly walks around as if she owns the place, and, in a sense, she does. Her husband may have pulled the *Post* into journalism's first tier through ballsy news judgment, but it was Quinn who single-handedly created a new kind of political coverage in Washington back when Tina Brown was still toiling at the *Tatler*. Many of the Style staffers who knew her only by legend were wondering what she would come up with on her second tour. It was not an auspicious return.

"I actually expected better. She has a reputation as somebody who could be cutting and interesting, and this was neither. The kindest thought I have is that it was a useful cinéma vérité peek into the grotesque, claustrophobic town we live in, but I'm not sure that's what she had in mind," says a colleague. Quinn's unparalleled connections did yield some nuggets: Who else could get that gasbag David Broder to state in very simple terms that "[Clinton] came in here and he trashed the place. And it's not his place"?

Quinn made that same point abundantly clear some months ago, telling the *Times*, "When you think about it, he's homeless." This from a person who wrote this week, "For reasons they cannot understand, Washington insiders come across to the public as judgmental puritans, shocked and horrified by the president's sexual misconduct."

Even though Quinn was determined to make her first piece back in the mix a reported effort, she couldn't help but interject the voice of civic hostess.

"Privately, many in Establishment Washington would like to see Bill Clinton resign and spare the country, the presidency and the city any more humiliation," she wrote.

There's nothing really private about the underlying message. Clinton had violated the narrow bandwidth of acceptable village behavior long before he began to sully the furnishings, and when he finally loads up the RV and leaves, Quinn and her buddies will regain custody of their city, if not the nation's interest. And maybe, just maybe, the next White House can crawl its way back onto the Georgetown A-list.

Who Asked You?

In an Opinionated Age,
the Written Word Is Not Part of the Argument

DECEMBER 25, 1998

WHEN WASHINGTONIANS SEEK a fresh take on the issues of the day, logic would dictate that they open up the Outlook section of the *Washington Post*. Outlook is an opinion-only enclave in the paper of record in the public policy capital of the world. Its editors have at their disposal the most provocative thinkers on every topic from Social Security to sexual insecurity.

But what should be a mosh pit for contestation is often a waltz of convention. Check out this gem from Sunday, December 13. Some key words have been edited out for effect. Stick in any nouns you want: "the Constitution," "Brussels sprouts," "swing music," or "the 105th Congress," and you, too, can write a lead piece for Outlook.

> Whatever one's view of the _____, there is little doubt that the _____ is in tatters. Long before the _____, all pretense of deliberation had vanished. The _____ conduct over the last month did nothing to persuade Americans that _____ had pursued _____. To the contrary, nearly all _____ seemed to have made up their minds before _____ was called.

It's just that kind of discourse that makes Greta Van Susteren seem like one of the more important public intellectuals of our time.

If it's opinion you want, you can just hit a random button and it will spill out of your TV in great, oozing batches. Opinions, it is often said, are like assholes—everybody's got one—and anybody with a remote can tell you that there are a lot more assholes out there. And if you prefer your CW in printed form, there's a Rolodex of spouters at the *Washington Post*, Slate, or the *New Republic*.

But you won't. Nobody reads that crap anymore—political magazines, op-ed outlets, or the intellectual webfests. People seem happy to ignore the words of the Novaks, Krauthammers, and Broders, huge, hulking hunks of gray matter who make big dollars to cogitate on the issues of the day.

As interest in the body politic has dimmed, the density of opinion has become overwhelming. There's a bull market on bull, and much of it arrives at a velocity that renders the average print bloviator vestigial to the informational needs of common folk. Last Sunday I didn't whip open the *Post* and the *New York Times* to find out what it all meant— not just because we were watching history with an asterisk, but because twenty minutes after the third article of impeachment was adopted, its nuances and implications were plain to every nincompoop in America, including me.

But there's another, more prosaic reason people don't pay much mind to printed thoughtfulness: most of it is no more informative than the average edition of Cochran & Company. The practitioners of opinionism—especially here in Washington—are stinking it up.

When's the last time you read something on the *Post* op-ed that you could remember by lunch, let alone care to talk about once you sat down? There's nothing but dead bodies on that particular battlefield of ideas. The page has gone from a place where consent was manufactured by far-thinking giants to a place where it is slowly codified, often to stupefying effect. How do you know that a *Post* op-ed reader has fallen asleep? His morning bagel falls out of his mouth.

In just the last week, we had a professor of strategic studies suggesting that Clinton's vid-game war won't touch Saddam Hussein, David Broder tagging Trent Lott as a partisan, and E. J. Dionne synthesizing those two bolts out of the blue by keening that even Saddam doesn't unite us. All true beyond argument—which is why they don't belong on a page that is supposed to be built on disputation.

Every day, the *Post*'s designated opinion meisters dodder about within a narrow bandwidth of opinion established by editor Meg Greenfield on some stone tablets an epoch ago. If it weren't for Michael Kelly's glorious jihad against Clinton—it's sort of like listening to Hendrix play guitar and wondering how he's going to find that one note higher—there would be nothing on this page your mom couldn't have told you last week or last decade.

Post Outlook, conceived as a Sunday hangout where a range of thinkers could spend time pushing the envelope on convention, has become an elephant burial ground, a place where tired, spent ideas limp into view and keel over. The discourse of academe, something I was thrilled to leave behind when I sneaked out of college, is there waiting for me every Sunday—but it's more like CliffsNotes than a grad seminar.

In recent weeks, Outlook has brought readers these polemic innovations: medical marijuana = bad, drug treatment = good (never mind that it ripped off an August Metro story by Peter Slevin that made a much better case), and Ronald Reagan = dead.

The *New Republic,* which once drove debate with regular curve balls and oddballs that changed the parameters of the national conversation, has become a must-not read. Forget plagiarism and fiction—*TNR*'s larger crime has been failing to make the smallest dent in the current debate before Congress, a story that it would have owned a decade ago. Yes, the magazine has always been full of eat-your-veggies policy riffs, but it used to be interrupted by conceptual scoops about current events that came out of nowhere. Other than Jeffrey Rosen's prescient pieces about the legal wreckage that will remain long after the particulars of this debate are forgotten—and those appear in New York titles as often as they do in Marty Peretz's playground—*TNR* has sat it out. The current regime, shackled by the publisher's agenda, has finally revealed the mystery of what the initials TRB stand for: Trite Redundant Bullshit.

The *Weekly Standard* has done a better job of staying with the story of the day, but it's a rubber room of ideologues who have been driven visibly insane by Clinton's endless political lives and the tendency of their Republican dreamboats to snatch defeat from the mouth of impending victory every single time. In the main, it's a marketing brochure for Bill Kristol's multimedia franchise—pity the schmucks who have to slug it out on short deadline to keep his name in the news.

Slate was announced as a place that would host a different paradigm, a blackboard for ideas as sprawling and unpredictable as the web itself. It has become instead the world headquarters of meta-journalism, an electronic exercise in smarty-pantsism where no one ever makes phone calls and everybody has thoughts about other people's thoughts. The archness—of the collective brow, the writing, and the arguments—is most manifest in the Breakfast Table, where cerebral celebs deconstruct the morning paper. "The wheel of history is spinning so fast that we're all getting dizzy. The headline news defies comment," writes Stephan Thernstrom, a history professor at Harvard University, before going on to do just that. Slate is ultimately like everyone's brilliant dilettante friend. Instead of calling to tell you that he just got back from an intense experience exploring Cambodia, and here's what it was like, he calls to say he just read a *New Yorker* article on Cambodia, and here's how they're playing it these days. In the meta-world, it seems that anyone who spends the time to get personally invested in anything—ideology, politics, emotion—is instantly an intellectual suspect.

Part of the reason opinionists don't have the inside track anymore is that there is no "inside." Guys like Walter Lippmann and Scotty Reston were able to own the public consciousness because government was nowhere near as transparent a few decades ago. Their priviness made them essential to citizens who hungered for understanding of what it all meant. Now there's no curtain to pull back. The sausage is made right before our eyes.

In fact, nearness to the process has become a handicap. How interested are you going to be in predictive, ahead-of-the-curve commentary that always turns out to be wrong? No one, not George Will, not James Glassman, and certainly not Robert Novak, knows what is going to happen next. The most seminal, farsighted commentary on the Clinton presidency turned out to be a movie script—*Wag the Dog.* Hollywood has the superior pulse on the land of ugly celebrity because surrealism is not a modality that plays well in letters. Historians will never accuse this decade of excessive thoughtfulness, but the past year has set new standards for vapidity and content-free current events.

Opinion writing, good or bad, doesn't stick out because there is very little of any other kind of writing going on, regardless of how it is billed. Every common ink-stained wretch has morphed into a commentator. Used to be that reporters would attempt subtle suasion by the way in which they knit some facts and left others out. Now, they just put an analysis stamp at the top—or not—and deconstruct events through the prism of personal whimsy and notional analysis. The pretense of objectivity has gone the way of the manual typewriter—magazines, papers, and broadcasts are so jammed with cant that it's getting pretty tough for papers—like this one—that used to make a living by just printing what they think.

Since TV commentary is the only cachet that seems to matter, formerly thoughtful people have come to view their columns as auditions for *Hardball with Chris Matthews.* Why bother with a fussy argument when a couple of quips about the Lewinsky affair will have producers all over town hitting their speed dials? Is it any coincidence that the only columnists worth reading anymore—Maureen Dowd (barely), Kelly, and Dorothy Rabinowitz—are the ones who refuse to endure the klieg lights of TV just to advance their visages?

When Andrew Johnson was impeached, it fell to the likes of Mark Twain and E. L. Godkin to give the first draft of history gravity and import. When William Jefferson Clinton got pinched, it was up to Laura Ingraham to put the events in context. The treatise is dead; long live the sound bite.

One Last Hitch

FEBRUARY 12, 1999

"MR. HITCHENS, YOUR table on the terrace will be ready in a moment."

"I had no idea the Palm had a terrace."

"We do now. Please go back out the front door and your table will be there presently."

Christopher Hitchens, every Washington dinner party's cuddly outlaw, took a flying leap into pariahhood last weekend. In a signed affidavit, he said that when his pal, presidential aide Sidney Blumenthal, testified to the House managers that neither he nor the president had been involved in any effort to trash Monica Lewinsky, he was, well, lying his ass off.

Oops. That's it for you, Hitchens. So what if your left-flanking maneuvers on Clinton in *The Nation* and *Vanity Fair* are galaxies more interesting than the jejune bilge Washington journalists manufacture by the tanker? There will be no more late nights discussing your boldly transgressive views on the fate of Kosovians over aperitifs in Georgetown. Expect death by a thousand whispered cuts from the gilded butter knife that is Washingtonians' weapon of choice.

"I guess my calendar has cleared up quite a bit, that's true. I'm not expecting a lot of invitations down the road," said Hitchens, managing to sound a wee bit wistful about all the stiff repartee he will no longer be able to enliven. All because Hitchens, who has a book on Clinton coming out this spring, trashed a long-standing tradition of Beltway omerta anytime a familiar is involved.

Part of the reason that his former patrons in the ruling class are ready to hoist Hitchens's ample noggin on a cocktail fork is that he has provided one last gasp of oxygen to those unmanageable managers on the Hill. He has some explaining to do, but since the story broke, Hitchens —a journalist who writes in real time on live television spots—has suddenly unraveled into a flummoxed, inarticulate naif.

Is he a great orator in possession of a bad set of facts? Or is Truth's own vigilante simply worn out by the grind of explaining why he threw his buddy onto the pyre of perjury? On CNN, Hitchens looked more like Ted Kaczynski than the charming and pitiless Clinton-hunter his adopted city has come to know and love/hate. It's as if his last friend had turned him over to the rapacious fangs of the House managers, instead of the other way around.

Hitchens defends himself by saying that he's not the one who told Blumenthal to adopt the duplicitous MO of his White House keepers. "If he is in a perjury trap of any kind, he was put in it by Clinton and his attorneys, not by me. And I will not appear in court against Sidney, especially if they let the perp [that would be the leader of the free world] slip the noose. I would go to jail first, and that's no bluff. Starr could still end up proceeding against Sidney, making him yet another of Clinton's victims. I think it would be very educational for the whole of society if this whole thing ended with both myself and Sidney going off to jail. It would be a most wonderfully symmetrical exercise."

Because Hitchens is believed to have transgressed the bonds of both friendship and confidentiality, the rest of Washington is withdrawing (anonymously, of course, because one never knows) the welcome mat for him, not his would-be cellmate. Forced to choose, colleagues all over the city are picking Blumenthal—this epic's Kato Kaelin, a man with an adjacency to great evil who nonetheless sees a conspiracy from without. And Hitchens, who once wrote a book attacking Mother Teresa, has been banished for whacking a revolving-door journocrat who served up the Clinton-concocted backstory in huge, heaping piles.

Blumenthal's lawyer, of course, made the famously grand gesture of releasing reporters everywhere from any oath of confidentiality. But in the best tradition of Washington manners (to which Hitchens now pleads ignorance), Blumenthal doubtlessly calculated that the code of journalistic repression — something he never seemed to have much use for back in his ink-stained days — would keep him out of the frying pan.

Besides, he argued in a deposition before the House managers, going tactical on Monica would have been off message: "We felt very firmly that nobody [at the White House] should ever be a source to a reporter about a story about Monica Lewinsky's personal life." All of those stories calling her "Elvira" and "the Stalker" that were attributed to White House sources? Well, they just emerged from the mists coming up off of Foggy Bottom.

But Republican investigators found out that Hitchens knew better. When they called, he volunteered that Blumenthal had bandied about Lewinsky's name in unflattering ways over lunch last March. Hitchens would seem to be the last person you'd dump the stalker angle with — it was already clear from his writing that he would choke the life out of Clinton with his bare hands if given a chance. But the conversation at the Occidental Grill was reportedly reflective of a pattern of patter that Blumenthal was engaging in at the time.

Blumenthal will likely maintain that it was all just chitchat among friends about what happened to be in the paper that day, but that kind of banter takes on a little more resonance when it comes off of "a highly placed White House source," now, doesn't it?

"He didn't have to draw me a picture on the tablecloth," says Hitchens, who hadn't seen Blumenthal for a while because of a six-month tour teaching at Berkeley. "When I came back, he didn't seem to be the same person. He was talking in this very sort of rugged manner about what was happening to the president, and I responded much more mildly than I probably should have and told him that this was no longer politics, that he shouldn't get mixed up in rubbishing these women . . .

In retrospect, I should have told him that you will rue the day that you ever went to work with this thug."

Hitchens maintains that he had already revealed the Clintonistas' dirty war on Monica in a column for the *Independent* of London back in September, so he doesn't see why everybody is in such a dither. Of course, there's a world of difference between a flaming column and a legal affidavit. When it comes to the fundamental question of why he threw up on somebody he sat at Seder with, Hitchens goes all gooey and naive—characteristics you wouldn't impute to the glibbest member of Washington's cocktail nation. In an op-ed piece for the *Washington Post,* he sounds as if he's expecting a call from Blumenthal the day after tomorrow asking him to dinner. The dinner will presumably take place between Blumenthal's strategy sessions with his recently retained and very expensive phalanx of personal lawyers.

Blumenthal's sad fate, Hitchens believes, has nothing to do with him, even if the thermonuke he aimed at Clinton hit Blumenthal instead. "He was already involved in a world of this before I came into the picture. He was intimately involved in a strategy to bodyguard the president's rash strategy of deception, and then he expects all of his friends to protect him. I don't think a friend can ask you to do that."

Presidential tours are not the only things subject to term limits in DC —when the terms of engagement change, friendships frequently evaporate. What a chum can and cannot do in the context of this blood sport between Washington's various estates was defined better by Tennessee Williams: "We have to distrust each other. It is our only defense against betrayal."

Goodbye to All That

APRIL 9, 1999

SHE IS SORRY, if you want to know.

Really. Sorry.

Sorry she plagiarized in the first place. Sorry she got nailed. And sorry she ended up in the same sentence as infamous fiction writer Stephen Glass. Ruth Shalit is mad as hell about that.

And you should know that the former *New Republic* writer is happy to have kissed off Washington and found a job as an account planner at a British-inflected ad agency in New York.

Really. Happy.

It's hard to remember that at a time when being a hot young writer in Washington was a big deal, Shalit was the biggest deal of all. As a featured writer in the opinion journal the *New Republic* beginning in 1993, she was a gorgeous stylist, with a gift for rendering the distant cousins of literary detail and policy nuance, often separated by nothing more than a comma. By the time she was twenty-four, contracts, assignments, and bouquets were arriving steadily from some of the most reliable brand names in the business: the *New York Times Magazine*, *GQ*, and the *New York Observer*, among others. Her first real job out of college made her famous and well-compensated in a business not known for either.

Somewhere amidst all the buzz and sizzle, Shalit made the quintessentially nineties journey from media employee to media celebrity. One particularly perfervid profile of Shalit mentioned her in the same breath as Hemingway and E. B. White and suggested that we will all anxiously await her memoirs one day. That may still be true, but those memoirs will now include an operatic chapter about her early rise and fall in the city of Washington, DC.

Her narrative became more complicated in 1994, when she used then–*Legal Times* writer Daniel Klaidman's prose in a *New Republic* story about the young Turks in the Clinton administration. Less than a year later, she was discovered lifting the *National Journal's* Paul Starobin's language about presidential candidate Steve Forbes. There were two other instances from the same period of linguistic kleptomania. Now, five years later, the twenty-eight-year-old Shalit is out of the business. But she's not done talking: The silkiest opinion writer of her generation has one more contentious issue to weigh in on — herself.

And it doesn't really matter who is doing the asking. *Washington City Paper* is one of the many outlets that savaged her on the merits. In 1995 the paper ran a skeptical profile of Shalit, then still a rising star despite the bullets she'd already taken over her reporting and her coziness with political conservatives. And she popped up occasionally as That Darn Ruth, a one-woman journalistic disaster area, in the media column I write. But Shalit is a tremendously self-involved person who is not particularly self-aware. At my urging, a request for a quick quote about her new gig mushroomed into a full-blown exit interview because there was a mutuality of needs: a journalist who wants to sell papers and a journalist who can't stay out of them, never mind what for. We made an appointment to talk later that week.

In Shalit's version of things, she left Washington because she finally decided to walk away from all of the hectoring windbags who would lay her low. She exited the *New Republic* at the end of January, but her departure actually came after months of quiet pushing from editor Charles Lane. Either way, Shalit is no longer a Washington journalist because she could not change the single most interesting thing about herself:

"People fall prey to a reductionist fallacy that the worst truth about you is the most consequential truth. [The plagiarism] was a truth about me and is a truth about me. But there are a lot of other interesting truths as well."

That's the voice of the massively intellectual daughter of a Wisconsin college professor, a kid who was reading her future heroes in the *New Yorker* by the time she was ten years old.

And then there's the voice of the ten-year-old:

"It's like when you are a little kid and you want to be popular and you want to get in the popular crowd. And when it doesn't go right, and they are just not having you. They're just throwing paper airplanes at you and kicking you. At some point, you have to admit defeat and go home and say, 'Guess what, Mom? I have to switch schools. I'm just not cutting it at this school, they won't have me, and I want to clear the decks and start over.' That's what I feel like I am doing," she says in one of several phone interviews from New York.

Both those personae reside in the same five-foot-four body—a combination that's nifty in an intern and not so in someone with a megaphone provided by some of the most credible publications in the country. In retrospect, Shalit's short years in the journalistic sun make you realize that much of the American publishing establishment is flying by the seat of its Dockers. (Former *New Republic* editors Michael Kelly and Andrew Sullivan declined comment, as did current editor Charles Lane.)

Shalit readily admits the reason that her run ended badly is the same reason it got off to such a rollicking start: she is/was a child playing over her head. Washington was completely charmed by her kinder-genius, complete with frilly socks. And until she got in trouble—and, in some instances, after it—New York editors relentlessly pursued a piece of La Shalit, a bubbly prodigy renowned for cultural literacy and political conservatism. But her attempt to hide in plain sight until the plagiarism became an asterisk didn't work. Nobody—not even her endlessly forgiving sponsors at the *New Republic*—wants to play anymore.

Unlike former *Washington Post* writer Janet Cooke—whose 1981 Pulitzer was revoked when it turned out she had invented the story and its subject—Shalit won't wind up selling clothes at a Liz Claiborne boutique; she'll design the commercials for it instead. In fact, in the context of the Gotham ad world, the noise from the tin can dragging behind her will be quickly overwhelmed by the buzz she can create on her lunch hour. If they hold a reunion anytime soon of former journalistic child stars, she will look great and seem even better. But her business in Washington is not finished. Shalit wants people to remember that all of the attention that preceded—and maybe foretold—her downfall was about her talent and not her defects of character. She needs people to understand that she was famous before she was infamous:

"People wrote pieces about Ruth Shalit 'failing upward' and implying the attention was beneficial to me, which is absurd. Well, guess what? I had the attention before any of this happened. My work was very well-received."

She excelled because she possessed a devastating eye for the cravenness of Clinton-era Washington, but she became what she assailed.

"But their slickness also has something a little disconcerting about it. The Stephanopoulites do not have burning consciences. They are not crusaders for social reform. They are baby-faced enforcers, directed to sand the sharp edges off their undisciplined elders," she wrote in the *New Republic* back in 1994.

As the covered and the coverers reached a new level of intimacy, stars such as Shalit began serving as subjects, rather than authors, of extensive profiles for the likes of *George* magazine. And, like those politicians who are handed gobs of power and adulation for no particular reason, Shalit became unaccountable. Her editorial enablers chose not to notice that their cherished phenom had not mastered the basics of her profession.

Jason Vest, another talented young journalist, who now works at the *Village Voice*, says that while he doesn't know Shalit personally, he questions whether they were ever actually in the same business.

"Journalism is supposed to be about thoughtful inquiry in pursuit of truth. From what I read and saw about Shalit, that didn't seem to be where her interests lay. She saw journalism as a route to celebrity and an opportunity to be intimate with power. Being a celebrity is not being a reporter. I mean, dancing with Newt Gingrich is a long way from speaking truth to power, if you ask me," Vest says.

All journalists—at least the ones I know—would like to be famous, read by millions, with contracts that other writers covet. (I'm not so sure about the dancing-with-Newt part.) And many journalists in Washington will do what it takes to get there—including stealing the work of a colleague. The story you're reading is full of efforts belonging to others—thousands of words and countless hours in reporting about Shalit that I downloaded and deployed to my own ends. Journalism is de facto appropriation. But it is a fundamental rule of the craft that when you steal stuff, you have to make it your own—through either creativity or industry. Steal people's intellectual property? Happens every day in Washington. Steal their words—word-for-word? Oopsie.

Starobin, of the *National Journal,* was one of the people Shalit lifted from. Because of the *National Journal*'s excellence and its obscurity, its stories and ideas frequently show up under some of the better bylines in town. But the appropriators usually at least shuffle the text.

"I have seen all kinds of rip-offs—the conceptual rip-off, where the words are changed but the idea is the same—but with what happened with Ruth, it was hard not to see it at some level as pathology," says Starobin, who holds no grudge by this time. "Her character has been fodder for all kinds of analysis, and some people chalked this off to a pattern of laziness, but I thought it was something more interesting than that. I just never figured out exactly what that was."

Neither has Shalit. She now admits the sin but pardons herself for youthful improvidence.

"I was twenty-three years old, I was writing *New Republic* pieces, I was writing cover stories for the *New York Times Magazine,* I was filing columns for *GQ,* and at the same time, I was bopping around and being a twenty-three-year-old and buying miniskirts with my *GQ* money. And yes, I loved it, but guess what? One false move and it all came tumbling down."

She thinks about this for a minute and then says, "Well, make that two false moves."

Plagiarism is not a fatal disease in journalism, regardless of how much huffing and puffing you hear from the Brahmins of the craft. Fellow journalistic it-girl Elizabeth Wurtzel lived to write again for a variety of titles after getting fired for plagiarism from the *Dallas Morning News*. The *New York Times*'s Fox Butterfield suffered only a one-week suspension after getting caught with the *Boston Globe*'s text under his byline. And NPR's Nina Totenberg's voice still resonates over official Washington, even though she plagiarized in the seventies while doing a piece for the *National Observer*.

Shalit was a misdemeanor plagiarist, shoplifting prosaic passages that didn't merit coveting; it was her recidivism that set her apart. Her career never regained traction because when her body of work was cracked open, it fell apart, yielding additional borrowed nuggets. There were too many instances of coincidental use of trademark language for her technical excuses to fully account for. And when she was in the middle of defending herself in 1995, she opened up a new front by delivering a massive whack at the *Washington Post*'s affirmative action policies that came up bad.

What she wrote was important and devastating—the *Post* is occasionally paralyzed by race—but wrong in serious ways. She cast *Post* writer Kevin Merida as some kind of poster boy for affirmative action when in fact he had risen in the business for reasons far more legitimate than her own. And her assertion that *Post* editors were disappointed when they found out foreign writer Douglas Farah wasn't Latino fell apart in the dustup that followed.

She remained in the gun sights after that, with normally measured *Post* editor Len Downie calling her work "big-lie propaganda," a right-wing-inflected bit of polemic that set out to demonize efforts to diversify the newsroom. And because she had incorrectly reported that city contractor Roy Littlejohn had "served time" for corruption when nothing of the sort had happened, this time there was more than angry letters. The *New Republic* was promptly served with a suit, and she was put on leave. (The magazine apologized, and the suit was settled with no damages paid.)

Shalit was allowed to come back from leave for reasons that are a mystery even to the people who decided to keep her. Her version of donning sackcloth meant crawling under the wing of the *New Republic*'s literary editor, Leon Wieseltier, and taking occasional turns as a culture babe in the back of the book. She did good work—much of it about the wrongly accused, it should be pointed out—and it seemed to be her own. But people who work at the magazine say she was still a nightmare to fact-check and remained confused about the gravity of what she did for a living.

Oddly enough, the mistakes that eventually left her too hemmed in to do her reporting came off another *New Republic* Beanie Baby: Stephen Glass. Many of Glass's pieces at the *New Republic* were made up, conjured from the space between his ears. Shalit's situation became untenable last year when she ended up paired with Glass in story after story suggesting that the *New Republic* was a hotbed of adolescently malevolent con artists with notepads. The taxonomy of journalistic evil has since become very important to Shalit:

"The headlines were all 'Kiddie Sociopaths Run Amok at *New Republic*,' and there was no distinction made between what happened with me and Steve Glass.

"Steve Glass was boring, a boring fabulist, the Milli Vanilli of journalism. There were all these sorts of pieces written about how he was this brilliant, misunderstood genius who was hemmed in by the literature of fact. I think that's wrong, that the appeal of his pieces was that they were supposedly full of all this great reporting. If you go back and read these pieces knowing that it was all made up, they don't seem fun anymore," she says.

"When people started writing pieces about Steve Glass, it all sort of got thinned out . . . It was 'Steve Glass, fabulist' and 'Ruth Shalit, plagiarist.' The rest of who I was and what I had done got dumped. And that was a drag, because if you stand back, there are good pieces with solid reporting, and that are true, by the way. To equate that body of work to the work of another writer whose entire oeuvre turned out to be this tissue of lies, that seems to be a large leap," she says.

In spite of her own circumstances, she has no accommodation in her heart for the likes of Glass, who is reportedly studying law at Georgetown.

"I don't think anybody at the *New Republic* has any sympathy for him. People there want to break his kneecaps. There are people there who are the nicest people I know who, if they saw him on the street, would take a swing at him."

When it was revealed that one of the better sentence writers to come along in a while had a tendency to steal the sentences of others, Shalit didn't help herself much. She suggested that it all came down to a butterfingered approach to cut-and-paste technology—that she had accidentally inserted passages from her notes that were actually the finished work of other writers. There are many who suggest that the problem was more split personality than split screen. But if she is a sociopath—a word both friends and enemies drop into anonymous chitchat—she is a very tough and well-adjusted one.

"I spent a lot of time trying to stand back and get some perspective on this. When the first few stories were written, there was a lot of armchair psychology about why I did what I did . . . I mean, *George* magazine even interviewed my poor father. And everybody was asking, 'What is wrong with her, and why is she so screwed up?' And I think a lot of that was pretty specious. I think the basic architecture of my personality was very strong and always has been. The story of what happened to me was basically the story of a young reporter who had ideas, energy, and talent, but who jumped on the Condé Nast gravy train, took on too many assignments, and had a hard fall. And that's about the size of it."

Washington, the *New Republic* specifically, was more than happy to accommodate her ambition, which is a mighty thing, even to this day.

"When I look back on it, I was probably ready to come in and be a *New Republic* intern and do the work of an intern. But things happened for me very quickly. After six months, I was getting calls from *Time* and

Newsweek. I was sitting down with [*Newsweek* editor] Maynard Parker eating cashews in the lobby of the Willard [Hotel]. I was so giddy, and I loved it. I don't want to sound too whiny and lame, because I totally set myself up for this."

In her version, she was a young reporter who did a bunch of stories that manifested the sin of sloppiness. At this point, that's good enough for one of her victims, Klaidman, who now works at *Newsweek.* "It's been years since the incident, and who am I to say that she hasn't learned her lesson? Frankly, I wish her well."

Someone who works at the *Post*—and therefore couldn't be caught dead saying a kind word about Shalit—says she will be missed, barnacles and all. "She took on brave projects at the behest of her cowardly editors and had a sense of humor and delight about what she was doing. There is none of that left now at the *New Republic.*" Still, she says, "I can't trust her on a personal level. I walked into a party and heard her just chatting away about her editor's deepest personal secrets."

Jacob Weisberg, a columnist for Slate, left the *New Republic* in 1994 after a brief period as Shalit's colleague. He thinks she got screwed.

"I'm sorry she isn't going to get a second chance. I think the Steve Glass thing just sort of snowballed onto her when, in fact, they had nothing to do with each other . . . It's like comparing a parking ticket to a war crime," he says, adding, "The punishment didn't fit the crime. I think there was a lot of piling on."

Shalit agrees, suggesting that the hounds would not give up because they were after her for sport:

"I had made enemies, and there were people out there with a motive to unbalance me, and it was very hard for me to keep my footing, but I tried. I tried to make good choices that reflected a sense of responsibility and maturity and poise. I tried to grow up, and I'm glad I kept at it for a couple of years and built up a new body of work by which people could judge me. And I would like to go back to it. [But] I got tired of making no money, staying up all night writing these pieces, and continuing to serve as a punching bag. It was like, Enough already. I knew that if I stayed in that environment that I would be irreparably altered."

In a place where second acts are routine, Shalit owns the form. She'll be back.

She certainly had a snug purchase on permission at the *New Republic,* judging by the way she held on in a Washington she deems unforgiving. She made it through myriad plagiarism charges, a blistering counterattack from the *Post,* a libel suit—and, it should be mentioned, three editors. That the *New Republic* would be so publicly in the unaccountability business is low farce. A shop that practically invented comeuppance, it specializes in tough-minded hit pieces that lay bare the shortcutting and self-dealing of countless intended targets. ("I wrote a lot of tart, skeptical pieces that probably did not increase world happiness in the aggregate," Shalit observes.) But the magazine never diagnosed the same sort of malignancy in Shalit.

"Ruth—and Steve Glass—embodies the opportunity the *New Republic* can give a young journalist," says a former colleague. "It's unmatched . . . [But] once you achieve this sort of star wattage, there is an expectation that builds around you. It's the kind of visibility that can be so out of proportion to what is deserved, or what you can handle, that this constant pressure builds up."

Another colleague says Shalit enrolls those around her in her dramas without their ever making a conscious evaluation of what they're buying into:

"Ruth has this weird charisma. People—really smart people—are interested in her and drawn to her. Many of them would end up punished for that interest, because she could be so high-maintenance and end up not being worth the amount of attention that you gave her in the first place, but it came to her quite naturally," says a former colleague.

Inside the brainy biosphere of the *New Republic,* Shalit was marveled at and feared from her first days as Fred Barnes's intern—the Phi Beta Kappa graduate of Princeton was coming off a White House internship at the time. She stepped into the light to stay with a mortally counterintuitive take on then-rising senator Carol Moseley Braun. (When her capacity to lay the mighty low is mentioned, she suggests Ray Bradbury's "small assassin" as an apt metaphor.)

Shalit swung from journalistic rabbi to rabbi, mostly men, who sponsored her through her epic rise and the worst of what followed. Eventually, even the support of stalwarts such as *New Republic* publisher Marty
Peretz, Wieseltier, and former boyfriend and *New Republic* writer Jeffrey
Rosen waned, rubbed out by Shalit's chronic Calamity Jane act. It fell
to Lane, the current editor, to finally tell Shalit that she needed to get a
new job. But it took a long, long time.

Shalit thinks her blend of gender, youth, and pixie affectation informed her rise and also contributed to her demise:

"I think there is something more pruriently interesting in profiling
a fallen woman, especially a young woman. There would have been less
sadistic scrutiny if I had been a man or if I looked like Sarah McClen-
don. But then again, it probably cuts both ways. My rise was probably
quickened by the fact that I was a young woman who wore short skirts
and lipstick. So, on balance, the gender thing is probably a wash."

As it happens, just about the time Shalit is dropping off the radar
screen of New York editors, another lippy kinder-conservative has
popped up. Younger sister Wendy Shalit—class of '97, Williams College
—is getting her turn inside the microwave of youthful success with the
publication of *A Return to Modesty: Discovering the Lost Virtue.* Its chaste
tenets make you wonder whether the two grew up in the same house.
(There is a dedication to her mother and father and "anyone who has
ever been embarrassed about anything.")

"I feel only unbridled happiness and excitement for her," Ruth Shalit
says. "I think it was Oscar Wilde who said, 'Every time a friend succeeds,
a little something inside me dies.' So maybe, if she were a friend, I'd be
wildly jealous. But she's my sister, so it's different."

The fluttering around the sister—"Miss Shalit, who is 23, hopes
to bring about nothing less than a sexual counterrevolution," wrote
the *New York Observer*—brings to mind another twenty-three-year-old
meteor-with-a-ponytail.

"I never sat her down and said, 'Oh, by the way, Wendy, you have
an older sister who just happens to be a cautionary tale of journalism,'
but I like to think that she learned from my negative example. I made

greedy decisions—I had never had any money, and then suddenly I was making over $100,000 with contracts, and I let it go to my head. I took on more assignments than I could responsibly deliver. Wendy didn't do that. She has had opportunities to commit to big contracts, and instead she hasn't. When she wants some mad money, she takes on a baby-sitting job." Modesty is as modesty does.

Wendy's sister Ruth has never projected modesty of any sort. She's still convinced that she is one of the best to come along in a while. She calls one of her assailed stories—the profile of the young Stephanopoulites—"a tour de force of original reporting."

Even people who used to say horrible things about Shalit at anonymous remove loved seeing her at parties, a cerebral confection of a person—you never knew what might pop out of those oddly colored lips.

The fact that she would continue to show up wherever she was invited gives a clear view of an inner core that seems to include some sort of titanium alloy. (She scoffs when it is suggested that she threatened suicide during the worst of her trials, in 1996, even though several colleagues say she brought it up when it looked as if she might be fired.)

Lisa DePaulo, who wrote a searing psychological deconstruction of Shalit for *George* in 1996, is struck by the resilience Shalit brought to her abasement.

"I have always respected the fact that even in the throes of the worst criticism, much of it deserved, she still got up every day, went to work, did her job, and went out socially. It took a lot of strength and guts," DePaulo says.

But her lengthy curtain call also says something about the city she made her way through: in a place where people come back from the dead to haunt their tormenters in nothing flat, nobody was willing to write Shalit off. Ambition and talent, and a fatal flaw to go with them, are run-of-the-mill here. Like Los Angelenos, people in DC are constantly looking over their shoulder before they frag someone. It's a fear-based work culture where who is ahead is the only score that seems to matter, and that could change at any minute.

"Ruth is not worth being an enemy of anymore. She is dead as far as

Washington journalism goes," says one longtime acquaintance. (Yeah. Sure.)

Shalit saw those people who are now busy discarding her like an old paper plate as her friends. They acted that way because that's how it's done here, and because she made them. She had the ability to co-opt people through neurotic neediness and a tsunami-like conviction that she was going to get through no matter what. But instead of seeing herself as someone who was granted endless chances, Shalit maintains that she was convicted and re-convicted as an outsider. At the risk of starting a death match of celebrity plagiarizers, she points to the *Boston Globe*'s Mike Barnicle as a media insider whom other insiders rallied around.

James Warren, Washington bureau chief of the *Chicago Tribune*, dubbed Shalit the "journalistic Unabomber" and took a hobbyist's interest in busting her out as a plagiarist, tearing the arms and legs off of the Reporter of the Moment in his Sunday column several times in 1995. He says the fact that she lingered so long is proof that she, and the business she perpetrated her crimes in, didn't learn much.

"Even as someone who believes in redemption, I think she stands as a warning sign to the perils and toxic mix of rapacious ambition, inexperience, and dishonesty. She got caught several times, fabricated the goofiest of explanations, but exhibited not a tad of contrition. She surely leaves town with some people wondering whether she will strike again," Warren says.

"It's possible, since advertising is inherently a business of smoke and mirrors, she will feel quite at home, but I think she would be better off turning to religion than to the hawking of detergent and underwear," he says.

Shalit's religion happens to be whatever she is working on—in this case, propaganda designed to manipulate human behavior to commercial ends. All jokes aside, she will likely excel. She has already acquired the vocabulary a few weeks into her job.

"I prefer to look at it as a fresh opportunity for creative exploration and hopefully a way for me to contribute meaningfully to cultural life.

I have always loved ads. I am a wonk, but I'm also a person who likes shopping, ads, and bad television," she says.

"I think that anyone who has an intense curiosity about human beings, to be . . . running these focus groups of people talking about their favorite breakfast foods and chocolate drinks, and what people like to do in their bubble baths, there is something very moving and interesting about that."

Shalit says little more than chutzpah landed her a job at Mad Dogs and Englishmen. It's the smart New York agency that does mannered takes on American products, including those weird MovieFone ads featuring deviled eggs.

"Look, I am not Monica Lewinsky. I had to hustle for this job. I cold-called [agency head] Nick Cohen and told him I was a journalist thinking about making the switch to advertising, and I went up there and I met with him, and he happened to say yes to me. That's how I got this job. Nothing was handed to me. I don't have a Vernon Jordan," she says.

Her pitch to Cohen was vintage Shalit—a sexy mix of high and low culture spun to the point of shiny brilliance:

"I just walked into his office and started talking to him about how breakfast cereals appropriate other foods, how you have Oreo O's, and Cookie Crisp, and Reese's Puffs, and this new spate of breakfast cereals that are actually based on traditional breakfast forms like Cinnamon Toast Crunch. How we have taken traditional breakfast icons and transferred them to more convenient forms. I just talked off the top of my head."

She will work as an account planner, someone who is "synthesizing a vast amount of information from the client, the research, and also from scanning the culture. It's looking at the same information everyone else is looking at and seeing the information in new ways."

Still, it's not doing cover pieces for the *New York Times Magazine*.

"If you were to inject me with truth serum and ask, is this what I want to be doing for the rest of my life, the answer would be I don't know. But right now, I am finding it terribly exciting," she says.

Shalit thinks she has found a job and a city that will be more accommodating to idiosyncrasies than the conformist's paradise she left behind.

"I live in a walk-up in Gramercy Park, and I'm wearing platform shoes and dyeing my hair again, and just sort of getting into it. Here, I am the most conservative person in my office. People at work make fun of me because I don't have my lip pierced," she says.

She likes the invisibility, not merely the kind that comes from living in a busy place full of exotic-looking people, but the version that derives from residing and working someplace besides Washington. She is tired of being Ruth Shalit, at least the one who has a comma and the word *plagiarist* behind her name.

"I think it's just a completely different culture. A completely different world. Outside of Washington, people don't know me like that . . . I don't have that kind of radioactivity somewhere else. And that's one of the problems of being in Washington. When I was trying to do reporting, there was all this sort of static around me," she says.

And she manages some self-parody when she's asked about her retreat from wonkdom.

"There is a part of me that is actually very interested in what Lamar Alexander is going to say in his speech to the New Hampshire Chamber of Commerce. It's a sickness, I know," she says.

She still admires the *New Republic* and sounds genuinely remorseful for the trouble she caused the magazine. She won't go into the merits of the various regimes that published her work, cracking wise instead about the contest the *New Republic* has sponsored in connection with its redesign.

"All I can say is that I really hope that I win the sweepstakes. I hear that if you win, you get to sit in on two editorial meetings, and that you get to go to the White House Correspondents Dinner. I really hope fortune will smile upon me."

She says she is happy to be out of the mix, but her exit strategy seems to have some options that would bring her back to where she started.

"I am not hustling anymore. I am not out there pitching stories. This really is a change. But there is a part of me that is always going to be a journalist. I think I wrote a lot of pieces that were good and fair and true. And I am sure, at some point, I will write again."

Like next week. Although she fails to mention it to me, Shalit will be writing an every-other-week column about the ad industry for Salon. Editor David Talbot says he's happy to publish Shalit's work, historical warts and all. "I did it with eyes open about Ruth's checkered past. My sister Margaret Talbot [since departed from the *New Republic*] was one of her editors there. We talked on the phone, and Ruth was very honest about her past mistakes and seems to genuinely regret them," he says. "She was quite prepared to leave journalism behind as a penance for what she had done and because she had decided that the profession would never forgive her. I was of a somewhat different mind. I think she has a wonderful talent, and this assignment is something she will do great things with. It keeps her foot in the door and gives us somebody with journalistic insight writing about the industry."

She'll be back, at least partway, but she will be writing about the flakes in the cereal bowl instead of the flakes on C-SPAN.

"Four years in the shark tank [of Washington] was a long time, by anyone's estimation. But I already miss those little relish trays at the Palm."

The phone rings at my home. It's Ruth Shalit. We have a spirited discussion about journalistic ethics. Mine.

It is one of many calls, full of lots of haltingly rendered but incredibly canny attempts at manipulation. Working with Shalit—even for a few days, even within the well-defined parameters of subject and reporter —is exhausting. She is not trustworthy, she trusts no one, and she is maniacal in pursuit of objectives. After several interviews, she learns that her picture may end up on the cover of the paper. She is horrified, reminding me, correctly, that this was not part of the deal and that she would have never cooperated had she only known. There is more indignant talk about my personal and professional ethics.

And yet, just about the time she starts jumping up and down on my last nerve with a voice redolent of need, entitlement, and wounded little girl, Shalit does a brainy fan dance that leaves me feeling stupid and ungallant for questioning her narrative about a bright kid who made a few mistakes born of opportunity: asked for a rearview look at DC, she delivers a rip-roaring parody, form tripping after function as the plagiarizer plunders every cliché in the book.

"Well, this is how I like to put it: to coin a phrase, 'Washington is a town that likes to destroy people for sport.' [laughter] 'A Town Without Pity?' [more laughter] No, wait, let me think. 'I've looked at life from both sides now?' [giggles] 'I've been down so long that it looks like up to me?' Really, I don't want to make any prophetic pronouncements about DC versus New York. I am just trying to have a life here."

She is scripted, maybe right down to the stammering about my alleged betrayal. "Ditzy like a fox" is how she describes it. I have been jerked around by a fading ingénue with no juice and few allies. No matter. Shalit will take Manhattan, for a time, anyway. She could land on the surface of the moon with nothing more than a Swiss army knife and have a decent coulibiac of bass ready by seven o'clock.

I remember my colleague John Cloud coming back from a session with Shalit when he was doing our story back in 1995 and being completely flustered. She had wept prodigiously and then promptly told him her tears were "off the record." I find myself getting similarly cornered because I want the story. When we talk, it's Rodan battling Godzilla, two versions of journalistic cons who should probably both go flying off the cliff. She is a lot more crazy-making than crazy, if you ask me.

But it's not a great use of her gifts. Precocity offers no second act, and her ambition to own the eyes and hearts of another generation of readers will take more than a bat of the eyes and the deployment of shimmering anecdotes. There are sound, very banal reasons that journalists used to have to work their way in from the hustings before being given broad audiences and permission to destroy people with what they say. That's partly why some of today's Next Young Things are turning into Ruth Shalit instead of Mike Kinsley. The time spent out on remote beats and in far-off places has a winnowing effect. Those who can't serve the twin—and not easily reconciled—masters of truth and buzz are dumped along the way. No matter how precocious they are.

Oral Exam

JULY 16, 1999

AFTER HE BOUGHT the *Washington Post* at auction in 1933, Eugene Meyer penned a set of principles for his new paper. Numbers 3 and 4 promised:

> 3. As a disseminator of news, the paper shall observe the decencies that are obligatory upon a private gentleman;
> 4. That what it prints shall be fit reading for the young as well as the old.

Guess last week's story about suburban preteen blowjobs wouldn't have made it onto his front page. But Meyer probably never reckoned that a sitting president would introduce the casual hummer to the national discourse. Given that much of a contemporary paper's information—whether it be news, entertainment, or gossip—derives from unholy congress, a journal intent on reflecting the experience of its readers will probably have to drop its pants every once in a while. And there is no more burning question in the minds of many newspaper-buying American parents than "What is that alien in the upstairs bedroom going to spring on me next?" With that key piece of market awareness in mind—and a dubious smidgen of evidence that your kids are on the verge of becoming mini-Monicas—the *Post* was off and running.

On July 8, Style writer Laura Sessions Stepp used a year-old incident among middle-schoolers to suggest that twelve- and thirteen-year-old kids had a Clintonian disregard for the intimacies that generally accompany oral gratification. Headlined with the teasing "Parents Alarmed by an Unsettling New Fad in Middle Schools: Oral Sex," the story was debated in the newsroom for months before it ran—and debated by readers for days after it finally did.

Stepp's piece, at the very least, isn't an example of the *Post*'s infuriating tendency to write up trends only when the government anoints them with an official report. As her article indicated, federal health officials had declined to survey this very aspect of teen sexuality because they didn't think Congress would fund research into such an unspeakable topic. So she did the honorable work for them—absent the scientific technique but accompanied by lots of alarming pronouncements about what your little Tricia or Mandy might be doing at her first boy-girl party. The piece came off as Soccer Mom's Worst Nightmare instead of a peek into an unlighted place. It was transgressive, all right, but not gratifying.

To begin with, Stepp recalled an incident at Williamsburg Middle School in Arlington where the principal held a meeting for a dozen parents and told them that their kids were having casual sex parties off school grounds.

"The news dropped like a bomb just over a year ago in the mostly upper-income community of elegant brick homes, leafy sycamores and stone walls, where wealth is acquired by working long hours at top professional jobs," she wrote. "These parents were unaware of a disturbing pattern of middle-schoolers' adopting an 'anything but intercourse' approach to sex. Eager to avoid pregnancy and hold on to virginity, an increasing number of teenagers are engaging in oral sex, according to school and health officials." Upon that narrow, unsturdy template, Stepp piled on the reporting, talking to people all over the region who deal with adolescent sexuality in its various manifestations. Dozens affirmed Stepp's underlying assumption that younger and younger kids are doing nastier and nastier things.

One District educator said she was thrilled to see the subject covered and found it even more refreshing to see a story about teen pathology with a dateline that didn't read "DC." My wife, who spends a fair amount of time wondering about what version of eleven-year-old twin girls we are raising, clipped and saved a "How to Talk to Your Kids About Sex" breakout from the story and placed it on the dining room table. No irony or isn't-this-a-stitch intended.

But not everybody was so enthralled by the *Post*'s walk on exurbia's wild side. A parent of a recent Williamsburg Middle School graduate —not involved in the alleged incident—was appalled. "I have no doubt that this sort of thing is happening all over the nation, but why was my kid's school on the front page of the *Washington Post* as an example of juvenile sexual misdeeds?" he says.

The parent blames Williamsburg principal Margaret McCourt-Dirner for speaking publicly about something that didn't happen on school grounds. In Stepp's piece, McCourt-Dirner comes off as an avatar of doom, telling parents of girls involved in the alleged incident that their kids are "at-risk." Parents of male students got no such talk. Maybe they were just fulfilling assigned gender destiny.

More important, the parent—who requested anonymity because he thinks Williamsburg parents have had plenty of attention already—says that one of the "elegant brick homes" achieved "by working long hours at top professional jobs" belongs to the reporter, Stepp. Her son graduated from the Williamsburg Middle School in 1998. That single fact raises a number of important questions. How involved was Stepp or her son in the discussions about off-campus sexuality at Williamsburg? Did her nearness to the incident enhance or obscure her vision of the larger story? And why wasn't her connection to the story disclosed?

Neither of Stepp's editors on the story, managing editor Steve Coll and writer Marc Fisher, had any idea that her son attended Williamsburg —which she described as "a school of about 1,000 students where test scores are consistently among Virginia's highest." The editors should have known, and they should have let their readers know as well.

After making some inquiries, Fisher called back and confirmed that Stepp's son had attended the school, but that he doubted it had an impact on what she wrote. "Her kid was not in the story," Fisher says. "And his friends were not in the story. What she did is use her knowledge of the community and information she found through friends, neighbors, and family to tell an important story. That's part of being a reporter."

Stepp says neither she nor her son was involved in the incident that she wrote about: "I would have to agree with my editors. We write about the lives we lead. This was not a story about Williamsburg or me. It was about a pattern of sexual behavior that our readers need to know about and have a conversation about." Any educated parent knows that junior high kids have always pulled capers out of parental view and still managed to reach adulthood intact. But that certainty goes out the window when it's your own kid — or his classmate — who's swinging from the chandeliers. Stepp's intimate knowledge and perspective as a mother of a young adolescent likely gave the piece a lilt of parental angst it otherwise might not have had:

> Many parents . . . instituted strict disciplinary measures. Some grounded their daughters for weeks. Several started reading their daughters' diaries and checking their e-mail. Some began staying home in the afternoons to make certain their daughters did, too. Some took their daughters to be tested for disease and at least one arranged for her daughter to see a counselor. One mother told her daughter she couldn't listen to rap music anymore.

Well, now, that ought to do it.

There is something sad and hilarious about parents who believe that the sexual revolution ended the minute they decided to sell out and settle down. Some of their kids — and neither the *Post* nor you know how many — have apparently decided that the sane response to AIDS and newly limited options for pregnant teens is to be sexual without having intercourse. By exploding out an incident into a trend, the *Post* may have been engaging in some risky behavior of its own.

"I think to disregard this story because it is based on anecdotal evidence is a bad idea," says Fisher. "Our job is to reflect what is going on. Now."

Coll says the *Post* only did what a good paper is supposed to do.

"The problem we confronted was there was no comprehensive epidemiological evidence about how early adolescent sexual behavior has changed over time . . . precisely because the government refused to fund it. The only available path was to go out and ask a lot of credible, well-placed people in the area nonleading questions about what was going on with early adolescents, and we heard very loudly and clearly that things were changing, so we wrote the story."

The parent from Williamsburg thinks any broader understanding of early adolescent sexual behavior among *Post* readers came at the expense of his daughter. "They more or less created the 'Williamsburg ho's' [a phrase used in the story], and that is how my daughter will be known next year when she attends Yorktown High School," he says. "That's a lot for a thirteen-year-old to deal with."

The thirteen-year-old has her own complaints. "The whole incident was hearsay," she says. "It happened over a year ago, and I know some of the kids involved, and it was blown way out of proportion. They are, like, saying that everybody from Williamsburg was mixed up in this, and hey, it didn't even take place on school property. I don't think it was a school issue, and I definitely don't think it was any of the newspaper's business. I was watching *Politically Incorrect* last night, and they were making jokes about it. It's disgusting."

Oh Say, Why Can't We See?

JANUARY 7, 2000

"IS THAT THE president?"

Three-year-old Maddie was peering down the Mall at the big screen next to the Lincoln Memorial. I could not tell who it actually was, although it looked and sounded something like Maya Angelou. Or Celine Dion. Or Kenny Rogers.

"Yes, honey, that's the president." Or at least as close as she was going to get to seeing him.

We climbed back up the rise we were camped on, two-thirds of the way down the Reflecting Pool. The view was impressive. I could see the naked guy romping in the pond, three drunks sitting in a tree in front of us, and the tip of the Washington Monument. The Lincoln Memorial, down the way through a thicket of trees, was out of the question. There was a dim screen visible through the branches on the other side of the Reflecting Pool, but the sound was so bad, it was like watching television with the mute button on. I really couldn't see the show, the talent, or the signs designating the year, but it was worth it just to ring in the new millennium with Will Smith.

Except we didn't see Will Smith. Schnooks that we were, we had biked down to the Mall, arriving two hours before the show was scheduled to start. The entrance we had chosen—it doesn't matter which one—was flanked by real-live mile-long lines on either side. When the show started, with Will Smith pretending to rap, my family was among the hundreds of thousands of stiffs outside the secured perimeter of the Mall. Whose idea was that? I'd happily soak up my share of a nail bomb rather than sit in that line—it never moved—for two hours. You want real terror? Ninety minutes into the standoff, Maddie looked up and said the five words that turned a bad decision into a nightmare: "I have to go potty."

Me too, honey. After polite Washingtonians finally got the picture of how deeply they were being screwed, they began squeezing over the snow fences. MPD chief Charles Ramsey finally convinced the National Park Service—may God bless you and keep you in this new year, Chief —that the jig was up, and they opened the gates. When President Clinton echoed Martin Luther King Jr. a couple of hours later by saying, "Let freedom ring," the folks trapped in the cheap seats only wished it were so.

At about exactly this time, Arthur Schlesinger, Sid Caesar, and Sophia Loren were slurping beluga caviar, lobster, foie gras, rack of lamb, and polenta. While we were all getting the full pat-down to make sure that we hadn't brought a drop of liquor—or plastic explosives—onto the Mall, all of the FOBs were taking their last tugs of champagne and then getting bused to VIP bleachers obscuring the memorial—which left them sitting pretty and the rest of us looking at the backs of their heads. Through binoculars.

"We raised over $16 million," presidential fundraiser Terry McAuliffe bragged to the *Washington Post*'s Roxanne Roberts about his financing of the party.

Yeah, Terry, and you spent it on yourself. For the rest of us, there was not a good seat on the Mall. All of it would have been fine if they hadn't issued a sucker's invite to plain old citizens, suggesting that all were welcome to a celebration "choreographed to celebrate the ennobling achievements of our country." The faux populism—"This is America, here," cackled Jack Nicholson as he made his way into the White House to pick up a goody bag with logo'd mufflers, hand warmers, and seat cushions—made it all the more cynical.

The regular old folks who showed up to a feast of anomie and disregard should have received day fees as extras for populating the long shots on camera. By the time I actually took a seat on the muddy grass, I was rooting for a Y2K episode that might, at least, screw up the delicate social choreography of the moment.

Down on Constitution Avenue, the District threw its own little party. It was DC all the way: cheesified, ethnic in goofy ways, and pretty damn fun. No-name bands cranked away while complete strangers compared glittering 2000 glasses. But people drifted away as the evening progressed, drawn by the promise of a "Midnight Moment, a spectacular sound, fireworks, and light display."

What "America's Millennium Gala" actually celebrated was a triumph of the monied, the haves, the powerful, and those in the know. This being the age of convergence, the morphing of power, money, and fame was in full cry behind the ropes at the Mall. Bill Clinton is America's celebrity in chief, and the historic moment was just an excuse for him to frolic in glitz. It was a televised private party that just happened to have half a million bystanders.

Sure, I'd feel differently if I had been inside the velvet rope, but I didn't belong there, and neither did most of the rest of America. I'm sure all the VIPs dug the show. A very spacious, very comfortable perimeter was built around the memorial—there was no risk of people dipping their furs in mud or getting beer splashed on them by the hoi polloi. When I think of clocking in the next year, century, millennium on the Mall, I don't think of sparklers climbing up the Washington Monument. I think of Liz Taylor's face burnished, lifted, and jammed with hors d'oeuvres.

While she was making an entrance at a secured portal near her seat, thousands of the unaccessed milled about, looking for someplace—anyplace—they could see something. The metaphor of a sanctified bunch enjoying themselves while the rest of us pressed our noses up against the glass was too true to the times to even ring comic.

I thought about pulling out of the crush around the Reflecting Pool, but where to go? The grounds of the Washington Monument were off-limits. The people's front yard, the most public of all places, was shut down, atomized, configured to create access and define privilege for the president and his pals. It was like being stuck in a four-hour motorcade.

In the moments before midnight, the night air was filled with poorly amplified blandishments from Clinton: "Celebrate the past," "Never forget," "Hateful intolerance." He seemed content to usher in the new year by listening to his favorite music—his own voice—but a countdown would have been nice. We went farther up the hill behind us for the moment of truth. It was quite a show. All thirty seconds of it. Must have looked swell from up on the dais. (I actually had a magnificent first few seconds of the new year. Our family of five danced in a circle, all wearing the same dizzy smiles and weird glasses—but we could have done that in our backyard.)

Better fireworks were scheduled for 1 a.m. By offering the bone of more fireworks later—Bono came on post-midnight as well—the Park Service was able to effect a "slow release" that allowed Clinton and his buddies to head back unimpeded to the White House for the rest of their "dusk-to-dawn affair."

Maybe Clinton stepped out onto the balcony and smiled down at all the people coursing around the Ellipse. Maybe he had a nice post-Midnight Moment, thinking about all those swell Americans and the big America's Millennium Gala he threw for them. If he had looked more closely, he might have noticed that all those folks were flipping him the bird.

5

Magazines

One evening at a DC cocktail party, an acquaintance of David's relayed some interesting media gossip. "Did you see that these guys Kurt Andersen and Michael Hirschhorn are starting an online magazine?" David, who often wrote about the slow-motion collision of newspapers and the Internet (after all, AOL was a local company in Washington), was intrigued; after more than five years at *Washington City Paper*, he was motivated to find a cutting-edge challenge. He traveled up to New York to meet with Kurt (one of *Spy* magazine's creators) and Michael (a highly regarded journalist and editor at publications such as *Esquire* and *Spin*); the more they spoke, the more promising the digital future seemed at their ambitious start-up, Inside.com. In May 2000, David began work there. He would report and write full-time, an inviting break from the editor-in-chief responsibilities he'd held for so long.

Inside.com garnered remarkable attention from New York's media elite, but its business model was not sustainable. *Brill's Content*, helmed by *American Lawyer* founder Steve Brill, merged with *Inside*; David chose to leave, signing staff contracts with both the *Atlantic* and *New York Magazine*.

Slower Than a Speeding Bullet

Washington Monthly, OCTOBER 1, 2001

THAT'S EPIC BRANDING, a Pavlovian depth of consumer affiliation that makes marketing executives hug one another. And it's brought to you by Amtrak, the rail transportation apparatus of the US government, an agency not historically celebrated for its warm relationship with the general public.

Every Tuesday afternoon, Hurley picks up Ryan and his four-year-old brother, Patrick, and heads for the Route 128 station outside Boston. They're all train freaks, the kind of civilians who live to be kissed by the wind of a passing behemoth. The three watch several trains go by before grabbing a local to the station for lunch, but nothing rivets Ryan like the Acela.

There's a reason for that. If a small child could conjure a grown-up train, he might make something that looked like the Acela Express. (The nomenclature is a conflation of *acceleration* and *excellence*.) Christened last November, Acela is a land jet with the nose of a 747 fronting a vast expanse of windowless grillwork that conceals tons of mechanical fury just waiting for a spark from the overhead wire. Back where the passengers sit, there's enough tricked-up gadgetry to put an arch in James Bond's eyebrow. On a northbound Boston trip recently, a guy in a suit stepped up to the whooshing electronic door at the end of the car and said, "Open the pod door, Hal."

An American version of the bullet train, Acela is capable of speeds in excess of 150 miles an hour and tilts niftily up on its side to take the steepest bends, the better to keep those nasty g-forces at bay. As a matter of design, Amtrak's high-speed entrant is bolted together to avoid the pushes and pulls of common rail conveyances, and is powered by electric motors less noisy than a lot of room air conditioners. Double-size windows suffuse the church-quiet transportation pod with light. The chairs—designed after careful market research on 25,000 riders in the Northeast Corridor—make the middle seats on a DC-9 seem medieval.

Such town-car amenities and aerodynamics didn't come cheap. The government-owned rail agency has sunk an unprecedented $1.7 billion into Acela, hoping to make the leap into the twenty-first century after largely bypassing the twentieth. To hedge its bets with the traveling public, Amtrak spent millions just on marketing its land yacht—a full year before there was ever a train to ride on. The promise of a bona fide American bullet train has certainly caught the attention—and the imagination—of the American public, but thanks to a combination of politics and performance, Acela hasn't quite lived up to the hype.

When it pulled into the Boston station at 9:30 one night last summer, dozens of people surged out to meet it. But they were there to get a look at the equipment, not the people it brought. Acela is that rare piece of hardware, like the redesigned VW bug, that makes people smile involuntarily when they see it. Hurley says Acela has riveted her grandson from the moment he saw it: "It's so sleek and beautiful. But our understanding is that as pretty and modern as it is, it doesn't really save you much of any time."

Grandma Hurley may have a soft spot for trains, but she's no sucker. The quickest Acela can go between New York and Boston is three and a half hours. Fifty years ago the New Haven Railroad's Merchants Limited made the trip in four. Three-quarters of the way into its maiden season, the best the bullet can do is save you the same thirty minutes over the Acela Regional, as the Northeast Direct is now called. (Between Washington and New York, people on the "high-speed" train can expect to pull in a whopping fifteen minutes ahead of those traveling on legacy technology.)

The meager minutes saved hardly match the mystique, nor do they derive from Acela's bulleting along at 150 miles an hour. The train hits top speed once, for a couple of minutes, on the flats on the Boston–New York leg; the rest of the time it floats along relatively prosaically under 100 miles an hour, something steam trains accomplished a century ago. The Acela Express only beats the old trains to New York because it makes fewer stops and doesn't have to switch to diesel now that the line has been electrified all the way to Boston.

In the end, Acela is functionally the same old Amtrak with a bullet-train bonnet, running on track that includes tunnels dating back to the Civil War and switching equipment not much younger. And it must share those tracks with freight rail companies. High-speed trains in Europe and Japan run on mostly straight, dedicated tracks between major metropolitan areas, and they are very fast. Those countries don't even consider a train high-speed unless it travels at least 125 miles an hour. Such technology typically blossoms in smaller countries that have the will to invest in infrastructure that make trains truly competitive with airlines and make cars seem silly. But in America, the term "bullet train" is more marketing rubric than paradigm shifter.

When pressed about the slowness of its high-speed train, Karen Dunn, an Amtrak spokeswoman, blames the media for hyping expectations, saying that Amtrak never claimed that Acela was a bullet train (an assertion somewhat hard to square with Amtrak's website, which promises that Acela "zips along at 150 miles an hour"). Dunn insists that the trains are meeting the agency's expectations and brags that they have shaved almost one and a half hours off the trip between New York and Boston. (Schedules show a difference of barely an hour, which stems from nonstop service, not the new technology.) While Amtrak expects to knock twenty more minutes off the New York–Boston leg, Dunn concedes that the United States will probably never have a true bullet train.

"We have a problem Europeans and Japanese don't: we are dedicated to our cars," she explains. "There's not enough room in this country to build tracks to accommodate high-speed rails."

There's something incredibly American about this particular failure. No other developed nation on earth would fall for a train that looked fast but wasn't. In Japan, the responsible executives would prostrate themselves and hint at suicide. European parliaments would convene, names would be taken and blame assigned. But here, performance is a vestigial issue and Acela simply another form of expensive techie jewelry.

Building a real bullet train would have required some very un-American impulses. In the United States, the good of the whole comes to a screeching halt just about the time Amtrak's congressional overseers interject pork-barrel politics and anti-government ideology that batters the "public" part of public transportation. And the idea of investing in infrastructure for a vehicle that can't be personally captained sounds almost silly. Trains? Who the hell rides the damn things apart from the rest of the known universe? In America, trains are for losers who have no place to go.

The promise of an American bullet train was born and almost immediately died in the months when Congress passed the Amtrak Reform and Accountability Act of 1997, which essentially laid the groundwork for dismantling the government's passenger-rail monopoly. While it allowed Amtrak, for the first time, to close money-losing routes and to add new ones, and infused $2.2 billion in capital funds, the law also required Amtrak to become self-sufficient within five years; if Amtrak didn't make the mark, a newly created Amtrak Reform Council could draft a plan to liquidate the entire system. (The council, which is supposed to guide Amtrak toward self-sufficiency, is co-chaired by rabid anti-government activist Paul Weyrich, and is stacked to the gills with conservatives appointed by Newt Gingrich and Trent Lott.)

Never mind that the national rail agency, christened in 1970, is no more likely to pull itself into the black than Congress is. After twenty-six years and $22 billion in federal operating subsidies, Amtrak has never made a profit, and it is so deep in debt that it could never survive without federal funds. But having been told to conduct itself like an American business, Amtrak has complied in full, blowing its wad on Acela, which is supposed to boost Amtrak's cash flow by 2002.

So far, the rail agency has spent $800 million on twenty new train sets, which are being produced by a consortium of Canada's Bombardier Transportation and France's Alston Ltd. (makers of the eye-popping TGV). Twelve have been delivered and another eight are due by the end of the year, despite the fact that there is not a single track in the country outside the Northeast corridor on which those new trains can run. And there won't be for many years, a problem Amtrak is well aware of. The new trains will simply replace the old Metroliners on the Northeast Corridor.

In bringing Acela to America, the agency ignored time-tested extant bullet-train technology and insisted on developing its own. It scrimped on the R & D, delivered the product late to market with unreliable technologies, initiated an ad campaign before the train existed, and has since used the conventions of marketing to obscure the product's failure to do what it was designed to do. You generally expect an entity with that kind of MO to be listed on the Nasdaq.

To build a real bullet train in the Northeast, an undeniable civic and national good, would have taken substantial money—at least $12 billion just to upgrade the Washington to New York leg—a lot of which would have gone to the kind of infrastructure improvements politicians can't cut ribbons on. (For the same reason, Amtrak spent millions renovating New York's Penn Station, even though the tunnels leading to it are decrepit and offer no realistic escape route if anything goes wrong. And now that Penn Station has been primped within an inch of its life, Amtrak has announced that it will use its portion of the station as collateral on a $300 million loan to meet operating expenses.)

Amtrak runs just like any other government program, which means that moneys have to be atomized across a broad constituency of politicians to cobble together a voting coalition.

The deals required to create that coalition explain a lot of Amtrak's current troubles. Already, former Senate majority leader Trent Lott

(R-Miss.) has successfully lobbied to get one of the ten or so scheduled new high-speed rail lines to go through—you guessed it—Mississippi.

The Magnolia State isn't exactly on the top of transportation planners' priority lists, but no matter. Money that might otherwise go toward developing better tracks from Los Angeles to San Francisco or safer tunnels at Penn Station may very well end up electrifying rail lines along that highly traveled "Southeast Corridor" between Meridian, Mississippi, and Dallas, Texas.

As John Robert Smith, mayor of Meridian (and Amtrak board member), told the National Conference of Mayors this year, "Southern Mississippi can be on the leading edge of the development of high-speed cars."

Because Amtrak can't offer customers speed, it has had to focus on selling the frisson of Acela. US Airways shuttle flights run on the hour between New York and Boston and New York and Washington, taking just an hour. Even factoring in ever-increasing delays and the hellish cab rides to Logan and LaGuardia, Acela can't compete in terms of time.

"They promise you prime rib, but what you are getting is good-looking hot dogs," says Joseph Vranich, author of *Derailed: What Went Wrong and What to Do About America's Passenger Trains.* "We now have a train that is attractive, with a number of really nice amenities, but it is insufficient to drive air passengers from the busiest air traffic corridor in our country. Even if it's successful from a financial standpoint, it will not cause the removal of a single commercial flight."

When Acela was christened last November, the former chair of Amtrak's board of directors, Governor Tommy Thompson of Wisconsin, suggested: "Every generation is marked by breakthroughs that profoundly affect our society. The launch of the Acela is one of those defining moments."

As I write this, we are limping over degraded track outside Stamford, Connecticut. Acela's fancy undercarriage banishes the clak-clak that has been part of train travel ever since John Henry first drove a spike. But the eerie quiet means that I get to listen to the guy across the aisle bray into a cellphone about his recent negotiation with a car salesman, all the time gesturing with a giant can of Foster's I'm pretty sure he didn't buy in Acela's Jetson-like café car.

One of every four seats is occupied. In the café car—the only such car in America offering draft beer—the bartender explained that this train wasn't on the original schedule, and so people weren't showing up yet. I suggest that this might also be because it costs twice as much as a regular train and takes three times as long as flying. (A one-way Acela ticket between Washington and Boston costs $162, compared with $69 for the regular train, and $168 round-trip for a ticket on Southwest Air.) The bartender says that travelers are choosing Acela Express for other reasons.

Acela draws a different sort of trade, he said, gesturing around, implying that his train was expensive enough for the busy business traveler to escape crying kids, fat guys chomping on smelly sandwiches, or grandmas brandishing an endless ream of photos. Indeed, Acela just doesn't have room for those guys. It has only 304 seats, compared with 700 on the European TGV trains—another reason the tickets cost so much. By granulating its audience through fares that grow to nearly match the airlines, Amtrak has made Acela a kind of rolling gated community, a clean, comfortable place where business can be conducted.

People also ride Acela for the same reason that they spend $200,000 on a powerboat that carries two people: because wasting money is fun and makes them feel alive. If only Amtrak could figure out a way to let passengers drive the train for the brief minutes it approaches top speed, they'd have a winner on their hands.

The inside of an Acela does have its merits. You could play racquetball inside the massive bathrooms, and it's nice to do your business standing up without having to put yourself in sync with the sway of traditional trains. The interior features that same odd combination of faux luxury cheesiness sported by the current crop of new cars—there's lots of that pristine ubiquitous plastic and fabrics that haven't hosted thousands of other odor-emitting humans.

But even on the level of service and creature comforts, Amtrak has a way to go. The airline shuttles offer nice new equipment, too, with televisions in each seat, lots of music to choose from, and, let's not forget, flight attendants. On the Acela Express, I did have a Maine lobster roll, but it cost $8.50 and I had to stand in line fifteen minutes to get it.

Amtrak didn't need lobster rolls to get in the game. If its high-speed trains had actually been able to get from New York to Washington, or Boston to New York, in less than two hours, they would have been swamped. Rail has a significant head start because of its relatively smaller footprint than those of airports and because it can be tucked underground in major metropolitan areas. The fight to get to LaGuardia or Logan, plus a growing collapse in the nation's air traffic grid, should have put Acela way out in the lead; instead, all the horsepower stays in the barn.

In order to convince people that Acela is the way to go, Amtrak has had to change the subject. The Acela Express is marketed the way airline travel used to be. Remember when traveling by airplanes was glamorous, when the flight attendants offered leis to travelers in between serving up recognizable food on fine china? Then came deregulation, and it was goodbye filet de bœuf and hello four-peanut polybag. The airlines' fleets became buses with wings, accessible to all at a manageable price, as long as they didn't mind riding with their heads in the armpits of the guys next to them. Now Acela is re-introducing the traveling public to fine china, at least in first class, in an age when time is the most desperately sought luxury of all.

Trains have defined and enabled progress throughout American history, but now, so manifestly overtaken, they cling quaintly to a very minor role in American travel. According to Amtrak, the federal government spent $33 billion last year on highways and $12 billion on aviation, while Amtrak had to do with $500 million, less than 1 percent of all transportation spending. People generally chalk up the lack of rail investment to Americans' dysfunctional relationship with the automobile, but it's really their submission to the clock that has sent trains running backwards. Once airplanes went supersonic, trains became rolling anachronisms.

And that's where they sit. As it is, trains are lying in wait for a perfect storm, a time when the country's air traffic and highway grid irreparably melt down. Even now, Amtrak gets a fair amount of business off the airlines when there's mayhem in the skies as there was last month, but it's hoping for more than referrals. Amtrak had hoped that Acela would inspire the kind of wonder that would renew the country's love affair with the train while filling its coffers (and saving it from congressional dismemberment), but there's little magic in a bullet that goes too slow to actually hit the target.

Details Reborn

Fairchild Gives Constantly Morphing Men's Magazine One More Launch

[Inside], SEPTEMBER 18, 2000

THE MAGAZINE LAUNCH ritual generally produces the hoariest of publishing clichés. Ads for the premiere issue are always *way over* budget. The young editor's nascent vision is judged a *revelation.* And—after frenzied scanning by journalists—the premiere issue momentarily succeeds, *wildly,* beyond everybody's expectations.

Details is living the cliché. The latest incarnation of the young men's magazine arrives at newsstands this week as well-fed (133 ad pages) and self-assured as its frat-punk editor, the twenty-eight-year-old Daniel Peres.

But the constantly morphing *Details* is a wounded brand, its equity tarnished. Conjured out of the downtown scene in 1982 by Annie Flanders, the magazine was purchased by Condé Nast in the late 1980s and turned into a hip men's magazine under a then hardly known editor named James Truman. It was the last time the magazine seemed to understand what the reader wanted. Since Truman was anointed editorial director of all of Condé Nast in 1994, the magazine has drifted between gay and straight, effete fashion magazine and babe-a-licious *Maxim*-alike—profits elusive all the while.

So six months ago Condé Nast chairman S. I. Newhouse Jr. killed *Details* and sent the cadaver over to recently acquired Fairchild Publications, home to *Women's Wear Daily, W,* and *Jane.* Initially, it was put forth that *Details* would return to its fashionable roots and become a small-bore attempt to corner the market on fussy men who spend a lot of time talking about, you know, ah, details.

But fashion is nothing more than an effervescent trope in the new old *Details.* Fairchild editorial director Patrick McCarthy and CEO Mary Berner apparently see *Details* as an opportunity to demonstrate to Newhouse, the media community, and their partners/rivals at Condé Nast that the recently arrived step-sibling was more than capable of conceiving and executing a general-interest men's magazine. And given McCarthy's enthusiasms and Berner's ambitions, no one will miss the symbolism if they launch a winner out of a brand name that the supposedly more beautiful and glamorous sister never got its arms around. Although he did not acknowledge a wisp of catty competitiveness betwixt Condé Nast and Fairchild, McCarthy says he expects that *Details* will be the first of "many, many launches" at the company. Whether he and Berner will be given the freedom and resources to do such launches depends to a significant degree on what happens with *Details.*

Given the hidden, but tremendous, stakes in play, it seems strange that much of the success is dependent on a guy who probably gets carded on occasion when he goes out clubbing. But Peres has been rapidly groomed through the ranks of Fairchild's various trade titles by McCarthy for a reason. He may be only twenty-eight, but having served as Paris bureau chief and European director of *W,* he has been in enough meetings with enough people not to be the least bit threatened or impressed by the parade of schlubby reporters coming by to sniff his magazine.

Peres believes that there is a third way between what he calls the "brands" of the men's niche, indicating the quotes around *GQ* and *Esquire* with crooked fingers, the service and adventure journals such as *Men's Health* and *Men's Journal,* and the wildly successful lad romp *Maxim.*

"I'd like to think that there are things that people like me find interesting besides a woman's breasts, although there's nothing wrong with a nice pair of breasts," says Peres, contributing a Seinfeldian irony to the interview. "But there is more to life than that," he adds.

All of Fairchild's assets have been leveraged to the hilt with *Details* to ensure this third way is a success. Creative director Dennis Freedman made sure that the rejiggered book is majestically lush, threaded with the kind of visual lilt and destination photography that has made *W* so much fun to stare at. McCarthy and CEO Berner made the most of extant relationships with fashion advertisers to goose the launch over three hundred pages. And perhaps most important of all, they kept ambitions for the new *Details* reasonable, so it can declare victory by achieving the same kind of numbers that shuttered *Details* last year. It's a tidy little play for 400,000 smart boys, a not-so-mass-market glossy that should eventually mean positive cash flow given Fairchild's more streamlined cost structure than its profligate sibling.

And it will work. Schooled at the neatly pressed knee of McCarthy, Peres has come up with a book that puts just enough twists and curves into the standard men's template to seem fresh, but won't be so idiosyncratic that the guys on the newsstand will tuck it in the back of the rack. The new *Details* is a general interest magazine in fashion drag—exactly the opposite of what it was first pitched as. Its fate rests with an audience of young men with a share of stupid money in their pockets and a self-consciousness about image and appearance.

"When my dad was twenty-eight, he had two kids, no money in the bank, and was at the end of a shitty marriage," Peres says. "This is the age of the twenty-five-year-old CEO and the thirty-year-old retiree. And we have to find something that fits his sensibility. And they have a lot more interests than the tits and ass and beer and babes and all that kind of shit . . . Beyond that, there has been an evolution in what it means to be a man. It used to be if you took an interest in skin care products or what you put in your hair, you were branded as faggy. Now those lines have been blurred. An interest in your appearance, in health or fitness, is no longer straight or gay."

Never mind the shirtless Robert Downey Jr. on the cover. *Details* is not a gay magazine or even a fey one in butchy drag. There's a nice androgyny to it.

But the cover, and the story behind it, won't provide much oxygen for the launch. The cover itself is on the cheesy side—the typography brings mid-seventies *Penthouse* to mind—and Downey's oft-told saga doesn't really invite further examination. (Neither do the other cover lines, a wooden collection that quietly suggests the reader might want to keep moving.) Downey—a late grab for the cover when other prospects fell through—already spilled his guts in *Vanity Fair*. His primary epiphany is the same one that all white people have after they go to jail: it sucks.

In spite of Peres's assertion that he is building a glossy refuge for ambitious comers who are winning on their own merits, there are four subjects in the magazine who found the limelight because they are a product of famous loins. Downey, Jakob Dylan, Cameron Douglas, and Eric Eisner all bask in reflected—and some self-generated—glory. There are a lot of home-run hitters in the magazine, but most of them seem to have started on third base.

But the magazine does enough other things right. The architecture of the magazine is completely logical and still manages to surprise. Dossier, the first section, includes decent short features and isn't cluttered with the infobites that seem to replicate across magazine titles. In this case, Charlie's Angel Lucy Liu, Dylan, recreational users of Viagra, and a supposedly reforming Hunter S. Thompson all get short, pretty rides. The section that follows, In the Works, serves as a lens on things and people that are in the process of becoming, including a massive redo at the Pentagon. Vitals constitutes *Details'* pause for commercial announcements, including the shiniest gadgets, fashions, trends, and design. The section breaks into single, comprehensible pages that scan nicely and don't interrupt the flow.

The features are hefty, including yet another look at how the nouveau mighty fall: in this case, Mark Hughes of Herbalife. Paul Allen's endless and fruitless attempts to gain a purchase on cool come off as an interesting thought well-rendered. Both stories succeed as mature narratives, but you wouldn't guess it from the hackneyed headlines—"Death of a Salesman" and "Revenge of the Nerd." A massive book excerpt about exploring Mars indicates that at a certain point, all of the additional pages kicked up by the guys in advertising became problematic. Still, there's a serious, lush look at the design of an otherworldly athletic facility outside of Berlin and an intimate portrait of the newest version of the oldest profession in China.

It isn't the *Esquire* of the sixties, but then again, it ain't *FHM*. It's a bracing corrective for all of the old geezers who believe that today's twentysomethings are a pack of self-interested young wolves. In feel, if not in look, it reminds of the early-nineties *GQ* when *Esquire's* David Granger was editing stories for Art Cooper. Granger hasn't seen the magazine but suggests that there's room for a men's magazine in which "the editor is following his own best impulses." Cooper thought it would be unfair to comment on a magazine he hadn't seen but offered the best of luck to a "brother publication."

He didn't say little brother, but there's been a fair amount of whispered patronization around Condé Nast. Why should they root for Fairchild to succeed with a title that bedeviled Condé Nast?

McCarthy says that if there is ill will, he hasn't seen so much as a puff of it. "From James Truman on down, people [at Condé Nast] have been nothing but supportive. He suggested writers and photographers and art directors. Remember that he was at *Details* and he wants to see its name live on and be a success. We all do."

One Condé Nast publisher sees nothing wrong with a little sibling rivalry for readers and advertisers. (And of course Si Newhouse, who views his magazine factory as the modern-day equivalent of MGM in the 1930s, doesn't mind his cherished cavalcade of stars stepping on one another's lines.) "I think it will be good for *GQ*," he says. "Condé Nast is a company that believes in intramural competition, and it is the better for it. I think that in a lot of ways, *Bon Appétit* has set the pace for *Gourmet*, and I really don't see how this is all that different."

There may be some gold in those hills as well, says Clay Felker, a guy who was around the last time Fairchild wanted a piece of the young men's consumer market (when it merged its flailing men's fashion title *M* with the editorial remnants of the brilliant eighties business magazine *Manhattan Inc.*). Maybe, the famed founder of *New York* magazine says, this time it will be different. "Young people are becoming more and more of an important audience, and if they figure out a way to access them, then it may be a good time for this to be coming on the market," he says. Although he's not fond of the name and is mindful of its conflicted history, Felker believes that Fairchild is a good home for the magazine, in part because of the corporate culture of feistiness inspired by former chairman John Fairchild.

"This is a place where nobody has an office and everybody pitches in on things, so you can imagine that everybody there—including Patrick McCarthy, a man who knows an awful lot about this business—is involved," he says.

McCarthy says that all of the speculation about what it means for Fairchild and Condé Nast is very much beside the point. "In this kind of publishing environment, everybody is going to jump on it and make very quick judgments . . . it's a very difficult environment to publish into. But I saw Si [Newhouse] last night and he said, 'All that matters is what happens on the newsstand. Nothing else really matters.' And he's right. I try not to get caught up in what the inner circle thinks of it. Either people will buy it or they won't."

Me, Me, Me™

FROM "21 BIG IDEAS FOR 2001," *[Inside]*,
DECEMBER 26, 2000

JOSH HARRIS, FOUNDER of the late Pseudo.com, sidesteps the pitfalls of Internet broadcasting with his weliveinpublic.com: it's just him and his girlfriend—plus a hundred cameras—in their home. (Dennis Rodman's doing the same thing, God bless him.) As theoretically commercial content plays get corrected out of existence, look for the reemergence of digital boutiques to recall the web's early promise as a flower bed of ideas. Today, everybody's a demographic; there's no persona too non grata for the web's cheap hosting and email marketing opportunity. Witness andrewsullivan.com, a virtual business-card-cum-publicity-site allowing the former *New Republic* editor in chief to post his contrarian views and pimp the Brand Called Me in both third-person ("In 1984, he won a Harness Fellowship to Harvard's John F. Kennedy School of Government") and first- ("Buy my books"). Unabashed self-promotion will evolve into comprehensive cultural verticals that find their own audience—especially with the kind of personal service offered by Florida dancer Cinnamon Rain, whose nastycinnamonsplace.com hawks her $25 undergarments: "I will wrap them in a zip-lock bag for freshness with a picture and thank-you card." No, thank *you*.

Who Needs Writers and Actors
When the Whole World Is Your Backlot?

[Inside], FEBRUARY 20, 2001

THE TV NETWORKS are displaying a distinct lack of urgency in their current negotiations with the writers' and actors' guilds. Might they be hanging so tough because programmed reality will soon obviate a major fraction of the need for the output of delicate—and increasingly expensive—artists? If things get bloody at the bargaining table, Hollywood producers could cut to the bone thusly: "If you continue to hold out for big residuals for video-on-demand, we have a large backlot called America that will fill the hole nicely. Our viewers will be so busy watching the *Millionaire Mole Survive Big Brother's XFL Temptation* that they may not notice you guys are on strike."

And they will be right. Reality programming in all its manifestations has co-opted tried-and-true dramatic motifs and wedded them to a new writer-and-actor-free process. (If you ask me, the made-for-TV XFL, a joint venture between NBC and the World Wrestling Federation, fits into this category as seamlessly as today's newsmagazines.) Producers concoct situations and then slice and dice the resulting footage. The result: the same operatic conflict followed by resolution with either a hug or a shiv that has become de rigueur in all network entertainment. Whether they're searching for an outlaw wide receiver to play for the

XFL's San Francisco Demons or the vote-stealing Florida shrew/bureau-crat, the industry knows precisely what to look for. Sports on steroids, enhanced news programming, and Darwinian game shows could shrink the window, and the need, for traditional sitcoms and dramas.

Reality programming can be as fake as a twenty-two-dollar wig, and people will still buy it. Viewers, especially younger ones, suspend dis-belief and buy the trope; after all, they've come of age in a tricked-up world. So they don't flinch at the conceits of Fox's *Temptation Island,* where a young hardbody with a tenuous commitment to a lover frolics in Belize with a girl whose breasts are fresh off the drawing board of a talented plastic surgeon. The situation may not scan as dead-bang true, but the hard reality always arrives in the consequences. If the hardbody screws up and busts a move on the fresh new girl, he will lose the woman he loves and rue the day long after the hottie he met on the TV show has dumped him, signed with an agent, and picked up a few small roles. But that guy's pain is the money shot of reality porn.

The industry version of "keeping it real" is not all that different from Thomas Hobbes's take on reality four hundred years ago. Hobbes cer-tainly would have appreciated Sue's nasty, brutish, and short speech that brought *Survivor 1.0* to such a deliciously hateful conclusion.

Cultural norms have mutated. The Velveteen Rabbit came quaintly alive by being loved; the characters on reality programs seem most epi-cally real when they have spittle in the corners of their mouths and a batshit-crazy look in their eyes. And it's usually a mite more compelling than the indignation pouring out of Martin Sheen's *West Wing* president when those damn politicians let the people down again.

In 1991, the first year of *Real World* and the beginning of reality's star turn—when Kevin went off on Julie for her dark, racist inner thoughts—we believed we were seeing a pure, unalloyed moment. But even if the transaction had the tang of reality, the template was pure, unadul-terated Hollywood cheese. Setting up seven cast-to-type kids in a cool house with a pool table turned out to be cheap and highly effective. The show's creators, network soap queen Mary-Ellis Bunim and documen-tary producer Jonathan Murray, made a virtue, indeed a genre, of necessity after they got stiffed on funding the fictional variant. No surprise it has legs a decade later—the business calculus hasn't changed, while broadcast network's numbers are looking more and more like MTV's every day.

French philosopher Jean Baudrillard suggested at about the same time as *Real World*'s debut that America had become little more than the sum of its mediated impulses. The nation as backlot is really just a matter of two worlds—one supposedly real and one a representation—finally meeting in the middle. Disney, having just completed Disney's California Adventure, could finish the build-out with an assist from broader cultural forces. Add a few more cameras to those middle places, and you have a broadcast version of *The Matrix*, a collective hallucination that makes a sitcom seem entirely beside the point.

That's not to say that in this post-writing, post-acting world, we will all spend our evenings gawking at one another on webcams. Intermediation and production values are critical. The unedited life is prosaic per se. But merely applying the principles of narrative and arc to the most mundane existence—mine, for instance—can yield impressive results. In one version of my life last week, I tracked down Tina Brown on an airplane for an interview, had lunch with a highly placed source, danced on the edge of ethical ruin, and screamed "Fuck" at my wife before breakfast. Pretty dramatic stuff. But in the other cut, the more realistic one, I wrote a crappy story nobody cared about, suffered twenty torturous minutes in a queue for the New Jersey bus, and watched my twelve-year-old twin girls get clobbered in basketball. Depending on which simulacrum you were viewing, I'd seem like a young Bob Woodward or the schlub next door. And the observed fantasy, as historian Daniel Boorstin noted forty years ago, would be "more real than the reality."

But there might be a self-limiting dynamic to reality's bullish run through the entertainment space. Like the lawyer working for a notorious defendant, producers will soon enough have trouble impaneling a group of people who are not already contaminated by the amount of mediation they walk through every day. Remember when the nascent television news would do a man-on-the-street interview back in the early sixties? Media naifs would blink into those bright lights, imagine the size of the megaphone they were speaking into, and barely be able to blurt out a few words. That same random MOS interview today is full of crisp sound bites, knowing glances toward the lens, and a tidy concluding statement.

It could ruin all the fun. Everybody now inhabits the voyeur dome; they not only like to watch, they're ready to vogue on cue. The contestants on *Survivor* 2 came to battle for the million, working off the Machiavellian script Richard Hatch used in version 1.0. The clueless prison guard was torched in the first episode for failing to internalize the lessons of the inaugural season, somehow thinking the game was actually about the camping skills she brought to the outback. *Who Wants to Be a Millionaire* was a huge hit when it was apparent that contestants were awestruck to be sitting across from Regis in all his monochromatic splendor. But by now, they all mug for the camera, each coming with their own ready-made, literally famous-for-fifteen-minutes schtick.

A friend of mine who writes television, good television—the kind that gets almost as many Emmys as viewers—says that if the lords of prefab reality really want to break through, they should take the next natural step: *Temptation Island* with pedophiles and child actors; *Big Brother* with a violent psychotic down the hall; *Survivor* without the producer-provided rice. *Then* you'd see some big numbers. And if vestigial norms prevent entertainment companies from physically jeopardizing participants, there's always the fig leaf of news to get the show on the road. The nice thing about ugly realities is that there are plenty of them to go around, and anybody who thinks that a prime-time execution is out of the question hasn't turned on a TV lately.

The Futility of "Homeland Defense"

Don't Even Try to Close the Holes in a Country,
and a Society, Designed to Be Porous

Atlantic Monthly, JANUARY 2002

GET OVER THINKING that America can be made safe. Defending a country as big and commercially robust as the United States raises profound, and probably insurmountable, issues of scale. There has been much talk of "Israelifying" the United States, but America has about 47 times as many people as Israel, and roughly 441 times the amount of territory to be defended. New Jersey alone is 753 square miles bigger than Israel, and home to nearly 2.5 million more people. Beyond problems of size, it's all too reasonable to assume that America won't be safe. Righting various asymmetries merely designs—as opposed to prevents—the next attack. When one target is shored up, nimble transnational cells that can turn on a dime simply find new bull's-eyes. Up against those practical realities, homeland security is the national version of the gas mask in the desk drawer—something that lets people feel safer without actually making them so.

If America is riddled with holes and targets, it's because a big society designed to be open is hard to change—impossible, probably. In 2000 more than 350 million non–US citizens entered the country. In 1999 Americans made 5.2 billion phone calls to locations outside the United

States. Federal Express handles nearly 5 million packages every business day, UPS accounts for 13.6 million, and until it became a portal for terror, the Postal Service processed 680 million pieces of mail a day. More than 2 billion tons of cargo ran in and out of US ports in 1999, and about 7.5 million North Americans got on and off cruise ships last year.

Group targets are plentiful. There are eighty-six college and professional stadiums that seat more than 60,000 people, and ten motor speedways with capacities greater than 100,000; the Indianapolis Motor Speedway seats more than 250,000. Few other countries offer the opportunity to take aim at a quarter million people at once. Also plentiful are tall buildings — until just yesterday the dominant symbol of civic pride. Fifty of the hundred tallest buildings in the world are on US soil. Minneapolis, a midsize city that doesn't leap to mind as a target, has three of them. And one of its suburbs has the largest shopping mall in the country, the Mall of America, with at least 600,000 visitors a week.

As for trained personnel to defend our borders and targets, the Immigration and Naturalization Service, which oversees the inspection of half a billion people a year, has only 2,000 agents to investigate violations of immigration law. The Postal Service has only 1,900 inspectors to investigate the misuse of mail. According to one estimate, it would take 14,000 air marshals to cover every domestic flight — more than the total number of special agents in the FBI. The former drug czar General Barry McCaffrey has pointed out that at least four different agencies oversee 303 official points of entry into the United States. After staffing increases over the past three years, there are 334 US Border Patrol agents guarding the 4,000 miles of Canadian border. The nation has 95,000 miles of shoreline to protect. "No one is in charge," McCaffrey says.

In all the discussion of building a homeland-security apparatus, very little attention has been paid to the fundamental question of whether 100 percent more effort will make people even 1 percent safer. The current version of America can no more button up its borders than mid-empire Britain could. Not just cultural imperatives are at stake.

America makes its living by exporting technology and pop culture while importing hard goods and unskilled labor. The very small percentage of unwanted people and substances that arrive with all the people and things we do want is part of the cost of being America, Inc.

This is not the first time a president has declared a war within US borders. In 1969, President Richard Nixon promised a "new urgency and concerted national policy" to combat the scourge of drugs—an initiative that has lurched along for more than three decades, growing to the point where the government spent $18.8 billion in 2000 trying to solve America's drug problem.

The drug war is progressing only marginally better than the one in Vietnam did. Adolescent use of most drugs has tailed off in the past year or two, but the hard-core population of 10 to 15 million American users can always find narcotics—and at a price that continues to drop. From 1981 to 1998 the price of both cocaine and heroin dropped substantially, while the purity of both drugs rose. From 1978 to 1998 the number of people dying from overdoses doubled, according to the Office of National Drug Control Policy. The Drug Enforcement Agency estimates that 331 tons of cocaine were consumed in the United States in 2000.

Counterterrorism is the ultimate zero-tolerance affair. Yet the same federal assets deployed in the war on drugs—the Coast Guard, US Customs, the INS, the Border Patrol, the CIA, the FBI, and the DEA—are the first and last lines of defense in this new war. The fight against terror involves a triad that drug warriors can recite in their sleep: global source management, border interdiction, and domestic harm reduction.

In both wars human ingenuity is a relentless foe. Create a new blockade, and some opportunist will survey the landscape for an alternative path. "What the war on drugs tells us," says Eric E. Sterling, of the Criminal Justice Policy Foundation, "is that people motivated by the most elementary of capitalist motives are constantly testing and finding ways to get in. Terrorists are as motivated as the most avaricious drug importer, if not more—and they are not going to be deterred by whatever barriers are put up."

Less than ten miles southwest of where the World Trade Center towers stood, the part of the Port of New York and New Jersey that occupies
sections of Newark and Elizabeth is back to work. On the day I went
there in October, straddle carriers—leggy, improbable contraptions
that lift and cradle containers—buzzed around in the shadow of the
Monet, a large cargo ship. The *Monet* is a floating lesson in friction-free
commerce. It is operated by CMA CGM, a French company, but owned
by the US subsidiary of a German firm; it is registered in Monrovia, and
it sails under the Liberian flag. Like everything else in view, it's massive,
capable of holding 2,480 twenty-foot-long container units—the kind
familiar from flatbed trucks and freight trains. It left Pusan, Korea, on
September 19, stopping in three Chinese cities before sailing across the
Pacific and through the Panama Canal and coming to rest in New Jersey
on October 22.

The Port of New York and New Jersey is no less international. It's the
busiest port on the East Coast. In 2000, the port moved approximately
70 million tons of general and bulk cargo, the equivalent of 3 million
containers, from hundreds of cities around the globe, and half a million
freshly built cars. The large containers it processes are stuffed, sealed,
and tagged in far-flung locations, and their contents move, mostly un-
checked, into the hands of consumers. A conga line of trains and trucks
snakes out of the port, bound for a metropolitan market of some 18
million people.

Smuggling goods in containers probably started the day after shipping goods in them did. In a sting last January, US Customs and the
DEA seized 126 pounds of heroin concealed in twelve bales of cotton
towels on a container ship at the port. That same month two men were
charged with importing 3.25 million steroid pills that were seized during
a customs examination of a container shipped from Moldavia. And in
May of 1999 the DEA and Customs seized 100 kilograms of cocaine
hidden under 40,000 pounds of bananas in two refrigerated containers.
Sometimes the cargo isn't cargo at all. In October, Italian authorities
found a suspected terrorist—an Egyptian-born Canadian dressed in a

business suit—ensconced in a shipping container. His travel amenities included a makeshift toilet, a bed, a laptop computer, two cellphones, a Canadian passport, security passes for airports in three countries, a certificate identifying him as an airline mechanic, and airport maps. The container was headed for Toronto from Port Said, Egypt.

Before September 11 only about 2 percent of all the containers that move through ports were actually inspected. At Port Newark–Elizabeth there is a single giant on-site X-ray machine to see inside the containers; since September 11, two portable machines have been brought in to supplement it. The Customs Service enforcement team has been temporarily increased by 30 percent, but even that means that a mere 100 inspectors are responsible for more than 5,000 containers every day. The service has been on Alert Level 1, which theoretically means that more containers are being inspected. But not even that vigilance—let alone the overtime—can continue indefinitely.

By reputation and appearance, the port is extremely well run, and it had tightened up security even before September 11. In the mid-1990s port officials began requiring every incoming truck driver to obtain an ID badge. One fall morning a man who appeared to be a Sikh, in a brilliant-orange turban and a lengthy beard, drew double takes from the other truckers—as he would anyplace else—when he stopped by the administration building to get his credential. When I was there, foreign crews were restricted from leaving their ships. The Coast Guard required ninety-six hours' notice before a ship arrived, and boarded every vessel before it was allowed into port. Two tugs accompanied each ship on its way in; if the ship were to head toward, say, a bridge support or some other target, the tugs would muscle the ship away.

But commerce, by definition, requires access. The port offers obvious targets because it is a place of business, not a fortified military installation. Tanks of edible oils sit behind a single cyclone fence; tankers of orange juice concentrate from Brazil stand unguarded in parking lots. Two squad cars, one belonging to the port and the other on loan from the Department of Corrections, were parked at one of the port's major intersections, but anyone can drive around much of the facility without having to pass a single checkpoint. A train moves in or out of the port four times a day, crossing under the New Jersey Turnpike and through a tangle of bridges and elevated freeways that carries 630,000 cars every day. Just across the turnpike, Newark Airport handles roughly 1,000 flights a day.

Testifying one month after the September attacks, Rear Admiral Richard Larrabee, the port commerce director, told a Senate Commerce, Science, and Transportation subcommittee, "As a port director, I cannot give you or my superiors a fair assessment today of the adequacy of current security procedures in place, because I am not provided with information on the risk analysis conducted to institute these measures."

If a container holding heroin slips into the United States, the street price may go down, gangs may be enriched, and drug use may rise. If that same container held chemical or biological agents, or a nuclear weapon, the social costs would be incalculable. Doing nothing to deter such events would be foolish, but doing everything possible would be more foolish still. "There are two things to be considered with regard to any scheme," Jean-Jacques Rousseau once observed. "In the first place, 'Is it good in itself?' In the second, 'Can it be easily put into practice?'" In the case of homeland security the answers are yes, and absolutely not.

Some measures, both quotidian and provident, will be taken. Practical approaches to making air travel safe again will emerge incrementally. Newly integrated databases will prevent a recurrence of the dark comedy of errors that allowed many of the hijackers into the country in the first place. Postal workers, it is to be hoped, will be tested for the presence of biological agents with the same alacrity that senators are. But the culture itself will not be reengineered. America will continue to be a place of tremendous economic dynamism and openness.

At the port the country's muscular determination to remain in business is manifest on every loading dock. But if one looks hard enough, the cost of openness is there to see. In a quiet spot amid the industrial bustle—behind Metro Metals, on the north side of the port facility—is a nasty clump of twisted metal. Some of the girders from the World Trade Center, another brawny symbol of US economic strength that also happens to be owned by the Port Authority, have come to rest here. The stink of that day—the burnt smell of implacable mayhem—hangs near, reminding us that great symbols make irresistible targets.

A New Mask

The Terrorists Temporarily Created
a Civil Society in New York — but the City
Can't Mind Its Manners Forever

Atlantic Monthly, NOVEMBER 2001

TO HAVE THE attention of a nation is hardly novel in a city that's been ground zero for more than a century. Living in the Mae West of municipalities, New Yorkers are used to people staring. People live here because they *want* to be noticed. But New York's starring role in history's most viewed piece of videotape — a whole new genre of terror porn — brings with it not just more notoriety but unwanted sympathy.

New Yorkers can stand anything save the nation's pity.

However well-meaning, and however important for those who give and those who receive, the sympathy alters only the isolation of the tragedy, not its dimensions. And once the questions from distant relations switched from Where were you? to How are you? people here did not know how to respond. As with the huge quantities of blood that arrived after the attack, New York is having trouble finding places to store all the consolation. Everyone in the city is so busy putting on a stiff upper lip — Damn that bin Laden and the disappeared 1 and 9 trains; I guess we'll have to walk — that the embrace of our countrymen becomes one more thing to put up with.

"The department moves forward," one firefighter told me, speaking with more firmness than defiance, even as he dug for 350 of his colleagues two days after the towers fell. "This thing was around a long time before me, and it will be around a long time after me."

In attempting to flatten civil society, the terrorists temporarily created one in New York. Of course, the city can't mind its manners forever. It's too much trouble. Yet returning to a reflexive leaning on the horn when some schmuck gets in your way—a civic necessity in the best of times—seems impossible while the rest of the country is draping your town in nobility. As odd as it sounds, the city's psyche is better equipped to answer back to Jerry Falwell's schadenfreude.

Deprived of both the smirks on our faces and the chips on our shoulders, we New Yorkers are looking for a new mask, one that will prove less corrosive to the wearer yet congruent with the threat. It's now okay to complain when the Brooklyn Bridge is backed up from here to kingdom come, but it will never be in good taste to wonder aloud if that's where it's going to be blown to.

Other cities do a much better job of being, without acting, terrified. Jerusalem, a place New York could end up resembling, was carved out of the hatred of others and makes no apologies for its means or its ends. Belfast residents, annealed by decades of neighborly enmity, know that there's no way to look good when you are running for your life. New Yorkers, raised to believe that showing fear is a felony, were left in the aftermath of the attack still wondering how to act when a bomb threat is announced at Grand Central. Probably not for long.

18 Truths About the New New York

New York, OCTOBER 8, 2001

IF SOMETHING IS both unthinkable and a cold fact, where to put it? The argument over what edifice will replace the towers has already been joined, but no one is sure what should supplant the city's collective sense of invincibility. It would be silly to live in fear, but it would be even sillier to go on the same way. As one friend said, "It's like having new priorities written in the sky." The effect on New York's skyline is writ, but it's worth wondering what kind of rubble the planes created when they pierced New Yorkers' collective consciousness. It's not over and never will be.

1. There is no such thing as too informed.
If the attack is something that cannot be explained, at least it can be known. The *New York Times* tripled its newsstand run, and the story pushed the *Daily News* over a million. Readers became expert on some palpable aspect of the monster. "Of 2,900 samples taken from remains at the scene, feasibility studies on 829 of them showed discernible DNA results, suggesting that the genetic material came from 289 discrete individuals," one self-appointed expert says. Beats wondering where all the bodies went.

2. Irony is not dead; it abounds. It's just reverted to form.

Kidnapped by twee practitioners, irony itself ended up in quotes and was used as a cover for collegiate snarkiness by a generation that never had to get serious about anything. Until now. The situational ironies compound horror: the rescuers who are also victims, the firehouse buried in disaster, and a death toll that inexplicably mounts at a site that yields few bodies. And civic discourse is now rife with rhetorical ironies: holy war, the gifts of tragedy, and heroic politicians. This has become a city where people can only smile wanly when its mayor describes New York as "the safest city in the world." That's irony in its natural state.

3. Everyone who comes after will never understand.

Not a new brand of New York provincialism but a cold fact. This is the place where the world seemed to end in a single morning. That day, as it was experienced here, was not televised.

4. There is no bridge-and-tunnel, no inner and outer, no us and them.

New York is no longer Manhattan. The attack took place downtown, but the collateral damage perforated the boroughs, Westchester, and close-in Jersey. Forget the wrinkled nose of condescension on the Manhattanite who encounters those who live on the other side of the river and those middle places. Red, white, and blue have suddenly become the new black: in choosing the flag decal as a signifier of the event, New York—a place that Spalding Gray once described as "an island off the coast of America"—has been repatriated. And people elsewhere are flying a different sort of flag in solidarity. "People here are hanging their I ❤ NEW YORK T-shirts in their window," says Minneapolis restaurateur Ed Nagle. They still hate the Yankees, by the way, just not their fans.

5. Everyone has a story, and everyone needs to tell it. Over and over.

Survivor stories always end the same way: *still here, not there, not dead.* The life-affirmingness of that narrative is matched by its singularity:

"This is something that happened to me." A woman in Midtown found herself in step with a stranger in a business suit. Apropos of nothing —and everything—he turned to her and said, "I was in the building." She stopped, reached out automatically to touch his arm. "What floor?" Everyone has a story, and everyone needs to tell it. Over and over.

6. The jumpers will always be with us.
Faced with the most horrible of all human choices, the kind of riddle that grade-school children use to torture one another, many leaped rather than burn. And as the debris falling from the top anthropomorphized into human beings, people watching understood that for the time being, we were all beyond help. "I don't remember faces, just bodies jumping out," says Alexandra Rethore, a second-year analyst at Lehman Brothers. "And the girl next to me was hysterical. She kept saying, 'They're catching them, right?' I said, 'Yeah, they're catching them. Let's go.'" It was a noble act, a message to loved ones: "I'm gone but not lost. I'm still here. Find me."

7. Everything going forward, apart from life itself, is a misdemeanor.
To complain about a job, a girlfriend, or an extra seven pounds in this new day is to invite disbelief. It ain't arms and legs, right?

8. Strangers aren't that strange anymore, unless they are.
Our interest in people we don't know cuts two ways. On the subway, we scan the car, examining people as potential threats—*Is he the kind of man who would sell me a bagel or blow this car up?* But after we've checked out features, backpacks, and mien, sometimes the eyes actually meet. And the look is returned with an understanding that at any minute, if things go wrong, we could come to know one another so much better. A woman on the 4 train sat down next to a man and began riffling through a document from the Federal Emergency Management Agency —the topic joined, they talked until she got off, sharing vulnerabilities, theories, and a ten-minute train ride.

9. The line between urban reality and urban legend is shrinking.
How is it that the most extraordinary acts in the history of Western civilization still prompt people to embellish? Yes, it is true that one of the firefighters was killed when one of the people he was there to save landed on him, but no, it is not true that a cop surfed his way down from the eightieth floor on a concrete slab. There's a high correlation between terror and gullibility, apparently. And then there is the sub-genre of stories that are true but too horrible to be told, such as that of the cop, trapped in rubble with two broken legs, who died from a self-administered bullet.

10. The house in the country has become the new cold war's bomb shelter.
What had been a signifier of status has become that other place where we will go when the shit hits the fan. Leslee Dart, president of PMK/HBH, closed down her office and sent people home by ten-thirty. By eleven-thirty, she—along with her husband, child, nanny, and a co-worker—was on her way to Garrison, an hour and a half north of the mayhem. "It felt like the safest place to be," she says.

11. It's good, not silly, to have a plan. And some running shoes in the drawer.
You leave breakfast with a friend, shaking your head about his interest in having an anthrax palliative on hand—and later find yourself surfing the web in pursuit of same. Then one of the cute girls in the office mentions that she's wondering how to accessorize her new gas mask that she plans on carrying with her all the time: "I can keep it in my handbag with my makeup and tampons, so no one will ever know." It's all good. If having climbing gear in your forty-fourth-floor office makes you feel one iota safer, rock on. Oh, and let's not forget sensible shoes. Now Manolos and shimmy dresses have given way to "flee wear," a look that's bound to flatter the girl who's running for her life.

12. Being scared and being tough are the same thing.
Tough is not insouciance and a leather coat. Tough is hanging in even though one of your friends is gone. Or going to work even though your

house is unlivable. Or heading down into the subway even though a sense of foreboding walks with you. "I feel like I don't want to stay here because I am scared, but I don't want to leave because I am more scared of people who haven't been through this," says Robyn Forest of the Lower East Side. The people who aren't scared are the people who have nothing to lose. Losers.

13. Below the radar is the trendiest place to be.
Low-rise, nothing-special-here New York seems like the last safe place. And New Yorkers now actually have a reason, other than pure snobbery, to avoid the places where tourists mass. Big is out, crowds are scary, as is anything that could be construed as an icon. Commuters still brave Grand Central but think twice before lingering for oysters and beer.

14. Evil now has an address.
Does the World Trade Center continue to smoke because it's still on fire or because a hole has been punched into Hades itself? No matter. There are six-thousand-dollar watches strewn about, a cache of gold in the basement, and lessons in the evanescence of human endeavors everywhere. It became immediately sacred, a construction site in reverse that also happens to be a burial ground. The most televised piece of real estate in the history of civilization can be comprehended only up close. "You can turn off the TV," says Diane Rooney of Minnesota, looking at the wreck. "Here it is real. All that you can think of is the sorrow and overwhelming loss."

15. There have always been people crying on the streets of New York. Now we know why.
Did you ever think the person weeping openly on the sidewalk in front of the bodega would be you? Public crying has become and will remain socially acceptable for a long time to come. Plane sound a little loud? Go ahead and bawl. Check a downtown avenue to get your bearings? Have a tissue. Wrong page of the Rolodex? Don't bother to close the office door.

16. Certain places in New York will never be the same.
Common parts of the city have been indelibly marked by uncommon events. The city work crews came through Union Square last Thursday morning and stuffed the impromptu memorials and sculptures into black garbage bags: "We're just finishing what the rain started." The square's status as a kind of holy place will linger even as children and dogs retake the park. Staten Island ferried in brave, talented men and got back an empty boat. And the armory's service as a nexus of human grief created ghosts that time won't rub out.

17. Trade Center metaphors are inescapable and in perpetually bad taste.
Five homicide detectives were drinking at Peter McManus on Seventh last week and telling work stories, including one about punching a perp in the face: "He was out of his mind. I hit him and he dropped like the World Trade Center."

18. The dust will be with us forever.
All the efforts at civic hygiene can't erase the past. That dust has become the spot that the Cat in the Hat could never get rid of. No one admits that it contains some fraction of the victims themselves, because to say so aloud would make it tough to draw breath. Underneath the rail at the downtown Chambers A-C-E stop, or in between the slats of a bench on the boulevard of Allen Street, the dust hides and waits, a tiny reminder of big things that never go away.

Gathering to Remember

New York, DECEMBER 3, 2001

STANDING ON LIBERTY Street, architect Bartholomew Voorsanger peers across acres of low-rise rubble to a ten-story dagger of façade — the last remaining bit of either Trade Center tower that still reaches for the sky. He'd love to put a tag on the massive Gothic detail, a signal to the contractors that it should be preserved. Except the façade weighs hundreds of tons; it shall not be moved, and will most likely end up demolished.

"You'd almost have to build the entire site around it," Voorsanger says. As one of three people chosen by the Port Authority to select artifacts for an eventual memorial (Marilyn Taylor, chairman of Skidmore Owings & Merrill, and art consultant Saul Wenegrat are also part of the effort), he has tagged dozens of items at ground zero, as well as out at Fresh Kills and Port Newark, where much of the debris has been shipped. He searches for totems that are less weighty but no less freighted with meaning: mundane signage, crushed public art, beams bent in ways that neither God nor man intended. In his office, he has a yellowed edition of the *New York Times* that was stuffed into a girder as the towers were being built (Monday, June 23, 1969: JUDY GARLAND, 47, FOUND DEAD).

Voorsanger, who just completed a redesign of the Asia Society building, has no idea what kind of monument will emerge from his work. It will be left to others to conjure—and fight over—a memorial that somehow satisfies the needs of the thousands who died and the millions who were affected. But he's ferociously interested in making sure that whatever is built captures the violence and loss of that day.

"I worry that the site is being sanitized," he says. Behind him, a dozen cranes, some twenty stories tall, dine on the remains of the seven Trade Center buildings. A lazy snowfall of office paper accompanies each bite. "It's starting to look almost normal. You have to see it, to smell it, to understand what really happened here."

Voorsanger and his colleagues have had to work in a big hurry. This being New York, practicalities required a massive push to get the site cleaned up, and the progress has been amazing (and divisive, pitting firemen against Mayor Giuliani). Now seven-foot-high chain-link fences surround the site, swathed in view-obscuring green fabric—as if what's going on were too shameful for civilians to witness.

"I think it's very important that we preserve elements of habitation," Voorsanger says, standing in front of an escalator in Building 7, which now leads nowhere in particular. A door with a nameplate, DANA MUR-NANE, SUPERVISING ENTRY OFFICER, opens to an office that in turn opens to the world because there is no exterior wall.

"For the memorial to be effective," he continues, "it has to speak to subsequent younger generations. You have to have metaphor. Now, there are plenty of bright people out there who can find a more effective metaphor than I can. But if you don't have a fragment of reality, then it's almost impossible to develop the metaphor."

That's All, Folks!

New York, DECEMBER 17, 2001

WHAT DOES IT mean when a corporate visionary such as AOL Time Warner CEO Gerald Levin—a guy with a reputation for seeing over the hill—looks into the future and decides he doesn't want to be a part of it? In the surprise retirement party he threw for himself last week, Levin indicated over and over that recent events made running a company seem, well, beside the point. But what if other, more mundane forces were at work?

Levin's unexpected exit could mean that he knows that the next couple of years will not be nearly as bright or bold as he once predicted. "This is typical Levin," says an editor at one of the company's magazines. "He made this move when he had enough time left on his contract to control succession." Retiring in May, a year and a half ahead of schedule, also gives him credit for the biggest media merger ever, while—just for instance—allowing him to forgo significant blame if all of those parts don't play well together.

Last January, Levin called the merged behemoth "a big monetization machine," but almost a year later it looks a lot more like an ad-driven company in the deepest media recession in years. Revenue growth has been half of what the company promised, and the stock is down 23 percent. (The overall Dow is down 4 percent.)

"A lot of us who know Jerry are wondering what he knows that we don't," says a senior executive in the publishing division. In other words, when it comes to Jerry, the timing might also be a little scary.

Close observers at the company pooh-pooh the idea that Levin is getting out while the getting's good, suggesting that he'd hardly name Time Warner guy (and personal friend) Richard Parsons CEO if there were a booby trap waiting. "I don't think it is anything but a personal decision," says Jessica Reif Cohen of Merrill Lynch, who has followed the company and Levin for some time.

Parsons's ascension over AOL's Robert Pittman, his co-COO, has been cast as the triumph of old media over new, of New York over Virginia. But it makes sense for the times: Parsons has become king because content is. In the vapor trail of September 11, concerns such as gross revenues seem, well, gross. Levin has spent a lot of time recently talking about the company's "sacred trust" as national storyteller.

It may be doing a good job of covering the biggest story in years, but AOL Time Warner still faces significant problems with its online service, which Levin called the "crown jewel" of the merger.

The plan to make AOL Time Warner a roach motel for consumers, a sticky village that would be easy to get into and hard to get out of, seems to be proceeding, but no one is spending money to reach those consumers.

"It is a great marketing machine, but advertising and commerce revenues are falling down dramatically and subscriber growth is difficult because it's working off a bigger base," says Cohen. The cost of acquiring those subscribers—freebies, promotions—is going up. Even though AOL actually raised prices back in July by two bucks, it's making less money per subscriber. And it's running out of seducible Luddites—most people know what the Internet is and have already decided either to use it or to ignore it.

But that's not Levin's problem anymore. There's more to life, he told the *Wall Street Journal,* than being a master of the universe: "I'm my own person. I have strong moral convictions. I'm not just a suit. I want poetry back in my life."

Some of the poetry is rendered in dark hues. Levin arranged to have an out clause in his contract after his son Jonathan—a high school teacher—was murdered by a former student in 1997, an event that left him fundamentally changed. Levin said that September 11 reminded him again that life is short.

"He is leaving on his own terms and his own time," says Scott Cleland, CEO of the Precursor Group. "Not many people get to choose their exit."

6

New York Times

The *New York Times* had a specific beat in mind when it recruited David in 2002. He was assigned to the Business section to cover what was then one of the city's most influential but rarefied industries—magazines. Time, Inc., Condé Nast, Hearst, and their ilk drove the water-cooler conversations and helped define the cultural landscape. While daily newspaper coverage of magazines was typically relegated to counting ad pages and chronicling masthead shuffles, David's reportage was never quotidian. He did the numbers, of course, but also managed to capture the myriad personalities and zeitgeist of a business entering a transition it barely understood. Soon David's assignments expanded to the Culture desk, where he created The Carpetbagger, an irregular series of reports about the motion picture world, especially Hollywood. David's pieces on the Oscars folderol became must-reading, and his appearances as one of the first *New York Times* reporters to file video reports brought him a new level of renown. With the debut of his Media Equation column, frequent television appearances, and the premiere of the widely seen *Page One* documentary in 2011, David became the unlikely face of the *New York Times.*

While David's first allegiance was to the *Times,* he managed to find time to write his memoir, *The Night of the Gun,* as well as occasionally contribute pieces to myriad physical and online publications. He began teaching a course at Boston University called Press Play, a class for aspiring journalists. After David's passing in 2015, his very idiosyncratic, demanding, and inventive syllabus for his students was widely disseminated; it is reprinted here, too, as an exemplar of David's thinking and a tribute to his never wavering soul as a reporter.

Neil Young Comes Clean

SEPTEMBER 19, 2012

DRIVING DOWN THE hill above his ranch in the Santa Cruz Mountains, south of San Francisco, Neil Young took a deep whiff of the redwood forest momentarily serving as the canopy for his 1951 Willys Jeepster convertible.

"I can still remember how it smelled when I first pulled in here—I was driving this car," he said, recalling the trip in 1970 when he bought the place and named it Broken Arrow, after the Buffalo Springfield song.

The author of some of the spookiest, darkest songs in the American folk canon seemed jolly on this late-August day. Even if he was accompanied by a reporter, generally not his favorite species of human, the motion soothed him. "I've always been better moving than I am standing still," he said.

Young, sixty-six, spotted this land out the window of a plane banking out of San Francisco four decades ago and now owns nearly a thousand acres of it. His song "Old Man" is a tribute to the caretaker who first showed him the place.

"I ran out of money, so I had to sell some of it," he said. "That's okay, because it was too big. Everything happens for a reason." He kept his eyes on the narrow road through the giant redwoods.

It was hard to reconcile the affable guy motoring along on a sunny day with his past incarnations: the portentous folkie of "Ohio," the rabid anti-commercialist who gave MTV the musical middle finger with "This Note's for You," the angry rocker who threatened to hit the cameramen at Woodstock with his guitar. He was happy partly because he was here.

"For whatever you're doing, for your creative juices, your geography's got a hell of a lot to do with it," he said. "You really have to be in a good place, and then you have to be either on your way there or on your way from there."

We would spend a few hours creeping along—he drove slowly but joyfully, as if the automobile were a recent invention—on our way there or on our way from there, the ranch where Young lives with his wife, Pegi, and their son, Ben. His longtime producer and friend, David Briggs, who died in 1995, hated making records here, deriding the hermetic refuge as a "velvet cage."

In addition to the studio, where more than twenty records have been made, there is an entire building given over to model trains, another where vintage cars are stored, and another piled with his master recordings. Llamas and cows roam under cartoonishly large trees. It seems like a made-up place, an open-air fortress of eccentricity meant to protect the artist who lives there. But what it has most of all is not a lot of people.

"I like people, I just don't have to see them all the time," he said, laughing. David Crosby, his bandmate in Crosby, Stills, Nash & Young, used to describe the complicated route into his ranch as "my filtering system," Young said.

He made a bunch of rights and lefts through the forest before getting out to unlock the gate. Others might have an electronic gate, but Young likes the mechanical experience of slipping a key into a padlock and swinging something open. He is fundamentally analog, despite the occasional electronic excesses in his music. He likes amps with knobs that go to 12 and things that click when you touch them.

I made it past the filtering system because Young was promoting his autobiography, *Waging Heavy Peace*, which comes out next week. The book is elliptical and personal, with little of the period poetics of *Just Kids,* by Patti Smith, or the scabrous detail of *Life,* by Keith Richards.

Young once promised he would never write a book about himself, according to Jimmy McDonough's biography of him, *Shakey.* But time passed, and then Young broke his toe a year ago and needed something to fill his time and refresh his fortune.

"I don't think I'm going to be able to continue to mainly be a musician forever, because physically I think it's going to take its toll on me — it's already starting to show up here and there," he said. Writing a book, he added, allowed him "to do what I want the way I want to do it."

Waging Heavy Peace eschews chronology and skips the score-settling and titillation of other rocker biographies. Still, Young shows a little leg and has some laughs. Yes, he partied with Charles Manson and tried to hook him up with a recording contract. He admits he saw a picture of the actor Carrie Snodgress in a magazine before he courted her, married her, and divorced her. He pleads guilty to having been busted for drugs with Eric Clapton and Stephen Stills. He even has a little fun with Crosby. "I still remember 'the mighty Cros' visiting the ranch in his van," he writes. "That van was a rolling laboratory that made Jack Casady's briefcase look like chicken feed. Forget I said that! Was my mike on?"

But as the book progresses, the operatics of the rock life give way to signal family events, deconstructions of his musical partnerships, and musings on the natural world. It is less a chronicle than a journal of self-appraisal. The book, like today's drive, is a ride through Young's many obsessions, including model trains, cars like the one we were touring in, and Pono, a proprietary digital musical system that can play full master recordings and will, he hopes, restore some of the denuded sonic quality to modern music.

Although he rarely meets the press, mostly out of lack of interest, there is no reluctance on this occasion. A plain-spoken Canadian from the tiny town of Omemee, Ontario, and a son who has done the work of his father — Scott Young, a Canadian journalist, wrote more than thirty books — he wants to be understood. Every question is mulled and answered directly, without ornamentation. But each time when I guessed which way we were turning, on the road or in conversation, he almost always went the other way. "Too many decisions to make with no sign of what to do," he said, laughing as he steered around a hairpin onto a side road.

Young has routinely fled success, severed profitable musical partnerships, dumped finished records, and withdrawn when it was precisely the moment to cash in. He is a person who will never leave well enough alone. "Sometimes a smooth process heralds the approach of atrophy or death," he writes in *Waging Heavy Peace.*

Doing as he pleases has worked out pretty well for him. As a young musician torn between the crunch of the Rolling Stones and the lyricism of Bob Dylan, he avoided the fork altogether and forged his own path. Over the course of more than forty records and hundreds of performances that date to the mid-sixties, he has backed Rick James, jammed with Willie Nelson, dressed up with Devo, rocked with Pearl Jam, and traded licks with Dylan. Some of it has been terrible, much of it remarkable. He has made movies by himself and with Jim Jarmusch and Jonathan Demme. He called out Richard Nixon, praised Ronald Reagan, and made fun of the second Bush. And he has little interest in how all of that was received. "I didn't care and still don't," he said, then went on: "I experimented, I tried things, I learned things, I know more about all of that than I did before."

His longtime manager and friend Elliot Roberts describes Young as "always willing to roll the dice and lose," and says: "He has no problem with failure as long as he is doing work he is happy with. Whether it ends up as a win or loss on a consumer level is not as much of an interest to him as one might think."

His records don't sell as much as they used to, but while many of his contemporaries are wanly aping their past, Young takes to the stage surrounded by mystery and expectation. And now he's doing so again on tour with Crazy Horse, a thunderous, messy concoction of a band that has backed him over the years and been a source of constancy amid all the hard turns in his career. "We've got two new albums, so we're not an oldies act, and we're relevant because we're playing these new songs, so that gives us something to stand on," he said.

It's safe to predict that people will come, critics will rave, and a sixty-six-year-old man afflicted with epilepsy and serious back problems (and who has had polio and suffered an aneurysm) will rock hard enough to become a time machine back to when music was ecstatic and ill-considered.

Dylan, in a note his manager passed to me, says it's clear why Young has not tumbled into musical dotage: "An artist like Neil always has the upper hand," he says. "It's the pop world that has to make adjustments. All the conventions of the pop world are only temporary and carry no weight. It's basically two different things that have nothing to do with each other."

Waging Heavy Peace faithfully catalogs the disappointment Young has produced in those around him, but he expresses little regret today. "I work for the muse," he said. When he swerved into techno and country after Geffen Records signed him in the early eighties, Young was accused of making "unrepresentative" music. He responded by taking a pay cut of half a million dollars for each of his next three albums. "I'm not here to sell things. That's what other people do; I'm creating them. If it doesn't work out, I'm sorry; I'm just doing what I do. You hired me to do what I do, not what you do. As long as people don't tell me what to do, there will be no problem."

Two nights before, at the Outside Lands festival in Golden Gate Park in San Francisco, Young headlined with Crazy Horse, their sixth performance this year after going the better part of a decade without playing together. Beck went on before them and covered "After the Gold Rush," and Foo Fighters followed, with Dave Grohl mentioning that the sooner he got done, the sooner they'd all get to hear Young play. (He stood at the side of the stage afterward for Young's entire set.)

The youthful festival crowd wore little more than tattoos on this damp summer night. Young and Crazy Horse took the stage looking like the Friday-night band at the local VFW: big shirts, work boots, and hair gone gray or just gone. Given the growing chill and a restless crowd, it would have made sense to begin with a song reminding the audience that a Big Deal Rock Star was at work.

Instead, the band kicked into "Love and Only Love," a remarkable song from Young's 1990 album with Crazy Horse, *Ragged Glory*, but hardly a sing-along. It lasted fourteen minutes, with Young shredding huge reams of noise and mixing it up with his fellow guitarist Frank (Poncho) Sampedro. Seeing them play was like watching an ancient steam shovel unfurl, claw the night air, and dig in. "We thought it was important to introduce ourselves, to remind people what Crazy Horse is all about," Sampedro said later.

Young, who has never been a graceful stage presence, lurched to the front. He is old—he began playing in this town more than forty years ago—and bent over his guitar, but he is not old and bent. Young has never been physically whole, but that brokenness has annealed rather than slowed him. He is anything but a frail man when he has a guitar in his hand.

His musical ideas work, whether plugged into a stack of amps or plucked on an acoustic guitar. As his solo career veered from unadorned folk into multiple genres, critics scratched their heads and fans felt whipsawed. But the *Rust Never Sleeps* tour in 1978 was bifurcated into acoustic and electric sets, a set of tracks he still switches between, which, along with his refusal to license his music for ads, has made him an emblem of authenticity for the next generation, the keeper of rock's soul. And after all his side trips, he always came back to Crazy Horse, as he had tonight.

Derided by more sophisticated players over the years, Crazy Horse is as much an ethos as a band. As Young says in his book: "The songs the Horse likes to consume are always heartfelt and do not need to have anything fancy associated with them. The Horse is very suspicious of tricks."

The band's music with Young is built around a long-running sibling argument between Young and Old Black, his painted-over Gibson Les Paul guitar. Young, born in 1945, is the older brother to Old Black, made in 1952. Through the years, Old Black has been souped up, tweaked, and rebuilt, but it has never been replaced as his musical partner. When he plays it, he often looks and sounds furious. (In explaining the equanimity that characterizes his book, he writes: "Sometimes it's better not to blow up at someone. I can save that anger and emotion for my guitar playing.")

Young can plink out a song on a piano, and play harmonica when it serves, but he has an intimate, if savage, relationship with his guitars. "If you wanna write a song, ask a guitar," he said to Patti Smith onstage at a book convention earlier this year to promote *Waging Heavy Peace.*

He played that night as if he were mad at Old Black, even if he smiled into the squall. The crowd remained enthralled as he tortured a single note with the whammy bar, although this kind of indulgence has worn out some of his other playing partners. "We've played that note, can we move on, Neil?" Stephen Stills says with a laugh over the phone as he recalls playing with Young.

The guitar owned the night, but the secret to Young's durability is his voice, a nasal-inflected borderline whine that was never a luxurious instrument but remains intact. He sounded as he always did, yelling the chorus to "Powderfinger" or plaintively singing "The Needle and the Damage Done."

Jonathan Demme, who has made three concert films with Young, including *Neil Young Journeys,* which came out in the summer, finds Young's playing and visage "irresistibly cinematic." "I saw Neil after a show and told him how amazing it was, and he said: 'Well, it better be amazing. Those people out there paid a lot of money to be here.'"

Part of the reason they pay to see Young in concert is that he respects the form. And they show up expecting the unexpected.

"You never know what you are going to get in a Neil Young concert because he never knows exactly what he is going to do," says Willie Nelson, a friend who started Farm Aid with Young and John Mellencamp in 1985. "That way everyone is surprised."

Tonight he was feeling playful, telling the crowd, "I wrote this one this morning," before starting into "Cinnamon Girl," one of a trilogy of songs, which also includes "Cowgirl in the Sand" and "Down by the

River," that he wrote in a single-day fever back in 1968. Later, he stepped to the mike and introduced a new song by saying: "We can't help ourselves, we're trained like chimps. They trained us to write songs, and we don't know how to stop."

The fourth song of the night was "Walk Like a Giant," from the forthcoming album with Crazy Horse, *Psychedelic Pill:*

> I used to walk like a giant on the land
> Now I feel like a leaf floating in a stream
> I want to walk like a giant.

The song ended with a solid four minutes of a repeating, thudding note as the band stomped in big steps, dinosaurs in full frolic. Boom. Boom. Boom. The audience tried clapping but finally gave up until the amps died down. It sounded like a hair-metal parody, but in Young's hands it had the aura of ceremony.

While Young played, I stood stage right with his son Ben, a quadriplegic with cerebral palsy who is unable to speak. When he was born, Young and his wife, Pegi, a singer and musician, put everything else aside to help him develop his motor skills. Now thirty-four, Ben goes on every tour. "He's our spiritual leader in that way," Young says. "We take him everywhere, and he's like a measuring stick for what's going on." (Zeke, Young's son by Snodgress, has a very mild case of cerebral palsy and works at Home Depot. Young's daughter, Amber, is a talented young artist who works in San Francisco.)

Ben Young, which is how his father often refers to him, was bundled against the chill and surrounded by friends. He looked over at me at one point, and I found myself wishing I knew what he thought about the proceedings. "I tell Ben everything, and he listens," Young would tell me later. "He knows everything, but who is he going to tell?"

Sitting with Young in his bus after the show as he ate a salad and drank lemonade—he's been sober for a year, the first time in decades that he has worked without drinking or smoking pot—it felt as if we were inside a guitar, the bus's rococo interior constructed out of layers of redwood sheets, built exactly to Young's taste. Money doesn't seem to matter much to Young unless he is out of it, but things matter plenty. With assorted companions, he builds and tweaks guitars, cars, buses, and trains.

Sampedro, along with the drummer Ralph Molina and the bassist Billy Talbot, passed through, all of them clearly pleased with the night. Young's manager, Elliot Roberts, talked mostly about how cold it got, but Young said, "All I felt was a cool refreshing breeze every once in a while."

True enough, the wind had picked up at the end of the set, when Young played "Hey Hey, My My (Into the Black)," a version of which poses one of rock's eternal riddles: Is it better to burn out or fade away? In the book, Young acknowledges that Kurt Cobain quoted the line in his suicide note and John Lennon disagreed with its premise. Young settled on a hedge: "At sixty-five, it seems that I may not be at the peak of my rock 'n' roll powers," he said. "But that is not for sure."

For no reason other than it pleases Young, the model-train barn near his home is framed by two actual railcars. Back in the day, he and his pals used to snort coke and drink wine and tinker with the model layout until it grew into three thousand square feet of track and trains.

Young picked up a controller that appeared to be capable of landing a rocket on an asteroid and reminded me that, as an investor in Lionel Trains, he invented Train Master Command Control (which allows you to run multiple trains at once), as well as RailSounds (which provides realistic railroad audio). Young lost a lot of money on his investment, but he's still a board member at Lionel and ended up with a lot of cool gear, so it all sort of worked out.

As different trains began to move slowly, Young choreographed and narrated. "There's all different buttons I can press to make them go fast or slow, but they're all going the same speed, so they're not going to run into each other except at a crossover," he said. "I am the Wizard of Oz in here. I can make anything happen because I know how it all works. Music is math."

When Young finds something he likes or cares about, he has a single mode: all in. With a team of technologists and investors, he has been working on an electric car for years—the LincVolt—and when there was an accident and it burned, he just started over. He still has plans to drive it to the White House and make a movie about the car. He can speak with authority about biodiesel, Chinese battery manufacturing, and the specific optical properties of 16-millimeter film.

"I worry about global warming," Demme says, comparing himself to Young as a man of action, "but I'm not out there meeting with scientists and funding research."

Young gets most worked up when he talks about Pono, the music system he has developed. It is beyond the hobby stage: Warner Brothers has agreed to make its catalog available on Pono, and Young and Roberts are negotiating with other record companies and investors.

We walked out of the train barn past a Hummer that runs on biodiesel and hopped in yet another car, a '78 El Dorado, to listen to the Pono system. Right now, it needs a trunk full of gear, but Young and Roberts are working with a British manufacturer to come up with a portable version. He gave a demonstration that replicated MP3s, CDs, Bluray, and then the full Pono sound.

"You are getting less than five percent of the original recording," he said at first. He put on Aretha Franklin's "Respect" and then switched to Pono. The horns jumped and the car was filled with lush, liquid sound. He madly toggled between different outputs to make sure I was getting it.

In the wake of *Americana*, a collection of folk songs recorded with Crazy Horse that was released last spring, he is already making another album and writing another book, this one about all of the cars he has owned. Roberts handles Young's business and artistic interests with a great deal of savvy, so Young is good at making money—which helps, because he is also good at making it go away. "I spend it all," he said. "I like to employ people and make stuff. It will be my undoing."

He has dropped a fortune making films, directing five under the pseudonym Bernard Shakey, including *Rust Never Sleeps*, *Human Highway*, and *Greendale*, and sharing credit on several others. His memoir is of a piece with his moviemaking impulse, but it's less pricey.

"Writing is very convenient, has a low expense and is a great way to pass the time," he says in *Waging Heavy Peace*. "I highly recommend it to any old rocker who is out of cash and doesn't know what to do next."

He decided to do it sober after talking with his doctor about a brain that had endured many youthful pharmaceutical adventures, in addition to epilepsy and an aneurysm. For someone who smoked pot the way others smoke cigarettes, the change has not been without its challenges, as he explains in his book: "The straighter I am, the more alert I am, the less I know myself and the harder it is to recognize myself. I need a little grounding in something and I am looking for it everywhere."

Sitting at Alice's Restaurant on Skyline Boulevard near the end of the day, he elaborated: "I did it for forty years," he said. "Now I want to see what it's like to not do it. It's just a different perspective."

Drunk or sober, he can be a hippie with a mean streak. He broke off a tour with Stephen Stills without warning and sent him a telegram —"Funny how some things that start spontaneously end that way. Eat a peach, Neil."

I asked if he was a good person to work with or for. "The fact is that I can be really irritable when I'm unhappy about stuff," he said. "I can be a nitpicker about details that seem to be over the top. But then again I'm into what I'm into, so a lot of people forgive me because of that."

In the book, over and over, he is there, and then he is gone—from Buffalo Springfield, from Crosby, Stills & Nash, from his love affairs— and not given to explanations. When he loses interest, he loses interest.

After we left the restaurant, we drove back to his ranch, but we stayed in the car near the house, because his daughter, who was visiting, did not feel well. Of all the obsessions that live on the thousand acres of his ranch, the family is the one that enables all the rest, he said.

Young could have crawled inside himself and remained there, huffing his own gas and reprising a storied, moldering past as so many of his peers have. But family life—a complicated, challenging one—suits and calms him. He and his wife, along with Roberts and a group of interested parents, created the Bridge School, a private institution for profoundly handicapped children located in Hillsborough, California, because the existing ones nearby were insufficient for Ben's needs. In a benediction near the end of *Waging Heavy Peace,* Young says much of his current battle is to be a person good enough to be worthy of his family's love.

In our crisscrossing the ranch, at one point we stopped in an outdoor graveyard of old cars, a white-trash tableau of desiccated, rusting sheet metal. He stroked the giant fin of a '59 Lincoln and said it may yet roar to life. "Every car is full of stories. Who rode in 'em, where they went, where they ended up, how they got here."

Both Hero and Villain, and Irresistible

OCTOBER 4, 2013

BEFORE THERE WAS a documentary about WikiLeaks—before there was a major motion picture about its founder—Julian Assange was a star.

With his mysterious hacker backstory and shock of silver hair, Mr. Assange burst into public consciousness in 2010 with WikiLeaks' release of the Apache helicopter attack video and, in the process of revealing millions of secrets, unlocked a rarefied kind of fame.

An unfolding tale of a swashbuckling avatar against powerful forces was a movie trailer waiting to happen. The mythmaking was underway long before the spring release of *We Steal Secrets*, the documentary directed by Alex Gibney, and well in advance of the buildup to *The Fifth Estate*, the Bill Condon movie due October 18, starring Benedict Cumberbatch as Mr. Assange.

The WikiLeaks-Assange story has snaked through countless twists and turns that played out on multiple platforms all over the world, scanning as a movie that has unfurled in real time. In that sense, the first film about WikiLeaks is the one that happened right in front of our eyes, one that left governments scrambling, media organizations gasping, and regular people guessing about his next move.

Given its high profile and cinematic elements, the WikiLeaks tale was catnip to the movie industry. At one time, there were five films about Mr. Assange in development, with the documentary and the new drama eventually winning the race and going into production. The movies, each directed by an Academy Award winner, have sparked enormous discussion and remarkable pushback from WikiLeaks and its supporters.

It is a measure of our times, and perhaps Mr. Assange's appetite for renown, that a technology designed to enable anonymity for whistle-blowers became an engine of celebrity. He is, even absent the attentions of Hollywood, one of the more recognizable faces on earth.

It helps that he inhabits the role of provocateur so well. Mr. Assange is Australian by birth, but his accent is transnational, reinforcing the impression that he is a new kind of human, a product of the Internet who lives on the digital grid and in our collective consciousness. But he wears white and black hats with equal ease. His critics say he has behaved carelessly, some say recklessly, a view of Mr. Assange that gained traction after he was sought for questioning about accusations of sexual assault in Sweden.

Handsome, dashing, conflicted, and pursued, Mr. Assange is a kind of freelance spy who engages in black ops against powerful multinational interests. How different really is that from every Bourne movie you've ever seen? Sure, the damage he inflicts is with a flick of the mouse rather than a fusillade of gunfire, but his credentials as international man of intrigue are unassailable. And the fact that the peripatetic globetrotter is now walled in by the Ecuadorean Embassy in London is a remarkably paradoxical third act.

"Even while he is attacking our movie, you can't help but feel how vulnerable he is in this moment," Mr. Condon said, adding that Mr. Assange was "stuck in a self-imposed cell, and there is something deeply tragic about that."

Mr. Gibney said that Mr. Assange expresses, and for some people fulfills, a durable human impulse.

"People desperately need and want a hero, and here you have some-one who can set up a computer and instantly be inside the neural path-ways of the entire web," Mr. Gibney said. "It's pretty hard to resist the story of a guy roaming the world armed with nothing more than his laptop."

In both *The Fifth Estate* and *We Steal Secrets,* technology is a persistent character. In the same way that *The Insider* (1999) seemed to make re-porters out to be action figures with weaponized cellphones—remem-ber Al Pacino as Lowell Bergman whipping out a clunky cellphone as if it were an AK-47?—*The Fifth Estate* is rife with scenes of Mr. Assange rushing into a room and snapping open his computer with a flourish. Laptops never looked so sexy or powerful, and the WikiLeaks story of-ten seems like a sequel to *Revenge of the Nerds* writ large.

By trying to stop the government's digital bots from taking over our lives, Mr. Assange would seem to be fighting on behalf of all mankind. He is Tom Cruise in *Minority Report,* Harrison Ford in *Blade Runner,* and Matt Damon in *Elysium.* But Mr. Assange also echoes a less modern cin-ematic type, the lone wolves of paranoid seventies cinema. As a man on the run, he brings to mind the CIA analyst Robert Redford played in *Three Days of the Condor* or the reeling Dustin Hoffman being chased through *Marathon Man.* You can go even further back and find an ana-logue in Frank Sinatra in *The Manchurian Candidate.*

Then again, Mr. Assange is fond of saying he will crush an opponent "like a bug." Through that prism, he is closer to a Bond villain—state-less, vaguely Euro-ish, with stunt hair and a remarkably cool demeanor.

But if we want to understand the appeal of a character like Mr. As-sange in the current cultural context, the small screen might be a better place to look. He is an outlaw who lives by his own code, as was Tony Soprano, but his closest counterpart is probably Carrie Mathison, the CIA operative on *Homeland,* skilled and omniscient but with a messianic zeal that tends to create a great deal of collateral damage.

On the big screen, the two movies cast Mr. Assange as a tragic and self-seeking figure, a leader of a cause that conflated his personal interests and the movement's. Perhaps no one could shoulder the scrutiny that Mr. Assange has lived through, but he does not play the game of making nice with the media.

As I have written before, I once had lunch with Mr. Assange in the English countryside, and while he was enormously gracious, fun even, in showing me and my family around the farm where he was under house arrest, he was also reflexively provocative, somewhat hilariously insulting me and the place I work for. In Mr. Assange's paranoid worldview, large, multinational financial interests have had a secret handshake with governments, principally that of the United States, and have together prosecuted a war on privacy, freedom, and economic fairness. The reason that paranoia is so appealing? He turned out to be mostly right.

Every time you open up a news site, the government seems to get its hands farther and farther up your skirt. In that sense, we are not just the audience in these movies; we are part of a target-rich environment, and so we root Mr. Assange on in spite of his shortcomings. Mr. Assange has made it clear that he hates both films, which comes as no surprise from a man who sees agendas and lies everywhere he looks. Mr. Gibney's film may be a work of journalism, but its rise-and-fall narrative did not sit well with its subject.

WikiLeaks put out an annotation of a partial script that takes issue with practically everything in the film, beginning with the title, which is described as "irresponsible libel." The memo adds, "Not even critics in the film say that WikiLeaks steals secrets." Mr. Gibney is accused of selective editing, underappreciating the historic nature of the organization's work, and rendering Chelsea Manning (previously known as Pfc. Bradley Manning) as a caricature, among many, many other complaints. Mr. Gibney, who has gone after many of the same targets that WikiLeaks has taken on, found himself dealing with incoming from its allies in the press and elsewhere. Chris Hedges, a former reporter for the *New York Times* who now blogs at TruthDig.com, accused him of making a work of "agitprop for the security and surveillance state," intended to marginalize WikiLeaks and Mr. Assange. Mr. Gibney said he followed the facts and told the story they revealed, nothing more.

"The degree of vitriol has been amazing," Mr. Gibney said. "He is a remarkable figure, narcissistic in the extreme, and, as they say, beautiful from afar, but far from beautiful."

Predictably, a work of drama purporting to depict real events has already picked up a great deal of withering reaction from Mr. Assange and his supporters. In a quotation sent by a WikiLeaks staff member—Mr. Assange is, as behooves a star of his magnitude, surrounded by layers and difficult to access—he suggested that *The Fifth Estate*, apart from being wrong about himself and WikiLeaks, is doomed commercially.

"Most people love our work and its ongoing David versus Goliath struggle," he said. "These people form the backbone of the WikiLeaks cinema market. But rather than cater to this market, DreamWorks decided to cater to other interests. The result is a reactionary snoozefest that only the U.S. government could love. As a result the film has no audience and no promotion community. It will flop at the box office and deservedly so."

In an email, Kristinn Hrafnsson, a WikiLeaks spokesman, said, "I don't recognize the Julian in these films, nor the fundamental essence of what we are doing."

In a phone call, Mr. Condon made it clear he was proud of his film. A narrative feature requires license to pack vast amounts of history into a commercially viable length, and Mr. Condon said the film is true to its subject, including its depiction of his alleged hypocrisy around organizational information and WikiLeaks.

"For a public figure, he is one of the most thin-skinned subjects I have ever seen," Mr. Condon said. "He believes and advocates for transparency, except where he is concerned. He doesn't realize it, but he has become the consummate tragic hero who sowed the seeds of his own demise."

The chronic, multifront war is a fact of life at the offscreen version of WikiLeaks. Even people at odds with Mr. Assange don't deny him his place in history.

"Julian was able to pull together the biggest news organizations on earth and get them to cooperate around a single leak, holding the story for three weeks," said James Ball, a former WikiLeaks associate who now works at the *Guardian*. "That is an amazing feat."

That Mr. Assange ended up in a dispute with Mr. Ball, his media partners, and just about everyone else around him adds to the myth. What is he against? Whatever comes his way.

"Most people avoid confrontation, but Julian escalates every single time," Mr. Ball said. "He has the guts, the arrogance, and the insanity to take everyone on. I think part of the reason that there is so much interest in WikiLeaks is that people respond to that."

Many of the great public debates show up in the movie house, so it should not be surprising to see a simulacrum of Mr. Assange on the big screen. And it's even less surprising that the nature of what is on the screen is the beginning of yet another debate. History, in this instance, refuses to sit still. The first draft is a web document, subject to endless annotation.

At Flagging Tribune,
Tales of a Bankrupt Culture

OCTOBER 5, 2010

IN JANUARY 2008, soon after the venerable Tribune Company was sold for $8.2 billion, Randy Michaels, a new top executive, ran into several other senior colleagues at the InterContinental Hotel next to the Tribune Tower in Chicago.

Mr. Michaels, a former radio executive and disc jockey, had been handpicked by Sam Zell, a billionaire who was the new controlling shareholder, to run much of the media company's vast collection of properties, including the *Chicago Tribune*, the *Los Angeles Times*, WGN America, and the Chicago Cubs.

After Mr. Michaels arrived, according to two people at the bar that night, he sat down and said, "Watch this," and offered the waitress one hundred dollars to show him her breasts. The group sat dumbfounded.

"Here was this guy, who was responsible for all these people, getting drunk in front of senior people and saying this to a waitress who many of us knew," said one of the Tribune executives present, who declined to be identified because he had left the company and did not want to be quoted criticizing a former employer. "I have never seen anything like it."

Mr. Michaels, who otherwise declined to be interviewed, said through a spokesman, "I never made the comment allegedly attributed to me in January 2008 to a waitress at the InterContinental Hotel, and anyone who said I did so is either lying or mistaken."

It was a preview of what would become a rugged ride under the new ownership. Mr. Zell and Mr. Michaels, who was promoted to chief executive of the Tribune Company in December 2009, arrived with much fanfare, suggesting they were going to breathe innovation and reinvention into the conservative company.

By all accounts, the reinvention did not go well. At a time when the media industry has struggled, the debt-ridden Tribune Company has done even worse. Less than a year after Mr. Zell bought the company, it tipped into bankruptcy, listing $7.6 billion in assets against a debt of $13 billion, making it the largest bankruptcy in the history of the American media industry. More than 4,200 people have lost jobs since the purchase, while resources for the Tribune newspapers and television stations have been slashed.

The new management did transform the work culture, however. Based on interviews with more than twenty employees and former employees of Tribune, Mr. Michaels's and his executives' use of sexual innuendo, poisonous workplace banter, and profane invective shocked and offended people throughout the company. Tribune Tower, the architectural symbol of the staid company, came to resemble a frat house, complete with poker parties, jukeboxes, and pervasive sex talk.

The company said Mr. Michaels had the support of the board.

"Randy is a tremendous motivator, very charismatic, but he is very nontraditional," said Frank Wood, a member of the Tribune board. "He has the kind of approach that motivates many people and offends others, but we think he's done a great job."

The company is now frozen in what seems to be an endless effort to emerge from bankruptcy. (The case entered mediation in September after negotiations failed, and a new agreement between two primary lenders was recently announced.) But even as the company foundered, the tight circle of executives, many with longtime ties to Mr. Michaels, received tens of millions of dollars in bonuses.

Behind the collapse of the Tribune deal and the bankruptcy is a classic example of financial hubris. Mr. Zell, a hard-charging real estate mogul with virtually no experience in the newspaper business, decided that a deal financed with heavy borrowing and followed with aggressive cost cutting could succeed where the longtime Tribune executives he derided as bureaucrats had failed.

And while many media companies tried cost cutting and new tactics in the last few years, Tribune was particularly aggressive in planning publicity stunts and in mixing advertising with editorial material. Those efforts alienated longtime employees and audiences in the communities its newspapers served.

"They threw out what Tribune had stood for, quality journalism and a real brand integrity, and in just a year, pushed it down into mud and bankruptcy," said Ken Doctor, a newspaper analyst with Outsell Inc., a consulting firm. "And it's been wallowing there for the last twenty months with no end in sight."

Mr. Zell has acknowledged that the deal has not turned out how he hoped. But noting a recent upturn in results, he said through a spokesman, "Tribune has made significant strides in becoming a current, competitive and sustainable media company. The measure of management's performance is reflected in the increased profitability of Tribune's media properties."

When Mr. Zell purchased the Tribune Company in December 2007, he bought into an industry desperately in need of new ideas. And Mr. Zell, a consummate dealmaker, had a barrelful.

Tribune, home to some of the most important newspapers in the country—the *Baltimore Sun,* the *Hartford Courant,* and the *Orlando Sentinel* as well as the *Chicago Tribune* and the *Los Angeles Times*—had been battered by big drops in advertising and circulation. According to Mr. Zell, the company was also suffering from stodgy thinking and what he called "journalistic arrogance."

"There's a new sheriff in town," he said, in speeches that were peppered with expletives, as he toured the Tribune's offices.

It was a message that some within the company initially welcomed.

"Sam Zell was sort of a rock star when he went around and toured the various properties," said Ann Marie Lipinski, the former editor of the *Chicago Tribune* who left less than a year after the takeover. "People had been living with uncertainty for so long, and they hoped something good would come from an owner with a proven track record of success in other businesses."

Mr. Zell's first innovation was the deal itself. He used debt in combination with an employee stock ownership plan, called an ESOP, to buy the company, while contributing only $315 million of his own money. Under the plan, the company's discretionary matching contributions to the 401(k) retirement plan for nonunionized Tribune employees were diverted into an ownership stake. The structure of the deal allowed Tribune to become an S corporation, which pays no federal taxes; its shareholders are responsible for all taxes.

The $8 billion in new loans used to finance the deal left the company with $13.8 billion in debt. But Mr. Zell was convinced that by quickly selling the Chicago Cubs and other assets while improving operating margins, the company could emerge as a valuable property. It was typical Zell: a risky approach to gain control over a large, distressed asset while minimizing his own exposure, something he acknowledged in a company newsletter:

"I've said repeatedly that no matter what happens in this transaction, my lifestyle won't change," he wrote to his combination employees/ shareholders. "Yours, on the other hand, could change dramatically if we get this right."

His second innovation was bringing in a new management team, largely from the radio business, that, like Mr. Zell, had little newspaper experience, which constituted more than 70 percent of the company's business.

Mr. Michaels, who was initially in charge of Tribune's broadcasting and interactive businesses as well as six newspapers, was a former shock jock who made a name for himself—and a lot of money for Mr. Zell —by scooping up radio stations while at the Zell-controlled Jacor Communications. Jacor was later sold to Clear Channel Communications for $4.4 billion.

In turn, Mr. Michaels remade Tribune's management, installing in major positions more than twenty former associates from the radio business—people he knew from his time running Jacor and Clear Channel—a practice that came to be known as "friends and family" at the company.

"Working at Tribune means accepting that you might hear a word that you, personally, might not use," the new handbook warned. "You might experience an attitude you don't share. You might hear a joke that you don't consider funny. That is because a loose, fun, nonlinear atmosphere is important to the creative process." It then added, "This should be understood, should not be a surprise and not considered harassment."

The new permissive ethos was quickly on display. When Kim Johnson, who had worked with Mr. Michaels as an executive at Clear Channel, was hired as senior vice president of local sales on June 16, 2008, the news release said she was "a former waitress at Knockers—the Place for Hot Racks and Cold Brews," a jocular reference to a fictitious restaurant chain. A woman who used to work at the Tribune Company in a senior position but did not want to be identified because she now worked at another media company in Chicago said that Mr. Michaels and Marc Chase, who was brought in to run Tribune Interactive, had a loud conversation on an open balcony above a work area about the sexual suitability of various employees.

"The conversation just wafted down on all of the people who were sitting there." She also said that she was present at a meeting where a female executive jovially offered to bring in her assistant to perform a sexual act on someone in a meeting who seemed to be in a bad mood.

Staff members who had concerns did not have many options, given the state of the media business in Chicago, the woman said. "Not many people could afford to leave. The people who could leave, did. But it was not in my best interest to have my name connected to an EEOC suit," she said, referring to the Equal Employment Opportunity Commission. (Indeed, there are no current EEOC complaints against the Tribune Company.)

There have been complaints about Mr. Michaels in the past, however. In 1995, Mr. Michaels and Jacor settled a suit brought by Liz Richards, a former talk show host in Florida who filed an EEOC complaint and a civil suit, saying she had been bitten on the neck by Mr. Michaels and that he walked through the office wearing a sexual device around his neck.

"They were like fourteen-year-old boys—no boundaries at all—but with money and power," Ms. Richards said in an interview.

During and immediately after Mr. Michaels's tenure at Clear Channel, three lawsuits were filed contending sexual harassment at the company. One plaintiff, Karen Childress, a senior executive, said she was fired after complaining about receiving lewd email from senior company executives. In her complaint, Ms. Childress also stated that women who slept with male executives at the firm were promoted. The cases were settled out of court. Clear Channel declined to comment on the lawsuits.

On December 11, 2008, the Tribune board was made aware that not everyone appreciated the new cultural dynamics at the company. The board received an anonymous letter detailing a hostile work environment and a pattern of hiring based on personal relationships and suggested that the company was leaving itself open to "potential litigation risk."

The letter also suggested that a senior executive and a female employee had been discovered by a security guard engaged in a consensual sexual act on the twenty-second-floor balcony. The board took the allegation seriously enough that it hired an independent law firm to investigate it. A company spokesman said the investigation found that the executive and the woman denied the incident and the inquiry could find no evidence that such an incident had occurred or that any harassment had taken place. But a person who worked in security at the time confirmed to the *New York Times* that a security guard reported seeing the incident. That person declined to be identified because of the sensitivity of the issue.

By September 2008, the historic Tribune Tower had someone new in charge of security: John D. Phillips, a former traffic reporter who had previously worked for Mr. Michaels. In June 2009, a party for management was held in the former office of Colonel Robert R. McCormick, the newspaper baron and grandson of the founder, on the twenty-fourth floor of the Tribune Tower. Smoke detectors were covered up and poker tables were brought in. Mr. Phillips posted pictures of the party on his Facebook page, showing Mr. Michaels and Mr. Chase, along with Lee Abrams, a former radio programmer who had joined Tribune earlier that year, playing poker and drinking in the ornate office. The Chicago media writer Robert Feder first reported about the Facebook photographs.

"We are in the office of the guy who ran the company from the 1920s to 1955," Mr. Phillips wrote on his Facebook page. "It's normally a shrine. We pretty much desecrated it with gambling, booze and cigars."

While the new owner and managers went about changing the corporate tone at Tribune, they were also under pressure to service the enormous debt. In his initial tour of the company, Mr. Zell promised there would be no job cuts. But like other media companies caught in the downdraft of advertising revenue, the company was forced to cut staff and slash budgets. Elsewhere, the company introduced promotions that seemed to have been drawn from the radio playbook. At four of the company's television stations, an event called CA$H GRAB, in which a viewer was led into a bank vault and allowed to scoop up dollar bills, was inserted in the middle of the station's newscasts. At WPIX-TV in New York, the viewers were cheered on by clapping Hooters waitresses, giving the station the appearance of televised shock radio.

Mr. Abrams, who describes himself as an "economic dunce," was made Tribune's chief innovation officer in March 2008. In his new role, he peppered the staff with stream-of-consciousness memos, some of which went on for five thousand typo-ridden, idiosyncratic words that left some amused and many bewildered.

"Rock n Roll musically is behind us. NEWS & INFORMATION IS THE NEW ROCK N ROLL," he wrote in one memo, sent in 2008. He expressed surprise that the *Los Angeles Times* reporters covering the war in Iraq were actually there.

James Warren, the former managing editor and Washington bureau chief of the *Chicago Tribune,* said: "They wheeled around here doing what they wished, showing a clear contempt for most everyone that was here and used power just because they had it. They used the notion of reinventing the newspapers simply as a cover for cost-cutting." (As a contributor to the Chicago News Cooperative, Mr. Warren writes a column that appears in the Chicago edition of the *New York Times.*)

In Chicago, Ms. Lipinski said, it became clear that Mr. Zell was not above using the newspaper as a tool for his other business interests. In June 2008, Mr. Zell approached her at a meeting, saying that the *Chicago Tribune* should be harder on Governor Rod Blagojevich. She reminded him that the newspaper had aggressively investigated the governor and that its editorial page had already called for his resignation.

"Don't be a pussy," he told her. "You can always be harder on him."

In a news meeting later the same day, she found out that Mr. Zell was in negotiations to sell Wrigley Field to the state sports authority.

"It was hard to avoid the conclusion that he was trying to use the newspaper to put pressure on Blagojevich."

Through a spokeswoman, Terry Holt, Mr. Zell denied he used the newspaper to business ends. "From day one, Sam vowed never to interfere with the editorial content at any of Tribune's media properties, and he has always honored that commitment," Ms. Holt said.

In a criminal complaint, federal authorities accused Mr. Blagojevich of trying to trade public financing of the stadium for the dismissal of some members of the Tribune's editorial board. An aide to the governor charged with pursuing the matter reported back that Mr. Zell "got the message and is very sensitive to the issue," according to a criminal complaint filed by the United States Attorney's Office for the Northern

District of Illinois. (In August, Mr. Blagojevich was convicted on one of the twenty-four felony counts he faced, lying to FBI agents about his involvement in campaign fundraising.) Ms. Lipinski said it was that episode and other conflicts with management that prompted her resignation in July 2008, just one month after Scott Smith, the paper's longtime publisher, left. "I was plenty used to crisis, in many ways thrived on it," said Ms. Lipinski, who had joined the newspaper as an intern in 1978. "But this nonsense was a form of intentional manmade distraction that made the work impossible. I couldn't protect my staff from what they could see plainly with their own eyes."

Mr. Zell's various approaches didn't slow the company's decline. In the third quarter of 2008, the company posted a loss of $124 million, and the recession made it difficult to sell the Cubs. His purchase of Tribune became, as even he described it, "the deal from hell," and the company filed for bankruptcy on December 8, 2008. It wasn't simply the huge debt that burdened the company; the performance under new management continued to slide. While its television division has since done well in the advertising rebound — overall, the twenty-three stations are on track in 2010 to pass $1 billion in revenue for the first time since 2007 — Tribune's newspapers have continued to underperform the rest of the industry.

Advertising has been inserted into the *Los Angeles Times* in new and unsettling ways. In March, an ad mimicking the front page for Disney's *Alice in Wonderland* was wrapped around the first section, and in July a fake version of the newspaper's section for late-breaking news, called LATExtra, was wrapped around the real one, promoting Universal Studios' King Kong attraction, with a lead "story" that read "Universal Studios Partially Destroyed." In April 2009 an advertisement posing as a news article about NBC's new show *Southland* appeared on the front page.

In July, the Los Angeles County Board of Supervisors, the governing body of the county of Los Angeles, sent a letter of protest, saying that the use of advertising disguised as news "makes a mockery of the newspaper's mission."

The ads do not seem to have helped. The *Chicago Tribune*'s circulation continues to slide, with weekday circulation down 9.8 percent in the first half of 2010. The *Los Angeles Times* is in worse shape, having lost 14.7 percent of its weekday circulation in the period. (Overall, the industry lost 8.7 percent weekly circulation in the period.)

Radio, which was the core expertise of the management, has had a mixed record since the takeover. After bringing in many longtime associates of Mr. Michaels, WGN-AM, the company's well-known talk radio station in Chicago, lost market share in 2009. The station manager sent a note last month to Tribune managers, asking them to call in to one of the new hosts, because few actual listeners were. But a company spokesman said that ratings in the morning were up 20 percent for the month of August. In an effort to shake up the station, the management jettisoned a sports talk show at night and installed someone with no radio experience, Jim Laski, an Illinois politician who had been convicted of a felony. Steve Cochran, a longtime midday host who has said he was dismissed as he was walking out of the bathroom this summer, said the changes seemed aimed at destroying WGN. "This was supposed to be their comfort zone, what they were good at, and they have ruined a radio station that has had an eighty-year relationship with its listeners," he said. "This is a collection of carnival workers who are only looking after their friends, giving jobs to their buddies. Blagojevich is on trial and you bring in a politician who has done time in jail?"

More than the Tribune's creditors took a haircut: the shares that about 10,000 nonunion employees received in the ESOP deal are now worthless as a result of the bankruptcy, although at the beginning of this year, the company replaced the ESOP plan with a cash incentive contribution. But if and when the Tribune exits bankruptcy, the value of the company will be worth substantially less than when Mr. Zell bought a controlling interest. Under a proposed settlement filed recently with the court, senior lenders, including the Angelo Gordon hedge fund and Oaktree Capital Management, would receive $5.5 billion, while other lenders with less priority would receive far less. The case is in mediation.

"How can anybody say that they have done a good job?" said Henry

Weinstein, a former *Los Angeles Times* reporter who filed a lawsuit, still pending, that contends that the use of employee pensions to finance the deal was illegal.

"Anybody can make money when you are not servicing the debt and cutting people. Zell and the people he brought in had no idea what they were doing."

And Mr. Zell? On August 13, his lawyers suggested that if other junior creditors were paid, he should get his money back as well.

Until the bankruptcy is resolved, Mr. Zell's handpicked team will continue to run the company, but it is frozen out of any large strategic alliances or purchases. The issue of who will run the company will remain unsettled until the bankruptcy is resolved. Mr. Zell remains the chairman of the board and is no longer involved in the day-to-day operations of the company.

Despite the company's problems, the managers have been rewarded handsomely. From May 2009 to February 2010, a total of $57.3 million in bonuses was paid to the current management with the approval of the judge overseeing the bankruptcy. In 2009 the top ten managers received $5.9 million at a time when cash flow was plummeting. Mr. Wood, the board member, said, "We think they earned those bonuses. They've done a fabulous job in very difficult circumstances."

At the time, the court-appointed trustee in the bankruptcy case filed an objection, writing that while the current owners argued for "shared sacrifice," they "fail to understand what the concept means when it comes to compensating their management," and then added, "now is not the time for yet another round of bonuses."

Other proposed bonuses on the table for 2010 could bring the figure for management pay enhancements to more than $100 million, and those bonuses are heavily weighted to top management. (Earlier this week, management announced that beginning in 2011, it would award merit raises to nonunion employees of about 3 percent.)

"You have advertising wrapping around sections and being disguised as news and empty desks all around you, and then you read about these ridiculous bonuses and feathering their nests with severances, you want to scream," said Steve Lopez, a longtime columnist at the *Los Angeles Times.*

The creditors, which also include JPMorgan Chase and the Deutsche Bank Trust Company, have acquiesced to the lucrative bonuses in part because they fear that antagonizing management could further hold up the company's emergence from bankruptcy, according to two lawyers representing creditors who did not want to be quoted publicly during bankruptcy negotiations. "No one is in charge there," said an adviser to one of the senior creditors, who declined to speak on the record because it was not in his business interest to be in conflict with the current board or management.

Mr. Michaels suggested in public statements that his current team was very much in charge. According to the company's monthly statements, cash flow is on the rise and the company has $1.6 billion in cash on hand, about half of it from the sale of the Cubs, which Mr. Zell eventually managed to sell. "We are just getting started," he said in the announcement.

And management still is confident that the new thinking has Tribune on the right track. The company recently announced the creation of a new local news format in which there would be no on-air anchors and few live reports. The newscasts will rely on narration over a stream of clips, a web-centric approach that has the added benefit of requiring fewer bodies to produce.

"The TV revolution is upon us—and the new Tribune Company is leading the resistance," the announcement read. And judging from the job posting for "anti-establishment producer/editors," the company has some very strong ideas about who those revolutionaries should be: "Don't sell us on your solid newsroom experience. We don't care. Or your exclusive, breaking news coverage. We'll pass."

Ezra Klein Is Joining Vox Media as Web Journalism Asserts Itself

JANUARY 26, 2014

AFTER A WEEK of speculation, it turns out that Ezra Klein, the prolific creator of the *Washington Post*'s *Wonkblog*, will be going to Vox Media, the online home of SB Nation, a sports site, and the Verge, a fast-growing technology site.

His change of address could be read as the latest parable of Old Media cluelessness—allowing a journalism asset to escape who will come back to haunt them—or as another instance of a star journalist cashing in on name-brand success. But it's more complicated than that.

Mr. Klein is not running away from something, he is going toward something else. Vox is a digitally native business, a technology company that produces media, as opposed to a media company that uses technology. Everything at Vox, from the way it covers subjects, the journalists it hires, and the content management systems on which it produces news, is optimized for the current age.

"We are just at the beginning of how journalism should be done on the web," Mr. Klein said. "We really wanted to build something from the ground up that helps people understand the news better. We are not just trying to scale *Wonkblog*, we want to improve the technology of news, and Vox has a vision of how to solve some of that."

In making the switch, Mr. Klein is part of a movement of big-name journalists who are migrating from newspaper companies to digital start-ups. Walter Mossberg and Kara Swisher left Dow Jones to form Re/code with NBC. David Pogue left the *New York Times* for Yahoo! and Nate Silver for ESPN. At the same time, independent news sites such as Business Insider, BuzzFeed, and Vox have all received abundant new funding, while traffic on viral sites such as Upworthy and ViralNova has exploded.

All the frothy news has led to speculation that a bubble is forming in the content business, but something more real is underway. I was part of the first bubble as a journalist at Inside.com in 2001 — an idea a decade ahead of its time — and this feels very different.

The web was more like a set of tin cans and a thin wire back then, so news media upstarts had trouble being heard. With high broadband penetration, the web has become a fully realized consumer medium where pages load in a flash and video plays without stuttering. With those pipes now built, we are in a time very similar to the early 1980s, when big cities were finally wired for cable. What followed was an explosion of new channels, many of which have become big businesses today.

The same holds true for digital. Organizations such as BuzzFeed, Gawker, the Huffington Post, Vice, and Vox, which have huge traffic but are still relatively small in terms of profit, will eventually mature into the legacy media of tomorrow.

More and more, it's becoming apparent that digital publishing is its own thing, not an additional platform for established news companies. They can buy their way into it, but their historical advantages are often offset by legacy costs and bureaucracy.

In digital media, technology is not a wingman, it is The Man. Kenneth Lerer, manager of Lerer Ventures and one of the backers of BuzzFeed and the Huffington Post, says that whenever he is pitched an editorial idea, he always asks who the technology partner is. How something is made and published is often as important as what is made.

It's worth remembering that Vox got its hands on the Verge because the people working at Engadget, a tech site owned by AOL, grew tired of trying to publish through the big, slow blob of a huge corporation. The staff came to Vox for the technology and used the flexible platform there to publish its way to an audience. Vox added Curbed, Eater, and Racked last year, so Mr. Klein's new venture will become part of a growing digital emporium. And from a standing start in 2011, the Verge has grown to more than ten million unique visitors a month, becoming a big player in technology and gadgets right out of the box.

"It is not as simple as journalists going to a digital site and doubling their salary," said Jim Bankoff, chief executive of Vox. "Many of these people, including Ezra, have a vision of creating something remarkable. There is a better way of doing things, and we like to think that we are using technology in service of creativity, journalism, and storytelling."

Mr. Klein, who is making the move with other colleagues at the *Post*, including Melissa Bell and Dylan Matthews, as well as Matthew Yglesias of Slate, said he was less interested in burnishing a personal brand than building a site that will go beyond politics and policy and serve as a prism on the rest of the news. "That's the theory, but that's all it is until we actually do something," Mr. Klein said.

But it still raises the question of why Jeffrey Bezos, who bought the *Post* in August and who has personally backed Business Insider and its founder, Henry Blodget, did not want to fund Mr. Klein's venture at the *Post*. He is not saying, but to start, the *Post* has long-festering problems with its core business. It has a strong editor in Martin Baron, who is making strides, but to invest time and money in building out another discrete brand—Mr. Klein reportedly wanted a big presence and staff that could cost millions of dollars annually—would be a major distraction.

Meanwhile, Business Insider sits at the sweet spot of digital content: high traffic, low cost, with a combination of sassy voices and viral content. Kevin Ryan, a backer and founder of the site, told me that he looked at *Businessweek* when it came up for sale for an effective price of zero dollars and found that it paid more than six times as much just for desk space and real estate per working journalist. While the ambitions of the journalism may be very different, Business Insider now has traffic that rivals the *Wall Street Journal*. And the skill set is not the same.

"Digital journalism is as different from print and TV journalism as print and TV are from each other," Mr. Blodget said by telephone from the World Economic Forum in Davos, Switzerland. "Few people expect great print news organizations to also win in TV. Similarly, few should expect great TV or print organizations to win in digital. The news-gathering, storytelling, and distribution approaches are just very different."

Great digital journalists consume and produce content at the same time, constantly publishing what they are reading and hearing. And by leaving mainstream companies, journalists are often able to get their own hands on the button to publish, which is exciting and gratifying. "If William Randolph Hearst and Bill Paley were alive today, they would think they were in heaven," suggested Sir Michael Moritz, chairman of Sequoia Capital.

But while the barrier to entry is low, one big obstacle to long-term media success remains: quality. The reason that Vice, Vox, Gawker Media's sites, and other players stick out is that they use their digital tools to make remarkable, unexpected content that people flock to. NBC did not team with Re/code simply because it knows the secret of the Internet.

"I have more flexibility, and can make decisions on staff and stories so much quicker, that we can keep up with organizations that are so much bigger than we are," Ms. Swisher said.

Staring into the whirlpool of content plays, it is easy to forget that building a credible news organization that people trust still takes time. Gawker is twelve years old, AllThingsD, which became Re/code, was founded seven years ago, and BuzzFeed has been around since 2006. It may not take $200 million, as it did to create a cable network, or $50 million as a national magazine might require, but creating a digital media company takes years. (And $25 million, give or take.)

With the price for web advertising dropping by the second and new competitors coming out of the screen at a very high rate, it would seem like a terrible time to jump in. But what we are witnessing now is not the formation of a bubble, it is the emergence of a lasting commercial market, a game that has winners and losers, yet is hardly zero sum.

When Fox News Is the Story

THE MEDIA EQUATION, JULY 7, 2008

LIKE MOST WORKING journalists, whenever I type seven letters—Fox News—a series of alarms begins to whoop in my head: *Danger. Warning. Much mayhem ahead.*

Once the public relations apparatus at Fox News is engaged, there will be the calls to my editors, keening (and sometimes threatening) email messages, and my requests for interviews will quickly turn into depositions about my intent or who else I am talking to.

And if all that stuff doesn't slow me down and I actually end up writing something, there might be a large hangover: phone calls full of rebuke for a dependent clause in the third-to-the-last paragraph, a ritual spanking in the blogs with anonymous quotes that sound very familiar, and—if I really hit the jackpot—the specter of my ungainly headshot appearing on one of Fox News's shows along with some stern copy about what an idiot I am.

Part of me—the Irish, tribal part—admires Fox News's ferocious defense of its guys. I work at a place where editors can make easy sport of teasing apart your flawed copy until it collapses in a steaming pile, but Lord help those outsiders who make an unwarranted or unfounded attack on me or my work. Our tactics may be different, but we, too, are strong for our posse.

Media reporting about other media's approach to producing media is pretty confusing business to begin with. Feelings, which are always raw for people who make their mistakes in public, will be bruised. But that does not fully explain the scorched earth between Fox News and those who cover it.

Fox News found a huge runway and enormous success by setting aside the conventions of bloodless objectivity, but along the way it altered the rules of engagement between reporters and the media organizations they cover. Under its chief executive, Roger Ailes, Fox News and its public relations apparatus have waged a permanent campaign on behalf of the channel that borrows its methodology from his days as a senior political adviser to Richard M. Nixon, Ronald Reagan, and George H. W. Bush.

At Fox News, media relations is a kind of rolling opposition-research operation intended to keep reporters in line by feeding and sometimes maiming them. Shooting the occasional messenger is baked right into the process.

As crude as that sounds, it works. By blacklisting reporters it does not like, planting stories with friendlies at every turn, Fox News has been living a life beyond consequence for years. Honesty compels me to admit that I have choked a few times at the keyboard when Fox News has come up in a story and it was not absolutely critical to the matter at hand.

But it cuts both ways: Fox News's amazing coup d'état in the cable news war has very likely been undercovered because the organization is such a handful to deal with. Fox is so busy playing defense—mentioning it in the same story as CNN can be a high crime—that its business and journalism accomplishments don't get traction and the cable station never seems to attain the legitimacy it so clearly craves.

There have been few stories about Bill O'Reilly's softer side (I'm sure he has one), and while Shepard Smith's amazing reporting in New Orleans got some play, he was not cast as one of the journalistic heroes of the disaster. The fact that Roger Ailes has won both Obie awards and Emmys does not come up a lot, nor does the fact that he donated a significant chunk of money to upgrade the student newsroom at Ohio University, his alma mater.

Instead, Mr. Ailes and Brian Lewis, his longtime head of public relations, act as if every organization that covers them is a potential threat and, in the process, have probably made it far more likely. And as the cable news race has tightened, because CNN has gained ground during a big election year, Fox News has become more prone to lashing out. Fun is fun, but it is getting uglier by the day out there.

A little more than a week ago, Jacques Steinberg, a reporter at the *New York Times* who covers television, wrote a straight-up-the-middle ratings story about cable news. His article acknowledged that while CNN was using a dynamic election to push Fox News from behind, Fox was still number one. Despite repeated calls, the public relations people at Fox News did not return his requests for comment. (In a neat trick, while they were ignoring his calls, they emailed his boss asking why they had not heard from him.)

After the article ran, Brian Kilmeade and Steve Doocy of *Fox and Friends,* the reliable water carriers on the morning show on the cable network, did a segment suggesting that Mr. Steinberg's editor was a disgruntled former employee—Steven V. Reddicliffe once edited *TV Guide,* which was until recently owned by the Macrovision Solutions Corporation—and that Mr. Steinberg was his trained attack dog. (The audience was undoubtedly wondering what the heck they were talking about.)

The accompanying photographs were heavily altered, although the audience was probably none the wiser. Mr. Reddicliffe looked like the Wicked Witch after a hard night of drinking, but it was the photo of Mr. Steinberg that stopped traffic when it appeared on the web at Media Matters side by side with his actual photo. In a technique familiar to students of vintage German propaganda, his ears were pulled out, his teeth splayed apart, his forehead lowered, and his nose widened and enlarged in a way that made him look more like Fagin than the guy I work with. (Mr. Steinberg told me that as a working reporter who covers Fox News, he was not in a position to comment. A spokeswoman said the executive in charge of *Fox and Friends* is on vacation and not available for comment but added that altering photos for humorous effect is a common practice on cable news stations.)

It's a particularly vivid example of how the Fox response team works, but it is hardly the only one. Julia Angwin of the *Wall Street Journal* wrote a profile of Roger Ailes in 2005. Again, her coverage was right up the middle, but that is not the way that Fox News saw it, and she was held out for ridicule over and over in items on various blogs penned by Fox News staff when she jumped the gun on the start date for the Fox business channel. (Ms. Angwin is on book leave and did not answer a message left on her cellphone.)

Earlier this year, a colleague of mine said he was writing a story about CNN's gains in the ratings and was told on deadline by a Fox News public relations executive that if he persisted, "they" would go after him. Within a day, "they" did, smearing him around the blogs, he said. (I did not ask him for a comment because the information was of a private nature.)

Some of the avenues of attack are easier to anticipate than others. Right now there are advance copies circulating of a reported memoir I wrote about my times as a drug addict and drunk. I've already been called a "crack addict" on Bill O'Reilly's show, which at least has the virtue of being true, if a little vintage. Expect a return engagement with some added detail. I have a bit of an advantage in that my laundry is already hanging on the line, and given that I have a face made out of potatoes, any Photoshopped picture of me will have to go a long way to make me any uglier than I actually am. Having pointed a crooked columnist finger at Fox, at least I have it coming. Not so for many of the beat reporters who go to work every day confronted by a public relations machine that will go feral if it doesn't get what it wants.

When I started calling around about Fox News, Mr. Lewis, the public relations head, made himself available on very short notice on the

Fourth of July. He patiently explained that while yes, the game had changed, it was hardly in the way I was describing. There are no dark ops, he said, and no blacklist—"a myth"—only good relationships and bad ones.

Mr. Lewis said that members of his staff were not in the business of altering photos, that they had no control over stories that appeared on *Fox and Friends* or other shows, and he pointed out that it makes their job harder when they go after reporters. He called my suggestion that there was something anti-Semitic about the depiction of Mr. Steinberg "vile and untrue." Mr. Lewis denied that his staff had threatened one of my colleagues or planted private information about him on blogs.

That comes as a surprise to reporters I talked to who say they have received email messages from Fox News public relations staff that contained doctored photos, anonymous quotes, and nasty items about competitors. And two former Fox employees said that they had participated in precisely those kinds of activities but had signed confidentiality agreements and could not say so on the record.

"Yes, we are an aggressive department in a passive industry, and believe me, the executives and talent appreciate it," Mr. Lewis said, adding that with the twenty-four-hour news cycle and the proliferation of blogs, a new kind of engagement and activism was required.

"We are the biggest target in the industry, and we accept that," he said. "We embrace controversy," but he said that he and his colleagues respect that reporters have a job to do.

Many of the television-beat reporters I called had horror stories, but few were willing to be quoted. In the last several years, reporters from the Associated Press, several large newspapers, and various trade publications have said they were shut out from getting their calls returned because of stories they had written. Editors do not want to hear why your calls are not being returned, they just want you to fix the problem, or perhaps they will fix it by finding someone else to do your job.

David Folkenflik, now the media reporter for National Public Radio, ended up on the outs with Fox News in 2001 when he was at the *Baltimore Sun*. After he wrote that Fox's Geraldo Rivera had not been at the site of an incident of friendly fire in Afghanistan as he had told viewers, Mr. Folkenflik said, his calls to Fox News were not returned for more than fifteen months.

"My sense was that it was designed to make it appear that I was having trouble doing my job, but also to intimate that the people who cross them will be shut out," he said.

Mr. Folkenflik said he did not take it personally because it was not aimed just at him. "I think it is a notably aggressive effort to manage the Fox News brand and image," he said. "I think it is suffused with a political sensibility, and I don't think it is any secret that it comes from the top with Roger Ailes. They behave less like a competitive news outlet and more like a political campaign when it comes to managing coverage."

But he holds no grudge.

"I currently have a perfectly good relationship with Fox News," Mr. Folkenflik said. "I touch base with them all the time, and I write the good and bad news as it occurs."

Bill Carter has covered television for the *New York Times* for many years and has always had a good working relationship with Fox News, but he was appalled to see what he viewed as an anti-Semitic caricature of Mr. Steinberg, a colleague and a friend.

"I have not had a big problem with them, in part because their success has been such a great story, but this seemed over the line and really hateful," Mr. Carter said. "It doesn't seem like you can deal with them professionally. You do this kind of thing to a guy who's writing a story for a newspaper?"

Fox News has long held that it is its politics and not its tactics that set it apart and require such vigilance. But working reporters have been shaking their heads for years about the nightmare of dealing with Fox News, and as a result, the antagonism they believe they are fighting against seems to be on the march.

Mr. Lewis made it clear that Fox News has no problem working with reporters when they don't have an agenda, and of course, I called with a very clear one. For the record, everyone I dealt with at Fox News in connection with this column was polite, highly responsive, and got right to the point, while still not giving ground on a single material fact. A guy could get used to that.

Deadly Intent

Ann Coulter, Word Warrior

JUNE 12, 2006

ONCE AGAIN, ANN Coulter has a book in need of flogging, and once again, people are stunned by what a "vicious," "mean-spirited," "despicable" "hate-monger" they say she is.

Ms. Coulter, who seems afflicted by a kind of rhetorical compulsion, most recently labeled the widows of 9/11 "harpies." It is just one in a series from a spoken-word hit parade that seems to fly out of her mouth uninterrupted by conscience, rectitude, or logic.

But Ann Coulter knows precisely what she is saying. Her current book, *Godless: The Church of Liberalism,* is heading to the bestseller lists in part because she has a significant constituency and in part because no other author in American publishing is better at weaponizing words. With five books and more than a million copies in hardcover sales, she plays to win and is happy to take hostages along the way, including the women she calls "the Witches of East Brunswick."

"These broads are millionaires, lionized on TV and in articles about them, reveling in their status as celebrities and stalked by grief-arazzis. I have never seen people enjoying their husband's death so much." That typical Coulter sortie was hardly a misstep on some overamped talk show. That doozy of a sentence was written, edited, lawyered, and then published. By now, she, along with Crown Publishing, has come up with a dexterous formula for kicking up the kind of fuss that sells books. It looks something like this:

She did not come out of the gate with such ruthless aplomb. As published at the height of the Clinton-Lewinsky scandal in 1998, *High Crimes and Misdemeanors* reflected her background as a lawyer and was fairly scholarly, considering what came after it. But once her lethally blond franchise became part of public consciousness, or at least the lower stem of it that feeds off cable talk, she quickly learned that hyperbole is best sold by the ton.

She has since suggested wistfully that Timothy McVeigh should have parked his truck in front of the *New York Times,* joked that a Supreme Court justice should be poisoned, and said that America should invade Muslim countries and kill their leaders. And she recently admitted that she is "no big fan" of the First Amendment that allowed her to say all of that.

"She is so smart that none of it is by accident," said Adrian Zackheim, the publisher of Portfolio, a business imprint, and of Sentinel, a conservative political imprint. "She knows that a few things she says are bound to get attention. She just probably doesn't know which one."

But once attention, negative or otherwise, turns toward her, she is all knuckles and know-how. When Senator Hillary Rodham Clinton suggested that her attack on the widows was "vicious," Ms. Coulter went casually nuclear, saying that the senator "should talk to her husband, who was accused of rape by Juanita Broaddrick."

The second-stage rollout—picking a fight with Senator Clinton is a way, as they say in politics, to "activate the base." Only the returns will be financial, not political.

"Every single book she has done has become an instant bestseller," said Bob Wietrak, a vice president for merchandising at Barnes & Noble. "Her fan base is phenomenal, and she is in the media constantly. When she is in the media, it creates more media coverage. And every single day, the book sells more."

You get the idea. Wagging tongue, wagging fingers, and before you know it, soon enough you have hundreds of hits on Google News for days to come (this column among them).

And just when things threaten to slow down, Ms. Coulter will saw into Cindy Sheehan, who lost her son in Iraq, describing her as "a C-list celebrity trolling for a book deal or a reality show," or accuse a disabled Vietnam vet she was arguing with on a talk show of being part of the reason the United States lost the war there. Her attacks on the maimed or the bereft engage the thermodynamics of the media marketplace to send her to even loftier heights.

An explosive device is now baked into every book. For *Slander: Liberal Lies About the American Right* (333,000 in hardcover sales, according to Nielsen Bookscan), she called Katie Couric "the affable Eva Braun of morning TV." We all tuned in for the ensuing cage match, in which Ms. Couric maintained both the higher ground and the upper hand. (That interview came to mind last week when Ms. Coulter, back on a Couric-less *Today* program, treated Matt Lauer like a cat toy.)

When she was pushing *Treason: Liberal Treachery from the Cold War to the War on Terrorism* (almost 400,000 in sales), it was all about the misunderstood genius and patriotism of Senator Joseph R. McCarthy. In *How to Talk to a Liberal (If You Must)*, she let readers in on the playbook: "You must outrage the enemy. If you don't leave liberals in a sputtering impotent rage, you're not doing it right." And her sales of 301,000 for what was basically a collection of columns seem to indicate that she has mastered the form.

Godless, which is already doing gangbuster business according to the folks at Barnes & Noble, suggests that liberalism "is the doctrine that prompts otherwise seemingly sane people to propose teaching children how to masturbate, allowing gays to marry, releasing murderers from prison, and teaching children that they share a common ancestor with the earthworm."

Does she believe any of this stuff? I doubt she even knows. When I profiled Ms. Coulter a few years ago, I never figured out the line between her art and her artifice. She picked at her plate of lobster ravioli before serving up Fred Flintstone–size slabs of red meat. For the duration of the media opportunity, she was playful and on point, other than fibbing about her age, because she cares deeply about the franchise.

Her sincerity is beside the point as long as people keep taking the bait. Mrs. Clinton, who is the perfect foil for Ms. Coulter—ambitious, allergic to irony, loathed by the people who will line up for *Godless*— simply added fuel to a fire that she was presumably trying to douse. All manner of televised talkfests, including *Today,* welcome Ms. Coulter's pirate sensibilities back aboard whenever she has something to peddle, in part because seeing hate speech pop out of a blonde who knows her way around a black cocktail dress makes for compelling viewing.

Without the total package, Ms. Coulter would be just one more nut living in Mom's basement. You can accuse her of cynicism all you want, but the fact that she is one of the leading political writers of our age says something about the rest of us.

Been Up, Been Down. Now? Super.

APRIL 20, 2008

LOOK AT HIM standing there, a great big movie star in a great big movie, the Iron Man with nary a trace of human frailty. A scant five years ago the only time you saw Robert Downey Jr. getting big play in your newspaper came when he was on a perp walk.

Yet when it came time for Marvel Studios to cast the lead for a huge franchise film, *Iron Man,* it bet on Mr. Downey. He is not only back in the game but at the top of it. Is this a great country or what?

For years Mr. Downey has been tagged with two shorthand references: "the greatest actor of his generation" (for his Oscar-nominated role in *Chaplin*) was usually quickly followed by "drug-addled lowlife" (based on multiple arrests and relapses). When it comes to that duality, Mr. Downey is elliptical, but there is no mistaking that beneath all that allegorical talk there is the beating heart of a ferociously ambitious actor. Now sober, highly productive (he'll be in Ben Stiller's *Tropic Thunder* this summer), and very much engaged as he sits in his home at the end of a cul-de-sac in Brentwood, Mr. Downey seems less surprised than the rest of us.

"The people who made this movie said they were going to screen-test some people, and I thought: 'Well, that's how I got *Chaplin.* Maybe this will work again,'" he said. "If you're going to spend a hundred million bucks on a movie, why not see who works?"

It doesn't take much more than a viewing of the *Iron Man* trailer to sense that Mr. Downey walked onto the set and said, "Yeah, I got this." And there is a sincere logic behind his casting in this estimated $130 million movie, scheduled to open May 2. The backstory of genius-inventor-billionaire-arms dealer Tony Stark is plenty textured: he likes big weapons and fast women and seems to have misplaced his conscience, so it makes sense that the man who steps into both his suit of armor and his role as superhero has manifest feet of clay. After a life of squandered promise spreading mayhem everywhere, our hero has a near-death experience and finds within himself the angel of his better nature. Ring any bells?

"There are things we know about just from reading the newspaper," said Jeff Bridges, who plays a surprisingly affable villain to Mr. Downey's superhero. "He doesn't have to do anything to make it happen. The audience brings that darker part of the story into the theater. And his wit and improvisation bring it home."

Jon Favreau, the writer of *Swingers* and the director of *Elf* and now *Iron Man*, said that casting Mr. Downey was far from a source of stress.

"Nobody went to see a movie about the pirate ride at Disneyland," Mr. Favreau said by phone. "They got interested in it because of Johnny Depp. When Robert was cast in *Iron Man*, it was as if a weight had been lifted off my shoulders. He was not the obvious choice, but my larger fear was making a mediocre movie; the landscape of the superhero is very picked over. I knew that Robert's performance would elevate the movie."

Although *Iron Man* is Marvel Studios' first self-financed movie — Paramount is distributing — Marvel did not consider casting Mr. Downey to be a risk. "That an actor of his caliber and talent was willing to submit to a screen test spoke volumes about his enthusiasm," said Kevin Feige, president for production at Marvel Studios. "And his past was not a huge issue. The fact that Disney had already cast him in *The Shaggy Dog* suggested that he was more than ready to do another family-oriented film."

Iron Man is a thoroughly mortal superhero, the product of Yankee ingenuity rather than a genetic mutation or spider bite. In the film Tony Stark is imprisoned by malevolent jihadi forces in Afghanistan but uses cunning, heavy metal, and an injured but increasingly palpable heart to perform a spectacular jail break. In order to do so, he builds a kind of supercharged exoskeleton that is the other star of the show, an anthropomorphized apparatus that takes some fashion tips from the Transformers but is radical and shiny enough to impress and perhaps excite a jaded action-adventure audience.

A trace of that armor still seemed to be in place early on a recent afternoon in Los Angeles. Mr. Downey used grand flights of rhetoric to glide past questions about his past, dwelling instead on getting mobbed at Comic-Con in San Diego by all the *Iron Man* nerds and rubbing his hands together at the planned global tour on behalf of the behemoth.

When serious actors take on jobs involving comic books and hours in machines and makeup, they generally plug their noses and take the paycheck. Mr. Downey is having none of that. At forty-three he is thrilled to be fit enough—he had spent the morning with the living room furniture pushed aside for instruction in wing chun, a Chinese martial art built on aggressive, close combat—to play a hero. He views the Big Comic Book Movie as a kind of arrival after years of lead roles in movies like *The Singing Detective* and *The Gingerbread Man,* which had cinematic pedigrees but little in the way of audiences.

"I've been in big movies before and never had a problem with them," he said, munching a carry-out lunch of sole underneath a gigantic Tobias Keene painting (one of two in the room). "What is creepy and obvious is that the market was suddenly flooded with morons who thought, 'If I've got five hundred thousand dollars, I can make a baseball cap that has a company name on it and say I'm a filmmaker.'

"On the contrary," he added, "I am thrilled to have made this movie with Jon. I seem to have been the person who's had to wait the longest for this kind of gratification." He leaned forward so that the multi-hued stone medallions on a leather strap dangled as he spoke. "It took a while. Richard Attenborough," he said, invoking the name of the director of *Chaplin,* "told me that one day your ambition will supersede all of these other impulses you have, and that will help set you straight."

Mr. Downey's ambition is getting some other room to work. Later this summer he will show up as Kirk Lazarus in *Tropic Thunder,* a comedy that throws multiple grenades at war movie clichés. Mr. Downey's character is an extremely mannered Australian Method actor who undergoes a pigment change to play a soulful black soldier. There is rich historical resonance in the turn. In his writer-director father's signature film, *Putney Swope,* the senior Mr. Downey substituted his own voice for that of Arnold Johnson, his black lead. (In *Tropic Thunder,* however, the racial co-option is mocked mightily by the character played by Brandon T. Jackson, a member of the platoon who is black.) And he has just finished filming *The Soloist,* about a homeless schizophrenic who nurses hopes of performing at Walt Disney Concert Hall.

So, superhero, arch comic in blackface, and sympathetic nutball. Not inconsistent with a career that has included *Chaplin, Natural Born Killers, Less Than Zero,* and *Kiss Kiss Bang Bang,* among some fifty other films.

Then again, he was extraordinary in other ways, once showing up to meet the director Mike Figgis two hours late, barefoot, with a loaded shotgun he could not quite explain. It was a while in coming, but in 1996 police officers who stopped Mr. Downey noticed he was packing an unloaded .357 Magnum, along with small amounts of heroin and cocaine. Just a month after that he was cited for trespassing and being under the influence of a controlled substance after passing out in a neighbor's (empty at the time) home.

There were rehabs that did not work, followed by jails that did not impress, ending in hard time, twice, including a one-year stint in a state lockup where he had to fight to find a place to stand.

A winking nod to that tumultuous history is baked into the banter in *Iron Man.* The movie opens with Mr. Downey's mitt wrapped around a tumbler of whiskey, rumbling along in a Humvee, AC/DC's "Back in Black" blasting on the soundtrack, and Mr. Downey acting all lusty and incorrigible. And when Gwyneth Paltrow's character, the dewy-eyed, ever-loyal assistant he sees with new eyes by the end of the film, learns about his alter ego, Mr. Downey's Tony Stark goes deadpan.

"Let's face it," he says. "This is not the worst thing you've caught me doing."

That running dialogue—between audience and actor, between Mr. Downey's past and present—gives the film a symbolic power not usually found in comic book movies. In the interview he preferred to leave that history between the lines.

"It has struck me lately that I don't have to talk about last century at all," he said with a dismissive wave. But he does so, obliquely.

"I have a really interesting political point of view, and it's not always something I say too loud at dinner tables here, but you can't go from a two-thousand-dollar-a-night suite at La Mirage to a penitentiary and really understand it and come out a liberal. You can't. I wouldn't wish that experience on anyone else, but it was very, very, very educational for me and has informed my proclivities and politics ever since."

(Suffice it to say he is not one of the Hollywood types who weeps over innocents trapped behind bars.)

His romance with mood-altering chemicals didn't end after he got out of prison. By 2003 he was an uninsurable serial relapser famous for being pulled out of hotels or other people's homes in an addled, disheveled state. As a movie star with a lot of pals, he lived a life beyond consequence until he finally wore out the endless mercies of the entertainment business. After he was fired from his spot on *Ally McBeal*, the bottom finally came, at a Burger King of all places.

On or around Independence Day in 2003, he stopped at a Burger King on the Pacific Coast Highway and threw all his drugs into the ocean. And while he was sitting there chewing on a burger, he decided he was done. This being America, five years later you can walk into that Burger King, and if you order a Happy Meal, you can get your own Robert Downey Jr. action figure, wrapped up in gadget ware. (And what does

Tony Stark want when he escapes his kidnappers? A good old American cheeseburger—from Burger King, natch.)

Today he appears to be happily married, to the producer Susan Levin, and to have a good relationship with his teenage son from a previous marriage, Indio, who stops by at the end of the interview. All of this has come to rest in a gorgeous but not gigantic house, in a room suffused with light that bounces off a grand piano that preoccupies the room and much of his free time. It's the kind of story that might make some misty, but Mr. Downey is more prone to the mystical.

"If I see somebody who is throwing their life away with both hands and is raging around and destroying their family, I can't understand that person," he said. "I'm not in that sphere of activity anymore, and I don't understand it any more than I understood ten or twenty years ago that somehow everything was going to turn out okay from this lousy, exotic, and dark triple chapter of my life. I swear to God I don't even really understand that planet anymore."

Mr. Downey, who has said that he woke up in a pool of his own blood a time or two when he was in prison, is a fighter. "Probably the biggest thing that Tony Stark and I have in common is the hardware of conflict, the courage under fire," he said, setting aside his lunch on a tray. "I don't really fit in so good outside the military bases with my mentality."

And he has strong, if mostly unarticulated, feelings about the people who raced ahead in the public consciousness while he was otherwise occupied. He noted that a picture of Leonardo DiCaprio was prominently displayed in the *Los Angeles Times* that day, even though Mr. Downey is the one with the full dance card.

"Yeah, to do this big globe-hopping thing for *Iron Man,* my ego is saying this is a victory tour," he said. "I'm all for chanting your own name, I'm all for that kind of pride, go with that a little bit, but that's just a firing pin to give you that energy to get through all the stuff."

Ambition of a very present-tense, urgent sort is part of what keeps Mr. Downey on the road away from trouble, as opposed to heading back toward it. The three bags of black tea in his mug are about as strong and wacky as it gets these days, but there will be trials.

"I don't think I will never go that fast again, but that is based on my behavior moment to moment, whether I'm able to maintain this nice groove I'm on or whether it will all go away in a second for something that I could justify or rationalize that was none of my own doing. But that isn't real. This," he said, gesturing around the nice house with the nice family supported by an increasingly nice career, "is real."

Before They Went Bad

ALBUQUERQUE — WE are back here, back in the place where mayhem lurks just a few steps beyond the cul-de-sac in the vast expanse of desert. With a downtown that has some teeth punched out, hotels that house only ghosts, and strip malls short on commerce, time is fungible here. Is it 2014 or 1974? And where are all the people?

In this forest of billboards advertising quick-buck lawyers and tattoo removal, Walter White is nowhere in sight, having gone down in a hail of gunfire after five seasons of *Breaking Bad*. What remains is the impulse to tell the story of a fictional version of this place, of the hustlers, gangsters, and losers who live like coyotes on the edge of this town.

For years there had been jokes in the writing room and on the set of *Breaking Bad* about the Saul Goodman project, the one that would take the indelible lawyer inhabited by Bob Odenkirk and wrap an entire show around him once Walter had sold his last barrel of meth.

Then something funny happened. The joke came true.

Sitting on the set in Albuquerque in September while filming the first season of *Better Call Saul*, which is to have its premiere on February 8 on AMC, Mr. Odenkirk remembers that when the bluff had been called and the *Breaking Bad* creator Vince Gilligan and writer Peter Gould were actually writing the show, he still had his doubts.

"It was clear that Vince and Peter were setting the show in Albuquerque, and I would be away from my family for a long time," he said in a trailer while having a quick lunch between scenes. "I was worried about what it would do to my family and worried about whether I would end up being the guy who, um, screwed up the legacy of *Breaking Bad.*

"And then I talked to my daughter, who is thirteen and incredibly mature, and she said, 'It's a big opportunity, we will be fine, and if it's bad, really, how bad could it be?'

"And I said well, it won't be bad. It's written by Vince Gilligan and Peter Gould; the worst thing is it's a really interesting misfire. If that's the worst thing it is, I'd be more than happy to be part of that."

Given that the writers and actors feel that they found something authentic and remarkable in *Saul* and that the show has already been renewed for a second season, that's a pretty good punch line for something that started as a joke.

In the increasingly cluttered marketplace of television — at a time when Amazon and Netflix are winning Golden Globes, and you can't click a remote without bumping into some version of quality programming — there is a huge advantage in spinning off a storied franchise. But building on the embedded awareness of the character from *Breaking Bad* also means dealing with all the expectations that go with it. That tension informed everything about the execution of *Better Call Saul.*

For one thing, it is a prequel, set six years before Saul and Walter became known associates. Mr. Odenkirk is not playing exactly the same character. Instead, he is Jimmy McGill, a knock-around guy with a law degree who cannot catch a break or a decent case. The series is the story of how a guy who struggled to stay between the lines and above the belt became Saul, a criminal lawyer who is more criminal than lawyer. In the time frame of the new show, Walter is still teaching high school chemistry, perhaps to Jesse Pinkman, somewhere offscreen, and Mr. Odenkirk's character, rather than guiding the events around him as Saul did, is lost, blown about by forces beyond his control.

Then again, it is about as far from a lawyer show as you can get, long on character and less concerned with classic plot lines or courtroom procedure. Without giving away (too many) spoilers, I will tell you that the show opens in the future, after Walter's downfall and Saul's dispossession of his greasy empire. Saul is in his own version of witness protection, tucked away in the kind of job no one sees in a place where everyone goes. He is a hunted shell of the smack-talking lawyer, who finds solace in running old tapes of his once ubiquitous commercials beckoning one and all to call Saul. It is grim and scary, but the vibe is as much *X-Files* (which Mr. Gilligan used to write for) as it is *Breaking Bad.*

And then the tape ends and we are back to where Saul started, as Jimmy McGill, a slip-and-fall shyster trying to walk back to more honorable pursuits by taking on public defender work. Short on real clients, he is looking after the interests of his brother, Chuck McGill (Michael McKean), a brilliant, successful lawyer who has lost his marbles and refuses to go outside. He also works hard at earning the interest of another lawyer, an icy beauty played by Rhea Seehorn, who sees right through Jimmy and still can't stay away.

She sees in Jimmy what we all do, which is a beautiful loser who trouble clings to like a halo of flies but who could talk the birds out of trees.

"I had no interest in doing some legal procedural," Mr. Odenkirk said in between twelve hours of shooting interiors with Mr. McKean. He told the writers to "push my character into really extreme situations."

Mr. Gilligan and Mr. Gould, the co-creator of this show and a writing mainstay of *Breaking Bad,* were happy to oblige. "Jimmy is a guy who doesn't know who he is yet," Mr. Gilligan said by phone from Los Angeles, where he and Mr. Gould were attending the semiannual Television Critics Association conclave of journalists. "He is struggling to be more than he is, and there is a poignancy to that."

Mr. Gould said Jimmy was determined to do the right thing, unless the right thing ends up being the wrong answer. "There are lines in the sand," he said, "but the lines end up shifting based on the circumstance."

Part of the reason they are continuing to write for Mr. Odenkirk is that they have not yet gotten to the end of what he can do. Saul was conceived as a little comic leavening for *Breaking Bad.* They decided a fast-talking consigliere would bring some funny to the proceedings and thought of Mr. Odenkirk—they were fans of his dating to *Mr. Show with Bob and David,* the 1990s sketch series on HBO. And then Mr. Odenkirk got to work, and Saul became less of a sideshow.

"The more we worked with him, the more soul and depth we found," Mr. Gilligan said. "We loved that he was funny, but there was so much range there. He crushed it so completely that we started to daydream about what else we could do."

It was still a dicey decision to take a fetish object like *Breaking Bad* and roll it backward. AMC, which produced the series along with Sony Pictures Television, said it was actually an easy call.

"There has never been a more challenging time to launch a series," said Charlie Collier, the president of AMC. "But Vince Gilligan and Peter Gould are storytellers, and when they tell you that they have more stories to tell about someone, you pay attention."

For a while, the co-creators, who could write their own ticket given the success of *Breaking Bad,* tried to talk themselves out of it, but they kept returning to Saul in part because they had fallen in love with the landscape and aesthetic of Albuquerque. "I was nervous about it, and I still am," Mr. Gilligan said. "Not everyone who takes a look will love what we did with it, but that goes with the territory."

Both Mr. Gould and Mr. Gilligan have made it clear they are making the first season of *Better Call Saul,* not the sixth season of *Breaking Bad,* and viewers should not expect to see Bryan Cranston or Aaron Paul. But we are in the same neighborhood, so it should come as no surprise that Mike Ehrmantraut, the beloved hit man played by Jonathan Banks, rears into view, his quiet fearsomeness contained for the time being by the parking garage booth where he first meets Mr. Odenkirk's character.

In *Breaking Bad,* Saul served as an odd sort of moral center, finding a thin reed of humanity in vile circumstance, all the while filling up the safe between fake Greek columns with lots of ill-gotten gains. His ability to pivot from the absurd to realpolitik is just as compelling to behold in its nascent state in *Better Call Saul.*

Until recently, Mr. Odenkirk was known as a comic, writer, and impresario who could pull laughs out of very unlikely places. Before that, he was an Emmy-winning writer for *Saturday Night Live, The Ben Stiller Show,* and *The Larry Sanders Show.* But in addition to his head-turning performance in *Breaking Bad,* in the past few years he had a well-reviewed turn in the FX series *Fargo,* and also received great notices for his film work in *Nebraska* and *The Spectacular Now.*

Mr. Odenkirk credits his acting run with a "poor sense of boundaries," nothing more. "People always tell me how honest I am, and the truth is I don't know how to be brave in that way," he said. "I just don't know how to play it any different."

On set, he admitted that even though he was filming the eighth episode of a ten-part season, he had no idea how the first year would end. "They offered to send me outlines, but I have enough to worry about learning the dialogue that I have for each episode and to be fully present for anything in that moment," he said, pushing back the hair that grew to be almost its own character in *Breaking Bad* but is now much more sedate. At fifty-two, he is playing a much younger version of his *Breaking Bad* character and has the kind of boyishness that makes it not much of a reach. There is a very un-actorly earnestness, a complete absence of vanity, to Mr. Odenkirk. Having led his own show and run a set, he requires none of the wide berth generally given to a lead actor. "Maybe I don't have the reverence for *Breaking Bad* that I should, but I love this show and I'm crazy happy to have been a part of it," he said. "And I already know that we are never going to repeat the social and viewing phenomenon of *Breaking Bad.*"

Mr. Gilligan agreed. "I would not predict for a minute that it would be as big of a hit as *Breaking Bad,* but I am every bit as proud of this show," he said.

Better Call Saul is driven less by macabre plot points than a character-heavy look at the burdens of the human condition and the price of one man's soul. It's less frantic than *Breaking Bad,* relying on an anchored camera that zooms in for long, hard looks. It is carefully constructed, with an emphasis on physical detail and sound that makes Jimmy's law office in the back of a nail salon seem more like a jail cell than a place of business.

It is a writerly series put out by people who scan as writers, first and foremost. "Peter and Vince are a lot more like playwrights and novelists than screenwriters, and on set, Bob is always reading three books at the same time," Ms. Seehorn said. "There are so many nuances to the work we are doing. We know where Saul ends up, but nothing here is played on the nose. There is always something underneath what is being said and done."

There will be a few surprises along the way, unpleasant for Jimmy but fun to watch. One trademark of the *Saul* writing team is rendering villains of epic proportions, and viewers might see a few familiar faces in Season 1. After all, finding compelling outlaws around here is as easy as spotting snakes in the desert.

Calling Out Bill Cosby's Media Enablers,
Including Myself

NOVEMBER 24, 2014

WITH PUBLIC REVULSION rising in response to snowballing accusations that Bill Cosby victimized women in serial fashion throughout his trailblazing career, the response from those in the know has been: What took so long?

What took so long is that those in the know kept it mostly to themselves. No one wanted to disturb the Natural Order of Things, which was that Mr. Cosby was beloved; that he was as generous and paternal as his public image; and that his approach to life and work represented a bracing corrective to the coarse, self-defeating urban black ethos.

Only the first of those things was actually true.

Those in the know included Mark Whitaker, who did not find room in his almost five-hundred-page biography, *Cosby: His Life and Times*, to address the accusations that Mr. Cosby had assaulted numerous women, at least four of whom had spoken on the record and by name in the past about what they say Mr. Cosby did to them.

Those in the know also included Ta-Nehisi Coates, who elided the charges in a long and seemingly comprehensive article about Mr. Cosby in *The Atlantic* in 2008. Those in the know included Kelefa T. Sanneh, who wrote a major profile in *The New Yorker* this past September and who treated the accusations as an afterthought, referring to them quickly near the end of the piece.

And those in the know also included me. In 2011, I did a Q and A with Mr. Cosby for *Hemispheres*, the in-flight magazine of United Airlines, and never found the space or the time to ask him why so many women had accused him of drugging and then assaulting them.

We all have our excuses, but in ignoring these claims, we let down the women who were brave enough to speak out publicly against a powerful entertainer.

Mr. Whitaker has said he didn't want to put anything in the book, which he wrote with Mr. Cosby's cooperation, that wasn't confirmed— which of course raises the question of why he wouldn't have done the work to knock down the accusations or make them stand up.

And given that the accusations had already been carefully and thoroughly reported in *Philadelphia* magazine and elsewhere, any book of the size and scope of Mr. Whitaker's should have gone there.

Mr. Coates recently expressed regret on *The Atlantic* website that he did not press harder on Mr. Cosby's conflicted past. In the course of his reporting, he said, he came to the conclusion that "Bill Cosby was a rapist."

He added: "I regret not saying what I thought of the accusations, and then pursuing those thoughts. I regret it because the lack of pursuit puts me in league with people who either looked away or did not look hard enough."

I was one of those who looked away. Having read the *Philadelphia* magazine article when it was published, I knew when the editors of the airline magazine called that they would have no interest in pursuing those accusations in a short interview in a magazine meant to occupy fliers.

My job as a journalist was to turn down that assignment. If I was not going to do the work to tell the truth about the guy, I should not have let him prattle on about his new book at the time.

But I did not turn it down. I did the interview and took the money.

I paid for that in other ways. The interview was deeply unpleasant, with a windy, obstreperous subject who answered almost every question in fifteen-minute soliloquies, many of which were not particularly useful.

After an hour of this, I mentioned that the interview was turning out to be all A and no Q. He paused, finally.

"Young man, are you interested in hearing what I have to say or not?" he said. "If not, we can end this interview right now."

Mr. Cosby was not interested in being questioned, in being challenged in any way. By this point in his career, he was surrounded by ferocious lawyers and stalwart enablers, and he felt it was beneath him to submit to the queries of mere mortals.

He was certain of his own certainty and had very little time for the opinions of others. Mr. Cosby, as all of those who did profiles on him have pointed out, was never just an entertainer but a signal tower of moral rectitude.

From the beginning, part of his franchise was built on family values, first dramatized in *The Cosby Show* and then in his calling out the profane approach of younger comics and indicting the dress and manner of young black Americans.

Beyond selling Jell-O, Mr. Cosby was selling a version of America where all people are responsible for their own lot in life.

He seldom addressed bigotry and racism. Instead, he exhorted individuals to install their own bootstraps and pull themselves into success. And while they were at it, they should pull up their pants and quit sagging, a fashion trope Mr. Cosby found inexcusable.

It proved to be a popular theme with white audiences and less so with black ones. A generation of black comics who revered other pioneers such as Richard Pryor found Mr. Cosby's lectures tired and misplaced.

But that moralism, which put legs under his career as an author and a public figure, made Mr. Cosby a target. In 2005, ABC News reported on accusations of a former Temple University employee, who said that the entertainer drugged and fondled her.

That was followed by a report on the *Today* show that he had done the same thing to Tamara Green, a lawyer in California.

The *Philadelphia* magazine article, with a more comprehensive list of victims, came out in 2006 and was followed by a piece in *People* magazine about Barbara Bowman, who said that she was drugged and assaulted. And then the story just died.

Mr. Cosby was (mostly) out of view, his lawyers pushed back and tried to knock down every story and victim, and no one in the media seemed interested any longer. Mr. Cosby was old news, he had been investigated but never criminally charged, and there seemed to be little upside to going after a now-ancient story.

But as Mr. Cosby's profile rose again when it became clear that he would get another ride on television with planned shows on NBC and Netflix, so did the scrutiny.

In February of this year, *Newsweek* published accounts from two of his victims, including Ms. Green, who called Mr. Cosby a "rapist" and "liar."

In the end, it fell to a comic, not an investigative reporter or biographer, to speak truth to entertainment power, to take on the Natural Order of Things.

On October 16, the comedian Hannibal Buress took the stage in Philadelphia, Mr. Cosby's hometown, and railed against the incongruity of his public moralizing and private behavior. He told the audience, "I want to just at least make it weird for you to watch *Cosby Show* reruns." (TV Land has since canceled those reruns, and both Netflix and NBC have shelved projects with Mr. Cosby.)

He said Mr. Cosby had the "smuggest old black man public persona that I hate. Pull your pants up, black people. I was on TV in the eighties. I can talk down to you because I had a successful sitcom."

And then he dropped the bomb. "Yeah, but you raped women, Bill Cosby. So, brings you down a couple notches."

Social media, a nonfactor when the accusations first surfaced, feasted on a clip of the set posted on *Philadelphia* magazine's website.

On the heels of Mr. Buress's routine, Mr. Cosby's public relations people asked his Twitter followers to make funny memes of the entertainer, and that promptly backfired in a huge way.

With NBC and his other former partners having jettisoned Mr. Cosby, his lawyers were left alone in the bunker, denying the charges and playing Whac-a-Mole against accusations from women that are popping up everywhere. And on Sunday the *Washington Post* published a comprehensive recap of the charges.

For decades, entertainers have been able to maintain custody of their image, regardless of their conduct. Many had entire crews of dust busters who came behind them and cleaned up their messes.

Those days are history. It doesn't really matter now what the courts or the press do or decide. When enough evidence and pushback rear into view, a new apparatus takes over, one that is viral, relentless, and not going to forgive or forget.

All Hail the Helix

DECEMBER 1, 2002

THE FOUR OF us gathered on the sidewalk in front of a downtown club after a glorious night, full of the self-assured chatter that suggested we were all at the height of our powers in the white-hot center of things. The tribal rite now complete, our hipness assured, it was time to say good night. My companions offered to share a cab, and then they remembered, "Oh yeah, he lives in Jersey." In an instant, a night's worth of easily won cachet vanished.

Human beings do endless things to keep dissonance at bay. In this instance, it was I who pitied them. While they would creep home through a tangle of tiny streets and cluttered neighborhoods, I would hop into my car, dive into the Lincoln Tunnel, and emerge on the Helix, a huge curve where New York, the greatest city on earth, would reveal itself in a mountain of lights and glory. The Brooklyn Bridge has its views, but for my money — five dollars a day — the wide-angle perspective on the Helix is the money shot.

If you ignore the lineup of cars and the drivers muttering oaths against their lot, the Helix is a graceful, improbable thing. Technically, a helix is a curve whose tangents are all equally inclined to a given plane. The shape can be found at the top of Ionic columns in medieval architecture, as a building block of DNA, or as a feature on some of the better mini-golf courses. Helix is also the name for a common genus of snails, but as a commuter, I find that particular allusion a bit too traumatizing to dwell on.

According to the Port Authority, the Helix feeds the busiest tunnel on earth, with 120,000 cars entering three separate tubes of belching combustion. In the morning, the traffic guy on the radio with the *whup-whup* of the choppers in the background often tells me that I will be spending a half hour of quality time in a conga line of cars waiting to snake into the thirteen-foot-high holes.

I either love it or pretend I do, taking the idle time as an idyll during which I peer through the morning haze at the crisscross of ferries and the undulating city behind it: the striving glory of downtown, the valley of the Village and Chelsea, interrupted by the sudden verticality of Midtown. When I cross my eyes slightly, a seductively Rubenesque outline emerges. I know it by heart and feel its effects there as well.

Having an adjacency to a place like New York, rather than occupancy, provokes a variety of reactions in New Jersey citizens. A retired Newark police lieutenant I know could not come up with the last time he had been in the city. Others simply lie and tell people next to them on airplanes that they live in New York or cut to a joke about the Sopranos. I cope by telling myself that I love coming to the city every morning and that I am just as thrilled to depart at night.

It is not all a lie. To live in Manhattan is undoubtedly a privilege and a convenience, but the majesty of the place is invisible from within. To see New York as one of humankind's greatest creations requires reverence born of altitude or distance, something New Yorkers generally leave to tourists. Like me.

The compulsion to come into the city—and that is what the tunnel is for; no one should pretend it is an escape route—is as old as the city itself. There was a time when the primary requirement for making it in New York was a willingness to get lucky, as E. B. White suggested, but these days, an E-ZPass is a safer bet. In the short distance of about eight thousand feet, a person from New Jersey can go from a place that is a punch line to a place that it is a pickup line.

For a time, I had the greatest commute on earth. I would hop a train to Hoboken and then a ferry to downtown. The sheer improbability of the Twin Towers, buildings I never knew enough to hate, rarely failed to thrill me. I would stand at the front of the ferry in all weather, humming something, probably Wagner, as we bounced over the waves. After the attack, I couldn't bear the daily intimacy with devastation. Instead, I hit the Helix and swore every time as the smoke rose for weeks on end.

I have since changed commutes. For a time I became a drone on the bus, a cheap and ostensibly easy way to go. But I quickly came to loathe it: No matter how sparkly the evening was in New York, the line for the number 66 bus at the Port Authority would vaporize the magic.

So, I drive. Therefore, I am a civic evil. Even if Manhattan needs me, it certainly does not need my car. Did I mention that it is an SUV? Among other things, it affords better views over the wall on the Helix. At night, hitting that curve where the city unfurls, twinkling and beckoning, I never fail to say good night or to revel in my good fortune for living as close to the stars as I do.

View, Interrupted

The Spoiling of Manhattan's Skyline

MAY 31, 2014

MANHATTAN IS AN island of serious wealth, endless ambition, and impossibly expensive real estate.

It is also an actual island, which means that some people are priced out for a variety of reasons and leave at the end of the day. That would include me. That means a bridge, a tunnel, or a helicopter. (Then again, if you have enough money for a chopper, you can probably live where you like.)

In my case, I live in northern New Jersey and commute through the Lincoln Tunnel, either by bus or by car, traveling on the so-called Helix. When it is not under construction, which is frequently, the Helix is an engineering marvel, a nearly circular switchback straight out of the roller-coaster school of architecture that allows cars and buses to descend from the bluffs above to the shoreline below, and reverse in ascent.

There are a lot of us at the Lincoln Tunnel: every weekday, more than 100,000 cars, buses, and trucks pay a significant toll in time and treasure to gain access from New Jersey to Manhattan, and then line up to flee at the end of the night.

It can be brutal. After a day of fighting for a place to stand on the island to get business done amid a thicket of self-important people in a hurry, we are again back in the queue, waiting our turn. But halfway up the Helix, the city we just left roars into view in side profile. Big on top (Midtown), thinner in the middle (Chelsea and Greenwich Village), and big on the bottom (downtown), the city is irresistible, a sexy colossus in Rubenesque recline. For a few brief seconds, we all stare at what many believe is the greatest city in the world.

It is, I have found, an easier place to love at this distance. Climbing the Helix each evening used to be an ideal time to assess my day of scurrying about at the feet of those majestic behemoths. Twinkling against a glowing sky, the city said goodbye in its own way, and I returned the favor. If on that day the city opened up before me like a giant, improbable rose — it happens — I would blow it a kiss. If, on the other hand, the city had had its way with me, punishing without mercy, I deployed one of my fingers as a gesture of rebuke. Most often, though, the city had both punished and uplifted. On those days, I still used the finger but gave the finger a kiss as I did it.

The hybrid gesture, weird I know, was an acknowledgment that even though the city or some of its inhabitants may not have been kind to me, I still loved it anyway. New York doesn't beg for forgiveness, but I and many others offer it unbidden. Even if I don't own a piece of it, it owns a piece of me — while I am happy most nights to leave it, I never imagine saying farewell for good.

But that reverie has been reframed and mostly ruined. For the past several months, two new apartment buildings have been creeping up over the lip of the Helix on the New Jersey side, obscuring what was once a million-dollar view. The buildings are ungainly in their nascent state and very much in the way. Regardless of how they will look once they are finished in shiny skin, they will be solid and opaque, stationed between the Helix and Midtown across the river, smack-dab in the way of New Jersey commuters who have, for decades, greeted the city in the morning or waved goodbye at night.

The Estuary luxury apartment buildings in Weehawken will rise to 90 feet, according to an article in the *Star-Ledger*, enough to block the view for many precious seconds but lower than the 160-foot office-and-apartment proposal that was floated back in 1999. I'm sure it will be a lovely place to live, with amenities that include a rooftop deck, a golf simulator, a yoga room, and a fire pit. And there is, of course, that incredible view.

I don't mention any of this in the belief that the township of Weehawken or the developers will come to their senses and stop in mid-hammer swing. What's done is done. (Speaking of which, after coming down the Helix and seeing downtown on fire after the attacks of September 11, I have watched the city rebuild, a time lapse of recovery the new buildings won't erase.)

But something glorious, a view held in common by thousands of people who come to New York for the same reasons people always have, will now belong to a precious few. It's not only a perfect metaphor for our times but a cold fact that I stare at every day. I often mutter oaths, not at the men and women building it—everyone has to work at something —but at the people who decided that a view that is the visual equivalent of Wagnerian opera was something to be auctioned off.

Weehawken's mayor, Richard Turner, told the *Star-Ledger* that some of the view will be preserved and that for those who want the full expanse, "my answer always is, move here."

I'd prefer to stay put. And I will continue the slog into the city, but there will be something missing from my ride.

There's still a brief interlude of New York cityscape I can see from my bus or car seat if I pay attention, but I don't look that way so much anymore. When I look toward the city, I don't see the glorious handiwork of human hands—I see what happens when those hands don't know when to quit.

I keep my own hands in my lap and my kisses to myself.

Breaking Away, but by the Rules

AUGUST 29, 2003

EVERY SUMMER FOR the last three years, my family has left our home in suburban New Jersey for weekends at a camp in the southern reaches of the Adirondacks in Upstate New York. Our getaway, a cabin with a tin roof—but nice floors—is framed by a low-slung mountain rising over Jenny Lake, a glorious little spring-fed oasis. To buy the camp, we sought and obtained membership in the Tawiskarou association, which governs our part of the lake.

In an official history that was written in 1976 to celebrate the fifty-year anniversary of Tawiskarou, there are two divergent translations of the name: "Bright and Sparkling Waters" or "Place of Chilly Winds." But when I bought the place from a friend, and I asked where the name Tawiskarou came from, he had another explanation. "Oh, that's Iroquois for 'Lake of Many Rules,'" he deadpanned.

The rules are mostly common sense, but strictly observed, as if a children's summer camp had suddenly been invaded by mature, scrupulously careful Eagle Scouts. The rules begin with there being no motors allowed on the lake—a glorious one, that—and then descend through a litany of evils that include fishing or boating in the swimming area, clearing trees without board permission, and listening to Eminem, or any other amplified music, on the beach.

By agreeing to abide by those rules, my family escapes the humdrum of daily life by embracing a more remote, but no less regimented, version of a civil society and has been rewarded with a summer of memories of a grand place that we share with splendid people. But this Labor Day weekend when we button up the summer house, deploying the mouse poison before we wanly close the door, we leave behind a burning political issue that is as much a part of life at Tawiskarou—or almost every other summer retreat—as evening bonfires and morning canoe rides.

The Hamptons has its bar wars, the Vineyard has its continuing development set-tos; at Tawiskarou, we have the diving board debate. A few years ago, the board on the floating dock gave out. As a diving board qua diving board, it never had much in the way of leverage; it was, in fact, little more than a hard plank that floated on barrels. But the argument over its absence has had plenty of bounce. At the annual meeting in midsummer, I suggested that the missing board had left a hole in our community's quality of life, depriving us of a launching pad for cannonballs and swan dives. During the run-up to the debate, I did some lobbying on the beach: "The right to dive is right up there with the right to vote as an entitlement of American life," I suggested. Thus informed, I expected they would take up pitchforks and lanterns to support an obviously worthy cause.

They formed a committee instead.

Polls have been taken, estimates are underway, but there are incipient signs of opposition. I was down at the tennis court the other day, and one of the Brahmins of the place mentioned that the Boy Scouts had outlawed diving altogether because of the liability issues involved. "Welcome to life at Tawiskarou," the old-timer said, all but pointing out that at three years in residence, I was a bit of an arriviste.

Down on the beach, where the heat of association intrigue is quickly surpassing the waning summer sun, the diving board supporters are madly speculating.

Of course, the people who serve on the committees and do the work that makes this place seem like paradise have no particular agenda beyond the common good, but that doesn't stop the rest of us from jaw-boning about various conspiracies that are afoot.

There must be some small but virulent part of me that wanted the intrigue. Even on my limited budget, if I wanted a second home where I could dive, burp, or do pagan dances at will, I could have made that choice. Instead, I leave a neighborhood where I know almost no one—and pay attention to even fewer of them—to spend weekends at a place where I actually care what my fellow travelers think of me.

In becoming a member at Tawiskarou, I agreed to abide by each and every rule. And so I have. More or less. The adult in me knows that the rules set us all free, but the weekend warrior within chafes at the strictures. The act of leaving the city carries the promise of freedom, one that seems all the more tangy and exciting when there is someone, anyone, willing to put a limit on it.

A crew of resident constables can be counted on to rise up from their Adirondack chairs when someone steps over the line. I am hardly immune to the mores of our Eden. When I saw some renters eating on the beach—a felony in our little world—I felt compelled to speak up lest somebody step on the crust of peanut butter sandwich on their way to the lake. "We eat up here," I clucked as I gestured to the grassy expanse behind the beach. "It makes it easier to keep the beach clean," I added helpfully. But the concern for the common good can make fun a little less common.

Now, I'd do anything to have a voice in those rules, except what it would take, which is running for the board and showing up at the meetings. I helped put in the docks this year and once cleared rocks on common land with an association member whose main form of recreation seems to be working tirelessly on behalf of the rest of us, but I'm usually a little too busy working on my table-tennis forehand to become too involved.

Last week, I was savoring a last, exquisite day at the beach when someone dropped her magazine and squinted into the sun as she asked me if I had seen the bulletin board. A notice had gone up asking for volunteers to help remove the beaver dam that had blocked the outflow and raised the level of the lake. It had come in for some anonymous annotation, probably from some children with time on their hands, who suggested that the beavers should be allowed to live in peace.

We live several hundred yards from the lake, so I have no dog in the hunt. The lake could go up or down and I would hardly notice, but some small part of me is worried that the beaver dam controversy will make people forget about the great diving board controversy of 2003.

7

All the Rest

The Wrestler

Remembering the Fights That
Philip Seymour Hoffman Won

MEDIUM, FEBRUARY 4, 2014

ONE OF MY favorite Philip Seymour Hoffman performances did not happen on or off-Broadway or on a big screen.

At the Independent Spirit Awards in 2008—a party on the beach meant to celebrate indie excellence the day before the Oscars—Hoffman was there to receive the best male lead award for his role in *The Savages*, a quiet film that unfolds into something spectacular. Rainn Wilson was the MC, and he did a great job, mugging, joking, and provoking. From the dais, he kept calling Hoffman, indie film royalty in this context, "the Hoff."

The event itself is always fun. Low stakes, lots of booze, and drunk celebrities in a tent on the Santa Monica beach. What's not to like about any of that? Even if you don't consume adult beverages—Hoffman was in that bunch—it was easy to enjoy the spectacle of actors in full frolic.

Somewhere near the end of the event, Wilson called out "the Hoff" once more, invoking, as I recall, their shared background as high school wrestlers. A gauntlet was thrown, and the two men collided mid-room, rolling under tables, grappling for their lives in a ferocious, spontaneous death match. Hoffman had a belly, but the man was not soft—he

gave as good as he got, huffing and puffing the whole time. One thing
led to another, his pants slipped, and he was selling a fair amount of
crack. It was not his best feature, but he did not seem to care, instead
concentrating on the matter at hand, which was fighting Wilson to a
joyous and crowd-pleasing standstill.

I saw him on the way out, and we walked back the match. I had wres-
tled in high school as well. "If I just would have opened a little stronger,"
he said, smiling. "He sorta got the drop on me to start." So . . . game,
ferocious, and always thinking about how he could have done it better.

Covering entertainment means that you come across people whose
faces you first saw twenty feet tall on a movie screen. They tend to shrink
when you meet them, but Mr. Hoffman was far from disappointing in
person. He didn't enjoy press even a tiny bit but knew everyone had a
job to do and mine, on occasion, was covering him during the awards
season. And he was always available for a quote about a fellow actor or
a project he was working on. He was a professional, and a kind, decent
guy to boot.

Some actors survive the press needs of the job by staying within a
narrow bandwidth of discourse, treating the world as a red carpet to be
endured as they step-and-repeat their way through interviews. Hoffman
wasn't like that. He listened to questions, thought about it, and actually
tried to answer them.

It's easy to get confused covering celebrities. You make fake friends,
born of transactions and mutual needs, but there is no human relationship under that. I was not pals with Hoffman, but he was uncommonly
gracious. He remembered my name, which is something of a parlor
trick given how many reporters actors see in the course of a career, and
gave me his phone number so I wouldn't have to run a gauntlet of fac-
totums just to ask a question or get a quote.

He also knew that I was in recovery, and we chatted about that a bit.
In that context, he was authentic and insightful.

Now that he is gone, much has been said about his failure, about his
fall. I don't really see it that way. He got in the ring with his addiction
and battled it for two decades successfully, creating amazing film work

along the way and doing the hard stuff to keep ambitious theater alive in New York.

And then something changed and he used. Everyone is surprised when that happens to someone famous, but it happens routinely everywhere else. Rooms of recovery are full of stories of people with long-term sobriety who went back out, and some of them, as a matter of mathematics and pharmacology, don't make it back.

Chemical dependency does not change—have one and you might die—and recovery does not change—have none and you might live. Addicts live between those two poles, but the hole that they once tried to fill with chemicals always remains, pushed back on a daily basis. Addiction, whether you believe it is a disease or not, is a pirate, constantly on patrol and looking for a weakness so it can climb aboard.

I have no certainty about what went wrong, but I can tell you from personal experience that what happened was not the plan. I have been alone in that room with my addled thoughts, the drugs, and the needle. Addicts in the grip always have a plan. I will do this, get this out of the way, and then I will resume life among the living—the place where family, friends, and colleagues wait and hope. He didn't make it back to that place.

We have the work, the memories, the films. I feel the loss, like all of his fans, but mostly I feel sad for him and those who knew and loved him. He built an amazing life while the rest of us got to watch, and somewhere in there he forgot or lost the ability to enjoy the promises that recovery had delivered. I don't blame him or condemn him or second-guess him. He did the best he could with everything that he had.

Press Play

Making and Distributing Content in the
Present Future We Are Living Through

COURSE SYLLABUS, BOSTON UNIVERSITY COLLEGE OF
COMMUNICATION, AUGUST 4, 2014

THIS COURSE, PRESS PLAY, aspires to be a place where you make things. Good things. Smart things. Cool things. And then share those things with other people. The idea of Press Play is that after we make things we are happy with, we push a button and unleash it on the world. Much of it will be text, but if you want to make magic with a camera, your phone, or a digital recorder, knock yourself out. But it will all be displayed and edited on Medium because there will be a strong emphasis on working with others in this course, and Medium is collaborative.

While writing, shooting, and editing are often solitary activities, great work emerges in the spaces between people. We will be working in groups with peer and teacher edits. There will be a number of smaller assignments, but the goal is that you will leave here with a single piece of work that reflects your capabilities as a maker of media. But remember, evaluations will be based not just on your efforts but on your ability to bring excellence out of the people around you. Medium has a remarkable "notes" function where the reader/editor can highlight a specific word, phrase, or paragraph and comment, suggest a tweak, or give an attaboy. This is counterintuitive, but you will be judged as much by what you put in the margins of others' work as you are for your own. To begin with, we will look at the current media ecosystem: how content is conceived, made, made better, distributed, and paid for. We will discuss finding a story, research and reporting, content management systems, voice, and multimedia packaging, along with distribution and marketing of work. If that sounds ambitious, keep in mind that in addition to picking this professor and grad assistant, we picked you. We already know you are smart, and we just want you to demonstrate that on the (web) page.

Together, we will make a collection of stories on Medium around a specific organizing principle — it could be a genre, topic, reading time, or event — which we'll decide on in collaboration as well. And once we get stories up and running, we will work on ways of getting them out there into the bloodstream of the web.

In order to have a chance of making great work, you have to consume remarkable work. *Fair warning: there will be a lot of weekly reading assignments.* I'm not sliming you with a bunch of textbooks, so please know I am dead serious about these readings. Skip or skim at your peril.

I will be bringing in a number of guest speakers. They will be talented, accomplished people giving their own time. Please respond with your fullest attention.

So, to summarize: We will make things — in class, in groups, by our lonely selves — we will work to make those things better, and, if we are lucky, we will figure out how to beckon the lightning of excellence along the way.

More info:

GRADING

30% final project

30% collaboration, based on assessment of your notes on others' work

20% class participation and demonstrated familiarity with the assigned reading

20% smaller assignments

I grade based on where you start and where you end. Don't work on me for a better grade—work on your work and making the work of those around you better. Show industriousness and seriousness and produce surpassing work if you want an exceptional grade.

PERSONAL STANDARDS

Don't raise your hand in class. This isn't Montessori; I expect people to speak up when they like, but don't speak over anyone. Respect the opinions of others.

This is an intense, once-a-week immersion on the waterfront of modern media-making. If you don't show up for class, you will flounder. If you show up late or unprepared, you will stick out in unpleasant ways. If you aren't putting effort into your work, I will suggest that you might be more comfortable elsewhere.

If you text or email during class, I will ignore you as you ignore me. It won't go well.

I expect you to behave as an adult and will treat you like one. I don't want to parent you—I want to teach you.

Excuses: don't make them—they won't work. Stories are supposed to be on the page, and while a spoken-word performance might explain everything, it will excuse nothing. The assignments for each week are due by start of class without exception unless specific arrangements have been made based on an exceptional circumstance.

If you truly have a personal or family emergency, your welfare comes first. But nothing short of that will have any traction with me.

If you are having trouble understanding expectations or assignments or instruction, please speak up. I care a lot about not leaving anybody behind.

ACADEMIC STANDARDS

This is a web-based course. We will transparently link to all sources. Failure to appropriately cite the work of others is a serious matter. Work done for Press Play may not be submitted for another class, and the reverse is also true. Do not use friends or Wikipedia as sources. All other

BU academic standards and the University Code of Conduct will be observed and enforced.

READINGS

Weekly assignments as noted in the outline. *The assigned reading for each week must be completed before that class.*

Before we begin the semester, do read:

"The Case for Reparations" by Ta-Nehisi Coates for *The Atlantic*

"The Empathy Exams" and "Fog Count" by Leslie Jamison (I highly recommend her whole book, btw, but it is not assigned as such)

"The Wrestler" by David Carr for Medium

(*subject to significant emendation*)

1. State of Play

Overview of the state of narrative and content. A foreshadowing of what is to come in class and in the media environment. A discussion of the production and distribution of content, with a focus on both editorial and business dynamics. Short introduction and tutorial about Medium. (*You can do yourself a world of good by signing in early to Medium before class,* so you won't be trying to figure out the content management system instead of actually writing in it.)

Random assignment into writing groups of four.

READINGS:

"Newspapers and Thinking the Unthinkable" by Clay Shirky

"2013: The Year the Stream Crested" by Alexis Madrigal for *The Atlantic*

"Baptism by Fire" by N. R. Kleinfield for the *New York Times*

"Why Did Jodon Romero Kill Himself on Live Television?" by Jessica Testa for BuzzFeed

2. Choosing Targets

Where do great stories come from? A discussion about how to choose persons, places, or things that lead to remarkable stories. Class will discuss and settle on an organizational principle for story collection on Medium.

Brief in-class writing assignment.

Due next week: A story on Medium that takes advantage of the format and can be read in under five minutes.

READINGS:

"Dr. Gilmer and Mr. Hyde" by Sarah Koenig for *This American Life* (audio)

"Consider the Lobster" by David Foster Wallace for *Gourmet*

"The Emperor Miramaximus" by David Carr for *New York*

3. You Are What You Type On

We look at various content management systems and platforms for making and distributing content on the web. A discussion of how, more and more, the medium is becoming the message.

Due today: First draft of Medium story #1 (under five minutes).

Due Friday, Sept. 26 at noon: Edits and feedback on group members' drafts —please make all notes public by Friday at midnight.

READINGS:

"The Remains of the Night: Sex, Trash and Nature in the City" by Elizabeth Royte for Medium

Glass, a blog on Quartz by Zach Seward (read a few days' worth)

"Deep Sea Cowboys" by Joshua Davis for *Epic Magazine*

4. Collaboration

How new and different eyes make things better. We look at how to provide constructive feedback without crushing the soul of the writer. A visit from an esteemed editor will be part of this class. There will also be some real-time edits in class.

Due today: Read the comments by your group members, professor, and TA on your work.

Due next week: Final Medium story #1.

READINGS:

"My So-called Stalker" by Anonymous for *Washington City Paper*

"At Flagging Tribune, Tales of a Bankrupt Culture" by David Carr for the *New York Times*

5. New Business Models for Storytelling

Historically, publications have created things people want to watch and read, and then extracted circulation revenues from the audience and advertising revenues from companies that wanted to reach that audience. Both those models have come under heavy pressure and pushed some media outlets—along with the people who work there—off the table. Are there other ways of supporting storytelling? A look at referral sales, branded content, and the vanity press.

Due today: Final Medium story #1.

Due next week: Just the readings.

READINGS:

"What Journalists Need to Know About 'Content Marketing'" by Shane Snow for Poynter.org

Google Hangout with Brian Lam of *Wirecutter* and Kevin Kelly of *Cool Tool*

"GE Becomes Legitimate Online News Publisher" by Lucia Moses for *Digiday*

6. Storytelling Innovations

What good is the fact that we now have the tools to do almost anything on the web if we don't do anything with them? A look at the new forms of storytelling, using data, video, sound, and scrolling to tell sticky, remarkable stories. I will be traveling, so you will have a surprise guest lecturer.

Due today: Just the readings.

Due next week: First draft of a short profile (1,000 words) on an interesting person of your choosing.

READINGS:

Arcade Fire's *Reflektor* by Vincent Morisset

"India's Toilet Crisis" by Emily Gibson for Berkeley Graduate School of Journalism

"The Most Deranged Sorority Girl Emails You Will Never Read" by Caity Weaver for Gawker

"Zombie Underworld" by Mischa Berlinski for *Epic Magazine*

7. The Holy Music of the Self

Personal essays can be dreary or magical — how do you pull yours out of the mundane? How to find the universal in the specific and render it in a way that aims toward transcendence, not self-aggrandizement? Special guest TBD.

Due today: Submit Essay 1 to appropriate collection; first draft of profile (peer edit your group's work throughout the week).

Due next week: Final draft of profile, incorporating any comments from your group.

READINGS:

"Amazon Is Killing My Sex Life" by Tricia Romano for *Dame Magazine*

"Me and My Girls" by David Carr for the *New York Times Magazine*

8. Voice Lessons

How to quit sounding like everyone else and begin sounding like . . . yourself. Who you are and what you have been through should give you a prism on life that belongs to you only. We will talk about the uses and abuses of a writer's voice, how to express yourself in copy without using the "I" word, and why ending stories with a quote from someone else is often the coward's way out.

Due today: Final profile draft, submitted to appropriate Medium collection.

Due next week: Pitch for your final project.

READINGS:

"Your Rape Fantasy Is Boring, Katie Roiphe" by Hamilton Nolan for Gawker

"The Princess and the Trolls: The Heartrending Legend of Adalia Rose, the Most Reviled Six-Year-Old Girl on the Internet" by Camille Dodero for Gawker

9. Distribution Models

So you made something wonderful. Now, how do you get anyone besides your boyfriend/mother/professor to read it? A discussion of social media marketing, the Collections feature on Medium, wooing the trolls of Reddit, and submitting to relevant digital and print publications.

Due today: Pitch for final project (due by email by start of class).

Due next week: Submit profile pieces to Persons of Note collection by start of class. Final pitch and proof of content due in class. (Have you made contact with any subjects? Can you prove your pitch is an achievable goal?)

READINGS:

"The Six Things That Make Stories Go Viral Will Amaze and Maybe Infuriate You" by Maria Konnikova for the *New Yorker*

"Click Print Gun" by Erin Lee Carr for Vice Media

"Statistics: Measure the Impact of Your Story" on Medium

10. Beyond Clicks: A Look at Reader Engagement

If clicks are overrated and traffic is a game, what is a meaningful measure of what is making a dent in a cluttered universe? A look at the new economics of audience, advertising, and paid content. This class will include a guest lecture, if all goes as planned, by Tony Haile of Chartbeat.

Due today: Final pitch and proof of content. Profile pieces should be submitted to Persons of Note by start of class.

Due next week: Come to class with what you have so far on your final projects, to workshop in small groups.

READINGS:

"2013: The Year the Stream Crested" by Alexis Madrigal for *The Atlantic*

"What You Think You Know About the Web Is Wrong" by Tony Haile for Time.com

11. Telling Stories in a Visual Age

If we are going to be writing for an audience of visual learners, can typing solve all of our problems? Probably not. A look at image-based social media, including Instagram, Pinterest, and Vine. And we will peer in on the video content economy — what works, how long is too long, and can serious content go viral on YouTube?

The formula for good narrative video: shot well, there are experimental elements to engage jaded viewers; a cultural nerve is hit and begets conversation and sharing.

Due today: Bring to class what you have so far on your final projects.

Due next week: Submit drafts of final projects to Press Play collection by start of class. Your small group, David, and Mikaela will make notes on them over Thanksgiving.

VIEWINGS:

"Life After Food" by Brian Merchant for Vice Motherboard

"Getting High with Russia's Spiderman" by Ralph Avellino and Masha Charnay for Vocativ

"Interview with a Cannibal" by Santiago Stelly for Vice

12. Pitching for All the Marbles

Is it more important that you fit in or stick out? At what point does a pitch cross the line from persistence to stalking? How to elbow your way in, get noticed, and leverage who you are and what you have done. A lot of miscellany, including how to target pitches, best time of day to send them, and how long to make them. Work for free or no? Send the whole story or just a pitch? And when to take "no" for an answer.

Due today: Semi-final drafts of final projects should be submitted to the Press Play collection by start of class.

Due next week: Make notes on your group's work, as early in the week as possible. Final projects due, along with a plan for social media dissemination, by start of class.

READINGS:

Media Equation column on Epic by David Carr for the *New York Times*

"Behold the Heart-Breaking, Hair-Raising Tale of Mexico's Monkey Woman" by Tim Stelloh for BuzzFeed

13. The Unveil

In-class presentation of final projects, with audience feedback, notes, and digressions on finer points of storytelling. Class stories will be assembled in collection on Medium, and we will push the button to publish. We will also discuss plans for dissemination via the social medias, US Postal Service, megaphone-wielding wildebeests, etc.

Due today: Final projects, along with a plan for social media dissemination.

Due next week: List of metrics on how your project was shared (be prepared to talk about distribution strategies, wins, and failures). Also due: a short critique of Medium as a CMS and learning platform.

READINGS:

Your classmates' stories!

14. So What Have We Learned?

A look back at the things we made and lessons learned about the art of collaboration and distribution. In the present future, is there really a dividing line anymore between print, web, radio, and video? We'll take a long, hard look at the media ecosystem and your place in it.

Due today: List of metrics on how your final project was shared, and a short critique of Medium (800 words or less) as a content management system and a platform.

READINGS:

"The Rise of the Personal Franchise Site in News" by Jay Rosen for
   PressThink
"Can Rupert Murdoch Hold On to Kara Swisher?" by Felix Salmon
   for Reuters
"Ezra Klein Is Joining Vox Media as Web Journalism Asserts Itself"
   by David Carr for the *New York Times*

Addendum

The good news is that this is the first time that I have taught this class, so boredom will not be an issue. It's also the bad news, because even though I have done a great deal of teaching over the years, it's the first time I've been an actual professor and have had to string together an entire semester. You are a beta, which means things will be exciting and sometimes very confusing. Let's be honest with each other when that happens. If you don't get where I am going or what I want, say so. I care deeply that I do a good job in all endeavors, especially this one. I expect you to work hard and want to respond in kind.

And just so you know, to speak to Mikaela is to speak to me. I lean hard on her and trust her judgment. Just saying.

Not need to know, but nice to know: Your professor is a terrible singer and a decent dancer. He is a movie crier but stonefaced in real life. He never laughs even when he is actually amused. He hates suck-ups, people who treat waitresses and cabdrivers poorly, and anybody who thinks diversity is just an academic conceit. He is a big sucker for the hard worker and is rarely dazzled by brilliance. He has little patience for people who pretend to ask questions when all they really want to do is make a speech.

He has a lot of ideas about a lot of things, some of which are good. We will figure out which is which together. He likes being challenged. He is an idiosyncratic speaker, often beginning in the middle of a story, and is used to being told that people have no idea what he is talking about. It's fine to be one of those people. In Press Play, he will strive to be a lucid, linear communicator.

Your professor is fair, fundamentally friendly, a little odd, but not very mysterious. If you want to know where you stand, just ask.

All That You Leave Behind

Bicycling, SEPTEMBER 3, 2013

I HAD ALREADY decided that I was going to stay on the bike no matter what. After weeks of postponements and calendar conflicts and over-time work hours, I was finally in the saddle and pedaling. The dread I had felt about riding—or really about all the riding I wasn't doing—began to fizzle away as I set off on a training loop near Great Sacandaga Lake, in Upstate New York.

It was early July, and I had set aside a few days to start preparing for a weeklong ride I was hosting a few weeks hence with a group of friends. I pedaled a circle around the top of the mountain near my cabin, just northeast of Saratoga on the first big rise of the Adirondacks. Then I dropped down a long, steep hill. There was only one way back up, so the real training would begin soon enough. First, though, I cruised over twenty miles of rollers on the shoreline that made for nice riding. My bike, pretty much custom-built with an elevated handlebar to accom-modate my unique physiological quirks, was running smooth, and I was starting to feel okay. The rugged ascent loomed.

About that dread I'd been feeling: I know it probably sounds odd. Most people with this sort of vacation on the horizon spend days and nights dreaming about quality time in the saddle. And the last time I headed out on a bike tour with some of the same friends, to Colombia,

I'd had one of the best weeks of my life. But I had trained hard for that one—the Andes have a way of getting your attention. This trip had snuck up on me.

Even with a decent amount of training, I'd be no threat to blow up a Peloton. A fifty-five-year-old with a complicated health history, I had dropped a few parts along the way. I have no gallbladder, no spleen, one kidney, and half a pancreas, partly because I had cancer and partly because doctors have permission to go most of the way toward killing you in order to save your life. Long-ago radiation treatments left me with a severely angled and constricted neck, which complicates my ability to see where I'm going. And in my younger days I'd spent more time bent over a shot glass, an ashtray, or a cocaine-lined mirror than a handlebar. During my twenties, which is the prime of many cyclists' lives, I became one of those skeevy crackheads you try not to stare at when you come across them on the street.

So, not the prototypical leader of a complicated cycling vacation, but here I was. Today's ascent back up the mountain would be ugly and wobbly, but I've done plenty of long climbs out of low places—so much so that I feel like the odds are in my favor when they're against me. It's familiar, comfortable even. I pulled over for water and to gather myself. But before I could unclip, I hit some sand and tipped over, pulling my arms in to protect myself. When I landed, my right arm cracked a rib underneath it.

I eventually got to my feet and looked up that hill with new eyes.

Adirondack Park, in spite of its proximity to the densely packed Northeast, is the largest protected area in the contiguous United States. At more than six million acres, it's bigger than Yellowstone, Yosemite, Glacier, the Grand Canyon, and Great Smoky Mountains national parks combined. It holds a relatively ancient place in the American narrative, with many roads dating to the Revolutionary War. There are soaring mountains, pretty lakes, and big wooded hollows—but it's not necessarily the first place you'd pick for a long-haul bike ride. Because any development arose from logging, the roads are few and far between and the towns are scattered. Unlike the nearby cycling paradise of Vermont, the Adirondacks make you earn every lunch, every cheap motel bed.

These logistical challenges were complicated by the fact that I had never planned a bike trip before. I entombed myself in a mound of road maps and cycling books and hammered away at Google until I eventually emerged with what seemed like a working itinerary—albeit one that was still partially based on hopeful guesses. My idea was to do a loop that made a necklace of various lakes, with the jewel of the High Peaks region in the middle: six days, about three hundred miles total. Our ethos would be to go cheap and ride until something beautiful pulls us off our saddles.

Your vision of such trips may involve a posse of fit, like-minded people who double-check their maps, their equipment, and their plans, then hit the road. This would not be one of those.

We were a loosely connected bunch of newspaper-reporter types who had two things in common: our chosen profession and John Otis, who had worked for me as an intern in Minnesota a long time ago. Afterward he had headed off to Mexico with a typewriter in his bag and minimal Spanish. He's been working in Central and South America as a journalist ever since. John is a strong rider, capable of gliding up the giant La Calera outside Bogotá, and an even stronger friend. His wife, Alejandra, is a Colombian journalist and the kind of relentless low-and-slow rider who can climb anything. About two decades ago, John began organizing come-as-you-may bike trips in far-flung locales. Unlike me, the riders who show up don't sit in a cube in New York City. The trips tended to attract folks like John—people who have worked as correspondents in Beijing, Kabul, Rio de Janeiro, Baghdad, and beyond.

The riders come and go in this bunch, but the vibe does not change. Someone initiates a thread of email that continues until a quorum emerges and a caper is launched. This time I volunteered to lead. There was a crisscross of emails about who was in. I knew John and Alejandra were bringing their young sons, Martin and Lorenzo. Tim Johnson, a journalist who has lived, worked, or filed stories from eighteen countries across Latin America, the Middle East, and Asia and now lives in

Mexico City, was coming with his teenage daughter, Sofia. And there were rumblings about an appearance by Shannon O'Reilly, who runs a bike company in Managua, Nicaragua.

I'd met Shannon, fifty-eight, only once, in his shop, where he mostly sells cheap commodity bikes, often from China, that workers use to get to their jobs. I'd heard he was a magnificent rider, but he was unimpressive as a digital communicator. He never confirmed, so as the days ticked down, I planned for the seven, including me, who had. In late July we all gathered at my home in Montclair, New Jersey, and began loading the van for the trip to my cabin. I was in the house when I heard shouts from the porch, where people were unpacking bikes from long flights: "Shannon's here!"

Sure enough, there he was in my driveway . . . accompanied by his wife, Ninoska, his teenage stepson, Gustavo, and his young daughter, Naomi. Shannon, a thrifty sort, had transported himself, his family, and all their gear to Montclair using public transportation. Their sudden appearance knocked me off balance—and where were the bikes?

Shannon pointed to a little roll-away suitcase. "My bike's in there," he said.

Aha, he had brought along one of those fancy fold-up models—although it seemed unlikely that even one of those would fit in that tiny piece of luggage. Then he opened it up, and there was a really dreadful child's bike, sawed into three pieces, with jerry-rigged iron connectors to bolt it together. There was also a saddle with a two-foot post so Shannon, six-foot-one, could ride the contraption.

This complicated the logistics, but I tried to roll with it—something that is not necessarily my strong suit. A few years ago, after someone told me I was "not nice," I came home to run it past my wife: *Of course I'm a nice guy, right?* "Well, it's not really what you feature," she said, delicately. Not fun to hear, but probably good to know. I have a kind of social autism, often speaking in brutally honest ways when I should not. And I am frantically impatient. Not the typical leader of a complicated cycling vacation. But here we were.

The next morning we set off from my house in the van, which we christened *Chancho Volador,* the Flying Pig, because I drove fast and hard even though it was stuffed with all eleven of us and had all manner of bikes and gear hanging off willy-nilly. We looked less like a bike-touring outfit than the Joads from *The Grapes of Wrath.* Up at the cabin we got the bikes assembled and tuned, and the following morning, finally, we pedaled away.

Few things feel better than those first few turns of the pedals, all fresh muscles and joy at being underway. I believe it's best to beckon gravity to begin a trip in good spirits, so we started a sixty-mile day with a lovely ride down to the Sacandaga River. Broken but serviceable asphalt gave way to mild gravel as we entered a cool tunnel of trees on the descent, the damp smell of woods reminding us that we were not just looking at pretty things but very much a part of them. On the bridge over the river, I promised the group if we all came back in one piece, we would hit the churning whitewater below in tubes.

We left the town of Hadley, no more than a crossroads, and entered a beautiful stretch of road to Stony Creek. We spread out over the rollers, our butts and legs beginning their long, individual negotiations with the saddles and terrain. Pedaling through a gorgeous, low-traffic, pine-filled valley, I fretted some about my lack of training and whether our newly formed, multiwheeled organism would grow and click over the next few days. The first fart joke — "Jet power engaged!" — came around mile 21. To our right, the first big bump of the Adirondacks loomed. My still-mending rib throbbed in unison with my labored breathing.

I looked around at our little pack. There were people who could ride rigorously and those who would not be fast if they pedaled every day for a hundred years. Some had the fat content of a can of diet soda, and others — no names need be mentioned here — were akin to bags of potato chips with legs. There were some who didn't speak English, others who didn't speak Spanish, and still others who were fluent in Mandarin. Gustavo was riding the spare bike I keep in my garage. Shannon's seat post on his toy bike looked like it was bending under his weight, while the gears and chain muttered and clanked. He had missed the last two trips for reasons lost to the mists of time, so I knew him mostly by legend. The stories were that he always showed up on rolling death traps built with knockoff parts—but also that he was strong, capable of pushing others up steep mountains with an outreached hand, even on his Frankenbikes.

John and Alejandra traded time driving the sag wagon so they could entertain Martin and Lorenzo, ages seven and four. Shannon's wife took a seat with their daughter, Naomi, ten, who regarded my attempts at friendliness with suspicion and found my forays into Spanish appalling. That left seven of us out on the road bikes . . . most of the time. My rib gave me tacit permission, I decided, to bail if the conditions got too tough.

That happened just after our first lunch, in Stony Creek. Faced with a long climb into the higher reaches of the park, I decided it was suddenly critical that I guide the group by sag wagon. It was a brutal rise, not like the endless switchbacks in the Alps or Andes, but rather a series of straight-up tooth grinders. At the crest we found swampy pine stands and empty roads. I struggled to keep the kids under control and the riders supported, but near the end of the day we were all more or less accounted for. I hopped on my bike for the last few miles into North Creek—the equivalent of Rosie Ruiz's faux finish at the Boston Marathon—then found out that our cheap motel was actually back out of town and many miles west.

I took my time during that last, unexpected leg, falling back behind the pack—not that I had a choice. I felt sheepish wobbling into the hotel, but the group was spilled out around the gravel parking lot, watching Martin and Lorenzo have turns on Shannon's teeny, weird bike. I took a few loops around with them as the others cheered.

The next morning we got up early and munched takeout pastries and coffee as we got ready. That day featured a fifty-mile haul to Long Lake. Some of us were eager to get on the pedals, and others needed to get kids squared, and before all the frogs were in the wheelbarrow we set off at different points without having huddled about route and destination. Oops. A few hours later, someone—that would be the fearless leader, the impatient one who wanted things to go just so—failed to wait for Alejandra at the turnoff into North Creek.

We ended up in town, in a small pool of shade in front of a coffee shop, while the van made ever-widening loops searching for the now missing Alejandra. Because we had limited cell coverage and a mish-mash of international plans, we had no phone capable of reaching her. The locals suggested calling the sheriff.

Allie, as her husband, John, calls her, is a talented rider and journalist, but her defining characteristic is a heart as big as South America. When I was going down to Bogotá for our ride there, she told me on a Skype call with her husband that she was "waiting for me with open legs." We had a long laugh about that, but it makes the point: I was able to imitate a human being because I was surrounded by other, good ones.

Still, as the minutes stretched into hours, I waited for someone, maybe me, to start freaking out. We were, after all, facing two immutable facts: One was that someone in our group had seemingly disappeared into the wilds of the Adirondacks. The other was that as the sun moved over-head and we remained off our bikes, my well-laid plans, and very cool route for the day, were on the verge of crumbling.

When I rode with this group in the Andes, I would swear off cigarettes forever on the way up, then want nothing more than to smoke one when I reached the pass. Silly, really, but there it is. And no one who knew me well would have been surprised.

Most of my life I have struggled with addiction of one type or an-other. I took to drinking early on. My first two-wheeled love had a motor, but that relationship lasted only until I took off in an impaired state, fell hard, and broke my foot. I never rode a motorcycle again, but I began to chase the booze with drugs. My boyhood friend Tim invited me on a few bike rides, but when I did the math on the quantities of schedule 1 narcotics I would need to load in the panniers, I waved him off. The only trips I took were long jags in rooms brimming with cocaine, light-ers, and pipes. The only campfires I sat around were the flames I bent over with other junkies, watching crack form or disappear into a swirl of toxic smoke.

When you are locked in that kind of addiction, people riding around on bikes might as well be wearing jetpacks. It seems impossible that you could pedal away from chronic abuse. Improbably, though, I wound up with sole custody of twin baby girls—which was when I realized I had to change things. As somebody you wouldn't trust to look after a ficus plant, I was an unlikely caregiver, but we found our way. Eventually I got sober. I got work. I got married. I got promoted. I ended up running a weekly newspaper in Washington, DC, where occasionally I would pedal around the neighborhood with the kids. Then one day I watched a guy who looked a lot like me climbing the hill next to the National Cathedral, and it came to me: *I could do that.*

A romance with cycling began in earnest. Around the block or in a big loop, the elegance and symmetry of the human-powered machine thrilled me. I began commuting from the edge of the District to Adams Morgan and back. Pretty soon, on weekends, there were rides through Rock Creek and along the Potomac. And soon after, longer loops out into Virginia and Maryland. I was never a serious roadie, but I strapped toe clips onto my hybrid and ran nice thin tires. Thirty miles, forty, then fifty, by myself, just taking it all in. My obsessiveness, which had long pulled me into the ditch, became something else on a bike: The series of discrete actions repeated over and over accessed the addictive autodidact in me. Like the weekend hacker at the golf course, I always expect my next swing will bring fresh glories. And sometimes that happens.

This is the point where you might expect me to write that the hard-earned endorphins of a good ride fill the hole left by the absence of chemically induced ones, but that is both true and not. Cycling helped me become a different person, one willing to wait for that moment when everything became aligned as opposed to trying to conjure it with mood-altering substances. I became more patient, someone willing to invest in the next pedal stroke to see what was around the bend. I fell off both the bike and wagon along the way. But to the extent I am good at anything other than falling down, it is getting back up, at overcoming low expectations—many of them my own—to do things I didn't think I was capable of.

While I had proven I could be part of (the back of) the pack, I worried that leading a trip would access the less pleasant aspects of my emotional machinery. I would see if I had evolved to the point at which I could be subsumed into the ad hoc democracy on which every bike trip —the good ones, at least—operates. And now as I waited, stewing over Alejandra's absence, I used a recovery-program triage before opening my mouth: *Does it need to be said? Does it need to be said by me? Does it need to be said by me now?* The answers were usually no. My best strategy, I realized, was to keep my piehole shut about my plans, try to be helpful in figuring our way out of this jam, and just let the trip happen however it might.

We waited. A cop stopped by after a few hours and said someone who'd been listening to the police scanner had found Alejandra at an ice cream parlor thirty miles north, which made sense because that girl can go. We hopped into the van to catch up, and I gnawed the bone of regret as we sped over a remarkable bike route. But the reunion was joyous, and the ice cream was good.

We all got back on our bikes, this time huddling before we set off. Riding along rolling hills through farmland, we came across a guy who had flatted and stopped to see if we could help. He said he was in the middle of a one-hundred-mile ride and had what he needed to get back on the road, so we took off again. Soon after, the lone cyclist passed our group on a climb, and he was so much faster, I felt like we were riding underwater. I watched him turn into a lone dot on the next hill and felt a surge of happiness that I was surrounded by my group. The anxiety of the day and my role in it—why hadn't I waited at the cutoff?—gave way to something else more abiding, a tribal feeling of belonging.

On a freakishly steep incline to the Adirondack Museum, I huffed my way along with my head down. I felt my pedals gain a sudden power and looked up to see Shannon beside me, pushing me up the hill. The legend turned out to be true.

The museum was a gorgeous place that provided a prism of history through which we could view the rest of the ride. And then it was all downhill, a sweet four-mile drop through lakes, bogs, and majestic pines. We stayed at a historic inn near Long Lake, and I snuck off and rented a pontoon boat. The kids did cannonballs while the adults nursed beers, taking in mountains that dropped right into the water. Naomi, the ten-year-old whom I had resolved to wear down over the course of the week, finally gave me the time of day when I invited her to drive the boat all the way back to the dock.

The next day we pushed deeper into the High Peaks. The smooth roads had generous shoulders, and I was starting to get my bike legs under me while my neck and rib went quiet. We fell in for the long ride toward Saranac Lake, which would put us just outside Lake Placid. I stayed with the others as long as I could, then let them gradually pull away, feeling less left in the dust than left to my own thoughts. I liked working my way up the hills with no one looking or rooting me on.

And I liked that even on a group ride you get plenty of solo time, accompanied by your own breath. I thought about how I was essentially the weird old guy among three families. My daughter Erin, twenty-four, had been eager to go, but I'd told her that she'd have to pay her corner of the expenses, and she decided it wasn't in her budget. I now saw that that was ferociously dumb—I would have plunked down large money on the spot to have her along, but the larger lesson will remain.

I thought about my first group ride, with some variation of this pack, in Minnesota's lakes region. I had been stunned by the dynamic. Bossy by nature but a weak rider in context, I quickly learned that the needs of the many sometimes pivot around the needs of one. People would look after me because I would, hopefully, look after them. In early recovery I had tried for years on my own to put down the bottle, to set down the pipe, then some kind of uphill would occur in my life and I would lose heart. I ended up in Eden House, a scary building in downtown Minneapolis—at least to my white, suburban eyes—full of last-stop knuckle-heads like me. And over the course of six months I went from regarding my fellow travelers with suspicion to understanding that I needed them in a very fundamental way if I was going to get anywhere.

When you're no longer caught up in the solipsism of addiction, you become tied to others with a yarn made of shared experience: *Did you see that hawk? Wasn't that meatloaf amazing? Why do they call it Arepa Hill?* I also learned that if you jawbone too long in the morning, you'll be left behind, and that as hard as it is to keep up, riding alone is orders of magnitude harder. I liked the shared rolling narrative—the roommate jokes, the stops for pie, the running cracks about my training cigarettes. All of it.

In Colombia, my second bike trip, John had set up a meticulous itin-erary full of remarkable descents, hellish climbs, and little villages that unfolded like the jungle flowers around them. We ate and slept as kings. I vowed many times on ascents I would never ride with these guys again, and at the end of the trip I swore I would never miss another.

At Saranac Lake, about 175 miles into the trip, we arrived at the wa-ter's edge and Gauthier's, our beau ideal of lodging: cheap, comfort-able, near good food, and with a drive-up vibe that made for encounters with others. Tim and Sofia were having an animated chat with a maid, and I approached only to find they were speaking Mandarin. I was ex-periencing parts of the globe I never would have without my worldly companions.

One of the great things about biking through lake country is that you're never far from intermodal transportation. There were kayaks stacked up right behind the motel, and not long after we got off our bikes we were again eyeing one another, talking smack. We lined up for races, then began paddling furiously.

The next day in Lake Placid was a shocker. After days of long rides and thin traffic, I found the bustle of the place overwhelming. We grabbed a picnic lunch and got out of there as quickly as we could. We set out through Keene Valley heading to Split Rock Falls, and it was the kind of ride you read about in, well, a cycling magazine, but rarely get to enjoy. The majesty and rideability of the High Peaks were astounding. The pitch of the hills allowed me to keep spinning at a good tempo, so I began to pedal hard on the descents rather than giving in to a rolling break. I rode with Tim then Gustavo then Alejandra, our legs pumping steadily while up in the saddle all was calm and chatty. I was having a moment.

Split Rock Falls was one of the amazing swimming holes I'd planned to hit along the way. I had been looking forward to showing the bunch how you can leap forty feet into a cauldron of foam, but a driving rain broke out soon before we arrived. No matter. We pulled up and began piling into the pool amid the downpour. It was starting to feel as if we had formed our own weather system, inside of which it was always seventy-five degrees and sunny.

We remounted and headed hard east toward Lake Champlain and the Westport Hotel, one of the nicer spots I'd booked. We were too ragtag by now for the fancy dining room, so we ended up at a restaurant on a deck down on the shore of Lake Champlain, Vermont beckoning across water reflecting the settling evening sun. For a time I'd agonized over whether I should have opted for the verdant lanes there instead, but as I ticked back through the past few days I realized the roads less traveled in the Adirondacks had made for a more complete adventure.

The next day was as remarkable as the one before, but in a very different way. Something about cycling along a huge body of water—first Champlain, then Lake George—makes the miles fly by. Six days in, riding for me had become more pleasure than struggle, feeling like second nature again. The last night on the road was in a place with a full kitchen just off the shores of Lake George. We decided to eat in, and I noticed how everyone scattered and came back together over a big dinner without any formal division of labor. We had become a working unit on the bikes and off.

Then all that was left was the promised whitewater run. Most tourists sign up with a rafting company, but we just grabbed a bunch of inner tubes and serious life jackets. We huddled together beforehand again, for the last time, and I gave a dry-land lecture about not standing up in rushing water, leaning away from the drops into big holes, and making sure we were in position for the pullout at the end. The river was a place I knew well, one in which I had guided many trips without any casualties. I looked into the faces of the people around me, a mix of big smiles and bike grease, and felt a lumpy pride from being with and in front of this amazing bunch. We slid into the water and used a wire, strung from the dam above us, to make our way into the middle of the river together. Then we all let go at once, laughing and screaming as some force greater than all of us grabbed us and took us wherever it would.

Cats

FROM *Cat Is Art Spelled Wrong,* EDITED BY CAROLINE
CASEY, CHRIS FISCHBACH, AND SARAH SCHULTZ, 2015

I DON'T HATE all cats. I like only one. Her name is Aligato.

Aligato is my neighbor's cat, and even though she craps in my yard as if she owned the joint, I've come to enjoy her charms.

She stays out late, she prowls. One of her eyes is either gone or permanently shut because, well, she's a bit of a brawler. When she does come on my porch, she always says hello and looks me right in the eye with her one good eye. She likes being petted, and she even comes when she is called. She is, in other words, a dog.

So my favorite cat—well, actually the only cat I like—is really a dog in a cat suit. The rest of them, the millions on the Internet, at my friend's apartment in the city, in the cat lady's house up the street, I do not like. It's not that I hate them, it is only that I return their indifference. Cat owners lavish love on their pets and are convinced they are receiving something in return. What exactly are they getting back? A rub against the leg or hand? It means the cat has an itch, nothing more.

I asked Ben Huh, king of all Internet cats and the dark overlord of I Can Has Cheezburger?, why, with all of the tropes, memes, and wild critters on the web, cats came to rule. He said it was very simple.

"The Internet is a playpen for cats where you never have to smell or clean the litter box," he said.

But why love something that won't love you back, whether it is on the Internet or in your home?

"Cats are like having a teenager. They just look at you over and over and say, 'Can I have more stuff?'" he said. "They don't really do anything; they lay about, so it's hard to tell cats apart from teenagers, except teenagers hang out at malls more. And yet people still love their teenagers. And their cats."

I will admit that some of my best friends are, and there is no nice way to say this, cat people. My cousin Peg in fact sent me a T-shirt from the Walker's Internet Cat Video Festival, assuming I'd be happy to sport some cat wear. I love the Walker and the fact that I am from Minneapolis, and I love rocking a vintage T-shirt that suggests as much. But cat wear? Not. Going. To. Happen.

I have no intrinsic problem with the festival; it's just that even though I'm sure there are tons of normal, fun-loving Minnesotans at the events, if I spread out a blanket there, I would end up with the woman who had two scrawny cats on leashes, a stack of photos as thick as a deli sandwich of Sprinkles and Ms. Diva doing their thing, and a sweater with cats all over it, both knit into the garment and, in a less organized pattern of cat hair, all over it.

I'm not unmoved by the sight of a cat on the web playing the piano, but unless they are going to kick into a decent version of Chopin's First Ballade, opus 23, there is going to be a limit to my amazement by this time.

Cat people can be nice people. A dear friend of mine lost his cat —the cat was old and led a very long and selfish life—and I felt terrible, but it was because I loved my friend, not because I loved his cat. I tolerate my friend's cats the same way they tolerate me. We don't look at each other, and as long as we are not competing for the same food, we get along fine. It is only when a cat hops onto a table—something a dog cannot and would not do—and begins snacking that I draw the line. A cat on the table is a deal breaker, more unappetizing than seeing the mouse scurrying in the corner that it refuses to go after.

All other domesticated animals that humans adore are working animals. It's a historical fact that cats were once prized for their ability to eliminate rodents, their one domestic chore, but most cats I know are on strike, content with being on the Meow Mix dole.

Cats were domesticated not for their usefulness but because they were mooches and hung around humans, acting all cute and cuddly just for the snacks. Dogs save people, sniff out bombs, pull sleds, herd sheep, guide blind people. Cats are mostly good at finding a sunny spot in the apartment and doing a series of lazy stretches that would not pass muster in a beginner's yoga class. On the Internet, the cats' greatest hits usually show them doing stupid stuff involving aquariums, television, and mirrors, which aren't really tricks so much as cats expressing their inner aggression and narcissism.

Yes, in most developed countries there are more cats than children, but as soon as we figure out how to train two-year-olds to poop in a box and are able to leave them home alone for hours on end, you can bet those percentages will reverse.

Whenever cat lore comes up, cat advocates will always mention that they were deified and mummified in Egypt, but let's remember that those pharaoh cat lovers enslaved thousands to build cats' pyramids, actual humans who were treated far less well. And throughout history, who were witches always hanging out with? Oh yeah, cats. The witch doesn't want a friendly labradoodle around; she wants a black cat as a like-minded familiar as she goes about her evil deeds.

In popular culture, the first icons that pop to my mind cat-wise are Garfield, Cat Woman, and Cat Stevens, all of whom have rather conflicted reputations. And who is the big star on the web these days in the feline world? Oh yeah, Grumpy Cat has six million likes on Facebook, all for her specialty of giving mean looks to everyone, which frankly doesn't strike me as remarkable—cats do that all the time.

I am not immune to the charms of the feline form. Cats, as the Internet has taught us, are cute because they are both ferocious and ador-able. They are predators rendered in miniature with all the tools of a killer—fangs, claws, a mighty pounce when they are not too fat—but they are harmless because of their size. That means that their hunting instincts are now aimed at rodents, hapless amphibians, and bugs. But make no mistake: when they dream, they dream large, of the days when they and their ancestors ruled the earth, loping along, scanning for food, and hitting the afterburners when they saw prey.

And if those dreams came true, if evolution reversed and they again became big and ferocious, the relationship with humans would both change and, in some ways, be the same. When you come through the door at the end of the day, your cat sees one thing: food. It knows that it is time to eat, and you will obediently get its kibble and put some nasty wet food on top because, well, you are its slave.

If cats suddenly woke up saber-tooth size, they would still see food when you walked through the door, except you would be dinner. You don't like to dwell on it, but you know if they were big enough, they would snack on you as if you were a field mouse. They might toy with you a bit, letting you make a feckless attempt to flee before they gath-ered you back toward their hungry maw with a swipe of their paw.

Remember Timothy Treadwell, the guy who thought he was a friend to all grizzly bears in *Grizzly Man*? They were not his friends, as Werner Herzog, the director of the film, says in the narration. Looking at Tread-well's filmed footage of his bear friends, he says, "I discover no kinship, no understanding, no mercy. I see only the overwhelming indifference of nature. To me, there is no such thing as a secret world of the bears. And this blank stare speaks only of a half-bored interest in food."

There is no such thing as the secret world of cats, or if there is, they own you instead of the other way around. Be honest with yourself: How many times have you looked into your cat's eyes and seen not the won-ders of the universe but "a half-bored interest in food"? It'd eat you if it could, and seeing as it can't, it just stares at you until you come up with something they can.

All the anthropomorphizing and speculating you do about what is in your cat's little noggin? For naught. Your cat's brain weighs under an ounce, is the size of an avocado pit, and contains just as many deep thoughts. Cats have mastered the art of looking wise, but that uses up all the gray matter they have—which reminds me of a boss I once had, but that's a much longer story.

Cats are different from us. You and I might hear a songbird and delight in God's creation. A cat will hear the same thing and do its best to kill and eat that bird, putting an end to the music and the creature that made it. Yes, they are expressing their inner, feral nature, but let's face it, any animal that will kill a pretty bird singing a song is pretty damn gangster.

My dog Charlie, a blond Lab and a girl, by the way, chases squirrels but does not catch them, a perfect version of the suburban wild kingdom. Every night she waits by the door and has a single question when I walk in: "Am I loving you enough right now?" She stares right into my face as she all but breaks herself in wagging with excitement. When she settles down and I ask for a kiss, she will stop what she is doing—unless she is eating—and come over to me. She will look up at my face adoringly and slowly place one paw and then the other on my leg and hoist herself up and give me one delicate lick on the nose. And then she sits back down. When is the last time you saw a cat do that? Put that in your Internet browser and smoke it.

You could say it is because my dog has no taste in companions, to which I would say, exactly. What I want in an animal companion is blind loyalty, unconditional love, and steady adoration. If I wanted another being to take me in with baleful indifference when I come home every night, I would have stayed married to my first wife.

So, in my family, we are dog people. That does not mean that if someone dropped a box of kittens on our doorstep we would ignore their mewling or their helpless adorableness. We would find a way to help them survive and find homes, but not ours, because kittens inevitably become cats, and that's where the problems begin.

My daughter Erin is an independent filmmaker and lives in Brooklyn, which is not code for unemployed and living off her rich father, because she does not have one. In Brooklyn, finding a place to live that you can afford is a war. Erin found such a place on the rougher side of Williamsburg, and she moved in with a guy she knew through friends. It is a nice apartment; she finds a way to make the rent, but somewhere along the way, her roommate picked up a cat named Latoya.

Latoya embodies all aspects of feline malevolence. She is a fat calico who hates everything, including my daughter, except yogurt, which she will stop at nothing to get a face full of if you try to eat it near her. She is mean because it is her nature, often walking into Erin's bedroom and staring her down as she takes a dump on the floor, or giving her a look over the shoulder as she pukes in the corner.

Like a lot of cats, Latoya sees ghosts everywhere, freaking out and clattering around when she spots some phantom menace. She does not like to be held and is skittish around everyone, including her owner. "When I look in her eyes, I see a reflection of all of the evil in the world," Erin recently told me. She and Latoya are in a Mexican standoff. Erin is not going to move, and Latoya is not going to change. Erin is a kind-hearted kid and would do nothing to harm Latoya, but she wishes Latoya would go for a stroll and never come back.

It is cheap and easy to use Latoya as a stand-in, like nominating an abandoned pit bull to represent all dogs, but when I see cats, I see Latoya. Perhaps she could have her own website where you could tune in, and she could return your digital gaze with a baleful stare 24/7. Grumpy Cat's agent could probably work with that.

I should say I don't mind looking at cats on the Internet, in part because they are ubiquitous and can't be avoided, and in part because I think that's where cats should live, on the Internet, imprisoned by my browser and one click away from being banished.

So, my little furry friends, go forth and multiply. Infest every corner of the web as is your nature. Chase that laser light, squeeze yourself into a glass bowl, freak out at the toy robot that your owner has set before you. YouTube is waiting, and people imprisoned in office cubes everywhere depend on you, cats of the Internet, to bring a moment of respite to the quotidian tasks that are on other applications minimized until the boss walks by.

We will continue to click because it is in our nature. We might even organize a film festival at a cutting-edge museum so that your splendors, your unique charms, can finally find the widescreen presentation and communal audience they deserve. But if we meet offline in the real world, don't expect me to ask for an autograph. I've interviewed and written dozens of stories about famous people who are riveting on-screen. They are, with very few exceptions, a huge disappointment IRL. And some are monsters, drunk on narcissism and transfixed by their own reflection in the faces of those who adore them.

You, cats of the Internet, may be hilarious and full of frolic when the camera is on, but once the lights go down and the set is struck, you are still a cat. I know who and what you are. As you do, Mr. Cat. Just don't tell the others, and you will be fine.

Untitled Essay

FROM *Worn Stories,* EDITED BY EMILY SPIVACK, 2014

I LIVE IN the New Jersey suburbs where the morning weather often bears little or no relation to what the weather might be like in the afternoon in New York, where I work. Many days I have miscalculated my clothing needs for the day—in part because I work in Midtown in a forest of tall buildings, and if there is a chill in the air it is multiplied by the wind that becomes amplified and focused by the canyon of structures around me.

I generally deal with the dissonance by refusing to go outside or by grabbing a fake cashmere scarf for five bucks off the street vendor tables in Times Square. I think there is a direct relationship between what you pay for an item and how long you hang on to it, so those scarves tend to come and go. (Though I do have a watch I bought on Canal Street almost a decade ago for five bucks, and it is still with me. I wear it every day and replace the battery every few years for more than the cost of the watch. But that's a different story.) Even if they last, I am a spiller, so they become a sort of napkin-cravat after a while and my wife quietly retires them without telling me.

On a very hot day last summer, I had the opposite problem. I left for work dressed for a rare television shoot, which means that I had put on a sport coat and dress shirt with a tie on top, and wore the usual black jeans and sneakers on bottom. After work, I was meeting a pal at the Frying Pan, which is a bar on a no-longer-seaworthy boat off of a pier in Chelsea.

The bar is aptly named. On a sunny day, the light and heat reflecting off the water mean that the people on the boat are slowly sautéed. Yes, a sunset on the Hudson is an amazing thing, so spectacular that even my home state of New Jersey looks majestic, but it can get very hot out there. It's also worth mentioning that Manhattan itself throws off a fair amount of heat because of the so-called heat island effect.

It was still very hot when I left my office at the end of the day, and even though I left behind my sport coat the sun immediately absorbed into the dark dress shirt I was wearing, so I walked down the street to the tourists' shops of Times Square for any old T-shirt that I could wear. Even at six bucks a pop, they were hideous, all of them swaddled in the announcement that the wearer was in fact, or had once been, on a particular island off the coast of America called New York.

I was just about to give up. My fading hipster cred—already suffering many hellacious blows because of advancing age—would not allow me to wear a shirt suggesting that "I ♥ New York." You can't wear a shirt like that ironically unless, say, you hate New York, which I do not. I still have an immigrant's ardor for the place, having come here a decade ago for a job. Before my family joined me, I lived in Tribeca for a few months. My second day in New York, I rode my bike into a fence at Broadway and Canal because I was looking up at a pair of tall buildings downtown. Those buildings are now gone, but the wonder, the sense of awe at traveling through one of humankind's greatest creations, remains.

And then I saw one—extra-large, thank God—in which the classic New York script had been misprinted upside down. I knew what to do. I turned to the guy running the shop and said, "This one is a misprint. I'll give you three bucks." He said nothing but nodded. I paid in two crumpled bills and quarters, ducked behind the rack, and put it on. As soon as I stepped out onto the street, people stared. I got on the C train to Twenty-Third, and a kid next to me stared at the logo over my burgeoning middle-aged midsection and said, "I like your shirt."

"Thanks, man. Three bucks."

Whenever I wear the shirt in New York, waitresses, bartenders, cabdrivers, they all say nice things about the shirt and ignore the fact that the rack it's hanging on could use some work.

When I travel, which is fairly often, and wear the shirt, which is less often, nobody ever says anything. I like that about my shirt: it is something that is intuitively understood in the City, as we insufferable locals call it, and is baffling to others, akin to many other aspects of living or working in New York.

I daydreamed for a while about getting some pals of my wife in the clothing business to crank out a few hundred. I even had a slogan for the back: TURNING NEW YORK UPSIDE DOWN ONE SHIRT AT A TIME. But then someone in the business explained to me that you couldn't trademark the idea of turning lettering someone else created upside down. So I just wear mine instead.

It won't last. It's white, for one thing, and a series of small food and beverage disasters have already begun to dapple its surface. One day it will accumulate enough stains and history so that it will mysteriously disappear from my drawer. I will miss it.

The So-Called Artist's Lifestyle

FROM *The Art of Wonder: Inspiration, Creativity, and the Minneapolis Institute of Art*, EDITED BY KAYWIN FELDMAN ET AL., 2015

SOME INSTITUTIONS LORD it over the cities they reside in, but the Minneapolis Institute of Art was never like that. It was born amidst and continues to be knit into the Whittier neighborhood. With its Beaux Arts grandeur, it should look out of place, sitting there on a nondescript stretch of Twenty-Fourth Street, but it never did, at least not to me. From the time I was a kid coming in on the bus from my suburban school, it seemed less a colossus than a kind of portal to a world built on history and far-flung lands.

To a landlocked, undertraveled kid from the Midwest—I never got on an airplane larger than a Cessna until I was twenty-one—it was physical proof that the places and epochs I had only seen in books and on television actually existed. But the existence and display of those artifacts did not make the museum any less mystical. For one thing, how could it be that all this treasure was splayed out in front of me, yet no one had asked me for money on the way in? And what of provenance? I would stare at a piece of African art or a piece of pottery from China and think long and hard about how it came here. Who had carried it here, and what had they given to obtain it?

The curators and directors who ran the joint seemed like some kind of unknowable priesthood. Did the museum guards talk about us after we left, or fondle the art in all the ways that were forbidden to civilians? In a city rimmed by lakes and cornfields, how could there not be secrets, some of them dark, about how this improbable place came to be?

As I came of age, I began to see that this was a world where the natural and commercial laws of the nearby Lake Street strip and the mores of the rapidly expanding suburbs did not apply. I didn't yet understand the civic impulse and cultural ambition behind it—what drove the mothers and fathers of the city to weave together public and private money, not to make more money but to make something that would last, that would be held in common by all for as long as the city was still a city.

Because it was always there, the institute's presence on the Southside always made sense to me. When I grew up and became a reporter, it failed to strike me as weird that a wild-eyed guy with a military haircut who hung around St. Stephen's homeless shelter for the food was also spending a great deal of time at the institute. He demonstrated a deep and loving understanding of the permanent collection when I went there with him one day. "Isn't this place amazing?" he asked as we walked out.

It was and is.

During the sixties and seventies, when I grew up, things came and went. The place where I first had chop suey in Saint Louis Park became a place that sold vacuum cleaners and then became a fitness center. But the 'tute—do they still call it that?—just stayed. Part of it had to do with the edifice, culled from a vocabulary that may have been common elsewhere but was rare in a town built on grain, trains, and rivers.

Minneapolis has many virtues—more with each passing year—but it's not a place where business and residential architecture generally aimed high. Everything I grew up looking at had a use, a narrative built on commerce and consumer need. The rivers and freeways that divided Minneapolis and Saint Paul suggested that even if I was going nowhere for the time being, everything around me was on the move, going somewhere else.

I eventually took the hint and got out of Dodge, hitchhiking over much of the American West as soon as I got out of high school, coming to understand how big and pretty the world was, and how little I knew of it.

To say that I was not an avid consumer of high culture does not begin to explain the deep hole I was working out of as a young adult.

My first purchase of something that had both aesthetic and practical value was an elaborately beaded roach clip I bought at the yippie camp-in outside the Spokane World's Fair in 1974, when I was seventeen. It was one of my fashion signatures for years to come, hanging off of greasy jeans and signifying to cops and potheads alike my most important affiliation at the time.

I came back from that long trip and began working at Powell's Candy in Hopkins. If there was fleeting artistic beauty in the tumblers full of colorful jellybeans I was making, I took note only in stoner passing. At the time, our family's financial fortunes had taken a tumble and it seemed sufficient to be getting by on my own. My dad had other ideas, insisting that I attend college. I finally relented and went to the University of Wisconsin at River Falls, just across the Saint Croix River.

By dint of temperament and hobbies, I fell in with a group of outriders, smart and druggy kids who left campus dorms behind as quickly as possible and began living on farms and retrofitting chicken coops or building teepees.

My bestie at the time was a guy from Chicago named Donald. Donald was remarkably handsome, quiet and contemplative when stoned and a hilarious menace when he drank. Donald had a thing with photography, which probably grew out of a high school interest in spending a lot of time in the darkroom. I played along, feigning interest in the work because I liked the guy who made the photos.

But if you look at art long enough, it begins staring back at you. It teaches you how to look, to see. Donald was something of a formalist, working mostly in black and white, and was very frugal in his choice of shots. I often commented on his comic willingness to lug a bag full of lenses and cameras around and shoot so little of what we saw. When he saw something he liked—usually a landscape, often a human-suffused one—he worked it hard, but the camera stayed in the bag most of the time.

He was still in the process of becoming an artist, and our lifestyle annealed his vision. In addition to a pharmaceutical diet of Mexican pot, amphetamines for studying, and lots of Leinenkugel's beer, we ended up with access to some of the very good LSD making the rounds at the time. The trips were strong enough that they required planning and careful consideration of set and setting. More often than not, we would begin and end those trips in a sinkhole off the banks of the Kinnickinnic River.

A writer in name only then, I embraced the period's fashionable library of drug-suffused books, reading Carlos Castaneda, Hermann Hesse, and, of course, Hunter Thompson. But if psychedelics changed what I was reading, they changed how Donald saw things. He actually began going to school when he didn't have to, working on large canvases with an airbrush, working on what he called "dot" paintings. It was a kind of pointillism, if you could count a single dot, a lone focal point, as a reductive expression of the form.

The paintings were gorgeous, with a limited but vivid palette, suggesting inner and outer space at the same time. Over time, the dots began to fracture, pivot on their planes, and interact with other geometric elements. Donald continued to shoot photos, but his paintings gained some attention in the fine arts program at school, which he always laughed off. No matter: my running buddy Donald had turned into an artist.

Various capers to go see the music of the time—Talking Heads, David Bowie, Naked Raygun, Big Black, Hüsker Dü, the Replacements—began to include daytime trips to the institute, the Walker Art Center, and, when we were in Donald's hometown, the Art Institute of Chicago and the Museum of Contemporary Art.

Donald had a weakness for the Minneapolis Institute because it shared his weakness for great photography and was willing to put it on equal artistic footing with centuries-old fine art. He was not a gallery talker, but I learned by what he paused in front of, where he stood, the low murmurs he made while looking. We talked about the work after we left, not as adepts but as collectors of experiences.

People scattered, but Donald eventually moved to Minneapolis, where I was already living, to work as a photo assistant. He was still painting and shooting, and I had begun to write, but our primary work of art was our inveterate pursuit of altered states. By now we'd moved on to cocaine, which took us to house parties in south Minneapolis that ran deep into the night.

Donald was an artist, and I, after a fashion, was a writer, but in retrospect we were junkies in training, hurtling through an endless oeuvre of dissolute youth that was bound to come to no good end. The so-called artist's lifestyle doesn't usually enable art. It obscures the impulse to make something — other than another phone call, to set up the next caper.

Near the end, in about 1984, we would head out on runs that lasted through the night and well into the next day. Much of it went off in south Minneapolis, and sometimes adjacent to the institute. We both had lost our jobs or soon would, so there was only the nonsense to see to. Many of the dealers we frequented did business in ramshackle duplexes on Stevens Avenue, which ran along the institute's west side, or two streets over, on Clinton.

After one of those nights in one of those dim, curtained caves, we came out massively tweaked, stunned that the day had begun so many hours before. At some point the previous evening we had left the car behind, and now we were walking in the brutal light of a summer day, both of us sweating in leather coats. We were making our way home on Twenty-Fourth Street, and Donald was a few steps ahead of me. He had paused at the corner of Twenty-Fourth and Third Avenue, and the institute — it might as well have been a spaceship, given the context — stared at us.

"You wanna go in?" he said.

I didn't say anything, just searched his face to see when he would start laughing at the preposterousness of the suggestion.

He didn't start laughing. I considered our busy schedule of figuring out where we had left the car and daytime drinking at the CC Club. My mind went to the doorway of the museum, to the inspection, to the eye-fuck we would get on the way in. And then I remembered you didn't have to pay, that we didn't really have to say much of anything.

"What the hell," I said.

We got nothing more than smiles on the way in, and the cool of the place became a stone respite against the blast furnace that had enveloped us outside.

I would not testify to it in a court of law, but as I recall, we skipped the permanent collection and went to an exhibition of—again, pretty sure —the work of Minnesota photographer Tom Arndt.

I think this because the work reflected my home. With their subjects' full-on embrace of the camera's gaze, the photos had little in common with Donald's work, but I can remember just letting go of the jangle, of the chase, and coming to rest in front of a carefully hung and lit narrative of the city we were living in. We actually sort of belonged in the work, two knock-around guys still wearing their clothes from the night before, way past their sell date. I think we saw our reflection.

Art has civilizing aspects, allowing even the most savage and lost soul to let go of the mania inside and see the world through someone else's eyes. We didn't talk much about it, but in Arndt's work, Donald probably saw sure-handedness, a mastery of lighting, a gift for making photographs that were highly thought of even though they seemed serendipitous, even casual.

For me, it was a reminder that the stories of everyday life—a day at the state fair, a walk past Moby Dick's ("For a Whale of a Drink") on Hennepin Avenue, a pause in front of Mickey's Diner in Saint Paul —were just as worthy of framing and preserving as a thousand-year-old sculpture of an enlightened bodhisattva.

Did Donald see himself there, drawing a line between what we saw and the creative work he executed when he wasn't in the midst of the self-induced chaos? I'm not sure he believed he was a member of the tribe of artisans and artists whose work was so meticulously annotated before us. But I did. Donald made some bad art, as any artist does, but there was rigor and vision in his best work.

When Donald was not busy being a knucklehead or working a money job, he was an artist. Not the kind who staked out a table at the New French Café and brayed until last call about whether cubism saved or ruined painting but the kind who made art when no one was looking.

We'd be dancing with a bunch of people we'd just met at the house he shared with his sister—Los Lobos' "Will the Wolf Survive?" was a perennial on our after-party playlist—and I'd see something new on his wall, something remarkable. Nostrils flared, sweat dripping off me, I'd ask, "Where'd that come from?"

He'd dismiss the work with a wave of the hand. "That's a piece of shit."

It usually was not. His work was coveted among his friends and ex-girl-friends, but the canvases were big—he often worked in triptychs—and I was itinerant enough that I never owned a piece. I didn't really have to. I was able to stay in the narrative, to see the work, by being his wingman in other pursuits.

I'm pretty sure the work endured—somewhere in the middle of the country it is scattered here and there—but Donald did not. I sobered up and eventually moved on and became a real writer, but we kept in touch off and on. Donald went back to school and began working as a landscape architect, but alcohol and opiates became a part of his life.

He ended up cornered in a one-room cabin in Newport, south of Saint Paul on US 61, with a radio and no television. There was room for a single canvas, but I learned not to ask if he was still painting or shoot-ing photos. It was grim, but he brought a gallows humor to his circum-stance, and we did manage a few last capers to the Wisconsin side of the river, where we'd fish, laugh, and talk shit about the old days.

I was on a trip back to Minneapolis a few years ago and turned on my phone as I landed, and it began ringing immediately. It was Donald's brother. It turned out that while Donald was in long-term rehab at a place in the woods, he'd had a stroke. His brother said I should come quickly, that Donald was at Saint Joseph's. I got to stop in and say good-bye.

I was in charge of the obit, so I called the guy at the place where he had finally put together some sobriety. He told me Donald had busied himself working on the grounds, using his skills as a landscaper to pretty up the place.

"He took a lot of pitchers, too," the guy said. "Never showed 'em to anybody, but he walked around with that camera a lot."

So Donald was working on sobriety, working on the grounds, working on his art. That's how he went out. His family let his friends go through his photos and take what they wanted. I loved the gesture, but at the time I missed the artist too much to take an interest in the work.

Over those years, Donald and I bonded over sloshing beers, over mirrors full of coke, but we also bonded over art. Both of us were too deeply ashamed of the druggy sewer we had created to act or talk like working artists, but we could look at the work of others—more a refraction of our ambitions in abeyance than a reflection—and admit by our presence that we admired beauty and creativity when we saw it.

Would Donald's work ever have made it into the institute? Doubtful. Art is a splendor, but it's also a crapshoot. He had never gotten it together to work with people who would have put up a show for him, so he was not bringing a lot of momentum to his career as an artist. All he did was make the stuff—he never really put value on it or knew what to do with it. He may have been a fine artist in his technique, but he was a folk artist by disposition.

In a sense, for both of us, the institute was a place between, a bridge connecting the nonsense we pursued and the excellence we wished we were a part of.

Great art is an argument against idiocy, against pointlessness, against the unholy music of the self. The fact that people, some of them long ago, decided to make these exquisite things and that other people did what was necessary to make sure we could all look at them, no matter what our state, is an affirmation of not just a civic impulse but a democratic and human one. Because there is nothing so special about art that regular people, even broken ones, can't look at it together and bask in something eternal.

David Carr's press pass from the *Washington City Paper*.

(Photo courtesy of the editor)

Acknowledgments

Final Draft is a reality because of the impeccable approach and guidance from David Rosenthal. With profound appreciation, I thank you. Flip Brophy, many thanks for your wisdom.

Thank you to the fine folks at Houghton Mifflin Harcourt: Beth Burleigh Fuller, Chloe Foster, Ivy Givens, Lori Glazer, Emma Gordon, Rosemary McGuinness, Brian Moore, and Bruce Nichols.

And with very special thanks to the *New York Times*: Dean Baquet, David McCraw, Sam Sifton, Alexander Smith, and A. G. Sulzberger.

Credits

"New Home Isn't Pretty, but I Came from Hell Anyway" and "Fishing Trip to Boundary Waters" both first appeared in the *Saint Paul Pioneer Press*. "Drinking and Flying" and "Faegre's 'Women Who Run with the Wolves'" both first appeared in *Corporate Report Minnesota*. "Brian Coyle's Secret" first appeared in the May 1991 issue of *Minnesota Monthly*. Reprinted with permission. "Even in Facing AIDS, Coyle Served Truth and His City" first appeared in the Aug. 27, 1991, issue of *The Star Tribune*, Minneapolis, MN. Reprinted with permission. Eight essays in Chapter 2 were originally contributed as part of "Because I Said So . . . ," a recurring column in *Family Times*. "Prodigal Clown," "Paranoid or Positive?," "IR Queer," "Still Life with Alien," "Indictment City," "Jackpot City," and "Public Dis'course" all first appeared in *Twin Cities Reader*. "Andrew Sullivan Out at *New Republic*," "Good News Traveling Too Fast," "Gored," "Sidney Blumenthal," "Sally Quinn on Vernon Jordan," "Kids Say the Darnedest Things," "Road Trip," "Crash Course," "Death March," "People (Not) Like Us," "Who Asked You?," "One Last Hitch," "Goodbye to All That," "Oral Exam," and "Oh Say, Why Can't We See?" all first appeared in *Washington City Paper*. "Slower Than a Speeding Bullet" first appeared in the Oct. 2001 issue of *Washington Monthly*. Reprinted with permission. "*Details* Reborn," "Me, Me, Me™," and "Who Needs Writers and Actors When the Whole World Is Your Backlot?" all first appeared on Inside.com. "The Futility of 'Homeland Defense'" and "A New Mask" were first published 2001–2002 in *The Atlantic*. Reprinted with permission. "18 Truths About the New New York," "Gathering to Remember," and "That's All, Folks!" all were first published 2001 in *New York Magazine*. The articles "Neil Young Comes Clean," "Both Hero and Villain, and Irresistible," "At Flagging Tribune, Tales of a Bankrupt Culture," "Ezra Klein Is Joining Vox Media as Web Journalism Asserts Itself," "When Fox News Is the Story," "Deadly Intent," "Been Up, Been Down. Now? Super," "Before They Went Bad," "Calling Out Bill Cosby's Media Enablers, Including Myself," "All Hail the Helix," "View, Interrupted," and "Breaking Away, but by the Rules" all originally appeared in the *New York Times*, are copyright The New York Times and used here by permission. "The Wrestler" and "Press Play" first appeared on Medium .com. "All That You Leave Behind" was first published in the Oct. 2013 issue of *Bicycling*. Reprinted courtesy of Hearst Magazine Media, Inc. "Cats" is from the collection *Cat Is Art Spelled Wrong*. Used by permission of Coffee House Press. "Untitled Essay" first appeared in *Worn Stories* edited by Emily Spivack. Copyright © 2014 by Princeton Architectural Press. Reprinted by permission. "The So-Called Artist's Lifestyle" is from the collection *The Art of Wonder*. Used by permission of Minneapolis Institute of Art.